The
Gold
Diggers

PAUL MONETTE

The Gold Diggers

Boston • Alyson Publications, Inc.

First published March, 1979, by Avon Books.

This trade paperback edition published by
Alyson Publications
40 Plympton Street
Boston, Massachusetts 02118

First printing: October, 1988.

ISBN 1-55583-144-3

To JK,
Ramblin' Ed,
and mon petit Cesar.

With my guineas I'll buy flowering trees,
flowering trees, flowering trees and walk
among my flowering trees and tell
my sons what fame is.
> —Virginia Woolf
> *Orlando*

Chapter 1

Rita was a mess by the time she got to LA. It wasn't enough that she hadn't had a real meal in two and a half weeks. Since the day she gave up men for good, in fact. The very day she called Peter and announced she was coming West. Because she was too fat to go anywhere, for days she ate bran muffins and little cans of grapefruit sections until she couldn't taste them anymore. Then she went on half-rations. The meal on the plane menaced her, it was so plentiful, and she handed it back untouched. The twelve lost pounds hovered in the air about her like stinging bugs. She'd seen the movie. Then, over the heartbroken mountains, the boy beside her lit up a joint and passed it to her. He looked about fourteen.

"Not on a plane," she said, shaking her head.

"But this is the safest place," he assured her. "We're in international waters. Besides, you get higher this high up."

"Why?"

"It's to do with the ozone," he said, going into something of a trance.

Interpol made no immediate move to eliminate them. She smoked away, if only to get her mind off the flaming nose dive into the Rockies. The boy, so seedy he looked as if he'd hitched the ride, apparently didn't want to pick Rita up. Now and then he narrated bits of the movie in her direction, though he didn't have the earphones and did a lot of guessing. *He* hadn't seen the movie before, so he got it all wrong. Rita tuned out, glad to slump by the window and wonder if LA wasn't a terrible mistake. She decided it was. Then the dope circled round from behind and socked her in the belly, and the next thing she knew, she was eating everything in sight. The boy had beef jerky in his pocket and a package of cloves Life Savers. That wasn't enough. Rita pleaded with the stewardess for a second chance at her dinner and got it, the chicken congealed and the cake like a frosted cardboard box.

"You shouldn't eat," the boy said as they began their descent. "You'll just come down."

"I've never met these people," she said. "I have to be normal."

"If you get high enough, lady, you can *act* normal. Just don't do anything that might attract their attention."

She stood now in the terminal feeling fat, attracting the critical attention, she sensed, of anyone pretty and tan and young. It wasn't enough that she'd sunk without a trace in New York, she thought, her accounts closed and all the signs of her tenancy flung to the four winds. She had to get smashed in flight and land without a brain in a future that called for the hawk eyes of an Indian scout. Swell, she thought, opening her bag to look for her keys and then recalling with a pang that they were all gone. She hadn't anything left that she needed a key to.

But she wasn't fat. That was just nerves. Nick, who was the first to see her except for the driver, would be struck by the full moon of her face and a rosy body like a duchess at the French court, the lines soft as a watercolor. No angles, no edges. And thank God she knew how to wear clothes. A Kelly green shawl and wheat-colored sweater, a scarf and a watch and locket around her neck, and cocoa satin pants with billowing legs like parachutes. Her hair did what it wanted, but it knew what it was doing. She didn't look ready for any one thing, not an office or a luncheon out or a lot of children. Because her time in New York had alternated between near careers and debilitating romance, she'd never been in one situation long enough to look like anyone else. She was almost forty, and she had the whitest skin. She had really gotten over not being thin long ago. The diet merely filled up the time before she left, and it impressed her as something constructive to do, now that she wasn't going to fall in love anymore.

She was trying to remember how she and Peter had left it when a dark, exhausted man appeared in front of her. He was fifty, maybe, and in one hand he had a ring of keys that he shook like a bell. It was a toss-up whether or not it was a voluntary motion.

"I'm here to get you," he said.

Even on easy days, Rita wasn't good at transitions. A moment since, she was in midair, and part of her was back there still, bracing for the crash, her whole body rigid as the foot she held to the floor in a speeding car. Where did the boy with the dope go? The fear shot through her that she was caught now in a drug ring. The boy had planted little packets all about her person while she sat unguarded. She was the middleman, and she had to go and deliver. She wondered what to do about her luggage.

"I have to wait for my friend," she said, clicking her locket and her watch together to drown out the jingle of keys. She tried to make the friend sound armed.

"Peter sent me," he said, tense because he wasn't getting

through to her, and as if he couldn't do a thing unless told to.

She suspected it all along because he didn't look tough enough to traffic, in spite of an accent she couldn't place. She was just making sure. She followed him out the door to a Mercedes parked in a tow zone, and he made her get in the back seat so she could be properly driven. Then he went back to the luggage bay, and at last she sank back and gave herself up to the woozy stage. The winter sky was milky here with haze, the air thick with the aftershock smell of gunpowder. But it came to her only faintly, because the bourbon smell of leather in the back seat knocked her over, too. She peered out a gray-tinted window that made things look separate and glazed, as though through a camera. After a bit, she heard behind her the reassuring thump of her suitcases being stowed in the trunk. Then the driver got in and turned the key. As the spark leapt, the car was filled with disco music and arctic air. There must have been extra speakers in the ashtrays and armrests.

They pulled out into traffic, and the phone rang. Or actually it buzzed. It was in a wooden case next to her on the seat, which she hadn't touched at first because it looked like the box with the button that the President's men carried around.

"I'm sure that's for you," the driver said.

It was like picking up the receiver in a random telephone booth. No one ever knew where she was, she thought. Assuming anyone ever looked. She said hello.

"How was your flight?" Nick asked. "I'm sorry the weather's lousy, but you can't have everything."

"I have everything I can think of right now," she said. Out the window she saw they were traveling fast along the flats. Bungalows all the way to the horizon on either side of the freeway. She knew Peter lived in the hills, though she couldn't see that far in the chalk-white air. "I feel as if I could take a bath in this car. All I have to do is find the right button. Are you Nick?"

"I am. Finally we meet."

"Is Peter with you?"

"We're going to meet Peter at the party." What party, she wondered. She hadn't been invited to a party. "He's had to do everything himself, because he's got photographers coming. So he won't even talk to us. But a party's a party, right? You'll be here in about twenty minutes. Do you want anything?"

"Give me a hint," she said.

"A drink. Or dope."

"No thanks. What I'm going to need is a little advice, Nick. I mean, about how to proceed here," she said, deciding she sounded awful. She should be letting him know she could go to a party in her sleep. She was afraid she sounded as if she ought to be left at home.

"Of course. You've come out to make your fortune, haven't you?"

"Oh no." She felt the heat on her cheeks. "I just meant I don't know what people expect. At a party, I mean." When the truth was, she didn't know what she meant. Would all the important things, she thought, have to be said from now on in cars? She had enough trouble with telephones that stayed in one place.

"Don't be sorry," Nick said. "It isn't considered bad form out here. Always remember that—you *can't* talk too much about money." She could barely hear him, and she had to raise her own voice unnervingly to get through. But the bad connection had done this for them—it heightened the moment, like a call across the ocean. "Nobody ever died of talking about it. If they did, this whole place would go back to the desert."

She was putting the place together as fast as she could. The only time she'd ever seen palm trees before was when she'd fled to the Islands, to try to rest up after one thing and another. Then she'd liked best to sit underneath and listen to the branches flutter dryly in the Gulf breezes. Here they had them any old place, as if they were just trees. And already she had the sense—picking them out here and there as they drove by, because they looked so odd—that no one sat and listened. If she'd said it out loud, Nick would have had her remember something else, that everything in LA was as shimmering with meaning as the palms, and, more to the point, that people couldn't help saying what the meaning was. If she'd thought about it, she would have said it wasn't much different from New York, as far as that went.

"Maybe on the way to the party," she said, "I'll let *you* talk about money and see if lightning strikes."

"It won't," he said. "The gods don't care. I'll see you."

She's stoned, Nick thought as he hung up. But he was relieved too, because he thought he was going to like her; and they both knew they had to for Peter's sake. He walked out onto the terrace now and lit a cigarette and stood on the lip of the pool. Below him, the hills of Bel-Air gentled down to the outside world; and he could look onto several houses tiered beneath his own. He also knew there was a line of houses at the very top that looked down on him, but he didn't think about it. It was part of the process of living in the hills to look down on, not up to, unless you were in the market for something. Besides, his house was so old it hid in the trees, and so it was just as good as living further up. There were unspoken borders between old Bel-Air and new Bel-Air, and Nick held the jigsaw of it all in his head. He knew his place was as old as you could get.

What about Rita, he wondered. He supposed he'd always heard the nice things about her, since Peter was so loyal to his past; and he suspected Rita had mostly been told how he could be a bastard. Peter phoned the Upper West Side like clockwork whenever he and Nick were fighting. Rita was always there. Nick knew that, six years ago, Rita picked up Peter in a taxi at his lover's apartment on Washington Square and raced him out to the airport. He was running away. And it was a secret. Nick was never sure whose idea it was, Rita's or Peter's. As Peter boarded the plane, the last words she said to him were, "Always order veal." She thought Peter should be taken care of. Nick knew, too, that Rita was the one who had tried to coax Peter back to his grandfather, the only one in his family he spoke to then or admitted to now. In a way, Nick thought, Rita invented Peter. All he needed was someone to give him ideas. The rest was just money.

Nick thought about Rita only briefly, until the sound died out from the phone call. He didn't have to think about her for twenty minutes yet. So he went back to Sam as if nothing else had happened all day. He had that morning sold a four-room house in the Hollywood Hills for a hundred and ninety thousand. He had sold it seven months before for a hundred and fifteen, and he scarcely paused to figure out what a good deal his day was turning out to be. All he knew was, he had to get over to Venice by one-thirty to meet Sam at the beach. The girl who lived in the house had cut a lousy album in November, and now she wanted something in the three hundred range. She would have liked to spend all day just telling Nick what to look for. He said he'd get back to her. She was on hold now, along with everyone else.

At least Sam was waiting at the café. He hadn't wanted to come, and he'd warned Nick that he didn't see anyone three times. It was forty dollars the first time and went up to sixty the second, but more and more money didn't make the third time worth it. Sam said he wouldn't need anything steady until he was twenty-eight or nine, and he was willing to make less now to stay unattached. He sat at an outdoor table, leaning back in his chair against the low stone wall, denim shirt open all the way to his waist and his face turned up to the feeble winter sun. His hair was black like Nick's, and his body was slim and taut, no bulk to his muscles because he moved like a runner. He always seemed about to leap away, even now, balanced on the chair's back legs and lost in the stars. It was as if he had enemies that preyed on more than him, that preyed on all his kind starting back in the caves, and they wanted him removed, but not for personal reasons. It was as if he didn't know who they were until they sprang. He was twenty-five, so twenty-eight was still far off, at an impossible remove.

Nick didn't know where to start. Until he got there, he hadn't really believed Sam was going to show up. Then he was afraid he'd waste the whole time convincing Sam to see him again. Why am I doing this, he thought as he walked up to the table, and he realized the question came up only when they were together. The rest of the time in the last two weeks, all he thought about was being in bed with Sam. He felt the knot in his stomach lift as he let go and pulled away from the shore. He knew he wouldn't have a moment to think until it was over. And he wished he weren't wearing a suit. He was afraid it made him look like a fool.

"They say this beach is littered with kids who want to be stars," he said, and sat down. "I wonder where they are today."

"Hey, coach," Sam said, stretching his arms in a yawn and rocking forward to face Nick at the table. "Maybe they all went home to Iowa. Besides, this isn't the beach anymore. The beach is up in Santa Monica."

Nick looked over Sam's shoulder at the wide lawn fronting the beach, where someone was flying a kite and a woman walked her dogs. There was not enough sun for much else, and the ocean was hidden in haze. Sam meant State, the gay beach. But the beach at Venice, because he had known it all his life, was for Nick the true point where the city met the Pacific. From the café terrace on a clear day, he could see north to the range of the Malibu highlands, blue above the blue water. And the odd stucco houses and cast-iron arcades of Venice still moved him with their waterfront gentility and foreign airs. Rust streaked the peeling pastel walls, and the new Bohemians had painted some houses burgundy red and electric green. But something had lasted here. All up and down the front, the wooden, parasol-roofed pavilions marked the course of the promenade. On nice days, it was still the perfect place to walk. Nick used to coax Peter to come in the middle of a workday, but Peter didn't want any part of Venice. Down on its luck. No money.

"My mother and father rented a place here every summer. For just two weeks. I used to think about it all year."

"That was in the forties, right?" Sam asked a bit tightly, as if Nick were in his forties, too.

"I was eight in 1950. It was more in the fifties."

Sam nodded. He wasn't very interested. Because the café wasn't open, they had nothing like coffee to turn to and no one other than themselves to watch. It was too late now to move somewhere else. Irrationally, though he knew Sam was going to care less and less, Nick felt he had to keep defending the old Venice. It had been years since he'd thrown in his lot with someone who always made him say the wrong thing. He knew he was going to ruin everything, and he went right ahead.

"My first love was a lifeguard in Venice. I must have been ten, and he was about your age. He had hunky shoulders and a hairy chest, and I'd sit for hours and watch him. He'd be high up in his chair, putting on oil and rubbing it in. It was a one-way thing—he didn't know—but I was so happy I could hardly breathe. Otherwise, I didn't do anything but go in the water. I was in the water all day."

"Do you live with someone?" Sam asked.

"Yes," Nick said, as if he hadn't been interrupted. Perhaps he hadn't been.

"I thought so. Is he older?"

"No. We're both thirty-five. Why?"

"You're like hustlers I've met who've settled down with someone," he said, then shrugged because Nick didn't prove the point. "Usually they pick some old queen."

Nick, and it was not like him, had to pretend not to be wounded. Sam talked about hustling the way everyone else in LA talked about work, as if the queer course of life and all the human ironies were just like the ones that went through the office. It wasn't that Nick questioned the notion that hustling was an image of life at large. Of course it was. But he didn't, like Sam, get all cozy inside about the noble solitary work that whores pursued. Sam seemed to think he was something like Thoreau, except he did it in bed. Well, all right, but Nick didn't want to be compared. He'd known the ones who ended up in silvery Ferraris too. They lived in Beverly Hills, the summer in Laguna, with gin-and-ice set designers, kept like human poodles. But he also saw others on the street, crow's-feet and too much tan, a thousand days of T-shirts and baby blue Levi's, who'd done it too long. Nick didn't think it was pretty either way. So he knew how little time Sam had.

"Have you ever been to the real Venice?"

"No," Sam said, still an edge on his voice—he would have gone there if he'd wanted to. "I'm not into Europe. I want to see Hawaii first."

"The reason I ask," Nick went on, but storing the remark about Hawaii, glad to have a thing they might do someday, "is when *I* went there, I'd had twenty-five years of seeing *this* as the real one. I fell in love with Venice, but the name never fit."

"I don't want to go to bed with you today, Nick."

"That's okay," he said, a second's glance into the boy's gray eyes. "Don't be so tense."

"Well, I don't know why we're here. I ought to be working now, or else I'll have to work all night. I don't like to just talk."

Nick suspected as much. They couldn't talk yet. He saw what he kept wishing for in men like Sam. Nick begged to be listened to in a particular way, because he was the only one he knew who was so enchanted by the destiny of things. Where other men were scared, or just confused, he noticed the course of things—the price drift from a hundred and fifteen to a hundred and ninety, the routing of the roads to plug into the freeways, the state of the royal palms along the street by his office. He felt an arc in almost everything he met, could tell where it would lead in the end, whether he saw a Caterpillar earth machine poised in a field or a wedding party milling at the door of a church. He'd never thought he could say it well because everyone else seemed dashed by the *meanness* of fate. Nick thrilled to the world in flux. His mind ran to pattern and process. If he really talked about it, he didn't know where it might lead. What he needed, he'd always thought, was the right man to say it to.

"You know, I'm not trying to play with you," Sam went on.

"I think you're terrific, and you turn me on. But so do a lot of people."

It didn't matter. Nick hadn't risked much on an aimless talk at an outdoor café. He had a better plan ready, just in case.

"You have the craziest idea of who you are," he said. He could feel Sam begin to freeze up, as if the muscles were about to take over and the feelings die away. He was ready to leave. The heart was best served if you treated it as just another muscle. "I exasperate you, Sam, but you must want to hear what I have to say. Because here you are."

"I came to tell you I'm not coming anymore."

"I have an option on some land in the hills above Malibu. A ranch." He spoke as if Sam hadn't; and as he did, he picked out on the lawn the figure of a woman gymnast stretching. She swung from one end of her body to the other, without a hitch. "They've just shut it down, and I want to take a ride up and look it over. You want to come?"

"Now?"

"Later in the week. Friday." It was Monday. "It's real. They used to board horses for westerns. Some guys from Texas ran it, trail men, so it feels like a cowboy's place. Nobody's messed it up yet and made it pretty."

"Are you a cowboy, Nick?" Sam asked him. He was gentler now, and he'd calculated in an instant that they were onto more uncharted matters. Nick, he seemed to understand, was more than a free man with money and a taste for infatuation.

"Put it this way. I've gotten more western since I've gotten gay."

"We could poke around the bunkhouse," Sam said. He put one hand in his shirt and massaged a muscle in his chest. "I'd need a new pair of boots."

"Of course. How much would they set you back?"

"Two hundred. Two-fifty, maybe."

Nick took a fold of bills out of his pocket and peeled off three hundreds and laid them on the table. He thought: I'm not like this at all. And then wasn't sure which role he was disavowing. It wasn't the money. The act of making payment caused him no dislocation, because he'd had it for free ninety-nine times out of a hundred; and besides, he used to be poor and so saw money as a windfall, no matter how much work he did to make it. It was more the singlemindedness of the pursuit that had him shaking his head in wonder. He'd kept his word for four years now, that nothing would get in the way of him and Peter, and he'd kept it with special care because Peter wouldn't promise. He'd never gone out of his way to go to bed with kids. They trusted sex too much, and they had a one-track mind about getting attention.

Somehow, Sam proved that Nick was never going to get over being poor and young, either one. It was nothing but the pursuit of pleasure that threw the last two weeks off kilter. It was not like love at all. The three bills lay on the table, fanned like a hand of cards; and the sun went in and out of the haze, as pale as a white-skinned melon. Nick felt the sweat in the fit of his suit. He'd be more himself, he thought, when they got to the ranch.

"I've died and gone to heaven," Rita said, breaking into his reverie.

This was what kept happening to time. Traveling back to Sam again and again was beginning to seem like a series of seizures, amnesiac episodes in which real life gave up. Twenty minutes here, an hour there, Nick thought as he turned from the pool to face her across the terrace, and no wonder he got nothing done. In the pearl light of late afternoon, she looked, tented in her green cape and brown pants, like a stray spirit of the woods of another country. The garden around the pool didn't seem various enough for such a wildfire pair of eyes. She was a gypsy, but that was only the beginning.

"Welcome to Crook House," Nick said. He sounded to Rita like the governess in a Gothic novel.

"What a name. Does it mean you stole it?"

"There are people in Bel-Air who'd call it stealing, but no. It's tucked into the fold between two hills. Built right in. That's why you enter down the stairs from the roof, and why you can't see it from the road. The road is above us."

"I know. It's like coming down the rabbit hole. And then *this*," she exclaimed as she spread her arms wide and capered up to the pool. She might have been about to burst into song, but in fact the moment struck her dumb. "This" was the whole of Los Angeles. They could see the reach of it through the trees of the dark green garden, miles of a plain with no borders but the haze. There wasn't an inch of it that didn't appear peopled and built, yet what held her immediately was the brute fact of the land. Rita's only previous fling at geography involved her perception at age four that Central Park had two sides, East and West. Yet already she knew the hills from the basin plain in LA, and she sensed that the contrasts were such that she could never go back to not knowing. Her head cleared.

"Where's the Pacific?"

"Straight out," he said, pointing west. "You'll see it one of these days. We have it almost all the time in the winter. How's New York?"

"The same. Too damn cold." She was sure that it was dangerous to criticize New York. New York ought to be protected. In New York, she used to protect Europe. She cooked French and bought Italian shoes and read Jane Austen. She was sure, since Europe was double the distance away now, she had no skills for this city. That is why she worried about not being beautiful. It would have been something to fall back on.

"Tell me about the house," she said, turning things to real estate because she'd heard it was what they talked about here instead of the weather. She was standing next to Nick, and when she looked up at him, they caught each other's eye. Being who they were, they learned a great deal from the gesture. He looks too beautiful to look so sad, she thought. His hair was dark and covered his head with light, thick curls. He had a wide mustache and great, rocky features. He didn't look gay in the least, she thought, mentally slapping her hand.

"It's Spanish, sort of. It was built for Rusty Varda in 1920." Then, because she didn't make the connection, he started at the beginning. "He was a Hollywood producer in the teens

13

and twenties. Silents. You've never seen any of them. They were lousy. He got bought out by better people. But in his heyday, every time he finished a movie he acquired another hundred acres in Los Angeles County. This was the desert up here when he came. So we live in a monument, if you can have a monument to just plain money."

"If there's enough of it, you can," she said. "J. P. Morgan's house in New York is kept like a cathedral. I think it even has nuns."

"Do you want to change for the party?"

"You mean my clothes? No. This is what I'd wear if I didn't think about it, and I don't want to think about everything. So what happened to Rusty Varda?"

She could tell Nick knew what she meant. She'd wear what she wanted. She probably could have said what she was afraid of, too, that she couldn't stand being alone any longer, and yet she had to if she gave up men, which she had to. But it wasn't all put into words yet. She only knew she was jittery, and here was someone who must have been, not long before he was sad, scared to death. He had an ambushed look about his eyes, like the victims of natural disasters.

"Nothing," Nick said. "He died. He lived here forty-five years, collecting coins. When you're rich enough, you get to collect money. He died without a will. No heirs. Enter the State of California."

"Did he die here?" she asked, looking down at the deep blue tiles, rimmed in gold, that paved the pool. She couldn't imagine why she cared. It was a jumpy thing to want to know, the young bride's line in the Gothic novel.

"Yes, as a matter of fact. He gave up the ghost one night in front of 'The Late Show' in his den. The house was empty eight years while they traced his phantom cousins and the lawyers siphoned off the liquid assets. We bought the house intact at auction. All the furniture in place. We junked just about everything. But we kept Hey."

"Who?"

"The houseboy. The one who picked you up at the airport."

"We weren't introduced," she said apologetically. Nick might get the wrong idea that she was snotty with servants. But he started to laugh.

"Don't worry," he said. "It's nothing personal with him. He has bad days when he can't stand people and talks to his parrot. Those eight years, he lived here all by himself." As he leaned forward and dropped his voice to a whisper, she realized he was as conspiratorial when he told stories as she was. "Twenty-five years ago, he used to dance with Balanchine. Come on. We'd better get going."

They walked across the terrace to the house, passing tubs of flowering trees and the big old white wicker chairs that sit on the porches of northern islands. The stones underfoot were slate gray. The house was built in a "U" around the terrace, with wide, rough-beamed eaves and a terra-cotta roof. Casement windows, mahogany like a ship, and stucco walls. Spanish, sort of. All the windows faced in, toward the pool terrace and, beyond it, the garden and the city. There were no windows to speak of on the outer skin of the house, where the hillsides came down steeply. Seen from above or, even more, from the back, it would have looked like a fancy motel; but it was sited so as to mask that view. It was built on an idiotic principle, hugging the shape of the hills so that it cracked at the seams in earthquakes and shook all the glass into powder. Hey used to say they'd toted up a thousand years' bad luck, just in cracked mirrors. Perversely, Rusty Varda loved the idea that the earth might swallow up him and his house and his sixteen thousand Greek and Roman coins at any moment. And these things equal out. It turned out that, when the fires swept down through Bel-Air, they tended to leap over Crook House, nestled as it was, burning the leaves off its trees as they passed and ripping into the houses on the bare hilltops.

It was like walking into an opera. The room at the center, airy and high—with the spiral stairway going up to a balcony, where the front door was—appeared to be swathed in peach silk. Waves of it draped the terrace window, and it wrapped around the sofas, the chairs, and the footstools. Close up, you could see it was embroidered here and there with exquisite little peach bees. But it wasn't a room intended for close-ups. It was a living room where nobody lived, designed for the view from the balcony. Nothing like a newspaper or telephone would have fit on any of the table surfaces. "Fit" in both senses. They wouldn't have been suitable, as having too much to do with people; and there wouldn't have been room either, what with the bowls of camellias and crystal eggs and covered silver boxes. It was a room that had to do with other rooms, measured against the way people lived who lived above the fray. Surprisingly, Rita was more proud of it than put off, because it showed how pure Peter's work had gotten to be. There were rooms elsewhere in the house, no doubt, where people could live.

Nick led Rita around behind the spiral stairs and opened a closet door which turned out to be a two-man elevator. As they rode up to street level, Nick ticked off the specifications of the house, but they didn't register because Rita was reeling with the incongruity. The elevator was painted inside, *trompe l'oeil*, to look like the view from a balloon. The wicker of the gondola was painted waist-high, then the guy ropes, and above their heads the bottom of the great gas bag. For the view, they were supposed to be floating above an English park. Rita didn't know what to say. Not wanting like a bumpkin to comment on everything, she let it pass. They got off at the balcony, walked out the front door and up a flight of steps shaded over by willowy trees, arriving at last at the driveway, high above the house. They took the Jaguar instead of the Mercedes. They drove down and down, out the east gate of Bel-Air to Sunset and left toward Beverly Hills. Nick tried to keep her posted on the lay of the land. She heard him all right, stone cold sober at last, but turned her mind to the string of vehicles. The DC-10, the Mercedes, the balloon elevator, and the Jaguar sedan. It was a very pricey game of musical chairs.

She was half in love with him already. It was just a manner of speaking, "half in love," and she'd use it to caution herself about men she shouldn't get involved with. The problem was, she more often than not went ahead and got involved, no one to blame but herself. Or worse, she'd fall all the way in love because the man in the picture didn't look twice at her, and she'd end up half-dead from the misery. Rita admitted she wasn't good at the matter of the heart. She'd had a bad run of married men, one after the other, as if she willfully refused to learn a lesson. What did she want? She'd never dreamed of asking, but it had to do with being alone. It simply never occurred to her that that was the very thing she might ask of a man. She thought that to ask it was to call the love off. Nick would say she was all wrong. For one thing, you can't be half in love, he'd say. He was a boy idealist about love, earnest and wide open. Tom Swift and His Pounding Heart. That's what Rita was half in love with, and they hadn't talked about anything yet.

"Have you lived here all your life?"

"In LA, yes. Not here," he said, taking his hands from the wheel for a moment and gesturing at the close-clipped lawns on either side of the boulevard. "When you're on your way up or down, you don't live anywhere long."

"Haven't you always been on the way up?"

"More or less. Not as much as Peter. He's the skyrocketing kind." He spoke without awe of the process, and seemed to relish it. He knew that Peter would never have become a decorator if it hadn't been for Rita, and he was asking her now to share the marvel of it.

"I don't even understand what happened," she said. The leather smell in the Jaguar was a shade sweeter than the Mercedes, like the difference between two perfect tobaccos. She was always good at hairline distinctions. "He got a job arranging pots and pans in a store window. Then it was antiques. The next thing I knew, he was decorating a yacht. The rest is history. My friend Peter, the star."

"Superstar, you mean."

"Is there a difference?" she asked playfully. She had got Peter his first job, doing the flowers at a wedding. She made a thousand phone calls to get him the next one, but he couldn't do it. His Village lover was jealous when he worked. Rita decided the Village lover had to go.

"I thought you'd never ask," Nick said. "I'm one of the handful of people who knows. With stars, history is the last three weeks. They have all the time in the world to get their hair done and go shopping. Time is what superstars give up. It doesn't exist."

"Peter doesn't have any time?"

"None. I wish I could buy him some, but he has more money than I do, so it mustn't be for sale."

He spoke evenly, the skin around his eyes crinkling with pleasure. Not because the news about Peter was pleasant. He seemed happy that he had a handle on the situation, that he knew Peter well enough to see him through the haze. She didn't think there was anything wrong between Nick and Peter. What was sad, what was making Nick talk rueful and portentous, was a split in their rhythm. Nick seemed to have all the time on his hands that Peter gave up. He had time to kill. Rita didn't know how she knew it, since she didn't have any idea of what it took to do a day of real estate. Maybe because he'd taken time for her this afternoon, she thought, and then thought it didn't say a lot about her self-image, if time with her was time killed.

"So LA is a gold mine," she said. She meant there were veins of it, and some people tapped into it and some didn't, and then it had to be mined, pick and shovel. It was a remark about how difficult it was, not how easy.

"You know those old prospectors they used to have in westerns?" Nick asked her as he turned into a driveway lined with freshly polished cars. "They're all grizzled, and they cuss and have rotten hats."

"Yes," she said, as if they'd seen the same movie that very day, projected in the middle of everything else, like a movie on a plane. "People who never make a strike. You wonder what they'd do with the money if it came to them now. After all that waiting."

"My grandfather," Nick said, shaping the irony into one

final photograph, sepia-toned and out of an album. "He used to go off by himself to the middle of nowhere and hunt for minerals. I don't know if it was a scheme about water or uranium or what; but when my father told me about it, I had a very clear picture of my grandfather putting a double handful of sand in a sifter. With a mule tied up nearby."

A boy who should have been in movies took the key to the car from Nick to park it, and the two of them made their way to the front of the house. It was an ordinary place, not so big, and Rita wasn't in the mood to go overboard about it. But she forgot until she walked in, shying behind Nick and edging through the crowd in the front hall, all of whom seemed to be kissing good-bye, that she was here to see the latest piece of Peter's work. If possible, there was more silk in this living room than in Peter's own, pale as cream on every wall, upholstered to the room itself. The furniture was variously English, provincial French, and just a bit of wild-priced American, all of it old and perfect and brought together as if by an inner will to be beautiful in a well-protected place. This was what Rita said to herself, adopting the eye of a country-squire magazine, or, rather, its breathtaken voice. She turned to tell Nick she loved it, but he was gone to the bar to get them champagne. Peter appeared as she drew in her breath, before it turned into panic.

"You look like you just blew in from the East," he said, grinning. "I can always tell, because you look as if everything here had a price tag on it, and you can't afford it."

"It's not that, Peter. I'm afraid they won't take traveler's checks, and I have to have that little chest of drawers under the window."

"The lady has good taste, I see." He was full of mirth, but he was looking sleek, his yellow hair cut close. He always looked like he'd just finished posing for a portrait six feet by four, but today he was an Art Deco poster, cool-eyed and angular. Not too thin, like he used to be in New York. No hunger about him at all.

"Maybe I could take it out in trade," Rita said, "because I

see now I have to have it. I can dust and do ironing and run the vacuum around. How long would it take me to earn that chest?"

"Oh, about three years. But you know, you can't eat a chest. They just sit there and hold up ashtrays."

They were so glad to be together again they were flying. Nick appeared with champagne, slopping it over his fingers, and they clinked glasses in a solemn toast before they went on laughing. Rita knew they had drunk to her arrival, but they also seemed to have paid their respects to the moment when they'd all three finally hooked up. It had taken them years and years.

"Go away now, Peter," she said. "You're busy. I'm okay. Nick is just who I needed. He's telling me about his grand-father."

" 'A Tale of the Old West,' " Nick said.

"Look," Peter said to her, "I have to talk to you right away. Nick, go find Jennifer and tell her the house is fabulous. I'm going to take Rita for a ride."

"Okay, Buddy." Nick took Peter's glass and poured what was left in his own. He lifted it to them both and began to move away. Then he called back over his shoulder. "What are the dogs' names? Poo-poo and Tinkle, right?"

"Pyramus and Thisbe, and they're angels, so don't tease them."

Peter led Rita through the room, and she noticed that everyone stopped to watch her. She understood they were keeping their antennae out for Peter, and they scrutinized her as something new about him. But it was odd. In New York, she was accustomed to centering herself in group after group at a party, until there was no line anymore between her energy and the party's. It tended to hide the fact that she was shy. There were perhaps thirty people in this room; but since it could have held sixty, the groups were islanded. As Rita and Peter threaded among them, she felt a whir and crackle around the two of them like a field of force. No one here, she realized, knew she talked too much. No one was weary of hearing she was wounded at love and so would hold out hope for her. Wouldn't have to *hope*. No one suspected her of less self-regard than the average. It made her feel fine, free to file for a new passport. It made everyone else seem easier to deal with, a little less than met the eye. She liked it that she'd been up three hours longer than anyone in the room. To make the point stick, she hadn't changed her watch yet.

When they left the living room, they went down several steps into the library. And there, suddenly, was Los Angeles again, this time through a mammoth plate window that showed how nervous it must have made someone to give up a whole room to books. Yet the books went on and on, rising to ten or twelve feet and scaled by ladders on tracks. But the first thing Rita saw was the swing. It was suspended on ship's ropes from the ceiling, more like a rickshaw with no wheels, or a sedan chair. It was painted, lacquered, carved, and beaded with stones like jade or lapis. From the Orient for sure, but Rita would have passed if asked what country. The rest of the room was more or less an English library. A Chippendale partners' desk and wing chairs by the fire, sherry and pipes, and a half-acre library table for magazines and bronzes. With this wedding cake of a swing chandeliered in the middle.

"What is it?" she asked, as he helped her up the matching portable stairs, a sort of jeweler's stepladder. She sat back plumply in the swing. It was padded in down pillows.

"It's a maharaja's seat," Peter said, hopping in next to her, the force of him sending the swing into motion. "It goes on top of an elephant. Pretend we're riding in a steamy forest in Rangoon."

"I can't. I've never been there."

"You've seen movies," he said, permitting no excuse. "Pretend."

They went back and forth above the refinements of the library. The sensation of gliding in the air while sitting cross-legged was like riding a flying carpet. As she looked down, it seemed to Rita that a scene out of Jane Austen could materialize here, which never happened in New York. Emma and

Mr. Knightly reading bits out of books to each other, years before they are ready to be in love. Rita looked up. As to the view, yes the view was lovely, though not as nice, she thought, as Peter's and Nick's in Bel-Air. She wondered if she was being discriminating or overly partisan. What, after all, did she know about the view? She'd never had one of her own.

"I can't believe I left New York," she said.

"You left it years ago, Rita. Are you in Rangoon?"

"A little. Peter, what am I going to do here?"

He sighed by way of answering, and fell back on one elbow into the cushions. The intervening years hadn't touched him. He would always be young to look at, Rita thought, and then one day go old in a flash. It had been the same with his grandfather. The only clue to Peter's given age was his good taste, which got rarer and subtler with the years—with the months, even. People with no taste might suppose he was still in college.

"What you have to do to begin with," he said, "is take care of me."

"Are you sick?" she asked dryly. "Because if you aren't, I can't imagine what needs taking care of."

"Rita, I don't know what I'm doing anymore."

"Aren't you happy?" she wanted to know, because if *he* wasn't, what with Nick and Bel-Air and houses like this to put together, then nobody was.

"I want to be an artist."

Now? If you're an artist, she thought, you'd have known before now. Because you can't just become one, unless you become *that* kind. By which she meant a con man with a gimmick, someone who was better at a gallery opening than he was all alone in a studio, who worked on the principle that the buyer was too cowed by "Art" to call his bluff about all those watery splotches. Rita didn't see why anyone would want to be that sort of artist if he'd already made it as a decorator. Decorating was as much of a con as you could wish for.

"What kind?"

"A painter, I think," he said. They floated on these pillows like angels on a painted ceiling, so art was as real as anything here. "I want to start at the beginning. I want to start lousy."

"But what about decorating? Are you giving up money?"

"No," he said, sitting up again and looking urgent. "That's where you come in. I can't trust anyone else. It's not as bad as it sounds. I'll make you a lot of money, too."

"I don't get it," she said, putting two and two together, "and I don't like it."

"I want you to work for me, Rita. All you have to do is spend money."

"No, Pete, please don't make me. I wouldn't know what to do, and I'm not dumb enough to start something new."

"Rita," he said, "you're the world's greatest shopper." He gripped her by the shoulders to buck her up, the producer sending the ingenue on at the last minute. Knock 'em dead, Alice Faye. "And you know why? You're totally dispassionate. You notice what's good for its own sake. Not because you want it."

It was true. Her happiest hours were spent adrift in stores. But it was at best an ambiguous virtue, she always thought, the quality of coming home from Altman's empty-handed.

"All you have to do is market it," Peter concluded. "It's your talent."

Rita had done everything. Opened a restaurant, edited a magazine, modeled, acted, taken in boarders, and minded ruinous children. She'd held a dozen nine-to-five jobs under Devil's Island conditions or worse. She could *do* this. But she was alert enough to know she had to heed what it said about her and Peter. She couldn't just take care of *him* because, for one thing, there was Rita to think of, here for her final assault on the future. Helplessly, she spent a moment wondering how pleased *Nick* would be if she came to Peter's rescue. A memory of New York went through her head like a stack of snapshots being spread out on a table. On an old pecan wood tea table she used to have, one she gave away last week. With Peter, she knew she couldn't look for the sort of way out that worked in New York, where she wouldn't answer the telephone for weeks to shake someone off. New York, until hours ago the works of the clock of the world, was time past. The job sounded good. But it had come so much out of nowhere that she hadn't had a chance to want it. She'd determined not to move until she knew what she wanted.

"I'm sorry, Rita," he said. "I've got it all figured out, and you haven't even unpacked. You get a vacation first. Have you met Hey?"

"He picked me up at the airport."

"Of course. Did he tell you about himself?"

"No," she admitted. She appeared to have evoked a contrary response out of Hey. She gathered he was everyone's dream of a long talk.

"He's not very good with women," Peter assured her. "It's because he's reincarnated, *he* says, and he's very close to his last life, when he was a woman. You must get him to talk about it."

"I thought he used to be a dancer."

"That was in *this* life," Peter said, having had more practice at making the distinction. "He told you about *that*?"

"Nick did."

"Hey never talks about it. He's closer to the lady he used to be."

Rita supposed she wouldn't get to Square One until people started telling her about themselves. When she'd decided to move to Los Angeles, she was fed up with her friends' predictable fads and self-delusions. She had heard the story ten times over of the wife-beater and the new girl who was different. Or the one about taking a house in the Hamptons to air one's head for the summer. Diets and sun signs and meditative breathing were only the tip of the iceberg when Rita got cornered over coffee. Was she a cynic? She'd always thought not, because she went on listening year after year, long after she'd seen the repeating patterns in people's fuckups and seemed to know to the day how long someone would still be sleeping with someone else. She'd never yet heard anyone out about a *previous* life. At least she could break new ground.

"Peter," she said, looking over his shoulder, "there's a photographer outside in the garden taking pictures of us." She said it as something of a warning, not because she thought it was the C.I.A. but because he might want to brush his hair or be seen with somebody classier than she. Besides, the photographer ruined everything. He took a cheap shot of the ride in the elephant swing and dispersed in the process the old, walled dreamworld of Peter and Rita.

"Oh?" Peter asked absently, not even glancing around. "That's just the newspaper people. You could be someone important. The *real* photographers are taking pictures of the house. Jennifer's a little insecure. She needs both kinds."

"Who's she?"

"Nobody. You'll meet her. It's really *my* house, of course, but as she paid for it, I let her live in it."

Peter spoke breezily enough, as if he didn't really mean it, but Rita knew what he was getting at. Back in New York, she'd always told him decorators got by on two lines. At the first appointment, they walk into the place and shudder audibly and announce: "Everything has to go." And when it's done, and they come back for a highbrow occasion, just another guest, they get a fix on the horrible new chairs and gasp: "What have they done to my room?" Everything rode on your attitude. This beautiful silky house had taken a year, Rita supposed. It must be strange to turn it over to someone else, she thought, even someone with the right to have human designs on it.

"The Bel-Air house is a dream," she said, bringing things around to something of his own.

"If we ever finish it," he said. "You think I can be a painter?"

"I don't know, Peter. I guess if you paint long enough."

"But how do I know how good I'll be?"

You can't, she thought about halfway through his question. A ripple of irritation ruffled the surface, and she automatically paused to let it pass. She'd never been angry at Peter, or, rather, she'd never said so. Other people, yes. She knew the only way around anger was right through the middle of it. But she'd long ago decided to go easy on Peter, even if she risked his behaving like a child. She knew from the beginning they might get locked into a game that got more unworkable the more it meant well. Then they would end up enemies. So she'd had to monitor spoiling Peter, all along keeping it to herself because the people she knew would call it queer. She made it work. But she knew already that something had to give if they did business together.

"It's none of your affair how good you'll be. Painters paint." I don't want to be serious, she thought, I don't want to. She'd been in the maharaja's seat long enough now to have given it a place in the pile of snapshots. She wanted the talk light like the air that fanned them; for here they were, together again for the first time in years. She'd planned on a talk in a private language for the first meeting with Peter, so what were they doing going on about Art?

"Well, I'd rather be good than not," Peter said. "*I'll* be able to tell, after all. I can't stand second-rate art, Rita, and neither can you." He turned his face now in the direction of the camera, as if he'd finally decided to cooperate. A string of pictures was taken as he went on. "Nick can. He says there's room for amateurs, and they don't do any harm. But you can't trust the things he says these days."

"Why?" Rita asked, leaning closer because he was in profile. "What's wrong with Nick?"

"Oh, Rita, who knows," he said softly. "I think Nick's in love."

Chapter 2

Peter's grandfather, Prince Alexander Kirkov, stood to inherit, among other more pedestrian properties which only generated rent, a summer estate that ran for a hundred and fifteen miles along the Black Sea. On Easter morning in 1912, when he was twenty-one, he opened a brassbound wooden box at the breakfast table in his parents' palace in Saint Petersburg. Inside it was a jeweled horse and rider done up by the house of Fabergé, the horse carved from a single block of midnight jade, the horseman paved from head to foot in precious stones depicting him in the uniform of an officer in the Imperial Russian army. The hint was not lost on Alexander that the least the very rich could do was protect the fatherland. What with a grand tour and two seasons of yachting, though, he didn't get around to enlisting until a couple of weeks before the unpleasantness at Sarajevo. He didn't pay it any mind. While the Kaiser and the Czar—Willy and Nicky, the prep school kings—burned up the wireless, Alexander had a daily fitting for uniforms with the tailor his father kept in residence and spent a whole day in the cellars choosing a cartload of wine to take with him.

He was blown away on the Eastern Front before the wine arrived. He spent the greater part of the First War being shuttled from one hospital to another and put back together, the doctors going in after more and more bits of iron and taking a turn at his ruined knees. He ended up in Paris for a couple of years, and by then he'd got almost everything out of order. He was all in one piece by then, but his head went. While the Revolution roared through Russia, he sat in a sunny window on the Ile St.-Louis, staring out and smiling, then seized with unaccountable fits of tears. His family was massacred, and he never knew. He got out of the clinic in 1919, and an exiled aunt and cousin gave him the number of his Swiss bank account. The balance was a trifle by a prince's reckoning. The safe deposit box was full of nothing in particular. He moved to Brooklyn Heights and stared this time at the cliffs of Manhattan. He lived modestly ever after.

The Imperial past came back to Alexander Kirkov in great operatic rushes over the years, like gleams of light in a swirl of fog. It was because the curtain rose unexpectedly one day in a downtown local train that Rita first met him. She was jiggling along, a copy of *Town and Country* open on her lap, reading how the world's ten busiest women took care of their hair. On the facing page was an ad for a Parke-Bernet auction, and to announce an odd lot of fat-carated stones, it carried a photograph of the horse and rider in the brassbound box. Alexander Kirkov, standing above Rita and happening to glance down, let out a Cossack's shriek and grabbed the magazine. Rita, a surreptitious reader of other people's papers, had a certain sympathy in these matters, but this old man had gone too far. She got a grip on the *Town and Country* and chided him. He held on like Gangbusters. She was fingered as a Leninist and given a speech, some of it in Russian, about the summer parties on the Black Sea and a ballet that appeared to have been performed on the Dowager Empress's train. Halfway through, he was weeping in her arms because she was the spit of his nanny, Tova, whose skin was like beaten cream. And so they ended up in Brooklyn, and she walked him home.

A heavily draped apartment, burgundy velvet and tassels. With a sea of photographs in Art Nouveau frames on the piano, like the stills from a long run of *The Cherry Orchard*. Alexander Kirkov showed her what was left, the silver and enamels, as if to prove his claim on the horse and rider. The marquis who was selling it at auction and the Texan who would buy it were in collusion, as far as he was concerned. Common horse thieves. Rita walked about, open-mouthed. She had long ago given up on her own ancestry—the poor, she'd decided, because they had their hands full of immediate family, kept the dead buried—and was a pushover for the Russian's stories about the vast prerogatives his people lived by, once upon a time. He unrolled for her the useless deeds and parchment titles and guided her finger through his family tree. She returned again and again.

And finally came face to face with Peter. She'd been aware for some time that the old prince—he must have been seventy-five then—didn't live alone, but she thought the rustling from the kitchen was a maid. Or a valet, perhaps, someone who'd laid out Alexander Kirkov's evening clothes ever since his first masked ball at the Winter Palace, except she was probably confusing it with the slaves in Mississippi. Then, one day, without preliminary, Peter came into the parlor carrying a tea tray, unbearably thin and pale, a young man made out of porcelain. He had finally decided to come out of hiding, as if he'd eavesdropped long enough to trust her. He wasn't shy so much as he seemed, like a deer, to be tuned to a higher world's rhythms, where the air was thin and the food music.

"Tell me," he said to her politely, "where you are exiled from."

The world at large, she might have said. From then on, Alexander Kirkov let the young man stay, and she pieced his story together from chance remarks. It seemed that Alexander Kirkov had ferreted out a Russian noblewoman shortly after he came to New York. They married and had two despicable children, a daughter who drowned herself and a son whom his father disowned when he changed his name to Kirk. Alexander Kirkov's wife took Peter in when the daughter went under— Peter was thirteen—and she herself died the following year. Alexander Kirkov could not keep it straight who was to blame for what, but that it was all someone's fault he knew for a fact. At least he didn't take it out on Peter, like Cinderella's stepmother. He sold an icon and sent him to prep school for two years; and when the school made Peter sick, he brought him home and brought in tutors. Piano, fencing, poetry, and art.

The art proved to be afternoon trips to museums with a melancholy pederast, also Russian. In fact, nearly everyone Peter knew when Rita met him was Russian, and most were nearly eighty. He was twenty-three years old, but something about him seemed to have stopped when he was thirteen. Standard American was no longer his native tongue. He took care of his grandfather gladly, but he'd ended up taking care of several of his grandfather's friends as well, aristocrats all of them. He took their treasures by the suitcaseful to dealers on Third Avenue. He went on all-day errands to buy tinned sturgeon and the best black bread. And while he plumped their pillows and made them comfortable, he heard the ceaseless lament for the lost world that stopped in 1917. Prince Alexander Kirkov never wavered in his belief that the Romanovs would be summoned again, and they would all return triumphantly to their estates and once more civilize the wilds of the earth. The old Russians tended to close their remarks with three cheers for Peter, whom they saw as if on a white horse coming home, restored to his ancient birthright. Alexander Kirkov didn't try to hide it from Rita. The young man was being prepared for a prince's destiny.

"Peter," she said one day in the midst of a brainstorm, for he had clearly begun to believe in the fairy tale ending and needed a dose of the real world. "I've always wanted to learn a little Russian. Come and teach me."

Because Rita was a realist, given to missing nothing when she walked down the street, casting a cold eye on her hit-and-run careers, she assumed her world was the real one. She was half-right. She harbored no illusions about herself, yet she had a habit of constructing castles in air around the people she loved. The Russian lesson was Tuesday and Thursday from ten to twelve at Rita's place, followed by lunch and a bit of shopping. It didn't take long for Rita to learn the truth about Peter, by which she meant his secret life, and it went two ways. One, he was gay. Two, he was mesmerized by Hollywood and spent his most rapturous hours at the movies. So he wasn't so un-American after all.

"It used to be that everyone wanted to be a prince," she said to him as they wandered through Bendel's. "Now even the princes want to be movie stars."

"I want to be an *actor*," he said dramatically.

"No, you don't. That's just because you're gay. You have to do something *practical*." She sounded insufferable. Don't be his mother, she said to herself. "What color scarf should I wear with a peach blouse?"

"Raspberry."

"Interesting. I was thinking green. You have to be able to think of both."

She wasn't always so controlling. This, the period of the Russian lesson, went on for more than a year, and the two of them were conspicuously loose and undemanding of each other. But Rita was under considerable pressure at the time, in love with a stock manipulator from Short Hills who could see her only during lunch. So she had to serve a meal and make love in the same hour on Mondays and Wednesdays, and it sent her off balance on Tuesdays and Thursdays when she saw Peter. She didn't absorb a hell of a lot of Russian. But it was a relief to be able to confide in Peter, who forced her to be hard on herself and abandon the men who fucked her over. Peter had less to own up to, since living with Alexander Kirkov meant he couldn't bring a man home to bed. An occasional visit to the baths, or he'd get himself picked up in a bar, but mostly he sighed for a perfect love and tried to imagine it to Rita.

She listened and didn't raise a finger to object, though here was exactly the place where the real world ought to have come down hard, without the flowers and the buff-colored birds. But see what Rita does. She rids herself so of Lancelot-and-Guinevere that she'll go get laid while the water boils for the speculator's coffee. And only one day later, she sits with her chin in her hands and lets Peter moon about the man in his dreams.

An actual, particular man, as it turned out. Peter was still getting over his first love. When he was sent off at fifteen to school in Connecticut, he had no friends and kept to himself. Rita imagined he must have looked like a changeling, unearthly in his navy blazer and white duck trousers. An older boy called Mark, the all-American sort, was charged by the grinning headmaster to keep an eye on the spooky little Russian who wasn't joining in. Peter didn't think he had anything to do with one thing leading to another. Mark was a senior and an athlete, and his body was a set of connections, perfectly in tune, between the way a boy moves and the way a grown man acts. Early on, before they even met, Peter watched Mark in the shower after soccer practice and would have turned him to stone if he could have, so as to run his hands over him whenever he wished. He wanted a Greek statue all his own, and he didn't much care if someone touched him back. When Mark first dropped by to say hello, Peter could barely put one word after the next. He slipped into Mark's room between classes and exchanged pillow cases with him. A week later, he rooted through Mark's laundry bag and took a set of dirty underwear and gym clothes to dress up in.

But he didn't know Mark had feelings of his own. Just before Thanksgiving, just at the end of soccer season, Mark came into Peter's bed one night late, and the lights stayed out. He arrived about midnight and stayed till nearly dawn nearly every night thereafter. As Peter told it, they got no sleep for the rest of the year. But they didn't look it, and the headmaster patted himself on the back and thanked God for the manly virtues that lit up his beautiful school.

That these things end is a matter of course, but no one had bothered to tell Peter. The head might even have remarked that it was just another case of boys being boys, nothing a caning or a lap around the track couldn't cure. June came, and Mark graduated, and Peter spent the summer in Brooklyn Heights, thinking, "*Now* what?" He couldn't believe it had come to nothing at all, but Mark didn't call, didn't write, and didn't come back in the fall to visit. He was too busy with freshman soccer at Dartmouth. Peter went up to Connecticut for another year and fell apart, though the only evidence of it was the silence that settled around him. The headmaster wrote to Alexander Kirkov that it was just what he'd expected, with the history of drowning and all. As the winter settled in, Peter had still another affair, but he never went into any detail about it with Rita. It was just something to do on the way down. By the end of the year, he was as tubercular, as bone-pale as any of the dead-tired heroes in Russian novels. Alexander Kirkov remarked on the resemblance.

Rita said he would get over it; but even Rita, who took things hard and lived on butterscotch sundaes when love went bad, had to admit that six years' brooding over Mark was tenacious beyond her experience. "Athletes die young," she told him. "You know what he'll look like in five years? I bet he'll be fat and surly." But her heart wasn't in it; and Peter, who had fallen in love with his own nun-like faith in the long lost boy, seemed to prefer to sigh and shake his head. Rita was maddened by it. He was stuck like a broken record in the middle of the first act. She applauded Peter's year of honeyed nights in the arms of his ancient Greek, but, after all, there were better things to do. She had an impulse to tell him what they were. She could have said that the second man got you over the first, the third the second, and so on. But she stopped

33

short. It suddenly gave her the creeps to think about giving him lessons in love. It made her seem like an old whore. And an old whore, she thought, would at least be doing her teaching in bed.

Peter and Rita got too close, so the language classes took a long summer break. She'd learned about enough to order a vodka at the Russian Tea Room. They spoke on the phone, and she still did a formal turn with Alexander Kirkov from time to time, a Sunday lunch or Tchaikovsky on the stereo and pound cake. Peter and Rita went about their business. The only reason they'd known each other for twelve years was that they managed to part for years at a time without any guilt. Peter really did want to be an actor until he moved in with his lover who didn't want him to work. Rita was just as serious about taking risks of the heart. They were never sentimental about each other because they knew that if they were, they would outgrow each other. Only the truest lovers, Rita thought, have the latitude to get sentimental.

Alexander Kirkov decided from the beginning that Peter was sleeping with Rita, and he was genuinely worried for Rita's sake. He knew she wasn't a whore. All he could think was that Rita was doing her part in a prince's education, that she was clever and mournful and had her own reasons, like Garbo in *Camille*, the only movie he had ever liked that wasn't Russian. He'd had so many qualms about the gap of passion in Peter's bringing-up. In his own youth, he had pursued his mother's lady's maid, and when he finally bedded her down, in the linen room at the palace, he was just fifteen and knew at the time that he'd settled the business of longing for his mother. Ever after, sex recalled the scent of freshly ironed sheets, which was as it should be. When he was sixteen, his father fixed it for him to make love to the very chorus girl he himself had been showering with bracelets and oranges. That went on backstage at a theater, and the echo of it spoke of lust as something more exotic than the smell of laundry. Alexander Kirkov was always glad he had had the two women to compare things against. His own son, the ingrate, peasant-headed

Kirk, had married at seventeen and so knew nothing at all. But Peter? Alexander Kirkov was beside himself until Rita appeared. Now he relaxed, sure that Peter had waited for the right woman. You could tell it was his governess Tova, not his mother, that he'd always wanted to cozy up to.

The news that Peter was gay knocked more of the wind out of his grandfather than it might have a year or two before, before Rita. Peter walked in with the steeping tea and bread and butter sandwiches—"The bread is just a vehicle for the butter, Peter"—and told him he was moving to Manhattan.

"Are you moving in with Rita?" Alexander Kirkov asked, a little irritated to be troubled at his tea. He thought it was possible to take these affairs too far, and perhaps it was past time for the boy to be over Rita. He didn't even know that Peter and Rita were having a cooling-off, since Peter still spent his Tuesdays and Thursdays on leave from Brooklyn Heights.

"Rita?" Peter asked helplessly, wondering how far away they would have to start, and then growing furious at the implications. He had been wonderful to Alexander Kirkov partly because they'd staked out a sexual DMZ, a no-man's-land where they were as neutered as a choirboy and a lofty, thin-legged cleric. Peter saw the whole dumb plot that had grown in his grandfather's head. The candle he carried for Mark flared in his hand; but, raised in a court's tradition, he kept things gentlemanly as long as he could.

"I have a friend," Peter said, who had in truth never had one in Brooklyn Heights. "He's made a room for me."

Somehow, Alexander Kirkov couldn't let it go, and he kept pumping questions. It was because he didn't see how he could let Peter go, but he was too proud to say that. So for the sake of a heart that couldn't speak its mind, he hectored Peter about wasting time. He trundled out the chestnuts about making provisions for male heirs and beefing up the stock with a wife one might have met over croquet in Sebastopol, one of one's own kind.

"I'm in love with a man," Peter said, upping the ante. "From Broadway." Here he stretched the truth to get an equivalent for the chorus girl, a story he didn't even know, but he needed a seedy shock effect his grandfather would recognize. It was true enough. Peter's first lover, bear-like Alan with the Diner's Club card in continuous use, put his money into things when he was flattered, and he'd put a bundle into plays that closed on opening nights. He was from Broadway to the degree that Broadway needed suckers. It would take Rita a year and a half to break them up because Peter got tenacious again, just to prove a point to his grandfather, who didn't even notice. Peter also nursed the pipe dream that he could be an actor quicker if he got hooked up with a fat cat.

Alexander Kirkov with the wind knocked out rattled like a serpent. He had protected this delicate boy in much the same spirit as his beloved Czar had protected his only son, the bleeder. Suddenly, all this refinement and faintheartedness of Peter's, far from being truly Russian and connected with a blood too pure, were just the frills that went with sodomy. If he'd known that Peter was going to walk out that day forever, that they were *both* going to go the route of dispossession and unbroken silence, he might have reconsidered the verbal blows he rained down on Peter's head. He was prince enough to long for Peter's happiness before all castles and estates. But he probably figured they would be railing at each other for months about the new kink in events. It was about time they had an argument. Alexander Kirkov's own father challenged *his* father to a duel before he was twenty, having to do with gambling debts. In a milder mood, Alexander Kirkov might even have said, sounding not unlike the headmaster in judiciousness, that fucking with another man was the sort of decadence to which an aristocrat might be momentarily drawn. Decadence went with the territory, so to speak.

In an hour it was over, and Peter had fled. The final shouting match got out of hand, the last recriminations animal and infantile—"Pig!" from the old prince, "Donkey!" from the boy. Alexander Kirkov had a sinking spell. He realized that Peter had gone beyond the need to justify or even win, and the argument as old as the wind on the Steppes, of who owed what to whom and who was to blame for the argument, wasn't going to take place in Brooklyn Heights. Alexander Kirkov needed to shout good sense at his loved ones because the shouting, he thought, kept it basic. The quiet in the heavily rugged apartment deepened into evening, and the prince skipped his dinner and ate a whole rice pudding—cried into it, really, and ate it as bitter herbs, because it was so cruelly humble. Cried for the whole hundred and fifteen miles on the Black Sea. And the Kirkov sapphires.

They were sewn into his pillow, five of them in graduated sizes from a pea to a kidney bean, so blue they were almost black. They were given to him in Paris when he got out of the hospital, by the cousin who gave him the keys to his Swiss accounts. The remnants of the Kirkov family who had made it to France after the revolution had grouped and voted to turn over the stones to Alexander Kirkov because he was the most highly titled. The cousin had smuggled them out of Russia by swallowing them. He was on foot for two weeks dressed as a peddler, stopped and searched a couple of times a day, and methodically every morning he did his business in the bushes by the side of the road. He dug the sapphires out of the shit and boiled them in a tin next to the tin where his tea water cooked. And then ate them again like vitamins, which in a way they were, because they kept him going. He had prized them himself out of a choker given to his wife—shot dead by revolutionaries with her baby in her arms—by the Empress Alexandra herself, as a memento of a trip through the fjords on the royal yacht *Standart*.

Alexander Kirkov received the sapphires gravely and brought them to America. During most of the transatlantic voyage, he was so nervous for their safety that he held them tight in his hand. He walked the decks with his fist balled up, as if he had taken a war wound somewhere in his arm and was clenching against the pain. Ever since, he would lie down in bed at night and feel for the sapphires through the feathers in his pillow, where they were wrapped in a square of dove gray velvet. He went to sleep with his head exactly over them. He

37

had never even shown them to his wife, since they had come to represent to him the Kirkov blood itself, the stuff of the male line.

Then his own son broke his heart and didn't deserve them. Peter was the only one who had a right, even if his mother had thrown away the Kirkov name when she married a fool named Gilmore. Alexander Kirkov always planned to hand them over to Peter as he lay near death. Over the years, he polished up a speech full of pearls that gleamed, when he thought of it, like beads of caviar. But the night Peter left, he moaned on his bed because it wasn't going to happen as he'd always wished. He pounded the pillow with his fist until he was panting. He hid his face in it and gripped it as if he would tear it in two. The sapphires worked their way out of the velvet pouch and got buried among the feathers. Somewhere, the empire bided its time, but the Kirkov line was done.

"How hot is it? Can you see?"

"Ninety-eight."

"That's not hot enough," Nick said. "And besides, I can still see you."

Nick and Peter usually made an appointment to meet in the steam room off their bedroom. Originally, they were being practical—no point in bringing the steam up twice. Lately, though, they were both so busy working that they made the arrangement to assure they would both get home at the same time now and then. They didn't say so, but each had a troubled vision of the other sitting in the gathering fog all alone, and it was insupportable. Not the same as coming home and finding someone has gone ahead with dinner or left for the party already. More like forgetting someone waiting in a restaurant, all dressed up, shrugging off the look of being left in the lurch. Yet the steam room was only as intimate as they wanted to make it, in that way not unlike the bed in the next room. They were just as happy sitting on opposite benches, heads bent and breathing eucalyptus oil, as they were talking and giving each other a rubdown. But the place had a peculiar intensity, maybe because they were both naked, their voices filling the room, and the act of sweating loosened the tongue like fever. In their case, it happened that they first met in a steam room long ago, or, rather, they sucked each other off and met when they stepped out afterward into the pest-ridden corridor. This was in the baths on Hollywood Boulevard, over near Western Avenue. Nobody went there anymore, but for half a year it was the thousand and one nights.

"It doesn't matter, Nick," Peter said, moving back through the clouds to where Nick sat. "I'll get Hey to call the steam man and raise the pressure. Let me do your head."

Nick leaned forward and hung his head down. As Peter stood over him and gripped his scalp and began to knead it, Nick reached up instinctively and took hold of Peter's thighs. Through the steam, it looked like something carnal going on, but the hold that each of them had on the other was classic as a wrestler's and just as cool. They stood still sometimes, Nick had come to think, in a world of ancient games and dances where sex had not yet taken place. Close up, one might have even called them innocent, except the innocent aren't conscious of what they do with their hands, and Nick and Peter were. The two of them *sought* consciousness in moments like these. As Nick's head gave in to Peter's rhythm, lolling and swaying, Peter had the feeling that he held Nick entirely in his hands. He knew what he would do for Nick and also what he didn't have to do. Peter liked the difficulty of the two of them, and he didn't mind the constant test of limits. As far as love went, he would have said, it was innocence that was a kind of sin.

"Did you take a look at the ranch?" he asked, and wasn't prepared for the tightening of the cords in the neck. He'd meant to be innocuous. What if the ranch was just a fiction? he wondered. Nick must have spent the day with the man who was tying him in knots, whoever that might be. They couldn't talk about it yet.

"Yes. This afternoon. I love it, Peter. It's like the middle of Montana or something."

"Are you buying it or selling it?" The ranch was real enough, it seemed. It must have been that Nick took the new man there with him.

"Both. I want to get it now and wait for a big buyer. Do you want to go into it with me?"

Peter lifted Nick's head and looked down at his face. He wiped the sweat off Nick's forehead and out of his eyes with the back of his hand, as if he could physically clear the air between them. Nick was dark and tough from a day in the sun. Cowboys, Peter knew, were his fiercest daydream.

"You must be thinking of someone else," he said ironically. "I don't like the West, remember? I'm the one who wants things civilized."

"You don't even have to see it, Peter," he said, curiously enthusiastic. "I mean as an investment."

"My money's all tied up," Peter said, letting Nick go and bringing up his hands to wipe his own face. He breathed in the smell of Nick's gypsy hair. A sorrow came over him because he was suddenly countering the wall Nick had thrown up with a wall of his own. Let's not talk about money, he thought. There were truckloads of property between them already, and not enough insurance, philosophically speaking. Lately, they did not seem able to decide together what it was they were trying to buy. The truth was, Peter just didn't have the time. But it probably seemed to Nick that if Peter's money was tied up, it was roped around with impossible projects. He was putting everything in his savings account, as if he were trying to bankroll a Russian palace and needed every penny. Nick thought they *had* to talk money because they had just moved into yet another new financial bracket, and they couldn't stay where they were, even if they'd wanted to. Meanwhile, the money ought to be a way to bring them together, to make certain bets and take risks as crazy as the two of them. But Peter knew what he sounded like just now. Threatened, as if the money had started to separate them. He didn't believe it, but he didn't know how to say so. Here, too, he didn't have the time.

"What are we going to do about Rita?" he said out of nowhere.

"Does something need to be done?" Nick asked mildly, going with the drift. "She seems terrific. Even Hey's in love with her. Isn't she good at the job?"

"She's fine." Peter hadn't told him yet about going into art, and he didn't know why. "I mean men."

"Are you so sure she's interested?" Nick said.

What had gone wrong, he wondered, in what he'd said about the ranch? Ever since this afternoon with Sam, he'd wanted to make Peter part of the desert territory he had happened on. He was too much off balance, dazed by the heat that he and Sam threw off. They'd sat on a fence and watched an old chestnut horse doze above a water trough. They drove the pickup, sliding in and out of wheel ruts, up a wagon trail to the top of a high hill, where the spread of the land was as far as they could see. Barbed wire crisscrossed in the near distance, running in lines between Nick's and the neighbors' boundaries, but Nick didn't care what was his and what wasn't. If he bought this place, he was doing it to get a ticket to all that space, whomever it belonged to.

And wherever they went, he and Sam were turning on more and more, but making no move until they couldn't hold it any longer. It happened in the bunkhouse, on a wooden bed with a stack of horse blankets for a mattress. They pulled their pants down around their boots and did it with their clothes on. He'd gone too far, Nick thought, and here he didn't mean sex. If only he could bring Peter into it. But he knew he'd picked the very place Peter had no use for. Somehow, he began to see, he was engineering things in such a way that he would end up unable to say what he wanted. Already he was hard put to talk to Sam or Peter about anything important because what was important now about each was the other. He did what he could to be with Peter now. But he might as well be all alone if Peter and Sam were going to cancel one another out.

"I know Rita better than you," Peter said. It was one thing

to find themselves at cross-purposes, Nick thought, but Peter was getting ornery. "Do we know anyone?"

"How about Amos?"

"*Amos?*" Peter laughed and sat back on the opposite bench. It must have gotten hotter because Nick couldn't see him now. "He only does it with himself. He can't even do it in front of a mirror, in case the other person looks like he wants something."

"But he's nice."

"Nice is not enough. Nice doesn't fuck."

"If I were you," Nick said after a moment when the pipes knocked as if someone were hammering them, "I'd wait until Rita asks."

"But you're not, right?" Peter snapped. Nick was not Peter, particularly in the timing of moral appointments. Peter shook his head benignly, not about to be trapped in Nick's system of cautions. And the gesture got through, even if, in the steam, it didn't register to the eye. Suddenly they were sitting in silence —actually, in something of a hiss, like the sound of a tropical rain. They would have called this occasion neither a fight nor a thin slice of the human condition, though they knew there was a white noise to which the missed connections led. They had learned at last, by way of each other, that the line in the liquor store, the misdelivered mail, and the fatal seating at a party were in the nature of things, pure and simple. They were alert for ways to love each other whenever they could. But they didn't expect, just because they were together, that a sort of order was restored. Peter was Nick's reality principle, Nick Peter's, but it didn't mean they could abandon themselves to expectations. The desultory talk in the steam doesn't *have* to be harmless, and the world doesn't go without saying. They let themselves bicker, if they had to, or come to no conclusion. They ran down sometimes like clockwork, right in the middle of something.

After several minutes passed, Nick made his way across to Peter's bench and straddled his legs where they stretched out in front of him. Peter was slumped like an unstrung puppet.

Nick squeezed Peter's thighs between his knees for no special reason, just to make contact. After the ranch, he was finished with desire for the time being, and his cock ached dully, like the root of a tooth. He leaned on the wet tiled wall against his elbows and buried his head in his hands. When he sagged forward sleepily, his belly brushed Peter's face. Peter slowly shook his head against the hair around Nick's navel, as if to wipe the sweat away. It was abstractedness that made their motions those of sleep instead of love. The sweating and the heavy air had slowed them down to a degree below passion. They beached against each other, their muscles full of cotton. They were so close that a third person coming in wouldn't have been able to tell from across the room that it was two people here and not one. It was funny. They twined about each other because the steam made them punch-drunk, and they got closer than they sometimes did when they tried to.

"Oh, Nick," Peter said, panting in the heat and giving up, "if I don't take a cold shower now, I won't be able to go out tonight."

"I don't want to go out," Nick said, very groggy, as if he'd gone nine rounds already.

"It's Friday." As if to say Friday was a law, bigger than both of them. Peter slid out from under him, touched him at random with both hands, and padded off. They had a dozen invitations between them that had accumulated during the week, and they hadn't even pooled them yet. A possible route would reveal itself when they did—two or three parties in the same neighborhood, or on a straight line to Studio One by midnight, where they could dance until it closed. Play was work on Friday night. By Saturday night it was a profession.

When Peter turned the shower on, at the end of the steam room near the door, the cold water gave off an aura that seemed to eat up the steam. The cold air rolled in, the opposite of fog. In a matter of seconds, Peter could see Nick clearly, still bent in a sweat against the wall. Peter stood with relief in the fall of water, his senses sharpening again. He watched Nick become aware that the cloak of vapor had disappeared. Nick brought his head out of the cradle of his arms like an animal waking to footsteps, as if he might have been confused for a moment about where he was. Then he stood up straight and stretched his arms behind his head.

Peter thought he was as beautiful now, shrugging his torso in the white-tiled room, as he ever was. Peter was not possessed by a wandering eye. He didn't want anyone else, no more than he did when Mark had emptied the world of everything but a soccer field on a hot fall day. Peter always made a lightning appraisal of everything he wanted—a Chinese jar, a chair, a watercolor—and he took home the very best, if it was for sale, and kept it forever and let it grow beautiful. Nick lumbered toward him. He slipped out of the shower to give it over, and he thought as they passed, one soaped clean, the other pouring sweat like a horse: I won't let you leave without a fight.

And if we have to fight about it, he went on to himself as he took an armful of towels and crossed the bedroom, I'll win and you won't leave after all, so don't try. He threw open three or four towels on the bed, flung the rest of the pile down for a pillow, and then lay back to dry off. He reached for the telephone and dialed his answering service, hardly listening to the string of names and numbers he should call. Nothing serious. They'd all call back. He was thirsty, but he didn't feel like tracking down Hey on the intercom to ask. He tried to make a picture in his head of his first painting. But he was trying to see it as if it were already done, so he tried instead to decide what it was a picture of. He couldn't say.

He heard the thump when Nick shut the door to the steam room, then the sound of him walking across to the armoire and the click of the latch as the double doors opened. Then nothing. He might have been staring inside at the stacks of shirts, sick of them all. Peter rolled onto his side and looked over. Nick was standing with his back to the room, holding the doors wide open with both hands, as if he'd surprised something going on inside. The muscles in his back stood out in perfect symmetry. He wore a towel hitched at his waist, not because it was modest but because it was sexy. He was looking over his arm and out the window, not at the shirts.

"I was a bitch, Nick. I'm sorry."

"About Rita?" he asked. "Don't worry. It slipped my mind already."

"She can take care of herself," Peter said. "She's got a line on everything. What are you thinking?"

"I cleared twelve thousand dollars this week," Nick said. "My father never made that in a year."

"Oh, that. Well, that's not going to get you anywhere," Peter said, whose own father's disappearance with his platinum secretary and a bag full of negotiable securities had driven his mother to the water. It would have cheered him mightily to hear his father died without a penny. But he'd heard all this before from Nick and thought it was beside the point.

"That may be, Peter, but that's the way I feel.'"

"Misunderstood again," Peter said lightly, and Nick turned to see what he thought was so funny. And the whole thing dawned on him as it had a moment since on Peter. The same old battle lines sprang up on the field while they weren't watching. Peter annoyed at the pain Nick felt, because it was unoriginal. Nick lost in the stars because he and his father were doomed by ironies. Nick had been on the point of accusations. You don't understand, he would have said in a minute, what it's like to be poor. Turning it around so that Peter was to blame. But Peter saw it coming and stopped it cold.

"Come here," he said gently, "and I'll dry you off."

Nick walked over to the bed and tumbled down next to him. Peter came up on his knees, took a towel in either hand, and began to pat Nick dry. Nick was still caught up in the twelve thousand twists of fate, but at least he felt them for what they were. It wasn't Peter's fault. Over the years, he knew, they'd had to call it a draw about the facts of life. Peter's life began when he finally believed he was all alone— Alexander Kirkov's cutting him loose from the dynasty and his arrival years later in LA were the two historic events. Nick was never convinced his life had really started *because* he was so alone. They avoided moralizing the worlds they inhabited before they met; and they lived with each other's motley crew —fathers, overnight lovers, and traitorous boys—as best they could. The past was a gift they couldn't refuse, after all. But they didn't have to keep it in the living room.

"You're very thorough," Nick said.

"It comes from washing cars," Peter said, rubbing him down inch by inch. "I always used to dry my Pontiac by hand. With a baby bunting. You know, my grandfather loved to tell me how much the family spent on things. They spent about twelve thousand a year on *roses*, for Christ's sake. His mother would only take her bath in Vichy water, and they shipped it to Saint Petersburg in boxcars. Think how long it would have taken your father to afford *that*."

"Is that what we'll do when we have a lot of money?"

Peter leaned on Nick's raised knees as he might have leaned across a bar, and he tilted his head to consider the reach of the question.

"We'll eat a lot of aspic," he said, "with the choicest things suspended in it. And cold bass. That's what they eat for lunch in magazine interviews. The water out of the tap gives me all the bath I want, so not that. Antiques and paintings, I guess. We have a lot of money already. What do *you* think?"

"Land," Nick said with a shrug, as if it were self-evident, but also as if he needed the Dakotas or his own archipelago to make the word work.

"Poor Saint Nick," Peter said. "Who ever thinks to fill *his* Christmas stocking? Is it because you were poor and straight at the same time that you need so much to fall back on now?"

"How much money is enough?" Nick said playfully, a question for a question, rocking his knees so that Peter swayed back and forth.

"Don't act as if we have too much already," Peter warned him. He knew the implication at large was that, if one of them lost his heart in his purse, it was going to be Peter and not Nick. "Think about what you really mean by land."

"I don't mean a place the size of Connecticut," Nick said, killing off the princes in Sebastopol. He was a storm of contradictions, and he knew it. He stamped his foot like Lenin over all the fat dominions on the Black Sea. He had a poor boy's bitterness about the overstuffed aristocrats who wheeled around on pastry carts, cakes and clotted cream on every side. On the other hand, he permitted the cowboy on the palomino in his dreams to ride his fences, half a day's journey at a time, without turning a corner. He let the lifeguard go home from the beach in an Aston-Martin. Nick wouldn't have raised a finger in a real revolution, because he didn't want things too equal. For him, money was one of the privileges of the hero. Anything the cowboy and the lifeguard wanted, they ought to be able to get.

Peter spread Nick's knees and pulled the towel loose.

"My balls are already dry," Nick said.

"I want to see for myself." And he bent down and put his face against the inside of Nick's thigh. He took Nick's cock in one hand and drew his finger back and forth along the skin behind his balls until the sack quickened and went tight. Nick began to swell, but Peter held his hand still and kept the pulse low. For the moment, he was doing something different from turning Nick on. Once, in the woods, he'd reached down and uprooted a handful of leaves while they were walking. He flattened them against Nick's face as if he would smother him, and at the same time whispered "Mint!" Nick tottered. Between the perfume and the word, Nick knew when he sniffed it in that a man could mean exactly what he said. Peter stroked him now, and the tension increased like the string being pulled on a bow. Just as it throbbed in response, he said, "When can you take me up to see the ranch?"

"Anytime," Nick said. "You really want to see it?"

"Sure." Peter let Nick go and sat back on his heels. "I have all that land in my genes, so I'll be able to tell you if you're getting a good deal. My family is supposed to have an eye for horses, too, in case you want to price livestock. Should I wear chaps and a rhinestone shirt?"

Hands behind his head, Nick watched Peter go into a pose, one hip thrown out and his hands in his hair. Then he arched way back and let out an easy laugh. Where Sam was a runner, Nick thought, Peter was a dancer. Both so lean that the flesh on their stomach muscles stretched like a drum skin.

"And a Stetson and a dusty kerchief? No," Nick said, aroused in spite of himself, and only three hours gone since Sam. "Pretend you're getting dressed to get picked up in a bar."

"Well, I'll wear my silk jersey number, then," Peter said. He fell down on his side next to Nick and pulled Nick over on top of him as easily as if he had been pulling up a blanket. "Net stockings. Patent leather pumps."

"No, you won't. T-shirt and Levi's. I'll get you some boots."

"I have boots."

"I'll get you some new ones."

"You want to fuck?" Peter said. It felt like they had just unpacked a trunk in a ship's cabin, and clothes were everywhere about the room.

"I guess so," Nick said, wrapping Peter in his arms and thinking he was just about to touch down again on earth. "I didn't think I wanted to."

"Well, your problem is you think too much," Peter said, willing to be unoriginal himself. "You forget what you already know."

"What's that?" Nick asked. He needed just a hint, and now, because in a moment he was going to be somewhere else, just he and Peter together, and he wanted a thread of reason to bring him out the other side. He'd spent the whole afternoon in a story, and he couldn't close the book as carelessly as he thought.

"Just stop thinking," Peter said sweetly, as if he would love him no matter what, "and it'll come back to you."

Rita, she said to herself long-windedly, if you want to get ahead, you've got to figure out why it is some people can't leave you alone and the rest look through you as if you weren't there. It had been happening forever. She thought it was about time to start *using* it. Here was a good example: In Rusty Varda's house, she was thrice blessed because all of them—Nick, Peter, and Hey—delighted in her and sought out chances to feed her and drive her and do her errands. But it could have gone the other way, she knew, and then where would she be? Besides, Hey was the type who made it a mixed blessing, coming on so strong he seemed about to faint whenever they met. She inspired reactions that were too extreme; and, consequently, daily life, the merest ordinary commerce, wore her out. And she never knew from one hour to the next whether it would be sticks and stones or a ring of kisses waiting around the corner. People tore up her magazines in subways. They passed her joints in airplanes. She made a blip in difficult people's radar, and they did their most difficult thing as they thundered by.

It crossed her mind again late Friday afternoon because Hey came in and fired a few rounds just as she was pulling herself together. She'd spent the day in the showrooms getting fabric samples for a list of upholstered pieces Peter had jotted down. She was fussy, and everything was ugly. Finally, she'd curled up in the back seat of Peter's Jaguar and doodled out a crewel design that really *looked* like a Rhode Island wing chair. She knew she couldn't spend her afternoons in parking lots. She had to make do with what was on the market. But she couldn't get out of her mind how everything *ought* to look, and four days of decorating let her know she wasn't going to be famous for sprightly solutions like red checked tablecloths done up as draperies. What kept her going was that, among Peter's clients, money was no object. So if the marketplace was barren, they could always farm it out with their own design to a custom-maker and wait a year and a half. Peter was always getting custom orders finally coming in when the clients were halfway through a divorce or, in one case, dead, leaving him with twenty-two rolls of wallpaper covered with bats and Japanese fans.

Rita was in no mood. She'd drawn a hot bath, and she was

doing a perfunctory bit of yoga while it cooled to a simmer. She twirled her neck in an arc and then got down naked on the white fur rug and did her best to be a cobra. As she rose to her feet, she felt a first glimmer of calm. Float, she told herself, feeling as if she'd come at last to a place where people took care of themselves the whole day long. She executed a slow tango across the room to the bathroom, a sweeping walk some-where between Isadora Duncan and Groucho, when suddenly there was a knock at the door. It was Hey.

"I'm doing a hand wash," he said, somehow getting by her and into the room. "Do you have anything you want done?"

"Oh, Hey, I'm not that organized yet. Everything I own is dirty," she said, pulling the seedy pink terry robe closer around her that she'd grabbed off the floor at the last minute. "I'll just throw it all in the machine before the weekend's over."

"I did some things already for you that I found in the closet," he said, and she felt a small chill creep across the back of her neck. "I separated out the delicate things for later. I can do the green shawl if you want."

"Please don't bother, Hey. I'm used to getting things done on the run."

"It isn't good for the clothes," he said, as if the clothes had some rights in the matter, too, whatever her penchant for barely making do. She knew he was offering her his services so he could fall in step with the rhythm of a woman, and she resisted them, but not because she was squeamish about his reasons. She supposed he was all charm and innocence when he gathered up her nightgowns and tights, and she wasn't inno-cent herself about the other ways in which a man could go about it. Rather, she was afraid she would start to pose for him, to pay in kind for all his small attentions to her. He wants to be my lady-in-waiting, she thought. Yet she couldn't help but envy his enthusiasm. He wanted so hard to hear the sea in the core of the shell that he brought it up out of the coursing of his own blood. The moves of a woman were a siren song to Hey; and Rita, just come from dancing in her room, was humming a few bars of it under her breath. No wonder people told her their life stories. She came across as if she'd lived them all herself. One on one, she flashed like a mirror.

"You know about Linda," he said, when it seemed to her the pause had gone on too long, and she heard his voice drop to the level of confidences.

"Linda who?" Was Linda the parrot's name? She'd kept her distance from the perch in the kitchen garden because the bird looked bloodthirsty.

"My previous life," he said, quite formal about it, and patient with others who weren't so lucky.

"Oh. Well, I did hear something," she said, and thought: Shut up now before you embarrass him. But she was too nervous to wait out the pauses while he picked his way over his English grammar. She tumbled on. "But you know who it is exactly, do you? I thought it was just a feeling. I mean, I didn't know you'd got an actual person."

He looked off rapturously and sat down on the bed. "My spiritual adviser tracked her down," he said. "It was a great breakthrough for him." Then, while she inwardly sighed for the flattening bubbles in her bath, he got quite moody. He began to get very interested in the crease of his trousers; and Rita noticed that, as he pinched it between his fingers to sharpen it, he affected a dressy lady's delicacy. He retreated into solitude as he sat and put his thoughts in order. There, like a widowed or banished lover who, without warning, still registers the most intimate expressions in his face, he seemed to be side by side exchanging knowing looks with Linda. Rita was a third party.

"I'd love to talk about it," she said, "except I have to take my bath."

"Yes, you'd better go ahead," Hey said, turning a placid smile in her direction. "They get out of here as soon as they're ready. You know, you can't waste a minute on Friday night. I'll get your things out."

You can't let that one go, she said to herself as she put the bathroom door ajar between them and hung the terry robe behind. She felt like such a coward sinking down into the bath. If she didn't draw the line now, she supposed, she would find him one day making up at her vanity table and dressed to kill. But she hadn't planned on being touched by Hey. She slopped the facecloth across her eyes as she lay back, because her throat had knotted and the tears were coming down. Unexpectedly, as if she were at a movie. She appreciated real commitment to such a degree that she'd gladly spend the better part of a year searching out a committed dry cleaner or drugstore. She could hold Hey back from laying out her party clothes on a Friday night, but at the risk of taking from him the chance to know a little further who he was. He might be crazy, she thought, but he had an idea inside him as pure as a fairy godmother.

"Linda revealed herself in the cards," Hey called out as he went about the room. For all Rita knew, it might have been a hand of poker. Softhearted though she was about the hands-across-the-sea between Linda and Hey, she took good care not to get involved in the method. She didn't want so much as a word of spiritual advice. "She ran a traveling Bible school near Sutter's Mill. Up in the mountains. It was during the Gold Rush, so Holy Brother and I think it must have been a cathouse, but we let Linda have it her way." He paused, as if to hold two blouses out at arm's length and pick a Friday color. "Which isn't to say she wasn't a lady," he went on, almost to himself. "Her card is the queen of diamonds."

"How does it feel?" Rita asked, not sure what she meant, but it had to do with being two people at the same time. She was floating after all, limp from the squall of tears and half-asleep. She knew from the sound of his voice that it must feel wonderful, so she gave him the cue to tell her so. Also, she guessed she'd be able to follow the story better if she encouraged him to talk girl-to-girl, so to speak, and underplayed the business of Linda's telegrams from the beyond.

"Oh, you know," Hey said through the door. "Men, men, men."

Rita blushed under the facecloth. She saw what a double

outcast Hey had come to be. There wasn't a woman she knew who wouldn't have scored him for his dimwit, one-word, definition-of-a-woman feeling. But at the same time he wasn't precisely gay. He didn't say what *he* wanted. She bet he used the woman who lived like an echo in him to pretty up his longing for a man of his own. She suddenly knew he'd had no sex at all, none to speak of, anyway, none that kept on happening. He had the strained, slightly hysterical up-and-down in his voice that she associated with aging virgins. His gestures had lost their dancer's logic. What, she wondered, had she expected? That he was as gay as Nick and Peter, probably. And that the Linda complication was another dimension still that connected him up all around. She'd wanted him exotic and wise like a hermaphrodite. A moment ago, when she was brimful of tears, she had turned him into a good-luck household god whose belly she could pat. Now he seemed instead just another out-of-touch and frazzled man cheated of love gratuitously. And she didn't want to know that much about him.

"You need *shoes*," he said in some dismay. "It's like trying to play tennis without a ball."

"Let me dance barefoot just this once," she said, standing up and taking stock of herself agreeably in the mirror, "and I'll buy them in every color come Monday."

"You can laugh if you want," he scolded her, "but shoes are invisible only when they're fabulous. You watch. Everyone's going to stare at your feet. I've got to go now. Hurry!" And she heard the door shut behind him. He went away, she thought, like a crone in a folktale who's done all the warning she can.

She mustn't let him get her overwrought, she told herself as she came back naked into the bedroom, letting the water drip where it may. Then she saw her things set out on the bed, an eggplant purple skirt and champagne blouse, a bra and panty hose, her least offensive shoes, a string of amber beads. She'd got it all wrong about the casting of the fairy tale. As to fairy godmothers, he appeared to be hers. That's when it struck her about the two sorts of people she fell among. Why didn't she know how to *use* it? She didn't mind Hey shadowing her half so much as she minded her own tailspin theories of who they both really were, deep down. Doubtless Hey was both the virgin in the maze *and* the double-sexed dream of life after life. The problem was Rita. Overinvolved again.

Which reminded her of Nick. She sat cross-legged at the foot of the bed and cranked the casement wide open to the garden. Rita was on the ground floor in the west wing, just a stone's throw from the silken, high-roofed living room. Nick and Peter were upstairs in the east wing; and it happened that, as her head began to clear around the chaos of Nick, she glanced up automatically, as if to measure the distance—the number of stones to throw—between her and them. And glimpsed him from the stomach up as he stood at the armoire lost in thought. The setting sun cast a pale banana light all along that wall of the house. In a moment he had turned toward Peter and walked away out of her field of vision. But she'd had time to catch sight of him peering inconsolably out at LA. She was just getting ready to tick off the meetings between them, all coincidence and coming-and-going. She went ahead with it—Tuesday noon at the pool, Wednesday breakfast, 5:00 P.M. in Peter's shop twice. The last, because it was the end of the day for all of them, had them driving away to play like children after school, Rita leaning forward from the back seat so that their three heads chattered in a row. And then, the most curious, last night over dinner. But the list went by without really getting her attention. She had too much to take in about his eyes.

She was in perfect control, or under it, at any rate. She'd thought so all week. She toyed with the charade that they were all set for the serenade scene, and all Rita needed to start a song was a guitar tacked up with mother-of-pearl. She laughed at herself for watching out windows like a schoolgirl, and the laughter convinced her she wasn't going to act like a fool. Nick, she supposed, was who she'd been waiting for all these years, but she knew she'd thought so half a dozen times before, and, besides, he was off limits. Not by being gay— which hadn't in the past been an impediment to a month of longing and a trampled heart—but by being Peter's. So it came to the same thing, that she had to use this, too. Maybe she couldn't help loving him, but she could do something with it that would rescue them all or set them free. It was a curious way to be through with men. It was dead-center certain to boot: She was going to get caught between two selfless courses of action, with Nick and Peter both, leaving her minus one self instead of the usual zero. She said as much herself. This was the girl who at fifteen closed *Jane Eyre* and for the next year wore her hair in a bun, sucked in her cheeks to look more like an orphan, and prayed for bad weather, preferably rain so fine it wet her to the bone.

But she was harder on herself than anyone, and so she didn't mince words when she told herself to stop it. None of the three of them needed Rita turning intrigues. To put her house in order, it was about time, too, that she stopped falling for men who were nice to her. She'd always said she was a woman waiting for a project in a world that did such things by committee. Things fell apart in her life in a sort of way, as if on schedule—about the middle of February, for example, every year, which was why she put on speed to be here fast, as soon as the last Christmas trees were put out on the snowbanks. In the general disarray, she tended to have her finest hour, tidying up. "I'm putting my house in order," she'd say over the phone when the March winds roared across the Hudson, confident she was quoting from the Bible, or at least the Gettysburg Address. It killed her to admit it, but she did: Cleaning up after her own messes was the project she could always count on. A committee would have tabled it.

It was simpler just to say she wasn't exactly in love with Nick, so that is what she said. She knew she could will it so, if nothing else. There wouldn't be any falling apart, and she wasn't going to let her good intentions go down like dominoes.

She didn't think it illogical to care all the same about what Nick was going through and how life hit him. She knew how he felt.

She stared up at their room, through the empty upstairs window, at the corner of the armoire. Peter was a prince in LA, she thought, and the difference between being one here and being one in Russia was a trick of culture. Peter wielded the same kind of power his grandfather had as a boy, and did so as effortlessly as he wore a tuxedo, because Prince Alexander Kirkov raised him to expect it as his birthright. The straitened circumstances of Brooklyn Heights had nothing to do with Peter's sight on the world. But Nick, Rita knew, had had it drummed into his head that everyone he would ever know was bound to fail. His father lapsed into the bitterness and suspicion that go with keeping doomed accounts. Nick had had to dream up the American dream all by himself, which hadn't been so hard as it might have been, with Paramount two blocks away and the ringing of hammers in Beverly Hills, where the family went for Sunday drives. But Nick acted now as if he had had no say in his own elevation to the rank of prince, as if there must be some mistake, some error in addition that would be spotted in time by a bitten-down accountant who looked like his father. It flew in the face of his own hard work and gambler's timing to see it that way, but he would have said that he didn't work hard anymore, and still the money poured in. He would have protested that it wasn't fair, and it scared him, except it was such a conversation stopper.

Except with Rita. He had laid out his rags-to-riches theory last night at dinner, the difference between his and Peter's expectations, and she filled in the narrowest pauses with "Go on. I'm listening." He talked about money, and she talked in her turn about sex, and it didn't take Freud to let them know they were parallel lines, sex and money, that defied the laws of geometry by meeting all over the place. Grown-ups talked about one or the other, Rita knew from experience, and more and more was what was usually wanted. But Nick and Rita

seemed to share a sense of missed connections between the
progress of desire and the daily life of the self. Nick was half-
ready to say he was through with money, to make the same
point that Rita made about men. He didn't really mean he
wanted to give it all up, and he told Rita she didn't, either. If
she went too long without a man, he said, she'd take up pride
and make the world atone for her illusions. Nick intended to
have it both ways, money *and* no illusions. The very juggler's
act he'd decided on with Sam, as well, though he was careful
to let on nothing of that to Rita. Rita had enough on her mind
without it. She tried to see the probabilities for an equation of
her own, about a *man* and no illusions. It sounded wonderful
when Nick described it. That was the problem.

What had she said about sex? She tried to remember as she
went back to the bathroom to get a towel. When she got
there, she found she was all dry. It must be late. More than
anything, she remembered, as she rifled through her string bag
among the five-and-dime cosmetics, the way they'd given each
other their invitations. Nick came home and got dressed up
and sat in the garden to wait for Peter. She came home and got
undressed and wandered out to walk by the pool in her flimsy
summer robe, expecting to be alone. While they talked about
the weather, Hey called out through the dining room window,
"Peter can't get away. He says to tell you not to wait for
dinner. What dinner?"

"No dinner," Nick said to reassure him. "Peter made a mistake." And the mistake, Nick told Rita after a moment when
they couldn't seem to get back to the weather, was forgetting
a reservation for two at Chasen's. "There's no point in letting
it go to waste," Nick said brightly, rubbing his head through
his curls like a sheepish boy about a date. "Why don't *you*
come?"

"To *Chasen's?*" Rita asked from the edge of the pool.
"Sorry. I'd have to spend the whole day getting ready. I'm
going to eat salad and an unwashed apple. For calories, I'll
drink Scotch."

"You can eat all that at Chasen's."

57

"I doubt it," she said, dipping the toes of one foot in the pool. "There I would be tempted to eat a whole cheesecake. Do you and Peter eat there all the time?"

"Oh, no. No one does. Besides, we don't get a very good table there. You have to be Louis B. Mayer or Irving Thalberg to get a good table. But we do it now and then to keep in touch."

"With what?"

"With the generals," he said. "It's the officers' club. The people who eat at Chasen's aren't hungry anymore, or not for food, at least. You have the feeling they would sing if someone at their table asked them to. Am I a cynic?"

"Not to me you aren't. I was wounded in the war myself," she said, her memory throwing out a snapshot of Peter's grandfather tied up by his knees in traction, an icebag over his eyes. "Is the food good?"

"Yup. Want to come?"

"Some other time. Stay here?"

"We'll flip a coin," he said, and stood up and dug one out of his pocket. He didn't care one way or the other, she could see. Really, she thought as he flicked his thumb and the quarter bulleted in an arc above her head, she didn't, either. She called it "Heads." It sailed in the air and plopped in the pool and sank. They stood side by side, waiting for the ripple to give out.

"Hey will get furious if we mess up the kitchen," Nick said.

"You don't know how simple this is going to be," she answered. "I'm not going to *cook* anything. We'll just eat enough so as not to feel faint in the morning. But how do you know you're not going to win? Don't you always?"

"In a way," he said, "but someone's been passing you the wrong information. *I* got stood up tonight, not *you*."

The quarter came to rest on the bottom, heads up. Within half an hour they were standing at the sink eating a basket of cherries where they could spit the pits economically. Then they sat at the kitchen table, hunched over a wooden bowl three feet wide at the rim, and ate a green salad with their fingers. They had not compromised about their clothes and so were still dressed in a dove gray suit and a dusty rose robe, the latter a Joan Crawford version of the terry number.

About sex, she'd said it was two different things. At first, she started out with a girl's three wishes, all of them the same: to get so naked and come so close, the self was all but lost. Intimacy, she decided at N.Y.U., would cure the migraine of too much consciousness, and the form it took for her was a man who would hold on tight until he'd finishing making the two of them one. She got mixed results. The other thing started later, in her late twenties, when the three wishes were all used up. Then all she seemed to need out of a man was a fucking machine. She didn't care if it had needs of its own, as long as they were carnal and not sentimental. She went to bed in those years as she might have walked onto the court for an equally matched game of tennis, in love with the game but planning to win. When at last the two sides of sex came together, she told Nick, slicing up the apple and parceling it out, she was well over thirty. By then, she said, anyone will make a strange bedfellow. Now, she didn't know what she wanted when she found herself involved. If a man got very intimate, she found she just wanted to fuck. If he came on like a rutting animal, she wanted promises as pretty as popular songs, claiming that love went on forever. It had happened that way so many times that sex itself, the diddling of the membranes, wasn't as important as the moods she was locked in whenever it happened. She sighed as if she'd given up the ghost. Was it ever that way for Nick? she asked him finally.

Yes, he told her, it was. Except he still believed in his membranes as if he'd just turned sixteen. And though he'd gone through a time in his own late twenties—he was still straight then, more or less—when he felt about fifty whenever he went to bed. The contrary moods that hit him when his cock stood up were not his cock's fault, he decided. A long time ago, he said, he must have separated sex from who he thought he was, feeling like a failure too much of the time and trying to keep something pure and simple. He knew it only *seemed* pure and simple. He was sure his detachment had caused him to boil ever since with guilt and a little boy's temper and a horror of the grave.

"But it still feels good to fuck," he said with a grin, "no matter who I think I am on a given day."

"Do you feel good after?"

"Oh, that," he said ruefully, bringing up his lower lip to stroke his mustache. "That's something else. Who said we're all alone in bed, no matter who we're with, but at least when we're there with someone we like, there's someone to be nice to afterwards?"

"Did someone say that?" she asked. "Whoever he was, he never went to bed with me."

She couldn't remember when she'd last talked sex with a man other than one she was sleeping with. At certain points last night, it had felt as good as the thing itself. By the time they had nothing else to say, he was pouring Cointreau over strawberries. It proved to be a nightcap. They both had to get some sleep because it was Thursday. Rita ate just the berries and let the orange blossoms lie, and she said "Good night" and slipped away at a quarter to ten, composed and self-contained, as if she'd said exactly what she meant.

Rita now took a last swipe at her cheekbones with a powdered sponge and went back to the bed for her clothes. They looked all right, but she had another sudden change of heart about Hey. It didn't do him any good to have her as a mannequin, she thought. She had no notion of what she should wear instead, but she went to the closet—across from the windows and beyond the bathroom door—to throw something on indifferently. The look Hey had given her was too studied. In the closet, as big as her bedroom in New York, with built-in cedar drawers and shelves for thirty pairs of shoes, she stood at the three-way mirror smirking. Then she reached out and took up a jumble of shirts and pullovers from the open top drawer. One by one, she disentangled them, held them up any-which-way at her breasts, and dropped them in the drawer again.

She didn't have a thing to wear, she thought, and the thought delighted her. It struck her funny because she was sure it was a remark being repeated at that very moment up and down the hills of Bel-Air. "I wept because I had no shoes," she said with a scowl to herself in the mirror, "until I met a man who had no feet," quoting her mother quoting—who knew—the *Reader's Digest* and Dr. Peale.

Laughing, she pulled the jacket of a black knit suit off a hanger and draped it over her shoulder, her hand on her hip like a toreador. Well, she thought, why not the widow's weeds? She did a bit of flamenco in the alcove of the three mirrors, winking at herself as she whirled by. Then she slipped, and her heel knocked the wall hard under the center mirror as she went down. There was a thud, she thought in midair before she landed, as if the wall were hollow.

But that couldn't be. She drew her knees up under her chin and sat in the pile of clothes that had broken her fall. She looked the alcove up and down. The three mirrors were set in and framed, and the ash paneling that lined the whole closet was pieced in a chevron pattern to the ceiling and the floor around the mirrors. This was the wall that, to move, you would have to move mountains. Rita was a stickler about her wonderful sense of direction, and she knew the closet corner of her room was cut out of the side of the hill. She'd already thought about the tons of earth crashing in on her if the earth should quake. The hollow sound would madden her if she didn't get to the bottom of it, because once she saw a thing one way, she incorporated it instantly and went on to the next. She didn't like the laws of matter changing on her when she wasn't looking.

"Rita, we're leaving," Peter called through her window from the garden. "Are you ready? You're not ready, are you?"

"I'm coming," she said, "I'm coming."

She went over onto her hands and knees and bent down near the floor of the alcove. She rapped the paneling under all three mirrors with her knuckles. Only the center one rang hollow.

She sat up again, and there she was, face to face. She was amazed at the look in her eyes. Then she turned her head to either side and saw how many Ritas felt the same way, though none could put her finger on exactly what it was. Rita looked the alcove up and down again, and she knew she was right.

The center mirror was a door.

Chapter 3

Nick stood in the doorway and watched the battered MG kick dust as it drove the trail over the hill from the main gate. Sam was going so fast that the car skidded badly out of the ruts and spun its wheels when he cornered to make the turn to the bunkhouse. He was out of breath and laughing, both at once, when he braked in front of Nick. He jumped out over the door.

"We did the last five miles on two wheels," he said. He was an hour and a half late. "I broke my own record, but it's unofficial, so I do it all the time. Some day you and I will have to go to Vegas together, so you can see me open her up. She likes that trip." He reached in behind the front seat and brought up a sweaty six-pack of Coors. He was talking too much. "I brought us a picnic lunch."

He came up the three steps to the porch and stared right at Nick, grinning, as he got closer. When Nick didn't move to let him by, Sam kept on walking until they were only an inch apart. Nick was leaning on one shoulder against the door, as mild as could be. They were both dressed western today, exactly alike, as if by common consent. Nick had changed out of his office gear and left it in the car. His grin still in place, Sam put his knee up and parted Nick's thighs in a gesture something like a caress, though behind it was the force that could double Nick over with a knee in the groin. Sam reached forward and got an open-handed grip on Nick's genitals, then leaned close and kissed the side of his neck hard, sucking in the skin.

"I'm here now," he said in a husky voice, and when he pulled back to look at Nick again, his face was quiet. Sam wasn't unconcerned, Nick could see, about the hour and a half, but he wasn't going to apologize, either. If he could, he would bring Nick out of it by being there now completely, but he wouldn't have a thing to say about the particular sorrows of Nick's afternoon. Now was all he had ever had time for. Nick wondered what it would be like not to care what other people thought. Sam didn't, and it turned Nick on. He liked careless people. They got that way because they were sexy rather than beautiful. Beautiful people took pains and, like Peter, moved to a kind of slow and cautious music. Nick liked Sam's attitude in spite of himself, knowing as he did that it had no plans and never gave ground.

"That car looks older than you do," Nick said, sorry as soon as he'd said it that he'd made a remark about anyone's age, but he wasn't alert because he was trying not to say: Where the hell have you been?

"Sheila?" Sam said playfully. "She's my twenty-dollar gold piece. I told you I was in New York for a while. I got back here answering an ad for a driver. A hundred and expenses to get an MG to LA in two weeks. And the guy never showed up."

"Where did he go?"

"Disappeared. I never found out." Sam shrugged, as if to say that people had to take care of themselves.

"How did you get the car registered to you?" Nick asked, but then decided to drop it. Peter called him Nick the insurance man when he started cross-examining.

"I met a guy who fixed it," Sam said. He opened a beer. He went over to the bed against the wall where the burlap and blankets were thrown, and sat back and drank. "You know, I'm not *that* attached. If you want to get me a Porsche, I'll strip Sheila down and leave her in a parking lot."

"So much for loyalty," Nick said. "Do you really get it on with people who give away Porsches?"

"No, but it never hurts to ask. It's not that people don't offer them, but it's usually got some strings attached. Like a long fuse."

"So maybe you wouldn't take it," Nick said, "even if I offered."

"Maybe. Why don't you take your shirt off and come over here?"

Nick could see now that he hadn't wasted the time alone. Because he wasn't hurt and wouldn't pout and didn't need loving. He felt a little leap of freedom, as if he'd just had proof that he wasn't going to get lost. He could not remember who it was, he or Sam, who'd started the teasing, but they made fun of one another whenever they were feeling wild and didn't care how it ended. Things weren't tense between them anymore. The separation and the white noise that blew about the lonely terrace, ten days ago in Venice, had vanished. Nick supposed they had laughed it off. So they teased, and Nick did all he could to punch holes in Sam, but he loved him still like knights and squires in a story that called for heroes.

"I thought you wanted to walk in the hills and scare up some ranch hands." Nick unbuttoned his shirt, pulled it off, and draped it on a rocking chair whose seat had rotted out. The chair sat back on its haunches. They'd gone off on foot the other day, charged with fantasies—over the next rise, what if they came upon men in chaps, branding and cutting calves. Or a wild horse in a corral, a rodeo rider breaking him bareback. Even as they laughed, imagining the dirty things they'd do, Nick had thought: The man we are after is still external to us both, even now. If asked to pin down who that man could be if not Sam, Nick would have said two or three things without thinking: He regularly wrestles some actual creature of the earth, and he's glad to be alone, whenever he can, and one day is so much like another that he doesn't hear them going by. It was another way of saying he had to be careless. Oddly enough, the cowboy lover in Nick's head didn't need sex and hadn't had a lot. He was pretty shy. And if he wasn't Sam, then Sam could not obsess him like a dream any longer. That meant that here they were at last, merely a man and a man, and Nick had the same power to be careless as Sam. He knew how much he preferred the dream.

"I never know what I want until it's time," Sam said. "You know what I thought about doing when I was driving up here? Going to your house."

"In Bel-Air?"

"I figured I ought to see how the other half's living these days. But then when I saw you at the door, I remembered I wanted to get laid."

Nick was standing at ease, halfway across the room, his hands in his back pockets. They both looked surly, as if it were a duel coming up. They were just out of range of each other's weapons, and they went through their footwork to loosen up. Sam was already hard as he slipped his Levi's down around his thighs. No underwear, of course. Sam followed the fashion in these matters to the letter.

"And after that?" Nick asked with mock weariness, as if Sam was going to have his own way no matter what. "Then would it amuse you to tour Bel-Air?"

"I won't know until it's time. I don't think ahead if I can help it."

Rita's right, Nick thought as he moved to the bed and knelt between Sam's legs. The flash of Rita brought back, like a second in a dream, the whole halting theory of Rita and the world. "Instead of growing up," she had said last week at dinner, "I read a thousand books. In books, the people start their letters, 'Dear So-and-so, I think of you so often.' After a while it made me mad. I wanted to say, 'But people don't *think* that often. About anything.'" And Nick protested. He never forgot a face himself, and it would have been the truth if he'd said it in *his* letters, because everyone he knew went through his mind from time to time, as if on cue. But Sam was the sort of person Rita must have meant. Meanwhile, the thought of Rita passed in a moment, but it was odd enough for *anything* to intrude among the cowboys and surfers that crowded Nick's heated brain when he went to bed. As to letters, he didn't know what he was talking about. His only commerce with the mails had to do with paying bills.

He held Sam's hips in his hands and sucked him up and down. It was as good a place to start as any, and it held him off from too much tight embracing, which made Sam nervous and shook him off. Also, he could be fairly certain for the time being that he wouldn't say the wrong thing, and now, at the first touch, he always fell into his most unguarded moment. If it had gone another way and he'd sucked Sam's ear, something he delighted in, he might have whispered, while Sam squirmed, the very antidote to his detachment. He knew Sam so well already that his cock seemed to have a taste all its own, which it didn't, but as it was in his mouth that Nick made the connection, taste was a way of thinking about it. Actually the texture and the shape had more to do with it, Nick thought as he worked it, since a cock was rumored to be just as telling as a thumbprint. What was he going to do about the paradox: four years of UCLA, no grade below eighty-five, and then two years at Stanford learning how to overdevelop the third world, and still he could spend an hour meditating the con-tours of a hustler's cock. Perhaps he shook his head in some dismay, just to think of it, and Sam groaned a little when the rhythm hit him at the root.

The truth was, the moral paradox didn't interest Nick, and it didn't give him sleepless nights that he had such a fix on sex. Ten years ago—when he blotted out the thought of sex in all its incarnations, and his own cock coiled in his pants and wouldn't sleep, for all his rising above it—his A's and his de-grees were all well and good, but he tossed on his bed all night and clutched his fevered pillow. He went around walking on eggshells, trying to find the nice girl life was preparing for him, and the moral edge he felt had a way of cutting like a blade of grass or a sheet of paper. It was quite another paradox that kept him haunted: Why, in the middle of making love, had his mind started to race? If it wasn't cowboys and gym gear, it was a stream of unspoken comments on the act itself as he played it out. It was true what he said to Rita, that he loved to fuck, but lately his fantasies fed on a thousand men before he came. So he didn't go wild imagining Sam when they were together. That went on all the rest of the time.

"What was funny," Sam said gently, reaching to clutch at Nick's hair with his hands and talking easily, as if his lower body weren't riding in heat, "the car turned out to be loaded with dope. One day a Baggie dropped out from under the dashboard. I dug out a couple of pounds, all tied up in ounces" —he rattled off the story as if it weren't supposed to make sense, as if it were the tune and not the words he was voicing —"in the spare, in the tool kit, under the seats. Why would anybody smuggle grass to *LA*? I mean, no wonder the guy got lost."

Nick lifted his head and sat back. All the while he was getting excited himself, but made no move to his belt or his boots. Sam's eyes widened a fraction, as if he were about to take his turn and had ideas he'd only just thought of. Nick wondered where it came from, his endlessly renewed enthusi-asm for another round. Sam went into detail readily about the high points of his career, and he gave indications of the sheer amount of work. But if he made you believe it was a job with special limits, like professional ball, the most confining having to do with what can be done with the time between games, he was all the more remarkable for his energy in the stretch.

"What do you want?" Sam asked, very civilized, as if he had swords laid out on a cushion.

"I don't know. I'm just an old dog without a bone."

"Is that right? You look like you couldn't unzip your fly because of the pressure. I want to do it on the floor."

It was a frivolous idea, sprung from his annoyance at the narrow bed—narrow as a grave, Sam had said, and it proved to him that cowboys didn't do it—a free-float longing for novelty. While Nick undid his pants, still kneeling on the bed, Sam drained the beer and flung the can in the deep stone fireplace, where it clattered and ricocheted. Then he slid off the bed and scrabbled, hands and knees, to the middle of the floor, where he rolled over on his back in the dust. His pants were down around his boots, but he kept his clothes on. He seemed to want to get them dirty. Nick would have gone naked if he'd had the choice, but the situation called for mirror images. He stood above Sam and released his own cock at last, which stood out straight and swayed a little. Then he came down on top of Sam, sixty-nine, and they mouthed each other like divers breathing out of hoses down among the reefs. They went over on one side, then on the other, and reached the point where it was all technique, no room for who they were to each other.

Sam heard it first, like a film threading through a projector, and he felt a rush of lust at the thought of him and Nick cavorting on camera. They were lying half on the bare floorboards, half on the hearthstone, a single slab greasy with soot and the sputtering of meat. In the fireplace, andirons strong as truck axles held up a couple of half-burned logs. From a long hook at one side hung a cast-iron pot. Someone had taken the ashes away and swept. The snake was curled beneath the logs, the rattled tail in plain sight, about a foot and a half from Sam's head.

Nick knew right away, and he spit Sam out and gasped, as if he had to come up for air. Then froze. Sam might have figured it out too late if the change in Nick hadn't hit him. He had to freeze, too, right away. Because the rattlesnake was moving. But when it did hit him what it was, he was horror-struck and went into a sort of spasm. Nick was still holding him around. He clamped Sam closer, and it seemed to still the shaking like a tourniquet. Buried as they were between each other's thighs, they were blind. They could only follow it by the rattle, and then, as it glided toward Sam, by the sandpaper sound it made on the fireplace floor.

It was as if the snake knew he had the upper hand, because he got out of the fireplace and, staying close to Sam, passed along the whole length of his body in a slow sleepwalk. He mulled the killing over. The noise that snapped him awake under the logs and filled his cheeks with vengeance on his enemies had ceased. He did a turn at Sam's feet and readied for a strike, but he didn't deign to make the first move. Let the beast breathing hard on the floor move a muscle, though, and he'd spring, mouth gaping, into the nearest swell of flesh, the calf or the buttock.

In an instant, the sweat began to pour out of Nick and Sam. Between their torsos, hearts knocking hard to be let out and flee, the sweat had them boiling with the heat until they thought they would suffocate. The rattle came now like a drummer biding time with a light, long roll. Nothing happened. Any other time, Nick and Sam could have fallen off to sleep in that position, but now the need to hold still even a minute longer made them shudder and cramp and beg to run. It was only twenty seconds, thirty at most, since they'd first noticed something wrong, when the snake cocked the trigger and got them covered. But already they were like two men on a tiny lifeboat who don't trust one another with the tiller or the gun. Nick took over, and he cradled Sam in his arms while he tried to figure out what to do when the worst happened.

Sam was more scared, and not just because he was closer to the snake. It was a death tied to a nightmare. Unable to even look it in the face, forced to take it in the back, he seemed to be delirious with fever, toxic, as if the venom already bubbled in his blood. And he didn't turn to Nick. Though Nick held on and would have let him know it was happening to both of them—at least that—Sam didn't believe in anyone. There was no safety in numbers.

"Can't you do something?" he whispered.

"I *am*." They might have been talking through a two-way radio. The sound was barely audible, but not the pitch of feeling and the tone of voice. "From here on, Sam, it's all luck."

"What's it going to do?"

"It'll go away. Don't move," Nick said. He didn't believe the one thing and sent the other up as a plea to all of them. Don't move, something kept saying very clearly in his head, and he meant the two of them and the snake, but a part of him meant the whole world, too.

The rattle's last effect was out of snake lore Nick had known all his life, though he'd had no occasion to recall it in the years since he learned it at school. So this is what it means, Nick thought, about the trance. As if a pocket watch were swinging back and forth, they were mesmerized. The sound was so insistent it seemed to set up a baffle in the brain, cutting the fear off, and it carried power like a current. The spell, Nick remembered, was a stroke of suspended time before the attack, so he knew when he gave himself over to it that one of them was marked. But he felt the same unwinding in Sam when he relaxed his arms. For the space of the snake's seduc-tion, they seemed to have left sixty-nine behind them and gone into a kind of yoga. Now, Nick thought, feeling nothing, do it now while we are numb enough. Not desiring it exactly, but accepting what would be required of him next. Maybe it was easier for him, because Sam was the target, after all. Nick just the medicine man.

But their luck held. The snake must have gotten the lore all wrong, because he kept up the rattle and made no move. It's not like drowning, Nick thought, since his whole past life slipped his mind. He and Sam were losing heat, and where their bodies touched, it was cool. There wasn't a thing they had to do. And when at last the snake slid across the room to the open door, Nick felt the world returning with a pang. Can it be I regret it, he wondered. The snake went away as if it couldn't be bothered. There were other shady places to hide in. As if a strike, to be worth it, had to meet with an outsize target, like a rearing mustang or a climber on a cliff face grabbing a blind ledge and coming down on the rattle. So they were safe. But as it vanished, as the tip of the tail disappeared, Nick felt something like fangs go in above his heart. The whole thing said: A snake isn't what you think it is.

Then the pressure fell. The plug got pulled out of the balloon, and the room sighed down to human size again. Nick and Sam fell over on their backs, head to crotch, and seemed to wait for ordinary life to come around, so they could jump on. They didn't see how ordinary it was again already. They hadn't seen the snake, either. It wasn't so much the feeling that it hadn't happened; it was as if something else had happened—a fight about nothing or a bad time in bed. Neither of them understood what had so suddenly isolated them. Each felt, perhaps, that he would have gotten over the rattlesnake fast if he'd been alone in the bunkhouse. Someone else being there meant someone else knew how insignificant the people had been. If someone had been bitten, they would have surfaced in the drama in the time-honored way, victim and rescuer, Nick making slits in Sam's thigh and sucking out the poison. As it was, the vast indifference of the Wild West was all they had to take their measure by. And they came out microscopic.

"Are you all right?"

"I want to go home," Sam said, but as if he didn't have the strength to go. He made it something of an accusation. Kidnapped and sold into white slavery, right off the curb where he hung out on Santa Monica Boulevard.

Nick sat up and looked him in the face. His color was awful.

"Whatever you want," Nick said, and when he put out his hand and let it rest on Sam's chest, he felt Sam flinch. "I won't bite you. Unless you want to be alone, why don't you come back to Bel-Air?" No response. "We'll have lunch," he added, inanely enough, but he meant to make it clear that the real world lay in routine. I won't touch you, Nick might have promised, except he left it open in case Sam wanted it. Purely academic of him. They'd both shrunk up as if they'd just had a swim in a mountain lake.

"What would have happened?" Sam demanded suddenly. "What would we have done?" He wanted to know how Nick would have gotten them out of it if the snake had struck. He was having a little fire drill here. Shutting the barn door after the horse was loose.

"But it *didn't* happen," Nick said sensibly. Not an attitude designed to cure hysteria. He might as well have admitted they were helpless. They would have done what they could, but it would have been a nightmare. Yet Nick resisted it. He strove to be matter-of-fact with Sam. Since the moment had passed him by to be tested by nightmares, he aimed to be as tough as he could in the letdown.

So he got them moving as if the only thing on his mind was getting them home in time for lunch. He stood and hiked his pants to his waist again, then reached for his shirt on the rocking chair and put it on. Sam was sitting up now, his arms around his knees and his head in his arms. Nick weighed the issue of going back to LA in one car and retrieving the MG another day. But that would leave Sam stranded for the intervening time, so was it all right to ride in caravan? Nick asked him solicitously. Could he drive? Of course he could. Put that way, as if Sam needed special handling, it dared him to be the weaker of the two. He got up and zipped himself and strode out the door to the porch. Sullen as hell but self-contained. The accusation phase had ended, but his mood was still tricky, as though the slightest thing would have had him all over Nick with his fists. No need, he said, for them to ride bumper to bumper. He knew the way to Bel-Air. Let them just meet

73

when they got there. We'll see, the implication was, who gets there first. Nick told him how to find Crook House up in the hills, the last leg of the journey, and then they split up, each to his own car, like racing men in shiny silver jackets. The other five beers were on the bed still, getting warm.

Because the Mercedes was parked further away, Sam seemed to wait, motor idling, until Nick was ready. Nick pulled alongside the MG as if there were a starting line drawn in the dust.

"Maybe you ought to tell the man at the gate about the snake," Sam said.

"What man at the gate?"

"Someone's there painting a sign."

"Oh." The sign that said "sold." Nick almost forgot that his bid had been accepted and this was all his. He'd clinched it at an early breakfast with the agent, at Schwab's on Sunset. Because they were both in real estate, they talked about the ranch as if no land went with it. It had to do with making an investment. Nick didn't talk cowboys at Schwab's.

"I'll check it out," he said.

As Nick pulled onto the road and led the way up the hill, he remembered that he'd planned all morning to tell Sam he'd bought the ranch. Now he planned not to. He looked in the rearview mirror at the MG. You're only as good as your last trick, Sam had said to him the day they met, untroubled about whether or not he was being original. It's too much the truth, Nick thought now, not to be the motto of all good whores or gamblers. Poor Sam. Today's trick was such a bucket of ice water that it might have been arranged by the Puritan God who lived in more seasonal fields than Southern California. Nick had a picture of the run of seamy endings Sam must have gone through—coupling interrupted by who knew what vigilantes, the wives and the toilet police. People didn't pay what they owed after they got what they bought. People got depressed, or they took out knives or locked themselves in the bathroom. Having survived it, Nick thought, Sam had earned a better deal. He wanted to make up for the snake, and a hundred ways sprang to his mind. Still, he wasn't going to say he bought the ranch.

The Mercedes took the lift over the hill without a bump, but he was going a little too fast to feel nothing at all. He had a moment when he went weightless, and it drew his eyes out of the mirror and back to the dusty, rutted road. At the gate, about a half-mile down the long hill, he saw a pickup truck parked broadside to him. He knew it right away, before he could even see the shop's name on the door, tan on gray: Peter's. Peter himself, standing a little way off in the fields, painting the sign, might have been anyone, might have been the cowboy who had eluded Nick and Sam all morning. After the snake, Peter wasn't the least bit extraordinary. He seemed to have work to do there, a little way off the road, and his light hair was blown about so that one would never know he had it barbered in Beverly Hills. If he was lettering a sign, it didn't spell anything yet. It was just colors. But no doubt it would say what it meant. Was Peter like the cowboy in his dreams, Nick thought as he narrowed his eyes, wondering how it could be that Peter looked as if he'd lived here all along.

Peter—because he was dazzling when he dressed to kill, because he was as serene as a yachting sailor when he went out for cocktails or walked into an opening—was too crown-prince for the Wild West. Peter walked through the weather of LA as if it were a shelf of olive trees above Cannes. But here he was. Nick was so spellbound by him, the figure in the miles of desert space, that he didn't stop to imagine how Peter got here, and why now. And he didn't think of Sam from the time he saw the truck till, cruising down the hill with the crunch in his ears of the tires on gravel, he braked forty feet from the gate.

Peter heard a noise like runaway horses. He turned and saw Nick and Sam when they were too close for him to think about. He walked back toward the road, and Nick only needed to roll his window down as he came to a stop. When he looked up, Peter's face was a foot away.

75

"I didn't think you'd come till later," Peter said, putting out his hands to lean against the roofline of the car. When he ducked his head forward, the usual world, about ten cubic feet, righted itself between them, deaf to everything but the truth. "I was all ready for four o'clock," he went on. "You would have found me sitting on the gate with a piece of grass in my mouth. But I was just guessing when you liked to come here. And I didn't dare go *that* way without you." He pointed up the hill and into the land without turning his head.

"How did you get here?" Nick asked wonderingly, beginning to see how odd it was. As if fate had dropped Peter in the path in much the same way as it had unrolled the snake.

"You mean, how did I find you?" he said with a smile. They couldn't ignore the MG much longer, but they could as long as they spoke in shorthand. "Your office told me. They even sent a map over to the shop."

"Is this the day you want to see the place?" Nick asked. Although he was asking out of it for now, he was still shot through with gratitude to have Peter here at last. And doubled up with guilt not to be staying on all day. "I would have planned it."

"It doesn't matter, Nick. I came up here to be alone and paint, too. I don't need *you* until four o'clock. I'll find you."

Just then they heard the MG growl. It backed up, as if to ready for attack, then screeched around Nick's car and sped out the gate. Nick and Peter watched it down the road as if they'd wound it up and set it going themselves.

"That's Sam."

"Very pretty. Or should I say he looks the part?" he asked with a smile. He spoke with less irony, Nick decided, than with the wish to pin it down precisely. "I'm sorry, you know. I wouldn't be so tacky as to follow you around. I have my price for practically everything else. But not that."

"Don't make me feel worse than I do, Peter. I'm the one who's being tacky." He hadn't mentioned Sam yet. This wasn't how he'd planned it. He felt a storm of sorrow start at the line where the roll of the hills cut the sky. "And I have to go right now, so I can't even explain. What do I do?"

"You do what you have to," Peter said mildly. "There's nothing to worry about. It's just a morning in the middle of the week."

It wasn't a choice, Nick thought. Between Peter and Sam, here was his real life, materializing in the spare winter green of the scrub and running weeds. Peter stood away from the car to let him go. There was irony in the smile now, as if he could appreciate the turn of events, even when they turned like a cat going after its tail. He's tougher than I am, Nick thought. Nick wanted to get it straight that he wasn't going to tamper for a minute with *this*, whatever he did with *that*. He said it all the time to himself. The two things were separate by nature, like earth and water. Of course, that was the quarter from which the fantasy came that he was frittering away his life on the beach, and it wasn't his favorite view of himself. Sam didn't matter to Peter and him, he was sure, but the other thing, the split in his head between what really happened day to day and what he imagined, he thought he had to hide. Mainly because it was tacky. Peter had no moral code to speak of, having lost it before he was born, in the revolution. Good taste was virtue enough. He fled bad taste like a virus, like the spots on the lung that his family used to favor for the last illness.

"Is that a painting over there?"

"Yes," Peter said, folding his arms and turning to eye it in the distance. An easel and a tackle box of paints beneath. "I'm painting it."

"Why?"

"Well, you ought to ask *it*. I'm just a medium, I assure you."

"You never did a painting before."

"That's true. This is my first one. Did you ever have a kid in an MG before?"

Peter wasn't going to leave it at an art lesson, no matter how pressed Nick was for time. There was a brief pause while the lighting changed. The noon sun had no character. It was indistinguishable today from the glare of midsummer.

"You know I'm not faithful to you," Nick said tensely. Not angry. Upset.

"Is that what I'm asking?" Peter was taken aback, as if he'd wounded Nick in play and wondered now what else he thought would happen if he juggled with grenades. When he went on talking, he found himself trying to describe wittily a thing he thought so sad it made him tremble. But even Nick didn't notice. The wit did its sparkle act and drew them back to safety. "I didn't mean sex. It was more to do with the stories I used to like. The old sort of romance. Two people in love who change their clothes a lot. If it was a movie, they had a lot of MG's in them. And drinks outdoors to catch the view. Very fifties. They don't do them anymore."

"It's worse than you think," Nick said wryly. "Sam works the street."

"Oh," Peter said slowly, getting it in focus at last. "Well, that's probably the story they're doing now, instead. I guess he's not as young as he looks."

"They never are."

"Younger than we are, though." He looked at the backs of his hands and then began to scratch out a stroke of yellow paint on his thumbnail. "Didn't you always assume we would stay the youngest of anyone? I did."

"I don't think that ever happens, even in stories, does it?"

"I think it used to," Peter said, but as if he couldn't explain how. "I made a reservation at Chasen's."

"So did I." They looked at each other then, and for a moment their faces were free of expression. It would have seemed nothing to anybody else. "Eight-thirty."

"Nine. Split the difference?"

"Sure," Nick said.

Then there was nothing to do but go. They'd done about as well as they could. Peter watched Nick's car out of sight and walked back to the easel. He didn't have a stroke left in him today. And he could see that he wasn't leaving it in the most opportune state, because it looked all pale and muddy. He needed to learn, he told himself, how to let it go along on its own. He'd let the idea get ahead of the paint while he was with Nick, half his mind still riveted to the canvas. He even felt the moment pass, as he and Nick talked on, when he knew it was no longer possible to get what he thought in the painting. It didn't signify a thing, he realized, capping tubes of acrylic that lay open on the easel tray. He hadn't expected art yet. In just two hours he'd already learned that he couldn't tell yet when the least square inch was done and ought to be left alone. And he'd watched himself mess it up time and again when the brush stayed too long in one place.

But the fact was, he couldn't keep it up because things were going crazy. When I have enough money, he'd always said, I'm going to do something hard. Enough was never enough, of course—he'd seen through that. It was harder to admit there was no point to going on today because of Nick. He'd never thought to think that way. The whole thing had literally ambushed him from behind. He had had it all planned, a finished painting before the sun set and a drink with Nick while they sat on the back end of the pickup. Now he packed the tin box and swirled the brushes around in a cup of water. He carried the canvas over to the truck and propped it on the passenger's seat, as if it might get inspired by the view. When he turned and stared back at the empty easel and the box of paints, ripe with possibility in the basin of the hills, he was afraid. It was the first time that he faced the worst: He could end up alone.

Peter didn't suffer from the human condition. Except for Nick and Rita, he had no patience for those who did, because they always overdid it. He chalked up his own bad years to the luck of being young, and that was all over. Since he'd gotten to where he was, there hadn't *been* a human condition. Hell might well be a cocktail party in Brentwood, but it didn't singe his hair or scorch his heart with a vision of his sins. He liked what he did. He hadn't gotten it right if Rita thought, the night in the howdah, that he had to paint because he didn't

79

have the strength to throw another petit point pillow on a sofa. He never minded going on about meaningless things, and he wouldn't have called them that. Wallet-headed women and fancy old queers who wore a lot of turquoise jewelry huddled with him on terraces and told him everything. He paid no attention to what they said, which they appreciated, but he loved to be confided in. And his opinion in matters of gossip, which he never gave, became more and more sought-after. It was madness, but so comical and innocent, Peter could have said, it fell outside the shadow of man's fate. This wasn't the same as saying any of them would escape it. It simply didn't come up unless someone died, and no one did that in LA until he ran out of deals.

Peter spent a good deal of his time out of the office playing with the stars—at pools, in saunas, of course in cars, passing a joint back and forth like an opera glass. Mutual success was the only thing they shared, but that one lucky circumstance gave off a certain glow in these encounters. Peter knew that Nick had a sweet tooth for anonymous and indiscriminate sex, and over the years he had come to see it as no more self-indulgent or significant than his own delight in butter-and-cream confections. Nick preferred to skip lunch and get sucked in the steam at his regular baths on Melrose, and Peter was more often than not a few blocks away at Ma Maison, eating a plate of avocado and lobster tails. They didn't push each other's faces in it. And Peter knew there was a precipice along one border for both of them. For Nick, it was letting it go too far and get too personal, so that he ended up involved with one of his tricks. For Peter, it was losing track of time, getting so caught up in power and glamor that he played more chess than he lived life.

But he couldn't, on the other hand, avoid the whole thing. Stardom was, to use Nick's word, Peter's fate. It was his subject and condition, and he spent his fantasy time fixed on the shine and shoot and fall of this one and that one. He was near enough to the top to pale the run of lesser lights that used to cluster around him just a year or two before. About making it big, he'd learned it was a problem either way—if you made it, you struggled to cope and hold on, and if you didn't, you worked at keeping the gun from your head. It wasn't for everyone. You had to be ambitious, to start with, and you couldn't know until it happened whether it was the up or down button the gods had pressed, so you never really knew which struggle to prepare for. Now Peter knew. Until a couple of weeks before, all he thought he would have to do from here on in was keep his drinking down, his checkbook balanced, and his ass clean in the LA *Times.* Then the bill came. He could have everything else but Nick or fight for Nick and put everything else on the line.

Because he couldn't do it alone. Nick was the only thing in his life that he bothered to keep like an island, temperate and ripe. And the funny thing was, he would have agreed with Nick that nothing was wrong with the two of them. There was the island, whole and long enchanted, ruled by a wizard and an exiled prince. But where things were always the same on the island, as against the thousand shifts and turnabouts in the world outside, the world's things had come more and more to be the same, too. The island and the world were still day and night, at opposite poles, but there were two poles now instead of one. He knew, from the moment he began the drive through Malibu Canyon and turned in at the gate of Nick's ranch, how far apart their dreams had ranged. The scale of the ranch told him what it was equal to in Peter's world. A first class stateroom on the *QE2.* The Cecil Beaton suite at the St. Regis. A hunting lodge once, in the Hebrides, that couldn't be reached except by plane, and then four hours in a Jeep that just about rattled his teeth out.

Yet even as the catalog began in his head, he knew it wouldn't satisfy him. As soon as the picture clicked, he saw himself shouting at room service over the phone. There weren't enough towels. Where was the ice? Short of the epic picture—the champagne cocktails on the Kirkov balcony over the Black Sea—he'd outgrown dream after dream because they turned out to be nothing special once he'd brought his suitcase in. So what he really should have seen about the dreams was this: Nick still had one strong enough to bid on, and Peter didn't. It was as if, to be a star, he'd had to give up the capacity to do something people who weren't stars needed to do more. In a word: dream. Life went on for days sometimes like a too deep sleep.

Leaving the easel where it was for the moment, he climbed into the pickup, started it, dropped it into second, and did a three-quarter turn to regain the gravel road. He headed up the hill. It was an idle enough desire, now that his plan to wait for Nick had gone awry, to see the other side. He probably wanted to know, too, where Nick and Sam were coming from, but not in any conscious way. He was right when he said he wasn't the type to follow people. Perhaps because he'd just told Nick he didn't dare go very far alone, he wanted to clock how far he did dare, now that Nick had driven off. He thought of LA, as he had most of the morning while he painted, though he was painting something right out of the Malibu hills. And not that anything here reminded him of the city that had no end. But he loved LA so much that he didn't like to be this far away in the country. Unlike Nick, he didn't care for California with a discoverer's lonely passion, though of course he thought it was beautiful and better than man and all of that. But LA was Peter's Paris-in-the-twenties. He couldn't imagine Josephine Baker or Schiaparelli or the Murphys footing it out to the farmland that lay a couple of hours in any direction from Maxim's. They stayed put.

Peter thought of Adele DesRoches, his big spender in San Marino, whose house he'd turned into a dream of wicker and travertine on the one hand, Persian miniatures and handwork on the other. Adele had lived in Pasadena and thereabouts for forty-five years and two and a half marriages. Once you had enough money, she'd told him, you ceased to live in California, even though it went on and on outside your windows. She'd bought a very airy Mediterranean place in San Marino for four hundred, and she budgeted—if "budgeted" is the right word— another hundred and fifty for interiors. Not including art.

"There is no Tahiti," she said one day, her sunglasses down on the tip of her nose. "What do you mean?" Peter asked. "It doesn't exist. I've been there," she said, and went back to working on her tan. And when you felt that way, Peter knew, it didn't much matter where you lived. Or you lived where Adele did, in the south of France a few blocks out of downtown Pasadena. He supposed there was no Tahiti wherever you looked in Beverly Hills. But Peter didn't buy it. He thought he lived at last in the center of the world, and the more people he met who thought LA was all dead-end, the rim of the abyss, the more there was for him.

When he crested the hill, he braked. It was more of the same, brush-covered hills—jade green, bottle green, sea-shaded —and a puzzle of fences. The bunkhouse leapt at him out of the distance, the one human thing. But he didn't for a minute think of cowboys. If he had had a notion of who lived here, he had them handcuffed to the land, dry-lipped and cheated and prey to bad weather. They hadn't a clue how to live in a house. Peter's mind worked like the mice in *Cinderella*—shutters at the sides of the windows, boxes of geraniums nailed to the sill, a knocker on the door, and coats and coats of paint. It was so sway-roofed and loose-boarded outside that inside must be old tin coffeepots and chairs made out of bent branches. Still, he thought, it was nicely proportioned for a single room. And there might be an attic in the peaked roof that would make a cheery loft for a bedroom. With a skylight over the bed.

He took off the hand brake and shifted into neutral and let the truck roll down the hill. An inadvertent glance in the rearview mirror, just as he left the rise, showed him the easel standing near the gate like a surveyor's upright. A flurry went up and down once in his stomach, as if for a moment the ranch was more real than he was and he, like the painting, not real at all. That's Nick's house now, he thought as he came down the long slope to the turn. In a way, then, it was his as well, and though he knew it was only an investment, just another kind of money in the bank, he suddenly thought they'd have to pull the bunkhouse down or fix it up. If it was Peter's, it had to be the best. All his life, he'd made do in a thousand different ways with nothing at all, just to avoid having anything around that was cheap or brutish or ugly.

He stopped again at the right-angle turn where Sam skidded the MG. When he got out to walk the rest of the way, a couple of hundred yards, he was slightly below the level of the house. From here, it sat low on the hill with a certain vividness and clarity, but he went toward it now as if he'd finished with it, his mind already somewhere else. He was going on only because he'd come this far.

He would have to tell Adele about Nick and Sam, he decided. He couldn't tell Rita any more about it, though he trusted Rita more, because she was in Bel-Air in the middle of it. It was close enough quarters as it was. He wouldn't admit that he might prefer Adele because she didn't know Nick. Or because Adele did what he told her to.

Just last week, the day he didn't make it home to go to Chasen's, he'd brought over to Adele's a tall blue and white vase from Isfahan. 1760. Thirty-two hundred dollars. That broke down to about sixteen dollars a year, he'd told her playfully over the phone, swearing it was a bargain. "Whatever you say," she said. She didn't even want to look at it first. So he picked it up at a shop on Wilshire and drove it over to San Marino, holding it on his lap. He walked right into the house, not bothering to knock. He called out for Adele and, because it was heavy, set the vase down on the travertine table in the entry hall. And it cracked. A hairline fracture about a foot long, starting at the bottom. The price went down to fifteen hundred, and he could hear Adele clattering down the stairs in wooden shoes. Like lightning, Peter swiveled the vase and turned the crack to the wall.

"Oh, Peter, it's too beautiful. I'm going to pass out," she said. "Tell me the story. Tell me about the little Iranian lady who spent twenty years painting my vase."

"Adele, it has to go right here. Don't touch it."

"But I thought it was for the bar."

"We'll find something else. This is where it belongs."

"Honey," she said with a dreamy smile, taking his arm and leading him into the wicker and travertine reaches, "I wouldn't move my bowels without asking you first."

Peter remembered it now, climbing up the steps to the bunkhouse porch, because whatever it was Adele saw in him was what everybody wanted. Except Nick. It was notable for Nick's lack of interest in it. Peter knew where he'd had his training in the styling and housing of Adele DesRoches: in his grandfather's study, turning over photographs of uniformed men and women in summer white. He used to go through a stack of dance cards, each as thick as a water cracker, as if they were pages in a diary. They had belonged to the woman Alexander Kirkov was signed up to marry after the war. Dead in a bombed train. A life lived out in a lost world, Peter always thought, and light-years removed from the gray and railing prince in Brooklyn Heights. It was the feel for that glimpsed and guessed-at life that Peter sold now on the open market. And only Nick seemed to know where the real Peter stopped and the romance began in people like Adele: Peter Kirkov, prince among men, his ancient blood like vintage wine, enameling greater LA with rich men's rooms like the bits and pieces of long gone landed estates.

The door was open. He saw the beer on the bed and went over and touched a can with his fingertips, as if he were taking its pulse. Because it was still cool, he opened it and sat down. He never drank beer. Better not to go home, he thought, in case Nick needed some time alone. He might as well drop by the shop. See how Rita was making out. He wasn't getting anywhere here, and it didn't do a thing for him to find Nick's trysting place.

What I'll do, he said to himself, looking around, is take those logs, as long as I'm here. One in each hand. I'll finish my Coors, he thought, and lug that wood to the pickup. He wanted to take it home for a winter fire. He imagined himself and Nick after dinner in the bedroom, making love in the firelight. It made him feel terrific. It wasn't a waste of time, once he had something to carry away. Peter was a star because he held old Europe in his heart like the jigsaw of a broken porcelain, and he passed it out like relics. He knew good wood when he saw it. He knew good everything.

Chapter 4

Rita wasn't in any rush. When she rode off on Friday night with Nick and Peter—clothes thrown on, her fingers tingling like a safecracker's—she was calm enough to realize that the door in the triple mirror might be more than she could handle. It might take a professional to get through. And the room beyond might be empty, or it might be the wine cellar or a narrow little safe and not a room at all, and Nick and Peter might already know about it, anyway. She didn't *believe* any of this, but she figured she owed it to the false god of luck to make the appropriate noises. She knew a crossroads when she came to one, if only because—especially because—it was her first. She'd been through doors with everyone, from Nancy

Drew in an old windmill to Howard Carter, live, from the Valley of the Kings. If Alice had stopped to wonder if the hole was full of wine, Rita reasoned, she would have lost the rabbit. Rita had the notion that you had to be ready to go, damn the luggage, the moment the story began. You ordered the cabbie to follow that car and hunkered down for the long haul. And you had to be in fabulous shape, in case the air got thin or the road played out. Your only tool was a nail file.

She was nice that night to all the absolute strangers, agreeing with everything they said. She stood with an untouched plate of fancies, a couple of feet from the buffet, purged of all her pedestrian hungers. She heard out a man who'd been through "total therapy" in Santa Barbara. The specialty treatment had him immersed in a tub of heated mineral oil, so-called "the French fry" by the patients. He swore that whatever it didn't do for the head, it did for the skin. Peter strolled by, and, putting his mouth close to her ear as she took a breath between exclamations, whispered that she was a cinch for the cover of *House and Garden* within a year. Rita grinned and nodded and agreed with him, too, though she had in mind something more like *National Geographic*. A border of yellow around Rita the intrepid, at the entrance to the pass to Shangri-La.

All evening, she was going through what she knew about locks and hinges—which, since she came from a New York apartment, was considerable enough. She knew it wasn't anything to do with a key. Captain Kidd, as she recalled, sank his treasure chest in a cave that showed its opening only in a certain tide that ripped in a certain weather. Off the Gaspé Peninsula or something. She guessed she was mixing it up with something else, but it gave her the feel of heavily treasured places, the "X" on the hand-drawn map—put her in the mood, so to speak. You didn't crack the enemy's war codes by knowing only the alphabet and how to count on your fingers. It took a different turn of mind, in this case a bird's-eye view of the course of a treasure—the source and the value in dollars, the owner, his heirs, his brand of paranoia, and his taste in gadgets. The lock on his secret room, Rita thought, was a plundering man's last stand against death. If you left behind a chamber hidden in a hill and stuffed with booty, like an Aladdin's cave, you had in a sense taken it with you. Because she understood the implications, Rita felt, she was the proper sort to break the seals. She took note of all the curses and went ahead and risked them, acknowledging that they went with the territory. It was all a matter of attitude.

So when they all staggered in at two or two-thirty, she stayed up an hour and drank iced coffee and sat on a little stool, staring at the mirror. Close up, she was able to make out, through the crack where the center mirror met the one on the right, a hinge mechanism that appeared to run without a break from top to bottom. Very tight and very strong. At the left, she ran a nail file along the crack and couldn't feel a bolt or a sliding bar. Couldn't feel a thing. She never once looked at herself in the glass. From this point on, in fact. Irrevocably now, the mirror was a door and not a mirror. If she still had staring matches with herself, as in the past, she had no conscious knowledge of them. Not a conventional lock, she decided as she sank into bed in the deep middle of the night. It must be tripped by the clock of a switch or a pencil beam of light. Swooning to sleep, her head beginning to bloom with a dream that took the shape of a vault like Scrooge McDuck's, mountained with dimes and quarters, she didn't even stop to register, as she always did in New York, that she was sleeping alone again.

During the weekend, whenever she had a free hour, she poked about for secret switches. Eventually, she broke the whole suite down into sections of fifteen or twenty square feet and went through it piece by piece—the bedroom, the bathroom, and the dressing closet. She tapped gently along the wall with a mallet for pounding veal that she took from the kitchen. No switches or buttons or plastered-over knots of wire. Before she finished, she already knew what it must be instead. It would take a coming together of two different things—like a key *and* a combination lock, both at the same time, or a skull that needed to be turned a quarter-turn on a sideboard, along with a certain book that must be pushed in along a shelf. The two things might be anything, of course, and you would never know if you had guessed just one or the other right, because nothing would happen unless you hit on both. Rita, however, was not whipped. The dabblers and the amateurs, the mere thieves, had been separated out by the difficulty. Perhaps that is where Rita came by the air of purity in her search—she hadn't the least desire to steal the least little thing.

It came to her Monday at work, just after a lunch when Peter taught her how to tell rugs apart, that she needed to start from the other direction. With Rusty Varda. There might be actual evidence lying around, an architect's plans and the like, but it mostly called for a portrait of Varda himself. And Hey, Rita expected, was the resident historian about the man who'd been emptied out of this house when he died.

They all had dinner in. That night at nine, when she thought he was finished with the dishes and ready to turn to his TV, she wandered in through the dining room. He was standing across the kitchen, just outside the door in the shady kitchen garden, his arms folded, a foot from the parrot cage. If Rita had interrupted them in heated conversation, there was no indication that they minded. The parrot, red head and yellow breast, jungle green in the wings, was doing all the talking. Like the static on a radio, with here and there a telegraphed phrase that sounded to Rita like "Machu Picchu." Now that she came to think of it, Rita noted, the rest of what the parrot said sounded like the purr and shrill of an Indian tribe, phrases that might well be spoken by believers in the sun. In that instant, Rita dropped hostilities toward the parrot. She stopped reacting as if it were a scorpion in that cage or, more to the point, a leaf-eating lizard with a scowl in the lower jaw. Things having turned out the way they had, he was no longer an alien. She decided to keep him on as a mascot. And she realized, as if in the same breath, the one thing bringing the other into focus, that she'd better get a car of her own.

She poured iced coffee from a white pitcher in the refrigerator—Colombian, filtered, floating a lemon peel and a thing that looked like a vanilla bean. She went to the doorway, and they said hello. Then they let a pause develop. When he thought to, Hey wore a white coat, and tonight it was luminous, his face far in the shadows.

"Was Rusty Varda very rich?" she asked. "How long did you work for him?" Clever Rita. She masked the baldness of the first question with the human-interest angle in the second.

"He left twelve million dollars, all told," Hey said matter-of-factly. Neither bitter nor proud. "We were together for ten years here. Did I tell you I used to work on my body six, eight hours a day?"

"Peter said so," she answered. "He mentioned you were a dancer." Perhaps it was the bird cage between them, so they could look at something besides each other, but they acted as if they'd say whatever they pleased. They didn't need to be roundabout. Besides, they weren't that interested in one another tonight. They were on their own. "What was he like," she asked, wondering: What can he say?

"Very, very private," he said, and Rita had to guess at the limits here. So private, it might be, that they had no right to inquire too much. "He'd already closed himself off from everybody else before he hired me. He had no outside world."

This all had the sound of an official position, Rita thought. What was he *really* like, she wanted to say, as if that were a more trenchant question. She needed Rusty Varda's most characteristic moment. What, all his life, did he used to *do* when his heart went empty and cold?

"The reason I mention my dancing is—I stopped training when I got to Crook House. I think it was the same day. I spent the morning at the gym, and a taxi brought me up here in the afternoon." He stared hard into the cage, as if the parrot might have an idea what must have happened. Then, looking through the cage at Rita, he smiled and finished the thought. "There's probably no connection."

"Rusty Varda got out of pictures in the twenties. Did he just *sit* here for the rest of his life?"

"I don't know. He was old in my time. The only thing he *still* did was juggle." It was a trump card, no doubt about it, and the story rose up to it. "He was a circus juggler before he came to the States. Long before the movies. I used to watch him out at the pool in the morning. He was lovely. He had a set of balls in every color, and you could tell the mood he was in from the balls in the air."

Juggling. Rita couldn't process it right away. She couldn't imagine what a juggler's lock would look like. It seemed as if it must be lighter than air. She might have to upend gravity to get through that door.

"What was my room in the old days?" she asked, turning to the map with the "X." "A guest room?"

"In a way. In the twenties and thirties, it was Frances Dean's room."

"She was his lover," Rita said, a whiz at following out a train of thought. "Right?" It also jostled something in her mind. Frances Dean, the fallen woman. It was either a movie or a run of tabloid headlines, Rita wasn't sure, but she felt several pieces interlock when she remembered it was a story out of the twenties.

"That's what everyone said, but it wasn't so. They were like brother and sister."

"What happened?"

"She was on dope, so he took her in," Hey said, as if it were worse to try to be polite about it. "He had a nurse here all the time, who lived in my room. *Your* room was like a sanatorium. But they finally had to take her to the hospital."

"That was all so long ago," she said. Frances Dean, Queen of the Silver Screen, was Rusty Varda's silent star. Rita wondered now if the girl's habit had cost him his production company. "Brother and sister" or not, they didn't get any extra sympathy from Rita. She was on business. "Did he leave the room empty after that?"

"How long is *so* long? You should have seen him lock himself in. He'd stay in your room a whole day sometimes. Sometimes overnight. Even the windows locked. I'd think he was dead in there. What would I have told the police? But I left him alone. It was between him and her."

"How often did that happen?" she asked slowly, her antennae beginning to sort and pick up signals. Something specific was coming in in waves. Like a set of directions—to the right, six; to the left, twenty. It wasn't numbers, exactly, because, of course, it wasn't a combination that did it. But the method was there, each step coming on the heels of the last, like a recipe.

"More and more," Hey said, all warmed up to it. "He'd go in there, and I'd say, 'Leave a window open, Mr. Varda. Just one, so you'll get some air.' But he wouldn't. My spiritual adviser thinks that he was doing self-hypnosis. It's very good for getting back the past, and that's where a lot of Mr. Varda lived." He stopped, seeming to listen to whether he had said too much or had given the wrong idea, and then went on. "It doesn't seem crazy to me, anymore. The past is where I live, too."

"I think you have to have a one-track mind, like the parrot, to live in the present." She raised a finger to the cage and twirled it, a gesture meant to tell the parrot she had loosened up. He recoiled a fraction, went silent, and made a stab at the bars of the cage with his beak. There was a clatter against the wire, and Rita jumped and drew her finger back into a fist. Hey didn't say anything. He was neither glad nor indifferent, but he appeared to think she had to learn it for herself. That was all right with Rita, though she would have felt differently if the parrot had made off with the first joint of her finger.

"Do you miss being a dancer?" she asked. She was so calm. She could feel the electric energy of the last three days resolve itself into a pinpoint of light that the lock on the door in the mirror couldn't blink away. She *knew*. It was as good as a telekinetic zap from the kitchen garden across the house to the secret room. It was as if she could hear the door click open.

"I guess so," he said quietly. "Do you miss being very young? It's like that. I was all shot as a dancer when I was thirty because I was a wreck from other things. I didn't have enough money to stay in it. I came out here to make it in the movies, like everybody else."

"But you didn't make it."

"Nobody does."

It might not strictly be so. Some did and some didn't, after all, depending on the market for types to people the dream. But she knew what he meant. The more she talked to Hey, the more amazed she was by his diamond-hard finger on the pulse of the world where dog ate dog. How did he put his two faces together, she wondered—the cynic whose eyes had dropped their scales, cheek by jowl with an open-eyed innocent who would believe anything, given enough Spiritual Advice. Hey was the household god of Crook House. Peter said he couldn't serve food hot, didn't see dust, could scarcely run a wet mop over the floor. But he was indispensable. He spent twice as much time there as Nick or Peter, and the house, accustomed to the motions of a cynical innocent, had taken the mood to itself until it touched each sunlit wall and earthen tile. Hey went as far back as a palace sage or a king's gatekeeper. The year that he moved in with Rusty Varda, Peter and Nick were still in high school, three thousand miles apart, mad about anything in pants.

"I'm sorry," he said to Rita, as if determined to see the things he said as good enough for him alone. Under any scrutiny, he seemed to say, they were fatuous and off-balance, and a woman like Rita shouldn't have a thing to do with them. "I realize now I wasn't meant to make it. But it's all right. The past is interesting, no matter how it's turned out." He lifted his chin as if to stretch his neck, then held it high as he went on, as if hearing the words from very far away. He looked at a patch of air just above her head. "I used to dress up as a woman sometimes. Now I don't have to because of Linda. But I must have been groping back to her all that time. There was a *reason*. Do you see?"

"Oh, yes." She was glad Hey trusted her, because she wasn't sure her face hadn't gone quite blank. She couldn't have repeated the moves that took them where they had just ended up.

"You'd better go now," he said, reaching up to unhook the ring at the top of the parrot's cage from the chain that hung down out of the tree. "He knows it's his night to fly. Once a week, I let him loose in the kitchen."

"How do you get him back in the cage?" She silently berated herself for lack of fortitude, for thinking right away of a dollop of parrot shit on the morning's rolls.

"I don't. He's gone back in by the time I get up in the morning. He just likes to stretch a little and limber up. He doesn't want to be free."

Hey shut and locked the dining room door behind her. Walking back to her bedroom, Rita cocked an ear when she passed the stairs up to Nick's and Peter's room. They must have gone out dancing, because there wasn't a sound, and they never went to bed so soon. Unless they'd locked their door to make love. We'll all be locked in, she thought, and the thought fairly made her skip the last few feet to her room. She didn't want to be free, either. She wanted to be in up to her neck. However wide the breezy sky, free was unemployed. Rita liked her circuits just this short of overload.

She began by shutting each of the casement windows facing on the pool, turning the latch to the lock position. Then she double-locked both the door to the hall and the outside door that led directly into the garden. She glanced around the room with a new delight in its details. Now that she'd pinned it down to Frances Dean, she thrilled to the scenes she planned to imagine having gone on here. But later, when she had more time. Now she had to move. She danced into the dressing room and saw right away that the mirror was the same as ever. She shut the door behind her and stood against it, leaning back on her crossed hands.

Now what? She couldn't deny she was stymied. It seemed so sure. She walked over to the triple mirror and pressed the flat of one hand against the place where a doorknob would have been if Rita's life had been a different story. It didn't budge.

Why did he lock himself in, the same way every time? she'd asked herself in the kitchen, and in a flash she'd seen the trick. Lock all the doors and windows, and the mirrored door releases, just like that. The secret lock, she suddenly understood, made a circuit with all the other locks. But it seemed that she was wrong. Something *else* was still required. She was mad, and for the first time she felt a desire to get a sledgehammer and beat down the door. She had a momentary picture of the scene: herself, ax in hand, standing amid the glitter of the shattered mirrors, and the others rushing in, thinking she'd gone mad because, poor thing, she wasn't as pretty as Frances Dean.

Calling it a day, she started back toward the dressing room door, determined to open things up again and sleep off her tension in the breezes off the pool. And at the last moment noticed a button in the center of the doorknob. It had never occurred to her to look. Wasn't it against the law for closets to lock on the inside? She pressed it in, click, and heard a sound behind her like a sigh of relief—no, sharper—like a gulp of breath at the end of an underwater swim. No sound of a lock at all.

The door was ajar, opening into the dark. She noticed it threw off the angle of the mirrors and, as she approached, that her own reflection registered crazily in the center, as if she were forever walking away. She stood on the threshold, pushed open the mirrored door, and couldn't see a thing. Saw an attic's worth of unfamiliar forms, oversize and many-cornered, shrouded in sheets. But the room was even bigger than she'd imagined. It seemed to tunnel deep into the hill. She had no candles, not even a match. But she did have the good grace to pay attention to the moment of crossing the threshold. She knew from her reading that you got only one threshold per expedition.

She peered in, her head held forward like a deer, stock-still. Curiously, she didn't plan on the horror she felt about the door going closed and shutting her in. Sometimes, she knew, the equipment didn't know the order of the story as well as the people did and, in its vast indifference, knocked the "off" button and brought things to a halt. She had to bring in a chair or something to prop open the door. She didn't even want to lean forward and grab the nearest sheeted object, for fear of slipping. She got so she could see a little in the dark. Under the sheet, she saw the corner of a heavy gilt frame, and she even took a guess at the patch of painting, a green and brown body of water and trees like broccoli. Dutch, she decided.

But for all that the first glimpse told her she'd found the very thing she wanted—though she hadn't, ever since Friday, been able to say exactly what it was—she was glad to pull the door toward her and save it for tomorrow, when she was better equipped. Anyone would have told her she had just failed the test of passion. What was she *doing*, restraining herself when all those boggling riches ached to gleam again in the light, whatever light they could get? But you could tell, in the languid slope of Rita's shoulders when she moved to withdraw, that the last people weeded out of the adventure were the ones who fell upon the treasure as if starved or high on a drug. Rita planned to do some thinking before she went on. About ownership, for one thing.

Then, in the final sliver of light that fell through the closing door, she saw a page of writing on the floor. And since it required her only to dart her hand a foot or two inside and pick it up, she did so, holding it between finger and thumb as she pulled the door tight. She didn't look at it until she was all unlocked again. She let the paper float down on the bed and then went in to bathe, taking her time. She thought about Hey in the tub, in fact, and shook the other business from her mind. Finally, she put a towel around her head and then lay down. Under the tiny light on her bedside table, she took the paper up and read it through. She was as cool as a scholar faced with something he'd never heard of, when he knew he'd heard of everything.

It was from Rusty Varda. To Frances Dean. All this part was guesswork, since the paper bore no names. Just a date, the numbers written big, with slashes in between—4/20/65. The brief text was in the high style, full of violins and the water sound of silk:

> We live in time, my darling, though I am betting it lives in us, too. If our ghosts come back, then let them meet here, if they still care to be together. I've provisioned them with all the beauty they may need. All I ask them is this one thing: *Remember us.*

The moment she got to "darling," she thought: Oh no, not this, on top of everything else. She was all braced for the mummy's curse. She'd mustered up some charity in case it was a futile cry of power Rusty Varda had set down: See how real I was, how far I got, how much I cost. Ozymandias, king of kings. But it was a bloody Shakespeare sonnet, instead. She didn't want a bit of it. If they couldn't work it out in flesh and blood, then let it go till doomsday. And if there must be ghosts, then let them be mean little spooks with tempers and tricks, and not the sighing kind. The dead could take care of themselves, Rita thought. Staying alive was a full-time job.

And yet, she sighed, and yet—notice how touching the present was in other people's lives. They wrestled with it and told you who they were. They had plans drawn up to collapse the past and put it in their pockets, at the same time saddling the future with carrying their baggage. Rita couldn't help it. She took a fix on 4/20/65 and slotted it in place in Rusty Varda's life. A couple of years *before* he died, so he either stopped coming here to his treasure room at the end, or he liked the symbol of the letter on the floor so much that he dropped by to watch it and arrange it. And otherwise he just juggled and felt this single-minded thought about Frances Dean. Wherever *she* was.

Meanwhile, Rita remembered, in the middle of the same chilly April, she herself had had it out with a man named Hank who couldn't do a thing until his mother died, and the mother had the genes of an Asian monk who lived forever on curdled milk. She couldn't imagine now that she could have cared, though she recalled exactly the feel of the tears that fell day after day. For Rita, the present had either turned out like the time with Hank, and she'd been sunk in herself from dawn to dark, or it didn't register at all. Most of the time, the present was just a way station. Rita appreciated people like Rusty Varda, who made the moment at hand a cause for gestures and manifestos. And they got what they wanted, she'd always observed, because they drew away the attention of others from things that didn't matter much.

She folded the paper into thirds like a business letter, just to show she wasn't going to treat it like the Dead Sea Scrolls. Then she tucked it in to mark her place in *The Ambassadors*. Letting *it* get stuck on page eighteen instead of her. Rita could see it was inevitable that she didn't read the way she used to, straight through from beginning to end, with incidental breaks for chores and errands, sandwiches and sleep. She'd read a tenth as much in the last few years. But just lately she could barely hold a book open in her hand. They weighed too much. They all sounded the same. They didn't *do* anything. She had to give Rusty Varda's ghostly letter credit—it had held her attention all the way through. It was just a conjurer's trick, of course, like a hundred books she'd read, in love with a world grown perfect. But at least, she thought as she sank into sleep, her head halfway to the lamp switch, at least Rusty Varda put his money where his mouth was.

The next night, she came in armed with a twelve-dollar flashlight, a Thermos of coffee, and a twenty-pound bag of sand. As she'd run into three different stores to buy these things, she liked the mystery gathering around her packages. No one would have been able to guess, opening her bags, what these three things were for. She cherished the feel of a secret life. Whatever people thought of her, they couldn't think the truth. It was too improbable. And she didn't experience the need to tell anyone about it, either. A switch from the old days, when the door would hardly close on Hank or his heartless equivalent—she'd be on the phone to Peter, to her cousin Marge in Gramercy Park, to anyone who'd still listen.

She sandbagged the mirrored door and walked right up to

the broccoli picture. It was Dutch, all right, but there wasn't enough *to* it to call it treasure. Somebody minor. She didn't even bother to kneel down and check the signature. Rita had thrown away every chance she had for a normal career by studying art history in college, and if she couldn't judge the Dutch with a flashlight in a dark room, then she might as well heave her Phi Beta Kappa key. Too bad, she thought. She'd hoped all day for a Rembrandt. But the Rembrandt didn't come until a few minutes later, after she'd thrown back the great canvas cover and gone through two stacks of paintings, propped upright one behind another like prints in a bin, except here they were all ornately framed.

She held in her arms the minor landscape, crouched to it, and held it like a loved one. Then saw behind it a Van Gogh oil of a bowl of red peppers on a yellow windowsill. And after that a nothing still life, and after that a phony Vermeer, a woman making lace in an autumn-lighted room while a small girl recited her lessons. Please don't let this be real, Rita thought, because there are only forty of his paintings in all the world. Or thirty-nine maybe, because one was lost in Dresden or something. But not a Vermeer *here*, for no one ever to see. Rita played the flashlight along the bottom, looking for a name, and a brass plate caught her eye. "Collection Galantine, Antwerp." A little museum too out of the way? So poor it sold a Vermeer? But why didn't it take the label off?

Well, so much for the Dutch. The neighboring stack was Italian—fourteenth, fifteenth century, two-paneled altarpieces and saints on boats, a red and gold curtain painted around the Virgin. Each of these was fixed behind glass, and they were less bulky. She went through them like files in a cabinet, letting them click against each other. She'd gotten B's in anything Italian, and it had proven to be the estranging issue between Rita and art history. She thought the professionals got too extreme about the Italian primitives. In fact, she was leaving the group without going through to the end when she flipped to the Rembrandt.

Himself at twenty-five in a brandy-colored velvet hat. The

eyes so direct they made you look away, toward the fur collar and the brocade vest. If Rita had a favorite way for art to go, it was here in this man's head, and she did a flip and didn't feel so badly about it being here unseen, because she wanted it protected. She clamped the flashlight under her chin so as to free her hands to pull the painting out, and the light splashed everywhere. She put the portrait in place in front, on top of the rest, and stared at it. This one, too, she thought, must be in catalogues. It even seemed familiar. *Someone* must know it's out of circulation. She wondered how anyone could have parted with it.

In a way, she'd seen too much already. She was glutted the way she was in museums. Without even lighting her way, she lurched from thing to thing and threw off the sheets. She just couldn't let it unfold anymore at a meditative pace. Where was it all going? In her heart's heart, it had never been Rembrandts *really* in the room. They were in another dimension altogether, where she played it like a game. She suddenly understood that a juggler was a man of concepts. She'd expected memorabilia, a stack of film cans, and a folded-up canvas chair with his name in script and a megaphone. Perhaps a blizzard of stock certificates as well, and municipal bonds a decade past redeeming. Money of some kind. And money in any form would have to go to the state, which had already reaped the twelve million and split it with the lawyers and then poured the rest away, Rita supposed, on a ten-mile stretch of freeway rehab.

But if you told a juggler those were balls in the air, and if he really heard you, they'd have dropped all over the room. Luckily for him, he wouldn't know what you were talking about because, to him, the balls were just a medium for a rhythm out of outer space. The dumb and stationary world going round and round in the air, thrown to the winds—it was a toy-maker's notion of making the rule of laws less absolute. And Rita was beginning to see the room of Rusty Varda's dream as just as brazen, just as unconcerned with the way things had to be. Plundering and bartering were one thing.

The goods mounted up, and the greed got fed, and the lust for more was a curious way of self-control. In a reckless man with power, money satisfied the lust to murder and make slaves. But this was a shy boy's valentine. Rembrandt and Van Gogh were no more actual to him than a cigar band gravely slipped on Frances Dean's ring finger. It was an old-school romance, and it could have been satisfied for images with ice cream and seashells. Varda just happened to have enough bucks to cast his juggler's balls in jade and agate.

Rita was sure he'd never set foot in a museum, that he hadn't had a clue to what he'd got. She played the light around her and found she was standing between two pedestals. On one was a Roman torso, cut off at the thighs and shoulders, the head thrown back and the mouth open. A javelin thrower, Rita thought. But now, without the gesture that defined him, he was focused somewhere else. His washboard belly and chiseled pecs were a shade too geometric, but the curve of his neck sent up a flow of something individual in his face. He looked as if the sculptor had caught him at the pitch of love. Rita turned around. The other statue was a woman who must have been made in Paris a hundred years ago. Rather, it was a woman's head and pretty arms coming out of a white marble statue of a dress, pleated in a hundred folds. It wasn't awful, but it was garden party art that ought to be surrounded by ferns, whereas the Roman athlete sent a chill up Rita's back. She knew already how the booty was going to divide up all through the room: sentimental junk on the one hand, the holy stuff on the other. About fifty-fifty. And Varda probably paid about the same for either kind.

She could see now boxes and crates and cabinets, a bookcase lined in leather-bound editions, and even a trunk ample enough for a body. The room itself was about fourteen-by-twenty. Rita had lived for years in a studio apartment that was roughly the same shape, with roughly the same amount of natural light. As she steered through to the back, she lit up along the farthest wall a little impromptu sitting area. A pair of tall, priestly Italian chairs and a twenties silk divan on a fabulous Persian carpet. An ivory-inlaid table covered with trinkets and costly playthings. And a cherry desk and chair where they might have signed the Declaration. Rita picked up from the desk top a book like a diary, but it was nothing personal. It proved to be a catalogue of every piece and every price in the collection. Then a column for the date it was acquired. And the final column gave the name of the museum. Rita looked up to think it over and stared into the middle of a thousand-flowers tapestry hanging on the wall. There was only one explanation, she thought, and she saw it dance across a page in an inch-high headline.

Black market traffic in stolen art.

She took the diary with her to work the next day and glanced at it all the while she was on the phone ordering fabric. She had a table of her own in Peter's shop, and though she'd been there only a week, it was already a half-inch deep in paperwork. So was the leather and chrome chair from Milan, and it meant that she worked sitting on the corner of the table, churning out memos and notes to herself. Rusty Varda's ledger looked surprisingly at home among the figures and the bills of particulars. She gathered that he had a regular dealer who delivered him things four or six times a year. He didn't buy anything a bum might be carrying under his coat. The amount of money paid was staggering when she added it up, but the price for individual things was sometimes bargain-basement. The Rembrandt—April, 1935—was only forty thousand dollars. The Van Gogh—Christmas, 1940—twenty-six. Rita tried to calculate in the margin of her memo what it worked out to in this year's dollars, and as a result she spent the morning disconnecting retail outlets and giving the wrong directions to delivery men.

By noon she'd put the phone on the answering service so she could take a long lunch. She found a fat envelope in the back-leaf of the book. She wondered briefly if the black market had gone the route of giving receipts or trading stamps, but it was clippings from the news about some of the thefts. As she settled down to read them through, she felt everything else turn off. She didn't touch her unwrapped sandwich. When Adele DesRoches walked in, she waved without looking up because she thought it was Peter. Nobody was expected. You had to have an appointment.

"Are you the person I talk to about upholstering a roller coaster?"

"Do I get a free ride?" Rita asked, looking up. Adele was so thin that you could have taken an X-ray of her with a flashlight.

"Not if I can help it. I'm Adele. Do you know who that is?"

"I've seen your floor plans," Rita said brightly. "More to the point, I guess you know who Rita is."

But that was as far as they took the shoot-out. They talked about her bedroom curtains, and they talked about New York. They split the sandwich Hey had packed her, and for a while they spoke well of Hey. Adele let Rita know she'd heard about Hey, about Bel-Air and Rusty Varda, the princes in Saint Petersburg and, oh yes, Nick. She asked smoothly what Nick was like. Rita pulled the bolt off the tiger's cage and said she really didn't know Nick well enough to say. In the end they spoke of Frances Dean, trying to recall when she died. A while ago, they thought. And Rita had to admit it was gutsy of Adele to walk in without pretext. Decked out in layers of tweedy Calvin Klein, fresh from modern dance and an hour's Tibetan massage, she apparently couldn't go on until she'd broken ice with Rita.

She's not half as bad as she must be when she's crossed, Rita thought. She'd so far avoided Peter's regulars, who kept him on forever as one project gave birth to the next. Peter laid the ground rule the very first day. He couldn't have assistants assisting too close in some people's houses. And Rita didn't care, at least for now. She took the messages in certain calls—she could tell by how much detail went into the variant of "Have Peter call me"—as if she were just a stock girl making room for Peter to create in. Rita didn't care how low they demoted her. She was busy learning the business, working up a head for figures, and getting things done the day before yesterday. She felt like Joan Crawford in a tailored suit with padded shoulders. Adele DesRoches was an enemy she'd left behind in New York for good. At last she'd found something Adele's set was poor in: big secrets. They shopped and ate lunch, and Rita used to think it took away the sting of time for them. But gossip wasn't secrets. To kill time required an impossible project. Adele looked starved on steak tartar.

By Wednesday afternoon, Rita was proceeding in two different directions. She brought to the shop a tiny Renoir oil, the head of a boy, lifted from a museum in Holland during the war. She wrapped it in tinfoil at home and put it in the bag with her sandwich. Later on, she ate the one and parceled up the other in cardboard and brown paper and twine, addressing it to Amsterdam and putting on a false return address in West LA. She guessed at the postage, slapped on stamps, and dropped it off at the post office on the way home. The same day, she had made a call to the *Times* and talked a clerk into researching the death of Frances Dean, saying she was from NBC and promising him a credit if they got it on the air. He called her back while the stamps were on her tongue. No report of the death had ever appeared in the paper. What, he wanted to know, was the project for NBC? To do with Howard Hughes, she told him, so it had to be kept a secret until everything was in place. Could she count on him? She could.

She spent the evening going through the jewelry. Not in the ordinary way. Not in a mirror. She felt less possessive of what unfolded out of these squares of black velvet than she did about anything she'd found so far. She knew they were erotic, the ones cut and mounted as women's jewels. And she realized how close the parallel was between Cartier gold and enamel and the wonders of King Tut's tomb. She brought them out of a wooden chest by candlelight. A silver cigarette case inlaid in a checkerboard of black and yellow onyx. A pear-diamond ring as heavy as a stone. A bracelet of pavé links, sapphires and emeralds. Erotic not so much because they were worn against flesh as because of the power that crackled between the lovers they were tribute to. Some were beautiful in a way that broke her heart, like perfect flowers that bloomed and died, except here it was the beautiful women who had owned them who died.

Rita let them run through her hands—art deco brooches, Tiffany earrings, a string of gray pearls—and she tried nothing on. But wasn't she being *too* pure? Anyone would have told her as much. Just because she'd passed through the mirror didn't absolve her of all vanity. She owed it to herself, to the war she'd had with love for twenty years, to try them on and feel how a certain class of man kept a certain class of woman. And yet, she thought not. She simply didn't want to be involved. She had beside her the diary list of the people whose vaults and lacquered cases had been rifled for each item. People from Sag Harbor and Hobe Sound and River Oaks and 78th and Park. She felt no welling urgency or sense of mission about returning these to their rightful owners, not the way she did about the art to the museums.

So, in part, the jewelry annoyed her. It was too sensational. Worth so much, it brought up the uncomfortable issue of telling the world outside what she'd discovered. She couldn't just ignore it. She'd hoped to pack everything off, but of course she couldn't. She couldn't mail the Ming plate either, or the crystal mouse. And what was rightful about the owners anyway? The jewels stolen in the forties belonged now to various estates and heirs, Rita supposed, and it wasn't the same as the women themselves. Of course, some of them must be quite alive, and some might be pining even now for their heavy gold chokers, but Rita wasn't in the mood to go out of her way for them. Let them go shop and eat lunch. She would have been quick to point out that her cooled-down attitude here was a form of vanity, too.

She leased a bone white Jaguar Thursday morning early. She couldn't be late for anything today because, for the first time, Peter had taken the whole day off and left no number where he could be reached. He was going painting. Rita had a meeting with the owners of a Continental restaurant in West

Hollywood who wanted the Spanish taken out. They wanted it to look as if it had been lifted from soup to nuts out of Harvard Square. She had a bout with UPS about the millionth delay on an order of sisal shipped out of Chicago. A man on Beverly Glen had just found out that the honey-finished cabinet Peter had bought him in Mexico, which had just arrived, wouldn't go up the stairs to the study. What the hell was she going to do about it? She sang him a lullaby of sorts and promised a house call at two o'clock. Then she finished her phoning and figured she had a couple of hours to kill, so she drove back to Bel-Air to pick up a medium-size painting.

It had to be small enough to fit in her overnight bag, because she couldn't just carry it out of the house under her arm. Someone might see it and start asking questions. She couldn't be choosy. She'd about decided on a *Crucifixion* from a monastery north of Florence when, tired of the Italians again, she took the extra time to crowbar the top off a wooden box. She'd still finished only about a third of the inventory, and there were any number of still unopened crates. This one proved to be English. Two Blake illustrations of *Paradise*. A Turner storm at sea. A Gainsborough boy and his dog. And then something that was just the right size: a Constable landscape. A little boring, perhaps. A ribbon of land beneath a swirl of dove gray cloud. There was a time when she could have written a paper about it overnight, a thousand words, and told the ways it was beautiful. Stolen from the library at New College, Oxford. Damn it, she thought, they probably haven't even noticed it's missing. The monks in Florence deserved to get their painting back much more, but what could she do? It was a little too big, and she needed to practice on easy things.

She had gotten so accustomed to locking herself up and setting herself free that she did it automatically, much as Rusty Varda must have done. She always put her head out the closet door before she came out, in case anyone should be looking through the windows from the garden, but otherwise she breezed about, opening and shutting, like a sailor who knows his boat down to the last screw. She went up the hallway, suitcase in hand, and squinted when she came into the brightness of the living room. The noon sun through the skylights pooled in three or four places, and she walked zigzag across the room in order to go through the sunny spots. No reason. She was happy. She was a little afraid, of course, to be so happy, and she hadn't done a thing about getting over Nick. She was still letting that happen in her head. But even so. That day, in the warm spots in the living room, she was at the exact center of her life.

Sam was standing on the spiral staircase, about halfway up. When she first caught sight of him, Rita thought he had just gotten out of bed. The sleep was still in his eyes. Then she saw it differently. He looked as if he'd spent the better part of his life in bed, but none of it sleeping. His eyes had a quality that could fix and stay like a painting, and they were older far than hers. She felt, when he looked down at her, like a fool eccentric who's neglected all the good things in life, doesn't have time for them, and in the end doesn't know what they are and can't go get them. She didn't desire an inch of him. On the contrary. She felt a bristling in her, so strong it shook her by the shoulders. He was sleazy. He looked like he'd given up on people years ago. He was beautiful, she had to admit, but it went no deeper than his tan and his sun-shot hair and carried with it the feel of its own exhaustion, like a Vegas showgirl's beauty. The sex was mean.

"Who are you?" he asked, genuinely confused.

"Rita," she said. Let him make what he could of that. She didn't like being down below, but she couldn't exactly order him down. She was furious at him for watching her crisscross the living room to stand in the sun.

"I'm Sam."

"Well, we mustn't be here to meet each other," she said ironically, "because we don't seem to ring a bell in each other's head. You know Nick and Peter?"

"Nick."

And she knew in an instant who he was. "Oh, Rita, who knows," Peter had said the first night at the party, "I think

Nick's in love." And as there was no follow-up—Peter didn't mention it again, and Nick was as normal as could be—she'd dropped the whole thing as unfounded, a way married people had of talking about the wild uncertainties of love. Her wish to protect Nick and Peter both was what had gripped her, and before she was conscious of summoning it. It sprang full-blown, probably because she'd taken such pains herself with Nick and Peter, in the struggle with her own sharp passion. About Nick, she had no expectations, and it made her free to go through the irony, the melancholy, and the tangle of being honest with herself. But not just yet. She hated this boy on sight for being so simple. And so carnal. She wasn't being repressive or righteous, either—carnal was all there was some-times, and when it was, it often worked. But Sam acted as if there were no other wisdom and no harder meeting. She and Nick and Peter had *done* all that, she wanted to say, even if she didn't know the details. They'd let themselves go, all three, for years. And all the same, they were split off on tangents, every one, and chasing each other around in a ring, trying to perfect a love they could live with. This boy wasn't one of them. He'd been through something else.

"Is Nick here?" she asked.

"He's on his way," Sam said, but didn't say from where. It was clear, though, that Nick was right behind him. Nick's going to walk in, Rita thought, and we'll both be changed as if by magic, and we won't have had anything to say about it. "Are you the one from New York who's starting over?"

"You could call it that." Is that how *Nick* would put it? "But it isn't fair. You know who I am, and I don't know who you are."

"Nobody special," he said. "I'm a cowboy. Why do you have your suitcase with you? Are you leaving?"

"Uh, no. I broke the handle. I mean the clasp. I'm taking it in to have it fixed."

"I don't own one." He came down the stairs now, strutted down, as if he meant to go on doing what he was doing before Rita came in. "I've never been anywhere far enough, I guess.

Sometimes I think I'll pack up and go to New York, though."

"To start over?"

"Sure," he said, face-to-face with her. "But I'm too lazy. Someone ought to pay me to just sit and drink beer. I'd be a rich man."

"I'll bet you could find someone to pay you for that," she said playfully, though giving him the option that he might not want to play with *her*. "People and their money love to be parted. All you'd have to do is convince someone you were the *best* at sitting and drinking beer. People love a winner."

"What do you do?" he asked. He looked now as if he'd forgotten what he was doing before Rita came in.

"Me? I put together packages. And I'm always on the lookout for time-saving tips. I save up time."

"What for?"

"I don't know," she said truthfully. "But I'll need all the time I can get when I find out."

Then they heard a droning from the dining room, and Hey walked in behind the vacuum cleaner. He had had no reason to suppose anyone else was home. They were all gathered here during an hour when the house was customarily his. For the briefest moment, his eyes took in Rita and Sam, and then, full of unconcern, he studied the rug in front of the machine as if he might pick up a stray diamond before the suction did. Rita could see he'd connected her and Sam up as a couple, and he meant to get out of their way, whatever sort of couple they were. He steered his vacuum meaningfully across the room, in the direction of the hall. Unlike Rita, he seemed to stay clear of the sun pools. Besides, he had his own reasons for getting some privacy. He'd made up his face as if for the stage—some red in the cheeks, a wide blue shadow on the eyelids, and a scatter of pencil lines to shallow his cheeks and soften his jaw. He looked like a washed-out clown.

"Hey, I'm just leaving," she said, and Hey looked up at her and cupped his ear. "You can stay. Sam can go out and wait by the pool."

It was the name that did it. Hey heard "Sam" and looked at

him hard for the first time, his eyes darting away from Rita. She watched the transformation happen in his face. He went white, and his eyes went wide with panic. So that's what people mean, she thought, when they say they've seen a ghost. It has very little to do with the ghost itself, who, after all, just wanders about in a sheet, who can't take hold of anyone by the throat because he can't take hold of a blessed thing anymore. But to see one, she understood now, is to stare your own death in the face. She didn't know what to do for Hey, he went so far away so fast. How could he have known Sam that many years ago, she wondered, because the first thing she noticed about his shock was how full it was of a thing long buried. Sam seemed to Rita like a teenager. Hey was old enough to be his father. So was she. It was between *them*, she told herself, and put on a smile and waited for Hey to compose himself. She didn't look at Sam.

"It's all right. I'm just passing through," Hey said, shifting back to her again. "It's already clean in here." The noise of the machine made it impossible for her to pinpoint the tone of voice. But clearly he'd decided not to show his cards just yet. "What are you doing with your suitcase? Are you going someplace?"

"No, no," she said. "I need it at the office. I need it for samples." Why am I lying two different lies? she thought, mentally kicking herself.

"Well," he said firmly, "you can't go around with that. Have Peter buy you a proper briefcase. Go to Gucci."

He sounded all recovered, and she couldn't hold him back. He zipped along and mowed the vacuum out of the room.

"It was nice meeting you," she said to Sam. "Make yourself at home."

Sam smiled and opened his mouth to say something nice. She could tell, she'd snowed him in spite of herself. People who lived in and out of their clothes appreciated Rita's velocity, her coming to the point and getting on her way. It was just as well that he liked her. She wasn't going to treat him like a ghost. That would amount to abandoning Nick, for one thing, and for another, she wasn't afraid, like Hey, of the kind of man Sam was. Hey thought he was dangerous. She thought he was like a delinquent boy, though she knew they both could be right. And then the nice things got left unsaid, because they heard Nick call down to them from the balcony.

"Nothing ever happens in the living room," he said, to mock them standing there. "If I'd come in time to introduce you, I think I would have arranged it in the garden. But my batting average is low today. I guess it's lucky we all got here in one piece." Rita and Sam, looking up together, looked like people plotting constellations in the midnight sky. Nick rained down his lightest comments on them. It had all stopped being in his control back at the ranch, the moment they heard the first rattle. Now he was doing what he could just to keep up. "Are you stealing the flatware?" he asked, pointing at the suitcase.

Rita grinned. "It's my secret life. I do a juggling act in Griffith Park during my lunch hour. This," she said, fluttering the overnight bag in the air at her side, "is where I keep my juggler's balls and my clown costume. You won't tell anyone, will you?"

"I never tell on my friends," Nick said, leaning from the waist over the railing, as if he might fly off. "But not because I'm virtuous. It insures that I keep hearing all their stories."

"I don't tell on mine, either," she called back, her voice a notch more cynical than his, the currents just as deep.

"Should we all have lunch?" Nick asked. He was talking to Rita. No one was talking to Sam.

"I can't. I have to go push an armoire up a flight of stairs. I just stopped here for a minute."

"To get the flatware."

"Something like that." She turned to Sam and said, "Take care of yourself," by which she meant "Take care of Nick, or else." She reached over and touched him, on the flat of his stomach, as it happened, and she thought of her statue. "Maybe next time we'll have a swim. Or just sit and drink beer."

"Will you hold my head under until I promise to be good?"

His voice was mild and even-tempered, and it struck her that this might be the nice thing he meant to say. He knows I'm a little hysterical, she thought. And she realized she'd had her first warning about Sam—he might be a kid, in love with himself and dispossessed of being human, but he wasn't stupid.

"I won't lay a finger on you," she said, knowing Nick was listening, and walked to the foot of the stairs. She could hear Nick starting down, so the last thing Sam spoke, intimate and dense with shadows, was for her alone.

"That's not the only thing you won't do, Rita. You won't tell me what's in the suitcase, either."

She pretended not to understand. She didn't really have to pretend. Negotiating the Samsonite as well as she could, she started up the spiral. When she and Nick met halfway, they made as if to slip past one another, but took more pains than they needed to, in order to draw out the time. Their voices fell to conspirators' pitch, as if by common practice. Still, there wasn't any time.

"I don't know what to say. Things have gotten a little out of hand."

"This is nothing," she said reassuringly. "Haven't I ever told you? I'm a tough guy."

"Rita, I'm afraid."

"So's Hey."

"So's Peter."

"Well, I'm not."

"Good," he said, the loudest thing he said. "I promise not to be, next time you are."

"It's a deal," she said.

Then the momentum of the stairs took over, and they were swept around the spiral, one up, the other down. She didn't look back, and the next thing she knew, she was out the front door. She put down the case and bent over, cradling the arm that had held it. She felt as if she'd never use it again. Her arm hanging lifeless, she was going to gimp around forever because she'd pretended it was empty when, in fact, there were pounds and pounds of painting in it. She stood between the house and the stairs to the white Jaguar. The shriek in her elbow joint abated after a minute, giving over to a throb that she could handle. She picked the suitcase up in the other hand and took a parting look down the green canyon below Crook House. From the kitchen garden, she could hear the parrot squawking. It was February twenty-sixth, she thought as she climbed the shaded stairs to the drive, and she no longer blamed the winter weather for what went wrong. That, right there, was progress.

Chapter 5

Sam didn't get the story straight for three or four days, but it was his own fault. He didn't pay attention the first couple of times Nick called. He made noncommittal noises here and there and kissed it all good-bye, because he didn't really believe what Nick was telling him. Sam heard stories all the time. He was used to scaring off married men and men with futures. As soon as it hit them they had gone too far, gotten too involved, they back-pedaled, threw the bolts, and went to unlisted numbers. *Sam* never got too involved, and his manner with any man went unchanged from the first encounter to the last, assuming he permitted more than one. They didn't have to worry about him sticking around. He always took the first hint when things were over, as he did now. All he knew was that Nick promised him Thursday afternoon in Bel-Air that they could make it in Nick's own bed the next day and then take steam and then a swim. And Friday morning at seven, Nick called and woke him up to cancel.

"My friend Peter was missing last night," he said. "He had an accident."

Sam knew who Peter was. He was the man they'd found painting at the gate to the ranch. And Sam figured the two of them must have had it out right there, after he took off in the MG. An hour or two later, when Rita left and he and Nick were alone again, they went on a tour of Crook House that was curiously formal, as if Nick were showing it to a buyer from out of town. If he only knew, Sam thought, he'd let *me* do all the talking. Sam could have walked these rooms in his sleep. Did, some nights. And yet he didn't mind Nick going on about Varda, the land he sold off in half-acre lots, and the will he never made because he was all alone. Though that was a lie, Sam thought, because what about Frances Dean? Why didn't he leave it all to her? Sam didn't say a thing out loud. He merely asked a tourist's innocent questions. Nick's version was just what he hoped for—it proved he was the only one who knew the truth.

"He's all right now," Nick said, "but I can't see you today. I'll call you Monday."

"Who knows where I'll be on Monday?"

"Will you call *me*?"

They left it open. Nick rang up again on Sunday afternoon, when Sam was just back from a heavy session with a trucker who'd driven straight through from Salt Lake City. One of his out-of-towners, who showed up every couple of months and paid top dollar. Sam held the phone in one hand and leafed through a bikers' magazine with the other. Feeling so satisfied with the animal scene where men said nothing, he was in no mood to give an ear to Bel-Air reasons. Nick seemed to want to tell him even more of the story, and he didn't know why. If you want to get out of this, Sam wanted to say, then just let go. He didn't care about Peter's accident. He didn't care about Nick, for that matter, and he had a certain specific contempt for Nick because Nick didn't know it. This was not the same as no affection. He *liked* Nick well enough. He liked everybody, really. Yet, as Rita had intuited, he had no interest in people, and the stories they lived out were all the same to him. And since he paid no attention to his own story, either, you had to admit he was consistent.

"It was the snake, Sam. The same snake."

"How do you know that?" he asked, suddenly aware that he might tip over if this went on too long. "Did it introduce itself?"

"It happened in the bunkhouse. Peter was fooling around in the fireplace, and it got him in the arm."

Sam felt his stomach tie up in a knot. Did it hurt? he wanted to ask. How *much*? But that was all. He didn't want to know the story because a hairsbreadth shift in the compass or the clock would have made it *his* story. But he let Nick talk on for a bit, waiting for some word about the pain.

From the moment the snake flashed, apparently, Peter moved as if he were being filmed for a documentary on the right thing to do. He made a quick tourniquet above the punctures. He picked up a Coors from the bed, pulled the tab, and used it to cut the sign of the cross in his arm, right in the middle of the wound. Then he sucked at it till the poison milked out into his mouth, sweet-sour, the sweet being the blood. Then he staggered to his pickup and drove out of the ranch and down through the canyon to the Pacific Coast Highway, where he floored it to a clinic he'd passed for years in Malibu. He walked in, held out his arm as if for a shot, said "Rattlesnake bite," and fell over in a dead faint. There wasn't a clue in his clothes as to who he was, and the slow-witted clinic crew didn't think to match him up with a car in the parking lot. He came out of the faint in a fever, and it was just before midnight that he dropped the long, delirious Russian tale of his crowns and estates and remembered who he was.

Sam tuned out. The pain stopped. It was just another story,

after all. There was so little that he bothered with beyond sex. The concept of pain still had the power to somersault Sam's certainty that he was self-sufficient, but even then it took the snake gliding close to his own body to bring it home to him. What's more, it would have required a bite in the small of the back, something that couldn't be reached, the pain going deeper and deeper, no truck, no clinic, to keep Sam riveted to Peter's danger.

"So I can't see you for a while," Nick said, as if he were betraying something.

"Why?" Sam asked.

"I just told you. Peter's got to take it easy. His nerves are shot. It isn't the snakebite, because it wasn't really bad. They think the snake must have just finished eating a mouse or something, and, besides, he was old. Anyway, I've got to stick close to Peter for a while."

"For a while," Sam repeated without inflection. "Well, I hope the two of you will be very happy together."

"I want to send you some money."

"Why? You want to put me on retainer like a lawyer? Or a private detective?"

"No reason. I just want to. What's your address?"

"I don't give it out."

"Really?" Nick laughed uneasily. "I guess you don't get much mail."

"None. That's the way I like it."

"Okay," Nick said, sorry now that he'd brought it up. "It can wait until I see you."

"No. I'll tell you what you do," Sam said, practical at last, and as if everything else he'd said so tonelessly were meant to be funny, though no one had laughed. "Leave it with the bartender at the Beau-Numero. They know who I am."

It was seven hundred in cash, and he couldn't figure out how Nick had arrived at the actual amount. It was certainly more than Sam expected or was accustomed to. Too much, in a way. It ended up irritating him, because he couldn't seem to communicate to Nick how to observe the proper boundaries.

He didn't see that Sam became extra hard and detached, just to compensate. Of course, he liked hundred dollar bills for their own sake, and he knew, the moment he opened the envelope, that he wouldn't have to work for a week. But what he liked best about the *business* of hustling was the cash flow, how it demanded not the slightest shred of his attention. He took it in and paid it out and worked when he wanted and never went hungry. He didn't need more, and since he didn't pay taxes, they never went up. He knew about inflation and, like a psychiatrist, added five dollars a trick every couple of years. The only thing that would have changed his rhythm was a *lot* of money, a vault of it in ingots, with neither strings nor a middle-aged man attached. That was why he'd bided his time for ten years to get back into Rusty Varda's house.

He didn't have a list of things in his head he'd been waiting to buy. If it had been seven thousand, maybe he would have gone after a secondhand Porsche, but his mind didn't run in that direction. All the same, he decided to take the day off and go shopping, struck with the notion of getting rid of seven hundred fast. It certainly didn't cross his mind to save it. He had no accounts, neither checking nor savings. He kept his money, what he didn't keep in his pocket, in a coffee can under his bed in the one-room apartment no one else knew the way to. Twisted-up tens and twenties and fifties. So much for security. When he was robbed, he chalked it up to the redistribution of wealth. He didn't even own a wallet.

He bought a case of Jack Daniels in fifths. Then a half-dozen tenderloin steaks. Though friendly, one-man stores made him jittery, he spent an hour in a rhinestone-western boutique in Hollywood, trying on fancy shirts. He tried on more than he needed to because the middle-aged glitter queens who ran the place were clearly so enamored of his torso. They held the discarded shirts over their arms and debated how marvelous he looked in everything. He bought a heavy khaki gabardine yoked with hand-sewn black and gold swirls, a six-gun embroidered at each nipple. In its way, it was as difficult to bring off as the overwrought three-hundred-dollar boots, but, on the other hand, Sam could wear anything. He lived so much at the surface of his body, at the nerve ends, that his clothes hovered about him like curtains billowing in front of an open window, going with the air.

Then a Stetson, off-white with a snakeskin band. He wore it when he drove up and over into The Valley. To Studio City, where he wound his way among a thousand houses where no one had ever worn *anything* that went for three hundred. He tooled into a driveway, leapt out of the MG, and went up and rang at a dead-end bungalow. Rust-streaked stucco and strangling geraniums. The old woman who opened the door couldn't have cared less who it was, so she wasn't his grandmother or his prep school Latin teacher.

"I thought you must be in jail," she said. "What do you want?"

"Two grams."

"Two, eh?" She seemed impressed. "You must have hooked up with a big tipper."

She padded into the house, and he followed her as far as the airless dining room, where three more women sat around the table, cards in hand, and waited. They looked like they'd forgotten what the game was, gone beyond it like yogis. If they'd once been the type to cluck at everybody young as reminders of their own children, they'd gotten over it. And no one took a second look at his torso.

The old woman came back from the kitchen with a parcel tied so well she could have sent it overseas. It was a hundred and fifty. She pocketed it and said, "Take care you don't ruin your nose. You won't be able to smell a rat when you need to."

That left him with a hundred and seventy-five, and he couldn't think of anything else he wanted. What would my father do, he wondered idly as he drove back over into Hollywood. Go out for dinner, maybe. Or buy a share of common stock. Or go get laid. Sam knew he had enough even now to fly to Vegas or San Francisco, the only two places he ever went. He always took his extra money one way or the other.

He liked them just about the same and found them very much alike. Like stage sets. All the people posed and spoke lines that wouldn't have gone over anywhere else and dressed so that they all matched. Of course, Sam could see that Vegas and San Francisco were the opposite of one another, too. But for him they were the two sides of LA, and narcissism was narcissism, whether it flowered in a desert casino or high on a foggy hill with a three-sixty view of The Bay. Sam would have gone right now, flipped a coin and headed for the airport, but he didn't want to put himself so far from Rusty Varda's house. He knew that it had to be only one thing. He couldn't splinter the last of the money. It waited in a wad in his pocket, to be risked all at once—on black, on red, on a single number even.

What'll I buy, he thought over and over, what'll I buy?

He went back to his apartment in West Hollywood. His nothing apartment. A double bed and a table with a big color TV that he'd bought hot. An easy chair, vinyl and motel blue. A Pullman unit built into a cabinet for pans and dishes. And a chest of drawers, every one open and spilling clothes. It existed hardly at all as a place to live. He passed the time there. He used it between tricks as a dressing room, though not necessarily so as to dress—more as an actor on location would have used it, doing a scene and resting, back and forth. Which is not to say that clothes didn't furnish the man. There was a layer of things draped and thrown on everything—Levi's and corduroys, gym gear, leather jacket, flannel shirts, swimming trunks, and two-toned jerseys for baseball, football, rugby. Street clothes. He lived here without declaring himself. And, of course, if someone had wandered in, a stranger from the world of laws and moral precision, he wouldn't have been able to accuse Sam of anything. There was no evidence.

He cut the cocaine and did a couple of lines. He poured himself a Jack Daniels over ice and turned on the TV to a game show. A half-hour later, when the coke had dropped its dazzle, he unzipped and pulled out his cock, spit on his hand, and jerked himself off. To keep him from going out on the street. He alternated that way for the rest of the day. Coke.

Bourbon. Every three or four hours a go at pumping himself. He was forever aroused. The only way he knew how to disconnect from his life on the make, since it was profession and fantasy-life at once, was to blur the edges and bring himself into a state of low consciousness and numbness of the groin. Unlike so many other hustlers on his beat, he didn't need a case of joints in his pocket, a six-pack in the bushes, or uppers and downers. He had to be alert to fuck, uncompromisingly fixed in the world at hand, so as to miss nothing in the region of his senses. His fantasies may have been more lush and slit-eyed with lust when he was wrecked, but he didn't shape them up and work them out in an actual bed unless he was feeling precisely where he was. When he was sober, he could get a hard-on right on cue, hour after hour if he had to. And since the places where he ended up were so unpredictable, four or five in a day sometimes, the real world was pretty much confined to other people's bedrooms, and it never failed to turn him on.

It was a struggle to take a seven-hundred-dollar vacation, even though he knew he needed it from time to time, and particularly now, with the Varda caper finally starting to happen. If he was going to lay low at his place and let the next set of moves come together in his head, then the fucking had to stop for a bit, because he threw his whole self into it and left no room. So, taking himself in hand, he skimmed off the excess juices until he was drunk enough, and then they ceased to boil and blow all by themselves.

But who knows what his reasoning was? He woke up the next morning and found he'd eaten two steaks and drunk a fifth of bourbon. The hangover had less to do with pain—a headache was kid stuff—than with a sense of being removed from his usual outlook, the mood he settled in when he walked his block on Selma. Normally aggressive, jumpy, unattached, he found himself sent back to a time before he lived by his cock alone. So he liked the morning after. Why he needed to go away as far as his youth in order to think about the present is a curious thing, but on that second day he had no need to will his solitude. He drank the bourbon with plenty of water and sat in the easy chair, head in the clouds, the look on his face like Tom Sawyer's. He waited until sundown to snort the coke. He walked around naked and tended to catch up his genitals in his cupped hand, kneading and stroking, no sense left of their function as tools. He sought asylum in himself because he'd never had anyone else to ask it of. And he got it. He disdained Nick and Peter for retreating into a couple "for a while" because it showed they weren't self-possessed.

He was just as drunk that night, but he woke wide-eyed on Wednesday morning, cooked a steak for breakfast, and headed out for the beach. It wasn't warm enough to lie down in a bathing suit, but he walked the tide-line with his shirt off. He went from the Santa Monica pier to the point where Sunset Boulevard spilled out at the Pacific—four, four and a half miles—and liked the feel of his shoulders burning. He had cruised the waterfront here a thousand times, but today he affected the air of a boy pirate, fashioning nothing for those who watched him. Indeed, he assumed as a consequence that he was next to invisible. In fact, it was a field day for men on the beach who would have been afraid most days to look him in the eye—men without cash, men who kept their shirts on. Because he moved for once without seeing himself in the third person, he was beautiful in a way that was quite unearthly, clean of sin and self.

If there was a way of keeping anyone, he thought, Nick was the sort he would go after. He always knew, when he met up with men who fell for him, the moment when they stopped wanting anything else. They surrendered the quest by believing that Sam was the goal of it all. *Sam* knew he wasn't. He would gladly fuck the whole world to prove there was no goal. There was only the accumulation of events. Sam couldn't get enough of new and better men, and he'd guessed right off that Nick was the same. They both wanted *everything* else, the search for which went on all the time and everywhere. Sam thought that if he could get Nick through the present phase—the cowboy buddies who sloughed off the world and set out for the wilds, their hearts unvalentined and freed to the weather—then perhaps they could go on to other things, each on his own. And they could use each other to measure themselves against. They could even try, for variety, to outdo one another in seeing how far they would go. And, of course, there would be the added business of Nick's money thrown in, share and share alike. To Sam, it had the earmarks of a perfect relationship, except for the fact that nobody ever stuck to the ground rules, even when they were perfect. That was why he was better off alone. But if he had his way entirely, he thought as he climbed up on a lifeguard's chair and lit up a joint, Nick was the man he'd bet on.

Wednesday night, he'd already decided, would have to be the end of his holiday because he had to make sure that his territory was clear for the weekend. He didn't want to have to fight it out on his block with some punk newcomer just hitch-hiked in from Dallas, his lifeless college diploma rolled in his knapsack. Anyone who knew the streets at all knew where Sam hung out. Three days wouldn't concern anyone. They would assume what the Studio City pusher assumed, that he'd landed a big tipper for a long binge. Or perhaps, they would think, he was doing penicillin for a case of clap he couldn't ignore anymore, for fear of making things sticky for his genteel customers. Sam knew he would be expected, on his return, to look like the conquering hero, as if he'd one-upped the regular work, where he normally went for thirty-five to fifty for an hour's hot job, not including the traveling time back and forth in air-cooled Jags and Mercedes. If he seemed the slightest bit shaky or even fatigued, the rumor would go out that he had started to slip. You were up or you were down in the higher-priced streets. If you got sick or you went too deep into the medicine chest, it all passed you by. There were other streets to move to, and the money was still quite good now and then, though you couldn't be so choosy about the clientele. Because he was aware of all this, Sam knew as the sun inched toward the Pacific that he had to be back in business before midnight.

He went home and ate the last tenderloin. When he went into the bathroom to get a blade to cut more coke, he stopped at the mirror to brush his hair and thus took the first step back to real life. When he was finished snorting, he pulled a red bandanna out of his pocket to wipe his nose, and the hundred and seventy-five tumbled out on the floor. He'd completely forgotten. Because he was ripped, he pulled up a stool, sat with his elbows on his knees, and grinned down at the curl of bills. How, he wondered, had he ever had a problem with what to buy? All he had to do was buy something mad. A three-piece summer-weight suit. Or a place setting of silver. Or a Christian Dior briefcase. Sam didn't know the names of anything, not by brand, not by store like Peter and Rita and Nick, but he had the most comical picture of all the junk he could afford. It was just what his apartment needed. A piss-elegant, pointless thing.

He dressed sexy, tucked an unopened bourbon under his arm, and headed east on Sunset to Hollywood. He'd *thought* he was going to go west, to Beverly Hills, so as to walk up and down Rodeo, looking in the windows until he'd discovered the silliest overpriced figurine dancers and bud vases. It must have been the dope, he would have said, that steered him wrong. He didn't think he was going to cruise Hollywood until he started to, the MG snuggling in among the Cadillacs creeping along the curbs. The silver-haired men with multiple rings and garish shirts leaned over to the passenger's window and haggled for blow jobs with fifteen-year-olds. Sam was a stranger here now. He liked all kinds, it was true, but he'd never developed a taste for chicken sex. Not that the Hollywood version wasn't lovely. Boys like high school lettermen, skateboards under their arms, luminous from so much sun. But the come-on pose as they leaned on the streetlamps was oddly androgynous—part wanton, part without meaning or balance, like a child playing dress-up in oversize clothes. They all looked the same. Do *we* all look the same, too, Sam asked himself—but as a joke, shaking his head no even as he asked it.

It didn't really matter which one he got. He pulled out from behind a Rolls where three boys were clustered at the window arguing among themselves about who was better hung. Sam stopped at the curb just ahead. He noticed a boy sitting on the sidewalk away from the curbside hustle, his back against a storefront, arms around his knees. The luncheonette sign directly above him, "JUST LIKE HOME," threw down on him a pale green light. He was smoking a cigarette. Sam stared until he stared back, kept on staring when he looked away. Finally, the boy got up, crushed the cigarette under his shoe, and ambled over to the MG. All of it reluctantly. It was a way of being tough without having to be aggressive. He was too shy to be tough in the usual way. Sam knew it backward and forward.

"What do *you* want?" the boy asked suspiciously, acknowledging the difference between Sam and his own regular trade. He may have thought Sam was a pimp. He wasn't seventeen, or he hadn't been on the street long, one or the other. His clothes, an army shirt with sergeant's stripes and green fatigues, were tidy, as if his mother still did them up.

"What do you like to do?" Sam asked. Rule one: Get it all out on the table.

"For twenty-five, you can blow me and I'll fuck your ass. For thirty-five I'll come."

How many times does a man say that, Sam wondered, before it sounds like nothing at all? This boy still liked the rawness of the bargaining—talking dirty, calling a spade a spade. About six months, Sam thought, narrowing his assessment of the time the boy had done.

"What about the other way around?"

"I don't *do* it the other way around," the boy said tightly, drawing back a fraction from the car. He took offense, as if Sam had said point-blank that he was queer. Oh yes, Sam remembered, this was the crowd that planned to live happily ever after, as soon as they had the down payment.

"Why don't you get in?" Sam said easily. "We'll work something out."

The boy climbed over the side and sank down into the seat.

He leaned against the door as if to keep his distance, turned sideways to face Sam, and then spread his legs wide as the MG allowed. He was full of crossed messages. He had jet eyes and, what was a turn-on because he was so young, the shadow of a heavy beard along his jaw. He called himself Eddie when Sam asked, though he seemed unused to the name. He changed it too often, Sam decided, driven still by the panic that he'd be found out, traced, turned in to his father or his parish priest. No, he didn't have a room they could go make it in, and when Sam said his own place was off limits because he shared a bed there with someone jealous, Eddie wanted out.

"Unless you want to spring for a motel, too," he said. "I won't do *shit* in a car."

"Why don't we just drive around for a while," Sam said. He decided suddenly he wanted nothing. What sent him to Hollywood, he supposed, was a busman's holiday. Men in the trade had pointed out to him classy old call girls, still in shape in their fifties, hearts like hard candy, who'd bankrolled enough to keep a young buck in residence to service them. Once again, Sam loved the idea of the cash flow. He didn't expect a good fuck out of any of these kids, but for a change, at least, he thought he'd enjoy the double hustle. His power in the scene would lie in irony, as it did for the powdered whores with gigolos. For him and a man like Eddie, he'd had an image in his head of two mirrors set face-to-face. Two hustlers together, the fantasy went, could turn a workout into a pitting of athletes. But as he drove up Franklin and went left and into the hills, he saw that what he'd wanted most was to hear a hustler's story. That's not like me at all, he thought, glad that for the moment they'd both shut up. It was as if, courting a kid for an hour, he'd wanted to learn where it all began. He'd never got caught before in the seethe of sentiment, and he took it as a warning. He'd been right, after all, to always cut himself off from anyone younger than himself. It was enough to go through it yourself. Watching someone else go through it could only slow you down.

"You can't get it up," Eddie said at last. It was an everyday remark. Where he hung out in LA, there was a sex therapist behind every tree. "I'm right, aren't I? A good-looking guy like you, you ought to be able to get it free. But something's happened to your confidence, hasn't it?"

"Mmm," Sam said, and his pride remained intact. Eddie's diagnosis, smug and impertinent, didn't even break the skin. Sam put his holiday away like a suitcase in the attic, and he threw his mind ahead a couple of hours, waiting on Selma for the start of the first dance. He only felt the slightest annoyance still about the unspent money. As for Eddie, he couldn't believe how dull it was.

"When you drove up," Eddie went on, "I thought you must be real kinky. Why are we stopping here?"

"Just for a minute. Then I'll take you back. You know what I'd like to do?"

"What?" Eddie said guardedly. The kink might be coming, after all.

"Make out."

"Meaning what?"

"Kiss."

"I don't kiss," Eddie said, throwing it out as if Sam were a tourist, used to the customs of a simpler country.

"Neither do I," Sam assured him. "But you know whose house that is?" He pointed at a bungalow, pale in the darkness, undistinguished. They were parked high on a hill in a cluster of houses, the nose of the MG headed down at a steep angle. Two invisible, penned-in dogs barked back and forth across the street. "Marilyn Monroe's."

"No shit. Is that where she killed herself?"

"It's where she died," Sam said, putting the best face on things. "So you see, it's a holy spot. When I want to go parking, I like to do better than Mulholland Drive."

"You're weird." But he said it without malice. Even in six months, apparently, he'd seen worse. "Why don't you take me back to the Boulevard, and we'll call it even. I don't use my mouth except to eat."

"Why don't we make it fifty?" Sam said. "You don't have to come. You don't even have to breathe heavy."

So it was agreed. For fifteen minutes, as if it were a taxi and they had a meter running, Sam leaned forward, and their open mouths met. The boy's tongue was dead like a slice of meat, and he held it close to the front of his mouth as if he were licking a stamp. Sam paid no mind to his delicacy. His own tongue probed and jabbed. He sucked the wind up out of the boy's throat, bit at his lips, and honeyed his whole lower face with saliva. It must have seemed to Eddie that Sam had developed a sudden obsession for him, and, scrupled or not about what passed his lips, he must have felt he was coming into the full range of his sexual powers. His kisses were going for about a dollar apiece. He didn't have to do anything. Pretty soon, he must have figured, they'd pay to just look. And that, as anyone on Hollywood Boulevard would have told you, was *their* dividing line between the stars and the suckers who worked.

But as the minutes passed, he must have wondered if it was really such a bargain. Because Sam ate him up. He tongued the corners of Eddie's mouth and clicked their teeth together till a shiver went up their spines. He didn't stop to breathe and didn't seem to need it, and Eddie must have wondered for a bit if he would suffocate. Sam leapt into this scene on the spur of the moment and for reasons he couldn't entirely separate, though none of them sprang from a passion for a sixteen-year-old boy. And not that he attached anything innocent to a kiss, either, since he tore through the virginal, light-lipped stages to get to the fevers and bruises. He didn't do it to kill his hundred and seventy-five. He did it instead of yelling and screaming. He did it to prove that Eddie had only scratched the surface of sex, and he intimated he could have done it just as well by just holding Eddie's hand or humping him through his clothes. Part of it he seemed to do for Marilyn, who didn't mean a thing to Eddie. Who hadn't ever lived in the little Spanish bungalow, either, but that was not the point. She'd lived *somewhere* around here, Sam knew, and she was the class item. She wasn't ever a punk fifteen, and she didn't have to pay for it at fifty. Sam kissed Eddie with his eyes and his mouth wide open. But he kept his hands to himself without even trying. For a quarter of an hour, he mauled that face with the single muscle of his tongue, which in its way was as versatile, as rife with moods, as his usual tool. In one long moment he worked Eddie over as if he could spit out the whole pack of lies men carried to his bed day in and day out. And when the time drew to a close he was ready. He had a built-in clock that could time a fuck like a football game. It would have been pretty, perhaps, if in the end he'd softened Eddie up. That is how Peter and Rita and Nick would have imagined it—that Eddie kissed him back. For all the gulf between them when it started, fire and ice, wouldn't it be fitting if the final kiss turned out to be Romeo and Juliet? But it didn't. When the meter ran out, Sam stopped, drew back, and wiped his sleeve across his mouth. Peter and Rita and Nick, revising their opinion, would have called the look in his eyes hatred. But it wasn't. It was nothing, which was the very thing he'd come to want out of this.

At first, Eddie didn't even close his mouth. He didn't move a muscle, and it looked like the lull before a counterattack. Sam wasn't sure. Completely as he felt he understood the way the boy worked, he hadn't given him a thought in the fifteen minutes. They might have to wrestle it out now, pull each other from the car and roll in the street, egged on by the pacing dogs. But it went another way, and Eddie's face fell sad. He wasn't going to cry, though, because hustling and tears excluded each other. Unless there was pain, and Sam didn't hurt people, even when they wanted him to. Hustling didn't exclude anything else but love, Sam thought, the Tom Sawyer smile on his face, and then he couldn't wait to be alone. It was the grief that follows knowledge in these naked matters that Eddie got a dose of, as if he were not old enough a half hour before. Sam hadn't himself had a case of the sorrows since he was eighteen, so he knew it wasn't terminal. Sad was the least of their worries.

"You should ask to see cash first, you know," Sam said, "especially if someone offers you too much." He leaned back against the seat and threw his hips out so that he could reach into his pocket. He disentangled a fifty from the bills. "And you're right to keep it clean in cars."

"Fuck you," Eddie said, plucking the bill out of Sam's hand. He spread it on his knee and smoothed it as Sam started the car.

"You must be a real terror when you get off. I mean, if you get all sullen and guilty from a kiss."

"I'm not anything, baby. I don't feel a thing," he said. He took a billfold from his back pocket and slipped in the fifty.

"Really? Well, you may go places, after all."

They drove the rest of the way in silence, and they looked from the side of the road as nice as brothers. If we're both as free of feeling as we say, Sam thought, it's a wonder we don't get along a little better. Himself, he didn't care if he never saw Eddie again. He'd have the same rush of pleasure passing him on the street and looking through him as he might have had meeting an old friend, if he'd had such a thing. He could have concluded from his fifty-dollar session that the men in this game were all alike, but it didn't come through that way. The nothing Eddie said he felt was different from the one Sam felt. Sam understood as he never had in the past that Rusty Varda wouldn't have let it go so far with just any hustler. He had probably brought a hundred other boys before Sam up to Crook House to swim and eat lunch, and they must have been as stiff and coarse as Eddie. Some of them, perhaps, stayed on and took steam. But only Sam—

"You don't have to take me all the way," Eddie said. "I can get a bus anywhere along here." Suddenly mild, his mind turned to the route he was traveling. He sounded as if he'd hitched a ride with Sam a couple of blocks back. "I'm through for the night, anyway."

"It's early."

"Yeah, but I promised my girl I wouldn't be late."

It would have taken a chemist to isolate the blizzard of elements in that remark. The slightest heavier stress on "girl" drew a line around him as powerful and impenetrable as a witch's circle. But he was no better than the johns who sucked his cock, Sam thought bitterly. When Sam went home, he didn't shed a disguise or resume it. He was as content in his room as a Greek philosopher living in a square with a crockery cup and a straw mat. He rested and drifted and kept to himself, no needs to speak of outside of the mirror to watch himself in, until it was time to go out again. The client class, by contrast, tended to Jekyll-and-Hyde their lives. Down on their knees, doing dark acts in public toilets. Upright in the dining room, carving the roast at a supper for eight. It had been that way forever, for all Sam knew, but he had it as a fact that his father at least taxied back and forth for years between a wife and a whore. It wasn't right. Sam was unbending about these things—Eddie had slipped beneath contempt, because he didn't have a right to live two lives if his girl was living only one.

He pulled the MG over. Eddie mumbled a sort of good-bye as he hiked himself over the door, but it was clear that he no longer remembered Sam's name, if he'd caught it to begin with. He looked very beautiful standing in the streetlight. Sam saw again what he'd taken in on the curb by the luncheonette —what he'd lost the whole time they sat in the dark car—that they had the same build and the same shape face.

"It's nice that you save it up for her some nights," Sam said pleasantly.

"It doesn't matter. She works nights, too, so we do it in the daytime." Which left unclear ˌwhat line she was in, though Sam could have sworn from the way Eddie said it that she was a hooker.

"Good-bye, Eddie," he said, speaking into the rearview mirror as he checked the traffic. "Some night we'll go to Valentino's old place and get it on like sheiks." And he sped away and waved without looking back. He laughed at the thought of what a pack of whores they were. Eddie and his girl were pooling, it seemed, so as to get the mortgage quicker and plump themselves down for good in a place like San Bernardino, happily ever after. Pretty soon, Sam thought, there would be so many more hustlers than customers that they would have to start going at it with one another, just to keep in shape. When Sam got started, it was a scandal to find a fifteen-year-old working a neighborhood like a combat veteran. Especially pained were the middle-aged middlemen from The Industry—the second unit craftsmen, the people in publicity, anyone who went out for an occasional pickup. They wanted children innocent.

Well, well, he said to himself as he drove along and sobered up, he might as well be on top of the business while he could. The boom wouldn't last forever. Sam had seen towns where the gold rush or the cattle rush had once swept through, where the grass now grew in the streets. He had a mounting conviction that he was the last of the breed, the boy Nero would have been feeding chocolates to while Rome burned.

He was this year's prize, and he knew it. The prize wasn't a trophy, of course, or fixed like a name on a plaque. It was more of a feeling, and he may well have been the only one to feel it. But he didn't require more proof than the intensities he inspired in those who stood by, at the end of an hour, while he slipped through their fingers. He was the best thing on the menu. He could see that he needed a holiday to put it in perspective, because he had to know he was damn good in order to push forward with the work he'd waited ten years for. He took the most exalted view of the nexus of forces. He was free. He had the ticket to Crook House in his hand. Lust fired inside him like a dollop of uranium. And he had no questions left about the world. The scene was set like a bomb.

In an hour he'd be doing gymnastics in a stranger's bed. But one last thing. He'd thought of it in the middle of the kisses. A hundred and seventy-five minus fifty. He rocketed along now, rooting to the center of the city, where the palms gave out and the air hung low, the color of sherry and the taste of lead. I'm a cowboy, he thought. And then: No I'm not, I'm a private detective, and I get to the bottom of things if it's the last thing

I do. A hundred and twenty-five. Somebody must have a gun they'd sell for that. Maybe a little thirty-eight. He drummed his fingers on the steering wheel by way of patting himself on the back. He knew just the sort of man to look for on the street. They had eyes blank as dimes, and they hadn't had a good fuck in ten years. You couldn't miss them. They were all over the place.

Sam had no past anymore before LA, but he used to. Until the day after Christmas when he was fifteen, he lived on East Sixty-fifth Street, in the pastoral quarter of Manhattan. He apparently thought it prudent to gather the aunts' checks in his Christmas stocking before he took off, and he pawned the watch his father had tied up in ribbon and set by his plate of goose and chestnuts. So he was less a New Yorker by reason of time than Peter or Rita, but Peter and Rita, knowing what they did now about the townhouse life, boxes at the opera, and boxes from Bulgari and Godiva, would have envied him the style he once was accustomed to, quite as if they themselves had grown up hillbillies. Sam, of course, thought lunches at the Plaza as dull and fussy as lunches at the Pierre. He was bored in New York, always, though he knew now it was being fifteen and under and not the city lights that made it so. By the time he was ten, he was in therapy twice a week, and at twelve he was sent to school in Connecticut. To a school, in fact, that played soccer and hockey with Peter's school. He flunked math and earth sciences, ran a respectable mile, and befriended the local toughs who ran the school kitchen. It took him a year to make connections, and he entered the tenth grade running about two hundred dollars every other week in drugs, mostly acid.

His mother and father, decked out like the sugar figures on a wedding cake, had always gone about their glittering business, and he didn't mind at all. Though he raged for something he couldn't name, he knew it had nothing to do with them. When his mother sickened and died like lightning in the summer before he ran away, he was terribly sorry for her but not for himself. He watched her stand stricken in front of her closets, wall to wall with clothes like a whole floor of Saks, here and there fingering a pleat and pulling out a sleeve. It was as if her things could reassure her that she'd done more than most did, that all the parties were just as lovely as they seemed. Something in Sam beat with its fists at the same door she did all that summer, shouting at how unfair it was. But all the same it happened outside him. Part of that, of course, was the acid he dropped, which made him see things as if underwater, but even then he had the wit to wonder when the detachment would stop. His father was worse. He treated her as if she'd brought down shame on his good name, as if she'd taken to drink or gone suddenly mad. The ruinous grief turned the house on Sixty-fifth Street into a kind of tenement. It might have gone on for months and months, but she lay one morning on her dressing room floor, an empty bottle of Seconal in the pocket of her robe, the vanity covered a half inch thick with designer scarves. It was at the funeral that he met his father's other woman. He was the only one dry-eyed enough to notice that, even underwater, she wore black crepe like a stripper. It proved to him what he hardly needed further proof of, that the only life he could keep in line was his own. And though he'd gotten to like the school's austerity and would have been glad to deal dope until he graduated—expecting by then to be able to get a piece of Reno or Miami—he knew it was time to go.

He went to San Francisco first, like a banker to Basel. He didn't feel much like a runaway—he took a plane, for one thing, and, like a pioneer in a Conestoga, he made good provision for a brand-new life. He had six hundred tabs of purple haze in his suitcase and four hundred dollars tucked in the crotch flap of his Jockey shorts. But he found he was two years too late with the acid, and anyone who might have still wanted a cosmic high couldn't afford the prices people paid in Connecticut prep schools. His market had fallen out from under him. He stayed three days and stayed stoned, but the hollow-eyed sorts he met in Golden Gate Park had fallen into gibberish, making him sound positively Shakespearean. It scared him. He went south, but again with no thought of LA. He had a vision of himself holed up in a stone house on the Baja Peninsula, getting his head together, by which he meant a toothless old Indian woman feeding him peyote buttons and giving him baths. He had been doing the little reading that is said to be a dangerous thing. He didn't consider drying out. He only wanted a change of medication.

But it ended up being decided for him. He hitched a ride in a beat-up truck in Monterey that was going down Route 1, delivering beer. For all his diverse chemical intake, Sam had hardly ever had a beer, and by the time they were taking the big turns on Big Sur, a drunken burr had insinuated itself in the midst of his hallucinations. The whole Pacific was, not to belabor the point, a purple haze. Then the trucker wanted to suck him off, and Sam said no. He didn't have room between the acid and the beer to feel panicky or flattered. He must have sounded almost bored, as if he were back in New York, refusing yet again to be waited on or entertained. And he thought that was the end of it. After a moment he showed there were no hard feelings by telling about his stash of LSD, promising to share. Then he needed to take a piss something awful. So he stood just off the road in a foggy meadow a half mile above the ocean, his cock in one hand and a beer in the other, while the truck drove off with his last key to the astral plane. It tooted its horn twice as it rounded the next bend. So long, sucker.

Odd, considering the drive that had moved him along at fever pitch ever since, how little thought he'd given to his cock. He'd noticed it was big, of course, about third in his tenth grade class of sixty boys, which was a relief. But he knew it wasn't going to be much use to him until later, so he let it be and played with his head instead, blowing it full of holes. The combined energy released through masturbation in his dormitory probably could have powered a turbine, and yet he genuinely preferred as an act of self-love to look at himself in the mirror without moving a muscle. He knew even then he was going to be a knockout. And he began to develop that eerie double life that only the great beauties live. At the mirror, self-conscious and self-absorbed, every feature put under a microscope. Anywhere else—in company, in crowds, especially in love—open and wild with grace and missing nothing, making free with the universe. Sam began to go back and forth, and it made him so happy he thought he would have it forever. Perhaps he would have, except that the balance is finally thrown off by the strain of making a living off it.

But that was much, much later. The day he walked along the coast road, gradually getting sober in spite of himself, he was as virgin as the flowers on the heath. Though the term here is purely literal, because at the same time he was badly shaken out of yet another sleep of innocence. He was down to four hundred dollars and the clothes on his back. He felt he was due for a stroke of luck. There was no lag in the flood of events in *his* world, even then. No pauses while time chiseled his fate in stone. He'd had his first roughing up, and he accepted it, used it, learned where he'd gone all wrong. He was ready to process something new in a couple of hours. The hills were ghostly gray. The fog wet him right to the skin. If nothing had happened, as it did to almost anyone else, and he'd walked the whole range till it ran down into civilization again, if he'd worn out his soles and learned how to tie his shirt like a kerchief on his head against the midday sun, he might have been a poet by the time he got to Santa Barbara. But he got his wish, and his good luck carried him away.

He took a road at random, winding down, and around dusk it brought him out onto the beach. For a moment, he thought he would die of the cold, and he ran around in a circle on the sand to keep warm. Until he spied a rose of firelight at the base of a cliff. He jogged on over, and in a moment he was staring across the fire, where a tenderloin was spitting on the grill, at a man with a halfback's build and a sandy beard, about twenty-two. Sam said hello to the next year and a half. "You look hungry," said Ben, and that was that. He cut the steak in two, poured him a Jack Daniels and water in a tin cup, and, when it was time, made room in his sleeping bag. They must have both lain awake for hours, curled like spoons, because they both noticed when the fog began to lift and the stars went on. They began to talk about the night as if there had been no lapse of time since they sat around the fire, where they talked about the four elements like characters in a medieval play. They stayed clear of talking about themselves, Sam decided in the dark in his underwear, because the tides and the plot of the North Star were more important. As to sex, nobody made a move.

For a while, it was assumed that Sam would be going off on his own again in a few days, and then suddenly it wasn't. They finished the week's hike and tramped inland, retrieved Ben's MG, and drove all the way to LA. Ben's house, a furnished bungalow on Norma Place, felt from the first like the opposite of Sixty-fifth Street, and Sam sat contented in the garden in the sun and looked at maps. Mexico and Central America. Then on across the Darien Gap into the jungles that went unbroken to the Amazon. Ben was away off and on day and night, but Sam felt no desire to know what it was he did. They slept in the same bed and, now that the sleeping bag didn't confine them to lying in each other's arms, kept a certain distance and talked less and less. What they both wanted wasn't something either of them seemed to think about. For different reasons, neither of them needed anyone else, and it was even better than being alone to have someone around who felt the same way. They were not out to be friends, let alone lovers. The nothing Sam would go a long way to feel years later came naturally to him and Ben.

It was the Southern California of the morality plays, perhaps —without humors, without reasons, without the characteristics of particular life in a particular place. It may be that they preferred to live in two dimensions, that they were more like photographs left about than people. Nothing happened on

Norma Place. Somehow the food must have got bought and the laundry done, because they didn't starve, and they didn't smell. But it was all very detached, and Sam left behind what little he still had of the past because feeling detached felt good. They assumed nothing. Assumption itself was tainted with good and evil, and good was the opposite of *bad*. No morals were involved.

Once settled, then, with nothing expected of him, Sam left his head alone and took hold of his cock. As naturally as if he were shifting languages between one country and the next. His schoolboy's line of reasoning, that it wasn't going to get him anywhere until he had someone to put it in, evaporated when it dawned on him—he was the one he was waiting for all along. He became his own man, literally. He didn't need to compare with anyone else because he had an eye for his own technique like an athlete who doesn't ever lose. And he didn't worry about his lack of experience because he loved to practice. He made his own experience up as he went along. It was very existential jerking off. He didn't do anything else for weeks.

So he woke one morning hard and got up to let it go in the bathroom. Closing the door, he looked over at Ben lying naked on the bed, taut with his own erection. Suddenly he knew— Ben was a hustler. Not that any street airs hung close about him. It was more that Ben seemed like a dream his genitals were having. Sam was years ahead of his time. He believed already that sex didn't have to leave the circle of the self at all. Wasn't meant to. He and Ben were the doubles of each other, he thought, and the world would have to feed on them to get tough. It came to Sam in the middle of things, something like a vocation. If it was love for Ben he was hiding, he was doing it all too well. They were born not needing love, it seemed. Their cocks, he thought as he stood there, were symbols of quite another force. Like the needles on sundials. Like radar. Yet even if Sam couldn't see it then, the two of them in the room on Norma Place—one half hidden behind the door, the other spread-eagle in a double bed, open to attack—looked like an allegory of love forever out of phase. Even if they didn't care what they looked like.

Sam got right into it, all by himself. Took a bus to Hollywood and walked the starlit streets till he found one set aside for kids. Dressed working-class, as if he were going to grow up one day and be a telephone lineman. He did his training on the job. He was amazed, in fact, at how little the old men expected of him. Fifty was the age that wanted him, and since it seemed an eternity to Sam, since he found them so unpracticed and so mute, he wondered what they'd been doing all their lives. He was almost never asked to touch them back. After a time, he hardly noticed them. His cock didn't care where it went, as long as it got a good rush. The older they were, the clumsier, the better, because it made it a snap to see nothing of himself. He did what he could to let them know what they *ought* to have done these thirty or forty years. Meanwhile, he got to know the cycles of the traffic in the street with a sixth sense. And, like a midshipman staring at waves, he felt kin to it all, as if the cars going by were one with the rhythm of his blood. Altogether, it was like getting paid to go to the movies.

He met Ben one day in the parking lot of an apartment house in Westwood. They were both walking—Ben in, Sam out—with men who could have been their fathers. They looked through each other as if they weren't there. And never brought it up. It may have been then, that night at dinner, that Sam began to get his bourbon neat when Ben made drinks. If so, it must have been a coincidence. This was not a fraternity they were in. Sam's debut in the business didn't fulfill a wizard's prophecy. And the upshot of it all was not kisses on Norma Place. Or to put it another way, there is more than one sort of romance. In the customary one, the knight and the squire meet by chance in the palace court, each carrying a freshly severed dragon's head under his arm. Their mail is rank with sweat. It is hard to say who is more proud of the squire's noble deed. But the torch passes on, and at last they are free to unbuckle each other's armor and bed down together. The monsters have all been taken care of. In the less well-known romances, the ones without the ballads, there are no knights and squires. There are no distinctions at all. Nothing is passed on. The romance comes from the going forth alone, time after time after time.

One other thing. Ben told him the story of him and Marilyn Monroe, and Sam understood he wouldn't have heard it *before* Ben knew he was hustling. To anyone else, it would hardly have seemed a story at all. Because it had no point. She stopped one day when she was driving past and asked him for directions. Ben knew who it was, and he knew she knew the quickest way to the Hollywood Freeway, too. But he told her. And they smiled at each other like movie stars.

"You know what I mean, Sam? I mean, if Marilyn Monroe doesn't know her way around Hollywood, then what the fuck are the rest of us doing here?"

The next time, she wanted to know the nearest branch of California Federal. Then, a week later, was there a college around. She was thinking of taking up reading, she said. Then a long time went by. Then, it was the day The Dark Lady brought flowers, she wanted to know where Valentino was buried.

"'Hollywood Memorial,' I said, 'but you don't want to go there.' 'Why not?' 'Because that's why we live here,' I said, 'to banish all that.'"

So it became a regular thing. She dropped by about every ten days, always dressed down, in a loud old Ford that must have been her maid's. Once Ben was at the curb talking with a john in a car when she drove by, but she didn't show that she noticed. They didn't talk about their work, in any case. They talked about the city, overgrown and seedy, and what it was like before, in Mary Pickford's day, in Garbo's day. They actually talked about the stars, and it turned out she didn't know any more than he did. He knew more, because he knew who was gay. They were strict about keeping their places— Ben out on the curb, Marilyn on the passenger's side of the car, legs tucked under her, elbows on the window sill. It went on for eight or nine months, until one day she said she was leaving town for a while. Ben knew she was going off to shoot a movie. He read about her, just like everybody else.

"I was going to buy you something," she said, "but then I didn't know what you'd want. What would you have liked?" He didn't know. He couldn't think of a thing. "Well, as long as it doesn't matter," she said, as if she'd guessed what his attitude would be, "then anything will do." She reached over into the back seat and brought forward a leatherette handbag, off-white, very fifties, with a rhinestone clasp. She opened it and held it out. "Close your eyes and pick something." And, when he made no immediate move, she added, "So you'll remember me."

Though he did it in broad daylight, it would have been hard for someone going by to know what he was doing. Not scoring dope or making change for the meter, because his eyes were shut. You don't shut your eyes on the street. But for a moment he'd suspended that part. His hand fished around among gum wrappers and eye pencils. He chose small and delicate and came out with a screw-on earring. A little disk of silver from which hung a cameo on a tiny chain. Just costume jewelry. Marilyn laughed and twirled a feather of hair.

"We'd better get you the other one, honey. You have to have a pair in this world."

"Pick me something else," he said, making as if to hand it over.

"Oh, no," she said. "You keep one. I'll keep one."

She wore no makeup except a sugar red lipstick, and she pursed her lips just then in a rosebud, as if to stifle a smirk. The sentimental hadn't got its hooks into her, she seemed to say, though she wasn't through trying to outwit it. Ben wondered if she meant, giving him a keepsake, that she couldn't see him again, even after she came back. That day, he could have asked her whimsically what was she planning, why was she paying him off. She didn't come back, in fact, not to him, and then she died a year or so later. By then she was once again the picture in the papers. He hadn't pinned her down on that last day because they were busy savoring how casual they were. They banished the future. It took itself too seriously.

"I'm going to have to pretend I lost one," she said, holding up the other earring and waving it like a little bell. "I can't imagine what *you're* going to say."

"I suppose I'll have to pretend I found one," he said.

For Ben and Sam, perhaps, it was the story of a relationship safely gotten through, from beginning to end. Sam found out later that everyone in LA had a story about a star, but it didn't diminish the one Ben told. The last scene especially, the pair of earrings, seemed to spirit them away to a green and lofty place where kings and mystics sat and watched sunsets. The present was the only sort of happy ending anyone ever got, and Ben had got it once with Marilyn Monroe. Only for an instant, but so what. That was part of the deal. "Don't ever lose it, because I'll know," she said as she drove off, wagging her finger, but Sam wasn't so interested in the telepathy that went with the good-luck charm. If her ghost still followed it around, all well and good—she was the sort of angel you could use in LA. But Sam cared more than anything to do a scene like that himself. Offhand, uninhibited, safe in an ordinary place on a nothing day.

He knew, though, that he couldn't just go out looking for the street life's happy endings. They just fell out that way every now and again. Like the night Ben told him all of this, as they were getting ready to go to bed, which they almost never did at the same time. Stripping out of their clothes, going in and out of the bathroom. They lounged like warriors in a tent. Sam knew, even as he listened, that he would never be so glad again to hear a story. He could see he was the only one Ben had ever told it to. Whatever there was to know was there. But he held himself off from naming it in case he should stray into sentiment. And then they went to sleep, and the past came and took the moment with it. From then on, the night of the Marilyn story played itself over and over in his head and left him thirsty and heartsick. He couldn't see why it didn't make him happy, as it had when it happened. He even thought to wonder if Ben felt the same when he thought of Marilyn Monroe. But he never asked, afraid that, if he was wrong, it would prove he was all alone.

It all fell apart without warning on Norma Place. A year and a half went by like nothing, and then Ben disappeared. He didn't come home one night, and Sam didn't pay it any mind, not then or the next day or the next. On the fourth day, he took the MG and went out looking. When he came back several hours later, there were cops all over, in the house and out, and Sam took off. This time he wasn't wearing Jockey shorts at all. All he had was an MG with an APB out on it. He drove to San Diego for a couple of days and hustled, got beaten up one night by a sailor he looked at funny, and came back to LA and bought counterfeit plates from a mechanic who took it out in trade. He wouldn't admit that Ben was dead, almost as if it were none of his business, part of the bargain of having no ties to each other. Ben wasn't coming back—that was clear enough—but Ben was all right. Sam regained his equilibrium by calling it a stroke of luck. Ben must have ended up on a yacht or a Lear jet, and somebody big, a magnate or an oil baron, was even now groaning under him and throwing out twenty dollar bills like streamers. Bound for the South Seas. Back to the spell of the four elements. Once he knew that, Sam's part was easy. He only had to go about his affairs as if nothing had happened. And nothing had, he told himself as he waited on the street. In a whole year and a half, not one thing.

Somehow, he would decide later on, it all served as a prelude to Rusty Varda. He had been in training for the main event since he left New York. And when the ink-blue limousine purred down Sam's block that morning, Hey at the wheel, in the back seat a cloud-eyed man, absurdly old, old enough to be the father of the men Sam tricked with, he tingled with the feeling that his own story had arrived. It was all luck. He never showed up on the street before 5:00 P.M., timing himself for the cocktail crowd, but now he needed extra cash to pay the security deposit on his new apartment. Ben had been gone two weeks. By Sam's reckoning, it was about time for a limousine. Hey stopped and got out. It wasn't clear to Sam that the old man had given any signal. The deal was simple—a hundred dollars for the afternoon at Mr. Varda's stately home, sex not required. He hadn't eaten lunch, had he? Good. And could he swim? Of course.

He'd said it before and since, that doing it was sometimes like being on film, but at Crook House he could almost hear the film whir in the camera. Varda sat in a wicker chair in the garden, facing the pool. He wore a beret. A round table had been set for lunch, and Sam saw that only one person was going to be eating. It was all arranged like a still life—peach roses, glasses for claret and champagne, a raft of forks on one side of the plate, spoons on the other. Hey reappeared, changed into butler's gear.

"Now then, Sam," Rusty Varda said, "you can go ahead and take your clothes off." The voice professional and direct as a doctor. He'd said nothing in the car coming home. Sam had sat up front with Hey, and he wondered if the old man wasn't afflicted with the aftereffects of a stroke, his vocal chords pulled like the lines on a switchboard. But it must have been the no-man's-land in the car that did it, he decided as he faced the wicker chair and unbuttoned his pants. Because this guy had the script down pat.

"A little faster. Fling them off and go for a swim. When you're finished, come out and have lunch."

And Sam kicked off his engineer's shoes and turned and dived in a single motion, as if he weren't going to listen to any more. As there wasn't a time limit set, he took deep breaths and swam the length of the pool underwater until he was all by himself. When he dolphined up and flipped himself onto the deck like a lifeguard, he heard the next set of orders as if they were no more than street noises, a radio turned on in a dream. He still did what he was told, but he began to think it was what he would have done anyway.

"Now don't dry off. I want you to shake your head like a

dog and then sit down. Hey will bring you lunch." He spoke in a sort of whisper now, as if he didn't want to get in the way of Sam's concentration.

He sat at the table and stared out at the beating city and the sun. He wasn't paid a hundred to ask, but he thought about men who wanted their sex in a three-act play. They dressed their hookers up as chambermaids and pleaded to be spanked. They wanted the door to the bedroom locked by a state trooper, and they fucked with the uniform first. The funny thing was, Sam couldn't say exactly what the fantasy was here because it was very like his own. Watched and served and left alone, all because he was beautiful. He had a cold green soup, a slice of salmon, then—one right after the other, more and more rapidly, it seemed—sweetbreads, salad, and a Black Forest cake so rich it gave him a headache. He let his belly go slack and leaned back and shut his eyes, listening to the clink of the dishes as Hey cleared away. When he opened his eyes, wondering what it was time to do now, the wicker chair was empty. He suddenly felt exposed, and he put on his clothes fast.

Hey proposed, driving him back to Hollywood, that he set aside one day a week. Mr. Varda, he said, would like to use him again. Did they have a number where they could reach him? No. Sam didn't have a phone back then because he didn't want his whole name on file with the phone company, where someone could trace him. Sam was all the name he had any use for. He tried to get gritty with Hey—"You could sure use a little, couldn't you? Doesn't it give you blue balls to watch a naked guy all afternoon?"—to loosen him up and get some information. They didn't hate each other, yet. Sam could talk smut to him and keep it easy and funny. Hey thought it was cute, or he thought it didn't matter, since a hustler's career lasted about as long as a ballet dancer's, and people who did it didn't grow up till afterwards. So at the beginning they played, driving back and forth in the car, and Hey talked bitchy and teased him, too. But he stayed tight with the information. To him, Rusty Varda was an artist, even if they'd taken the film out of his camera. The nude scene at Crook House was a movie. It couldn't be put into words.

But Sam began to figure it out himself, even without Hey's help. After all, he did the very same thing, pool and lunch, every Friday afternoon for five months—Friday perfect because it gave his cock a rest before the weekend, when it went into fourth gear. Varda gave him a few more directions—slow down his walk to the table, don't look at Hey—but after a while Sam was on his own. The scene had something to do with a moment from Varda's own life, Sam decided as he floated on his back or buttered his roll, and Sam was some man who'd obsessed him once. Someone he'd lost.

Then, a month or two into it, he changed his mind and thought instead he was meant to be Varda himself, and the scene at the pool was a picture postcard of LA success. He knew by then the bare bones of Varda's film career. The immigrant juggler who landed on his feet had bought a whole mountain of his own and built a villa. For forty or fifty years, he held his wide-screen perch above the race of the city, but his fullest memory of it all must have been the seven-course days of his youth. So he made this minor little scene of himself, Sam thought, a couple of hours a lifetime ago when nothing particular happened. It was just the kind of time Sam would have plucked out of his own life. He came in the end to play it like Shakespeare, though of course without the words, which he didn't really miss. After all, he did a lot of things as if in a silent movie—streetwalks and sex and drives in his car—so he had a technique to fall back on.

Sam didn't get tired of the show, but Varda became so still in his chair, he seemed half the time to be in transit between planets. No direction in weeks. No chitchat. When the menu began to repeat, Sam felt as if he'd used up this production—the play was too good for it. Five minutes before the end, one Friday in November, he called across to Varda as he spooned up his dessert. Hey was waiting with a tray of iced coffee just outside the door to the dining room. Sam felt it was mostly himself still happening here, still *playing* it.

"Mr. Varda, do you ever look at your pictures?"

To look at him, Varda had to stop looking off. There was a pause in which they waited for the stars to draw back into the planetarium.

"No," he said, "I hardly remember them." But it wasn't modest of him to say so, and he wasn't pleading the special case of old age. He had no wish to disparage them, he seemed to say, but he himself had gone on long ago. Sam knew two things about Frances Dean—he'd found them out, from asking around in bars—she was a pinup Cinderella, and she went to pieces at Crook House, where they kept her half-asleep for years. The change in her was the reason he had left his films behind, because it was like staring at a dead child to see her on the screen. Sam was guessing. "Where have *you* seen them?" Varda asked, glad to talk about it if Sam cared so much.

"No, I never go to the movies. I can't sit still." He put down his spoon, though he hadn't had half enough raspberry mousse, because he had a prince's manners when he was talking about himself. "I only meant—what do you do all day? Not including Friday."

"I juggle," Varda said, and though Sam knew it was an evasion, that he didn't do anything, the wand of the weather vane had moved, and the wind was from another quarter. How about a performance then? Sam asked politely, but as if to point out that he'd done enough performing himself and had to be spelled. Varda grinned, called for his box of props, and made his way to the pool. He was wearing his ice cream whites.

Hey could date his hostility to the moment he set down the iced coffee on a wrought-iron bench and went across the terrace to Frances Dean's room, to the walk-in closet where the juggling things were stored. He never stopped feeling threatened after that. Varda did a warm-up with three green balls, then Hey threw him the fourth, and they made a perfect circle in the air. Then one ball leapt about as he tapped it with his shoulder. He did rings next, seven or eight flipped up at once, so that in profile it looked like a team of bicycles. Anyone would have thought, watching him light three candles, about to spin and toss them like sticks and not snuff a single flame—you would have thought he was seducing Sam. But it was the other way around. Sam urged him on, and when Sam laughed to see five pieces of fruit go up in a circle and make a wreath revolving in the air, the laugh brought the morning glories open. He was standing, still naked, in front of Varda, cheering him on. Varda looked through the juggle he was doing as if it were a curtain. And Hey brought the last tray in and poured the iced coffee in the sink.

Well, before that he went to his room and got his Brownie Hawkeye. He stood in the dining room window, which was shaded by a tree, and snapped a half-dozen shots of the scene at the pool. Collecting evidence. He'd had enough of ballet to know the thunder and lightning were gathering force offstage. The two men outside faced each other through a circus act, hardly like two men at all. To Hey they were Beauty and Beast, princess and frog, and he knew which was which. Some great catastrophe followed on the heels of their coming together. Hey remembered the night Frances Dean took a razor to herself. Remembered it from the pictures in the papers, long ago when he was young and lived in South America. Crook House had a well of violence down in the core, he'd felt it the day he walked in, and it shot to the surface whenever it had to. But whatever was tremoring now, Hey planned to survive and not get arrested for it. He went back to his room and hid his camera under a pile of shirts. Then changed his mind, took the film out, and went and put it in the parrot's cage deep in the sawdust. What else could he do? There was no point trying to stop it. This boy had come to take everything.

And the boy didn't even know it himself. Nothing irrevocable ever happened to him, after all. Two or three Fridays later, they started spending an hour in the steam after Sam did his scene, Varda wrapped in towels head to foot, and then an hour in bed. Sam lay there and let it happen and didn't care. He knew whatever it was would come, and he was right.

Because Varda said one day as he stroked Sam's skin, out of who knew what set of erotic associations—"There's a treasure buried in Crook House." It was as if Sam had known it already and only needed reminding. And week after week he begged for more from Rusty Varda. But as it was the one thing he had to be coquettish about, Varda stretched the story out and rambled on about Frances Dean. Still, in another month Sam might have learned the secret of the mirrored door. Bad luck for him, it ended before he even knew what the treasure was.

It was so much on the tip of his tongue that he knew, ten years later, that Rita had a piece of it in her Samsonite. What and where—that is what he waited ten years to go after, and he was like a man serving time. As for the thing going wrong when he was right on the brink of it, there was no surprise in that. Rusty Varda died in his arms, of course. One moment holding on to Sam for dear life, the next a bag of puppet's bones. And Sam got dressed and ran downstairs. Then crept back up and waited till it was the same time as usual. He was no use to Varda now. Varda wouldn't want him in trouble. He went to the kitchen to get Hey, said he was ready, and Hey looked over his shoulder from the parrot's cage and guessed, just like that. He pressed the intercom to Varda's room and politely said his name. He looked like he had enough evidence to hang.

Sam ran out. He crashed downhill through the kitchen garden and landed in the yard of the next house below. No one screamed, though a servant here and there came to the window and stared until he'd passed on through. It didn't matter, not this one any more than Ben, as long as he didn't stop. When he got home, off a bus up Sunset, he decided not to bother with his apartment. It wasn't that he was out of time. As he climbed into the MG, he knew he could have gone up and packed. He had left almost three hundred in cash leafed in the pages of a Gideon Bible. And a set of barbells and a tapedeck. But what the hell. He had a hundred in his pocket from Hey, delivered as usual in advance, in an envelope. The earring was where it had always been, in the glove compartment. Always left behind whenever the car was rifled, because nobody wanted just one. He drove east, toward New York. And didn't return for two and a half years, by which time he had no past. As far as anyone knew, his second time in LA was his first. He might never have come back at all, except there was a treasure in his head.

Chapter 6

Peter walked out to the pool, stark naked. Rita and Nick, laughing like kids, were bent over something on the table at the far end. Peter struck a meditative pose, as if he were getting his wind in rhythm before throwing himself into a game, tennis or track and field.

"Didn't anybody hear me?" he asked a little wearily. They looked up as if he'd found them making love. They moved in front of the table like curtains and stood together side by side, so he wouldn't see.

"What are you doing up?" Nick wanted to know.

"I got up to find out why no one was paying attention to me. I bet I hollered for ten minutes."

"I don't see how that's possible, Pete," Rita said sensibly, looking up to their bedroom window as if to measure the distance. "We were right here."

"You will both be glad to know," he said—and he looked as if he'd decided he'd rather not be naked now, but there were things he'd come downstairs to say, and he'd say them first— "I'm getting up for good. I've put away my hot water bottle and my flexible straw. I want to have a party."

There was a slash of red on his right forearm, inside it the purple lines where he'd slit to get at the poison. It hurt, but not a lot.

"When?" said Nick.

"Tomorrow night." It was Saturday morning, ten after ten.

"Who do you plan to invite who won't have plans? Hey and Rita and me?"

"Among others. It's a business party, to say that I'm back in business. We'll ask all my clients. If they've made other plans, well that's all right. That's up to them." It wasn't all right at all. Peter smiled, because he knew he was setting up a crazy test. At least, the smile went on to say, he wasn't testing Rita and Nick. "I want it very simple. Quiche and salad and mousse."

"Are you going to order it all in?" Nick said, pursuing a line of questioning, as if to say their power had limits. Who took Sunday orders Saturday morning?

"I did already. On Wednesday."

"So really what you're doing is just inviting us," Rita said, glad to get it straight, relieved of the responsibility. She turned around to the table, like a figure in a clock going back in. She'd got so she paid no attention when the two of them crossed swords.

"Well, no. We all have to work, because I want to bring a lot of things up from the shop. Look, let me go get dressed, and then I'll explain."

He turned and strode through the dining room door, but it seemed hardly necessary now, because he'd been talking as if he were fully clothed. He didn't take poses in order to draw them out. Enough was enough. But Rita called "Pete!" and when he came back to the door expectantly, she drifted across the terrace with a package held out in front of her. About the size of a book, done up in foil and black velvet ribbon.

"This is a get-off-your-ass present from Nick and me," she said. "But I guess it's belated. I don't know what Nick and I are going to do with ourselves, if you're telling the truth. Take it anyway. You may have a relapse."

"You can all laugh," Peter said, "but you know, five hundred people die of snakebite every year. Five hundred are *reported*. Who knows how many just shrivel up and die in the bushes."

He wasn't paying any attention to what he said. Opening a present was his favorite ceremony in the world. He had the loot to prove it, because his friends were glad to know someone who cared so much. He sat down on the doorsill and put it in front of him on the shady terrace floor. He pulled the bow apart as if it were a magic trick. "I hope it's something to wear," he said dryly, to make a joke about his body, since he knew it had to be a thing. Needless to say, his friends found him less and less easy to please. He was always touched by the thought, but it could be a burden on an end table. It was safest to buy him something fleeting, like Dom Perignon. From Rita, though, he'd always won a prize, because a different order of intuitions came into play when she was giving gifts. She had sent him things in the past that took their places on tables and held firm until the tables wore out from under them. "Why didn't you think of getting me something like *that*?" he'd wanted to say to other people when the tissue stopped flying, pointing across the room at Rita's Haitian mask or Rita's Ethiopian basket.

Today she'd given him a frame for a photograph, meant to sit on a desk. It was gold to begin with, scrolled and etched with a jungle of fruity vines. The berries were pearls and polished pieces of nephrite. At the top, like a pediment on a Greek temple, was a pale blue enamel ground around a large yellow diamond, shining like the sun on the vines below. The center space, for the picture, was empty, just a pad of red damask under glass, but it looked like a photograph would fade or burst into flame if you tried to mount it there. And on the back, signed in Russian: c. FABERGÉ 1912.

"I got it because of that time your grandfather couldn't afford to buy his own horse and rider back from Parke-Bernet. I thought, Peter must be the only prince in the country who doesn't have a scrap of Fabergé in the family."

"But this cost a fortune, Rita."

She shrugged. In fact, it had cost Mrs. Lisle Beatton of Baltimore fourteen thousand dollars in 1924, which was a bargain. Then it was paid as part of a ransom in 1933. Rita didn't like the looks of the heirs she tracked down in the Baltimore Social Register, especially the ransomed daughter. But she was checking it out only halfheartedly, having already decided it had to be Peter's. She had returned to a small museum on a horse farm in Delaware a silver tankard by Paul Revere, so she figured she'd done enough for that part of the country, anyway. Rita couldn't be sure what a fortune was anymore, if this was one. To her, the picture frame was like a box of chocolates compared to most everything else in the secret room. The day before, she'd sent back to Paris a diary and a square of needlework, both interrupted, left on a plain pine table when Marie Antoinette was led from the cell at the Conciergerie to give her life for her country. Pinned to the needlepoint canvas was the account by the priest who heard her confession and stayed behind and slipped both things into his surplice. Rita didn't know what to say. She would have given Peter a Cézanne if it wouldn't have raised so many questions.

"It's nothing," she said lamely, trying to play it down a little. The diamond suddenly seemed to her about the size of a raspberry. She realized, here in the light of day, what the whole thing would be worth chopped up and strung on a bracelet. "The problem is," she went on, as breezily as she could, "it doesn't really go with anything, does it? I mean, it makes you want a Louis XV desk, and then you have to have the chair—there's no *end* to something like this. You're the only one I could give it to, Pete, because you have all that breeding to bear up under the burden."

"What about you?" Peter asked, turning from Rita and calling across to Nick.

"Oh, I just let Rita put my name on the card. I didn't know you needed a picture frame crusted with pearls, but she said you did, so you must."

"Well, you're both nuts," Peter said, standing up and letting the wrappings lie. "Maybe I'll have a picture taken of the frame and put it in the frame so I'll never forget how much you both love me." He went back into the dining room, holding it out in front of him. "On the other hand," he said as he walked off, his voice dying away across the room, "maybe we'll start the other way around and throw out everything else. Because this is going to need a hell of a lot of room."

Rita started to laugh, and she stooped and retrieved the black ribbon before she turned around again. "Well, doctor," she said as she sauntered toward Nick, "I believe the fever's finally broken. Tell me the truth now, didn't you think it was a hopeless case?"

"Some of these things, my child, are in higher hands than mine. He has been spared to do great work."

They were both grinning as they met at the pool's edge. They had to wait now for their orders. It wasn't stated out loud, but they had both been more or less planning to spend the day together. They were there in Saturday clothes, with no other plans. Before Peter came down, Rita was about to propose a day at Disneyland, if only to get her mind off beautiful things. They were clever enough to keep it from themselves as well as each other how clear they kept their calendars lately. After all, they would have said, they were thrown together more often than not by circumstance. Living in the same house and all. In fact, they were shy at times, and they'd never been that when they first met. The more time they spent with each other, the more care they took about intruding. It wasn't their fault if they were all tangled up. Peter had been in bed, in and out of it but in the house, for fifteen days.

Rita and Nick had meanwhile logged half a dozen dinners out, four late parties, and an opening or two. Partly, they thought they stuck together because it was easier to answer questions about Peter's accident and lingering rest cure. The rumor was that he'd had a breakdown. And then Peter kept insisting that they go. "I'll feel better," he said, "if you two are having fun. Do it for me." So they did it for him. It was a tribute to how much they loved him, really, that they were glad just now to see him so well.

"We'll have to stop meeting like this," she said ironically. It was a hard-won irony, to be sure, but it showed how much confidence she had in the run of excuses they had collaborated on.

"Time has had enough of us," he said, staring into the water for all the world as if it were a stream dancing over a bed of rocks, "and now it rushes on."

She knew where *her* line came from, more or less, but she couldn't place his. He sounded a bit like Rusty Varda. And though he was mocking men who spoke too much of time, it wasn't fair for Nick to act so grave, even in fun, because her own irony hovered just this side of hysteria. I don't mean hysteria, she thought—it was more like going balmy, as if she would be prone to curious noises, overly chummy with strangers, if she lost her footing just once in the balancing act with Nick. It was nice the way it was. She would be crazy to ruin it now by talking out of turn. They were about to touch down again on earth, and that was that.

"Maybe he'll let *us* go to bed for a couple of weeks," Nick said, "so we can decompress." He meant the sickbed variety of bed, of course, but her cheeks burned as if he'd suggested the other. Which was pretty odd, since she hadn't blushed about sex in fifteen years. Worse, she and Nick had stopped talking about it.

"I'll take a raincheck on that," she said. "I'm sure I'll have a snakebite of my own before long, and then I'll want all the pampering I can get. Peter will have to change my ice water every couple of hours."

He's acting as stilted as I am, she thought, and only a moment ago we were grinning like a tap-dance team. She hadn't thought about what to say to Nick for days and days, but here she was, trying to make conversation. But what's *his* excuse? she wondered ruefully. He'd just gotten his lover back.

"Are you two ready?" Peter was upstairs, leaning over the windowsill in the bedroom. He was decked out in three pieces of Yves Saint Laurent, camel with a pale orange stripe, so he'd presumably assigned the furniture moving to one of them. "Rita, all you have to do is invite everyone."

She flung the ribbon away to her left, into the garden, and followed it with her eyes as if she hadn't heard. Then she said distinctly, between her teeth, "Groan."

"Look, I'd do it myself, except they'd all want to talk for an *hour*. It'll be like their psychiatrist coming back from vacation. Nonstop. Besides, they all like you."

"They do not all like me," she said defiantly. "Half of them would put out a contract on me in a minute if they didn't think it would make their draperies late. Some of them think that I've drugged you like Frances Dean, that I keep you prisoner here."

"You're too sensitive, Rita, you always were." Up where he was, pots of fuchsia hung from the roof beams in baskets of rope and moss. He seemed very, very happy. One did not have to be overly sensitive, for instance, to appreciate a window flooded with purple flowers. "Nicholas," he went on, "I know you'll say it's the last minute and all, but we can't have a party with this crummy sound system."

"You're joking."

"Alas, no. But if you get the most expensive, they'll install it on a Sunday. You'll see."

"What are *you* going to do, Pete?" Rita asked.

"I'm keeping an open mind about that. I've been working on this for three days, and I need a break. I'm going out. The Fabergé has inspired me." He sounded as if he were going to enter a monastery. "Let's all meet about five and have some bubbly and fish eggs. My treat."

He couldn't stay another minute. He vanished from the window, and Rita and Nick were both so railroaded by it all that they couldn't come up with the words to hold him. Crook House was an absolute monarchy today, and Rita and Nick were the masses. They turned to each other as if to ascertain whether they'd been hearing things. And when they saw that it was real, they wasted no time clucking their tongues. They'd had a suspicion all along that it would end in a burst of theater. And they had to do it. On the other side of the party, everything was going to go back to normal. All Peter required was a ceremony grand enough to trample the rumors underfoot. Or so they all hoped. Peter was a star in part because he was good at cracking a bottle of Piper across his own bows. Somehow he could do it without getting wet.

"When you signed on for this trip," Nick said, "I'll bet you didn't count on so much suddenness, did you?"

"I suppose we're lucky it's not tonight. You know, it never occurs to him something can't be done. He's that way with people's houses, too."

"I know." She sounded sad to him. She ought to be angry if it didn't sit right. She understands me better than I do her, he thought. And then he said, "I get scared that some day he'll come up against a wall and beat his brains out on it. Because he's gotten his way so much that he doesn't see."

"He'll be fine," Rita said, "as long as no one ever puts a ceiling on the money. And the clients never do." She paused to gather up half a dozen examples, then let them go. You bitch, she told herself, you leave Peter alone. "You know, if I don't start these calls right now, I'll probably run away. Good luck in the technology race."

Nick, least of any of them, had had no thought he would end up by himself today. It was either Peter or Rita or real estate, every waking hour for the last two weeks. So when she walked away through the garden, head bent, hands in the pockets of her big Irish sweater, he felt a little ulcer start to blow its bellows in his gut. She closed the door as she went into the living room. What now, he thought in a panic, and he meant: What am I going to do about Sam? He wasn't ready yet. He'd thought he had at least until the middle of next week before Peter was up and about. He'd even come close to asking Rita what to do, convinced she'd got Sam's number in the couple of minutes she'd spent in passing. But everyone else, he knew, would say only that it was easy. Nobody else had been in love with Sam. Oh, that was what it was, Nick was sure, and part of the suffering that put its hooks in him now was disbelief that it was over. He was afraid he might never have loved any better than two weeks here and two weeks there.

"Nick, I have to talk to you."

He turned to see Hey on the other side of the pool. He couldn't imagine where he'd come from. Up the hill out of the bushes, he supposed. He was relieved just then to be given any sort of diversion at all, but it also flashed through his mind that Hey had been listening in.

"About the party?"

"He doesn't understand. He thinks it's a goddamned vacation for me because he's got a caterer coming in. But I have to make sure they don't pocket the silver. And it takes two days to clean up after them."

"I know." Hey had been on edge ever since Peter's accident. Nick decided he must have a morbid fear of snakes. "I wouldn't have let him go ahead with it, Hey, except it got him out of bed."

"That's another thing," Hey said, as if he'd just remembered. "I told him the other day, I'm not going to climb those stairs one more time. *That* cured him fast."

Nick laughed. "Why don't you take a few days off? You can have the whole of next week if you want. You want more money?" It was only a formal gesture, like the first draft of a treaty. Hey shrugged and looked away. Nick had known from the beginning, when he'd agreed to stay on with them, that Hey was not moved by time and money. He kept his loyalties simple—the house and Rusty Varda. Nick suspected they were lucky, he and Peter and Rita, that Hey had come to include them in his vision of Crook House. If he hadn't, the whole lot of them would have vanished into thin air. In any case, it was not like Hey to speak to one of them about the others. Hey fought battles on the spot. In fact, he was more likely than Nick was to convince Peter that Sunday was out of the question. Something else was up.

"He'll be all right," Hey said, his voice quite gentle now. That's just what Rita said, Nick thought. It was as if they all knew it wasn't snakes but Nick and Sam. "It's about Linda."

"Oh."

"Holy Brother says she's going through a transitional phase. She's got to fall back on the physical plane for a while. That's me."

Nick nodded. I am not embarrassed about this, he said to himself. He was troubled about the rip-off, though, and he wondered again how much Holy Brother charged for an office call. It was never clear what the medium was, crystal ball or tea leaves or tongues. Nick didn't think Hey was crazy. He did think Hey was gay, and the elaborate machinery of other selves was a camouflage for a self he couldn't face. But it had worked for Hey for four or five years, and Nick had a tough streak that would fight to the finish for anyone's right to do what worked. He realized suddenly that, though he didn't yet know what to do about Sam, things were going to be all right once he'd done it.

"And what exactly does that entail?" he asked Hey.

"I don't know, Nick." He looked down into the water, as if to catch a glimpse of Linda passing across his face. "Maybe nothing. Maybe I'll just be a vessel and never know. But I want to be free to move if the rhythm hits me. What I need to know is: Do you care how I look?"

"Of course not," he said. Hey meant drag. There had been no mention between them of the makeup he wore when he walked in on Rita and Sam. Was it going too far? he wondered. What if Hey served them lunch some day in spike heels and an off-the-rack dress? Peter wouldn't like it. He was irritated as it was by Hey's proprietary air, where Nick was charmed, and besides, Peter wanted to get a French couple some day and dress them up starched in black and white. But Nick meant it when he said he didn't care. We all look okay to me, he thought. So many of the things power and money had brought him had turned ambiguous or dumb or dull, but at least, he thought, we have come far enough to do what we want in our own house. He meant for Crook House, above all things, to be home for a troupe of consenting adults.

"Thanks," Hey said, and, as he made his way around the end of the pool, he walked with the care and stillness of a mannequin coming down a couturier's runway. "You know, at the beginning I thought I was two separate people. I was real schizo. But lately I see that we're both the same, Linda and I. There isn't any difference."

"Between a man and a woman there is, isn't there?"

"No," he said emphatically, putting his face close up to Nick's. "That's what I mean. *No* difference."

Well, Nick thought, that's just what the rest of the world still has to learn, so bravo for Hey. Nick had only been trying to point out the matter of genitals, and now he felt a little foolish. It showed he was still tied up in a neuter view of women, still penis-fixed, as if he were back on the beach at Venice ogling the rise in the lifeguard's trunks. Hey's virginal passion had brought him like a bark canoe to the source of two rivers. And Nick realized that he'd been feeling something of the same sort about him and Rita. They saw most things alike. Even more, they both believed their sex lives had nothing to do with their real lives—though they'd never actually said as much to each other. For years, Nick had exulted over the change he'd made between straight and gay, because once he'd made it, it proved to him he was finally alive. Now the range of the erotic was centered in his head and not his cock. Sex was a door to a suite of imaginings. Hey was right. After a certain amount of experience, everyone was the same.

"As far as I'm concerned, Hey, she's free to come and go as she pleases."

Hey was content. He left Nick standing there unarmed, in need of the next diversion, and then he stopped at the dining room door. He turned around as if he'd forgotten just one more thing.

"The three of you," he said. "You're all right, aren't you?"

"Of course we are," Nick said, his eyes narrowing. He felt a bubble of anger rising. What does he mean, the *three* of us? "Why?"

"You were all so sad a couple of weeks ago. Now I don't know what you are."

"We're fine," he said. Weren't they?

"Good." And then it seemed he would go. But he couldn't contain himself. He had a theory. "Because you're all perfect for each other, you know. Holy Brother says it almost never happens. Two's easy—it's what everybody does. But *three*—" He put up the palms of both hands, as if he were a bishop blessing a crowd. He couldn't bring out the phrases that told how rare it was. Finally he did it by way of The Beyond. "It must have taken you all dozens of lives to get here. And we think you must have done time in ancient Greece."

"I don't think it's a good idea," Nick said, as aloof as he needed to be, "for you to include us in your religion. We're just who we are."

"Oh, I know I talk too much, Nick. Forget it." Yet his parting shot throbbed with sentiment, as if to say *he* wasn't going to forget it. "You all have to get on with your destiny. There aren't any words for it anymore."

Well, Nick thought as Hey disappeared into the house, I've made my rounds this morning. They can't say I'm neglecting them. He already had his checkbook and credit cards in the pocket of his painter's pants, so he went off without further ado to put a dent in his accounts. When he passed by Rita in the living room, pillowed on a sofa soft as an English cloud, the phone at her ear, he waved, but she didn't look up. He got into the elevator, thought hard as he went up about Hey's fruity notion of the three of them, then dismissed it as he went outside and leapt up the steps to the car. The three of them were terrific, of course—Nick knew that—but the rest was just a fairy tale. Nick might have parried: What about Sam?

What would Holy Brother have to say about *four*? Nick bet it would rank right up there with the loaves and fishes. Hey didn't really want to get under his skin like this, did he? After all, he knew what Judith Anderson had come to in *Rebecca*.

In principle, of course, Nick fully agreed with Sam. See a man a second time only if one of you doesn't get it right at first—assuming, that is, that the one who *does* get it right is fabulous. Or do it to go that one step further, to push through to the other side of the fantasy, to the place where even the cowboys haven't made trails. After that, there is no excuse for doing it again. The third time, people are all too real. They start to do what they do at home. Nick let the Jaguar float down the curves of Bel-Air, and he swung by paneled trucks parked up and down the hill, delivering bottled water and dry-cleaned gowns and babysat kids who'd stayed all night. The sprinklers misted the lawns, and the only sound inside the houses was the Bloody Marys being mixed in pitchers. The world was full of systems. Nick's rules for the conduct of extramarital sports fit right in, and he wished he'd played the same with Sam as he did with anyone else. He could see how a man like Sam shook the method of things. He was like an ambulance pulling up at the lacy gates of a Spanish Baroque pile on Bellagio Drive, the siren cutting a swath through the lemon trees and putting greens. Even if only one house had the mishap, the stopped-up artery and the sudden widow, the ruckus alone brought down values all over the neighborhood.

Nick had had sex with a couple of hundred men in the two years they had lived in Crook House. If that looks to be about two men a week, then the figures are deceptive. He had gone a month or six weeks sometimes without so much as a double-take when he passed in the car a Greek statue with its shirt off. He had fucked with four men in a row, though, at the baths, four or five hours under a dusty rose light, accessoried with a cock-ring and a box of poppers. Not once had he brought a man home until Sam. He had gone up badly lighted stairs and done it in rooms with no linen on the bed, and he'd rented rooms by the hour in motels that didn't go in for details. Nine times out of ten, he had no more connection to it as he drove on home than a roll of dirty photographs strewn in his head. Moreover, the men he went with were in it for the same regulation match. They'd had enough of their conference calls and their cliffhanger deals—or their chemistry texts if they were young—and they didn't want to be anybody else for a while but a man fucking.

Nine times out of ten. The tenth time, Nick's heart went to water at the unexpected sight of a blond and thoughtless surfer running out of the waves at Zuma or—it could happen anywhere—an out-of-work actor in the checkout line at Ralph's. He wasn't even looking for it at the time. As a rule, Nick was as philosophical as the next fellow about the longing for the unattainable man glimpsed through a window when two trains pass abreast. Momentary as it was, it was the closest he ever got to perfect love. Wait, he'd want to call out, overcome with the certainty that he'd found at last the man in the shadow at the back of the mirror, and already the trains would be rocketing off, respectively, to Cincinnati and Santa Fe. Something as melancholy as a distant whistle would linger and haunt for the rest of the afternoon, fading finally into things that lasted longer than a moment. It happened to everyone, Nick supposed. The problem was, in LA the boy with the water streaming out of his hair might lock eyes and freeze, and the next thing Nick knew, he was rolling around in the back of a van. Or the actor would say, helping Nick unload his groceries onto the belt: "I have forty-five minutes before I have to be at Unemployment, and I live about two blocks from here. What do you like to do?" And what was meant to come and go in a flash, never meant to be, had a chance to dig its heels in and sing. And what it sang was a ballad, which always tells a fateful story. The lovers are smashed to bits by quakes and runnings aground and holy wars.

Nick came away shaken from coupling with dreams, afraid he couldn't readjust to the world at large. Forty-five minutes was time enough to make sex take on the feel of Paradise, if only it would never stop. But of course it did, and *then* the trains went flying to opposite places. In the falling dark, the ride home was full of red lights and bottlenecks. Nick would get so depressed for the next day or two, he'd think he was going to collapse, run off, start bawling in the midst of some trivial, mechanical thing he did every day. What else *was* there, his nerve ends kept insisting, remembering a perfect fuck, what else but the wrestles of passion? Everything else was all alike—repetitious, pointless, stale. It took Nick too long to get back to normal, so he didn't even welcome it anymore when fate put a cowboy in his path. He wasn't good enough at feeling nothing. He preferred the faceless goings-on at the baths, where he was in control of what it was about. He preferred his own indifference. When he emerged again into daylight, the pressure off in his crotch, real life took on, by contrast, a sharp and tonic air. He'd go get a package of ten-cent cupcakes and throw them down with a swallow of black coffee. Then he'd be ready to buy and sell. He stood on the hills of LA and raked the land in like a croupier.

So he knew what he was letting himself in for, from the very first day with Sam, from the moment they checked in for an hour at the jail-gray motel. The thing grew like a virus. Nick's life outside it went on by force of circumstance, powered by inertia. Right away, he saw no reason to throw up the old line between fantasy and reality—Sam was too exactly what he wanted—and he decided to let the borders establish themselves in their own way, like a waterline according to the weather. He was like a heavy drinker who decides one day he's no longer going to chalk the mark in the dirt at five P.M. And then it was as if the story he started had been waiting all along offshore, like a hurricane feeding itself with every passing wind, and it came down on his tidy systems in a fury. Within two weeks he'd bought the ranch.

Why am I doing this to myself? he thought as the pain heaped up, hour after hour. To see if I can survive it, he'd say. Get rid of it once and for all. Go down with the truth at last. He was lying. He liked it, or at least he needed it, because he couldn't handle the run of good luck that choked his wallet with bills too big to break. The image he'd had all his life of losing control—before Peter, before his personal boom in real estate—was an image of attack by nightmare, like a cancer or an incendiary bomb. Now he'd grown up to be Midas, and the merest bungalow in West Hollywood—tile-roofed, Taco Bell version of a tarpaper shack—turned out to tap into a gold mine. Nothing ever went wrong. And it made him feel out of control. Like drowning in whipped cream.

Well, it was and it wasn't the niceness of life, still as an unruffled pool, that sent him after Sam. Nick wasn't the type to self-destruct. He didn't just look for a ruinous force. He believed in the man in the dream, enough to take a lot of enemy fire in pursuit of him, and even though he'd have to let him go in the end. True to the whole story, Nick went along with the scene where the cowboy rides off alone at the end. Nick just wanted to watch for a while, to ride through town at the stranger's side, passing the time of day. As usual, of course, there was no sex at all in the fantasied meeting—maybe the knees of their buckskin trousers touch when they rein in their horses and stare out at the grasslands, but it's by chance— because the fantasy had been around longer than the itch in his groin. He could listen to Sam talk about nothing for hours— his MG, his acid trips, the river of violence he skirted in the street, the men he met who couldn't hide a thing from him because what they wanted laid them wide open. It came through to Nick like a movie. He read into the grit and bitter herbs of Sam's disconnected anecdotes the points of a symbolic journey. Sam lived one of his lives for him. Other men did it with football teams.

Whatever it was, it changed forever on Thursday night, the twenty-sixth of February. Nick waited upstairs to go to Chasen's, flat on the bed in a suit and tie and no lights on, and he thought once again about Sam. That afternoon, when they'd taken the tour of Crook House, Nick had an obscure feeling that he was showing much too much of himself. He guided people who didn't know what they wanted through a dozen houses every week, so he figured he'd seen all the possible reactions. But whatever he said about *this* house—impersonal, statistical, the usual—Sam would seem to take a second look and slow them down, as if he were putting two and two together. Two and two *what?* Nick wondered. He could feel him taking note of where Nick and Peter ate and slept, what made them mad, what things they'd owned the longest. The life of the house was meaningless to Sam, Nick could tell, but all the same he seemed to be running his hands over everything. Not casing the joint exactly, not like a thief going through a jewelry box. More like an animal making a mess to get at food, except here there was no mess. Nick thought and thought, but he couldn't get it right what he'd lost that day. It was *he* who'd lost it, though. Not Sam.

And then, around eight or eight-thirty, he began to worry where Peter could be. He called the shop, called Adele's in San Marino, called Chasen's. He knew it must be the ranch, but he was reluctant to get in the car and drive up there, in case Peter was already on his way home. He didn't want to get accused of hysteria, not now anyway, not since he'd shoved Peter's face in it this morning at the ranch gates, when Sam had screeched away and left him no option. For Peter's sake, for *his* and Peter's sake, he had to be as blasé tonight as a cocktail pianist, to prove that everything was just the same as usual. But it got worse and worse, the thought of Peter crushed beneath a harrow or a caved-in shed, and finally at ten he got in the car. In LA, as Rita had observed, people feel they are doing *something* in a crisis if they can only drive off somewhere. At the ranch, Nick tore around in the dark looking for the pickup, and a couple of times he got out and stood on the hood of the Jag and called at the top of his voice. But by then he was just as sure it was over, and Peter was dead or alive but somewhere else. He drove home calmly, summoned in Rita and Hey to tell them, and as they all settled down to come up with a plan, the phone rang. "We have a man here with a snakebite," they said, and the world fell into place again.

What would he have done, Nick wondered now. How far would he have gone with Sam? He drove down Robertson

Boulevard sixteen days later, on the lookout for a sound store
where money would talk, still numb from the turn things had
taken as time went on. Simply this: He had gotten over Sam.
He hadn't meant to—on the contrary, he'd intended to keep a
candle lit in his head night and day. He thought it would
persist all by itself. The first weekend, when the telephone
calls to Sam were rotten with apologies and he left the seven
hundred at the Beau-Numero, he imagined there must be a
black cloud just behind and to the left of him, hurling down
thunderbolts. If it had only held off a little longer, he might
have made it. He'd wanted to have it both ways—the cowboy
and the Black Sea prince—and in the process he'd thrown the
switches too soon, put the tracks crisscross, and brought about
a crash. The first few days, the empty place ate into him like a
grave being dug in his belly. He expected nothing left by the
time he got back to Sam, but Sam was to blame for that. He
blamed him in advance for a foregone conclusion, and by the
end of the first week he was pelting the place himself with
small arms fire, in a rage at Sam's little faith. Two superhuman
fucks was all it amounted to. The third was a draw on account
of the snake. But Nick was the only one who could hold onto
what little there was and so protect it. He locked it up like
Rusty Varda. He had to protect it even from Sam. And still it
paled until it was as thin as mist, until the slightest movement
through it blew it out of shape.

So he hated him after a while. It didn't feel especially odd at
first to have his feelings change, and if he couldn't pinpoint
when it happened, it was because it was hidden deep in the
nature of things. As if the eye of the hurricane had passed over
Crook House sometime in the night when he wasn't looking.
While he sat on the bed with Peter and Rita, reading aloud the
personals out of a New York paper. And before he had really
stopped to notice, the trees were bending the other way. Suddenly, he hated Sam for having no fantasies of his own, because it meant he had no past that had gone wrong. He hated
him for sticking to himself. He'd got to be terrific at fucking
so as not to have to see how people really were. Didn't have to

be bored by their husbands, bury their mothers, wait with them dazed for the bad results of their biopsies.

Can it be that I hate him, though? he had to ask. After all, it may have been himself he meant to hate, for squandering too much on men who added up to nothing. He was going on about it still, all day long, as much as when he loved him and suffered and loved that, too. But now it only made him think his life wasn't in order, which always sent him back to Peter. He had to hold Peter in a bearhug, first things first, and look over Peter's shoulder to see what he could do without, cut loose, give away. And it was Sam. He and Rita may have snapped at Peter now and then in his convalescence, putting down their foot like Hey and saying it was all *Camille*. But it was the most time they'd spent together without a program in a couple of years. Once he got up, noon or after, Peter painted the ranch from memory, canvas after canvas, one a day, and Nick took lunch hours half a day long. He spread the whole of their finances out on the bedroom floor and lectured, speculated, profited, and lost. The days of the second week went by, and he didn't hate Sam. He'd just outgrown him.

"What you really ought to do is read to me," Peter said at the easel. Toward the end of the second week, the bunkhouse began to appear in the paintings, first at the edges of the canvas, then bigger and bigger, as if Peter were focusing a zoom. "Why don't you read me poems? In Italian."

"I don't speak it, for one thing," he said. "And neither do you."

"Oh, that doesn't matter, does it?" he asked, brush in the air.

"Don't be fruity, Peter." Nick held up a pen and a power-of-attorney for him to sign. Peter put the brush between his teeth, the paper on Nick's shoulder where he sat on the floor at the foot of the easel, the pen to the dotted line. They were mostly quiet, absorbed, and meticulous, and it looked on those afternoons as if they could have changed places and gone on without a pause, as if they were two monks gilding the facing pages of a prayer book. They weren't restricted by separate energies,

weren't tied to artist and banker. They were playing, after a
fashion. Not play like cowboys and Indians for once, toys and
reckless outdoor games. Play like the play in a rope—elastic,
room to maneuver, the line going out and coming in. They
were so undriven and so afloat they were half-asleep, their
heads like globes of brandy. They could have been lying in bed
after making love.

All told, then, Nick thought as he pushed through the doors
of the warehouse and the music jammed his circuits, he'd had a
five-week thing with Sam, maybe six. Now it was up to him to
call up Sam and break it off. He wasn't as sure as he'd been a
couple of weeks before that Sam had given it the finger all on
his own and leapt in the saddle and gone. Nick wanted to just
forget it, but he didn't dare. Sam knew where to come back to.
In the meantime, he couldn't successfully divert his attention
to stereo components, because he had a tin ear and his mind
went blank in front of machines. Peter hadn't sent him on this
errand for his expertise. It was because he could handle—and
Peter couldn't, not for an instant—bleak and noisy stores
where they banked the TVs row upon row and turned them
all on to the bowling matches. So he put on a pleading look
and collared a salesman and nodded a lot for the next half
hour, full of encouragement, nicely tuned out. He spent
twenty-one hundred dollars gladly, grateful to get it over
with. And not including a hundred to the salesman and another to the trucker, to see that they had it blaring disco to
shake the walls by 5:00 P.M. on Sunday.

Driving home, he let Sam go, convinced he couldn't do
much till Monday, and tried to think straight about Peter and
Rita. *They* were what he was going to do about Sam, and the
rest was just a phone call, another packet of hundreds, and—
what the hell—maybe a new MG and *really* end it. Funny,
though. He could feel his cock shift with a will of its own
from first to second at the thought of Sam. There hadn't been
a peep out of it for anyone but Peter in well over a week. He
didn't still want a piece, did he? Let go, he thought, let go.
He'd come too far, he told himself, letting the fantasy go on

for a bit but turning the lights out on it, to make it faceless. Nobody else would ever be quite so right for the cowboy's ride as Sam, but he'd make do. He knew now what the problem was. Allowing himself to get too well-known, he'd begun to see in Sam's eyes, instead of a wild idea, a zeroing in on who Nick really was. As if Sam couldn't sustain the fantasy. Not his fault—a lot of static and interference from God knew where, like men who couldn't keep it hard. Maybe because he was a hustler and had to be bookkeeping all the time. But it was a dead end for Nick. Peter was the only one he wanted to look at him for real. And now Rita. Sam was nobody compared with them, and Nick understood for the first time who was riding away from whom. Sam wasn't the cowboy stud at all. He was.

Peter and Rita and I are just three friends, he thought, and yet, since none of us has ever gone in much for friends, that's more than we're used to. And I'm the luckiest, he had to admit, with a lover among them and someone old and someone new. Peter and Rita had had each other so long, they were already well-connected when Rita arrived—*were* each other in certain moods and certain seasons, certain public places. They could take it for granted. Peter, of course, had Nick the way Nick had Peter, but not really, for the field that drew Nick like a magnet to ripe naked men left a space like a blank in a film that Peter had to grapple with. Rita had old and new, but she was the one without a lover in the group, which made her more alone, even if she wanted it that way. No, he thought as he went under the arch of the East Gate and into Bel-Air, they don't have it as easy as I do. We all have the three of us, but I have more. As with the money, of course, the pots of gold at the end of every arc he traveled, having so much was the very thing that threw him. It made him lose track of what it was for. In the end, it sent him scavenging for men with nothing, men like Sam.

He took the curves and wound his way among the islands and half-acre kingdoms of people doing well. The midday air at the end of winter was as clean as they were going to get in

LA, and the noon sun, he saw, had brought the Bel-Air villagers
out to their pools and paddle tennis courts to go through another round of staying alive. Everyone meant to survive who
made it here, which is why they put tomato juice in their
Saturday drinks—a vitamin is a vitamin, no matter what company it keeps. The houses, Rusty Varda's and some few others
excepted, weren't there fifty years ago and wouldn't be, what
with the fires and the Palmdale bulge, fifty years hence. So no
one survived by monuments. It was your body or nothing,
three-score-and-ten with a shot at a century. And if it means
I'm cynical to think so, he thought, then cynics are not as
black as they're painted. He loved his checkered neighbors
in the hills, for all their ironies and lunacies, not in spite of the
gimlets gulped before and after the perfunctory swim but because of it. Consenting adults wherever he looked. And we can
be just three friends, he decided, without a lot of scrutiny and
fitting in boxes. No big deal.

Rita's car wasn't there, and Peter's car wasn't back. I'm first,
he thought contentedly, leaping down the steps as if to get
things ready and surprise them. Set them a gingham picnic by
the pool, perhaps. He put the key in the lock, but the door
gave only a couple of inches when he pushed, because the
chain was up. "What the . . . ," he said. He poked at the doorbell till it rang like chimes. He could hear Hey apologize from
several rooms away. But he got more and more incoherent the
closer he got, running through the living room and up the
spiral stair. He squinted out and saw Nick pressed against the
door like an invading soldier.

"Oh, what are we going to do!" he cried. "The parrot's
gone."

"Let me in first," Nick said with deliberate calm. He stood
back while Hey closed the door and then opened it wide. He
was stricken.

"It doesn't matter," he said, his voice all ashes, though a
moment before he was shrieking. He was like two different
characters, now up, now down. "You can open all the doors
and windows now. I thought he was just loose in the house.

But he's out *there*." And he looked over Nick's shoulder at the outside world as if it trembled with death like a jungle.

"Tell me what happened," Nick said quietly, summoning up the proper attitude. He and Peter hated the parrot, gritting their teeth whenever they thought of him on his nightly spin in the kitchen. He wasn't pretty to look at, and his jaundiced eye and his weathered beak appeared to be spotted with tropical fevers. But he and Hey went together as if they captained a sailing ship between them. They had been housemates during the lonely years of litigation after Varda's death, and the parrot was a fixture by the time Nick and Peter came.

"I was cleaning the cage," Hey said. Nick guided him into the elevator and kept his arm around Hey's shoulder as they started down. "I never bother to close the door to the dining room, because he *knows* it's just for a few minutes. He always waits on the towel rack. But I turned around, and he was gone. I ran all over and closed the house up, but I knew it was no use." Then he raised his voice again, in a tone of lament he must have carried in his genes. "Oh, *Christ*! Why does it have to happen *now*?" He could take it, he seemed to say, but he had his hands full just lately, with Linda swooping in out of the blue to put him on like a coat.

"He'll come back," Nick said, and they stepped out into the living room. He could tell the house was sealed. It seemed under pressure and somehow far too still, as if they'd been away on a long trip. "As soon as he's hungry. Besides, he knows he can't do without you. He's just like us."

"That's very sweet of you to say, Nick. But if I were him, I'd be halfway to San Diego by now. Compared to flying," he said, looking about distractedly, "all of this is shit." He started to cry, with tears welling out of his eyes and a gathering heave in his shoulders. It was the sound of someone homeless.

"You go lie down and take an aspirin," Nick said. It was on the tip of his tongue to say they'd get another one, but he saw it would be insensitive. Besides, he didn't want another one. He wanted a dog.

"I don't know how I'm going to get through this fucking

party," Hey said brokenly, and Nick led him through to the kitchen and told him not to think about it. Hey's room had a separate entrance off the kitchen garden, so they had to pass by the empty cage, its barred door ajar and the floor all freshly papered and covered with gravel. Hey went into a full sob. Nick put him to bed, gave him a Valium, and said it was aspirin. He sat on the bed until Hey stopped crying and closed his eyes. Then he went around and opened things up. All the sliding doors to the garden and, one after another, the casements, locking them open at different angles to catch the slightest breezes. It was his imagination, but he seemed to smell bird shit in every room, and he aired them all out, once and for all. Good riddance, he thought. Now maybe they could get a Lab or a collie, both of which Peter thought mawkish, too doglike. Peter wanted something nobody else had, a Rolls-Royce of a dog, he didn't care what. Hey wouldn't hear of it, either way. He said he had his hands full with the bird. And listen to you, Nick berated himself, it's all you think about, what you want. Like a saint keeping points on his out-of-church acts, he dropped the dog and thought kind thoughts about Hey, who'd lost his other half.

When he got to Rita's room, he realized he'd been saving it till last so as not to compromise her privacy. He half hoped she'd come home while he was at the upstairs windows, and then she could open up her own. But at last he propelled himself over the threshold, if only because he didn't want to be making exceptions and getting too courtly. It was hot as a sauna. She had the whole row of casements along the garden side, and when they caught the high point of the sun in spring and summer, the light lit it up like a stage in the middle of the day. There were clothes thrown over everything as if they'd all floated down out of the sky, as if she had to have them all in plain sight to know where to start. New things still in their boxes, tumbling out of the tissue. A storm of magazines all around the bed. Nick felt giddy with affection. There ought to be at least *one* room in Crook House, he thought, set aside for chaos. He had been hanging his own clothes up the minute he took them off for as long as he could recall, as a hedge against the letting go that went with being broke. The terminal house he grew up in was full of things that fell where they may as if they'd given up. He disentangled a scarf from the clump on the end of the bed and threw it like a streamer, and it lilted in the air and settled slowly in a splash of red and gold. Nick laughed out loud. It rang in the cluttered room like a cheer or a whoop as he turned to go.

But a sound like the clatter of poker chips made him stop. It was coming from the walk-in closet across the room, and where he might have thought mice at any other time, he knew without looking that he'd tracked down the wayward bird. Damn it, he thought as he skirted his way among the clothes, you're supposed to be in San Diego. He had an urge to go get it, tuck it under his arm, and fling it out one of Rita's windows. But with his luck, he thought, putting his head around the closet door and peering in, it would settle itself in the garden and wait for Hey and be forevermore out for Nick's blood. He snapped on the light, and there it was, sashaying back and forth along the clothes bar that ran the length of one side.

"Hello, you little fungus," he said, advancing into the closet and standing eye to eye with it. "Have you crapped all over Rita's clothes?"

"Machu Picchu," said the bird. He skittered away to the left and out of Nick's range. He stretched both wings in front of him, as if he were adjusting a chieftain's cape, then folded them back along his body and stood up straight and still. Nick had been dismissed. The parrot's forward gaze took on such a spiritual air, he could have been posing for Audubon.

So there's someone for everyone, Nick thought wryly, even the lowliest, and the parrot had Hey, who was more than he deserved. Nick decided he'd bring the cage to the bird and not the other way around, since he couldn't picture the parrot perched on his forefinger all the way back to the kitchen. Better yet, he'd wait till Hey woke up. There didn't seem to be any violence or mess, and anyway, the closet was practically empty. A few things hung on hangers, but most of Rita's clothes appeared to be strewn about in the outer room, as if she were saving the closet for something else. It was because he couldn't *do* anything yet that Nick took such a long look around. He was keeping an eye on things. And the packing box on the floor was pretty conspicuous, even with a sheet thrown over it. Even then, he only meant to lift it at one corner, to get an idea. But what was it? The first, fast glimpse only tantalized him, and before he knew it, he'd snapped the sheet off like a real magician.

There in the box, propped on a bed of shredded newsprint, was a girl's two hands in marble, holding a ball. The rest of her was left behind a couple of thousand years ago. Nick bent down and lifted out a folded paper that lay alongside. It was notes, in Rita's hand, but too disconnected to follow out the train of thought. "Found at a dig at Cnidus, August 1921," it said at the top. And then a lot of comparing it to other things, but that was all too technical for Nick. "200 B.C." he understood. But "stolen at site" didn't make much sense because, if it was stolen, what was it doing here? "Who needs it? British Museum?" Well, how was he supposed to know. He folded up the paper and put it back exactly right. He chided himself too late for overstepping on Rita's ground, and he sagged inside with a variety of guilt which threw him, since he was an expert only in the sexual kind. Nick didn't know a thing about art, he always said. He didn't even know what he liked. He left all that to Peter and went his way, and part of the reason he wasn't a curious or gossipy sort was that he didn't much register the price of people's knickknacks. But even he had ideas about the British Museum—big bucks and no bullshit. So Rita had a sideline, good for Rita, he thought, trying to be jaunty. But he couldn't get it out of his head that he'd had the kind of accident that he and Peter and Rita were going to be a long time recovering from. Even if he kept it a secret.

"It's all your fault, you know," he snarled at the parrot, bringing his hand up menacingly, as if to cuff it. The parrot scooted further away along the bar, blinked once, and went back into his trance.

And then, more or less, the sky caved in. He heard a rustle of packages out in the bedroom and knew he'd been caught red-handed. He had no choice. He held his breath, glared as if to say the parrot was a plucked chicken if he squawked, and determined to wait it out. She didn't use the closet, after all. In a minute she'd probably go out to the pool or something, because it was so hot in her room. Or if she'd just go in the bathroom and take a pee, he thought, he could sneak out easily. Though now he was almost reluctant to go. It was cool in here, and he had to admit, he wanted to hold the hands—because they were old, not because they were art. If she'd only go, he thought. But the next sound let him know how little he knew. She was shutting the windows.

One by one, he could hear the casements bang and the locks turn. He knew precisely how long it would take, since he'd done the very same thing ten minutes before, going the other way. He should have known then it was all over. But did he really have no choice? Couldn't he have walked on out the moment he heard her and pointed inanely at the parrot on his shoulder? He would never know now. But he probably would have said, given time, that his hiding was a reflex, and it had to do with leaving Rita alone. He had no right—to be there at all, to poke around among the ruins, to involve himself with her in any way. As if he weren't involved already. I don't have to know your secrets to love you, he would have liked to say to Rita. Whatever she told him was all he needed. And if that is how he would have put it, then he must have felt much more than she how well they had made it work in the last two weeks, being together so much. We did it without getting involved, he must have thought. What did he think they were instead? Like brother and sister, maybe?

It didn't matter. When she shut the eighth and final window it began to happen very fast. She must have flown across the room to the closet, because she was standing in front of him, the door slammed behind her, the lock locked, before he could change his tune or whistle a warning. They looked into each other's eyes for an instant, long enough for Nick to see she was feeling caught, just like him. How will we ever get out of this? he wondered. But all in a split second, because the mirror swung open, too, the moment Rita shut them in. The two of them turned at once and stared into the dark, as if someone might step out and save them. Then, when Nick looked back, he saw how her eye was caught by the uncovered box. She studied it wistfully, not as if she regretted its betraying her, but as if the marble hands might be the best way to begin. If she was angry or even surprised, it didn't show. She accepted the new situation as fast as it happened—she and Nick had gone on to the next step, whatever it might turn out to be.

"Where's Cnidus?" Nick asked casually, trying to let her know he'd gotten the lesson by heart, trying to give her a cue.

"I don't really know," Rita said. "A city, I think. Sacred to Demeter, the goddess of crops and marriages."

"Is that whose hands they are?" He was so interested. They might have been picking each other up in a museum.

"No. That's Aphrodite," she said with something like awe, as if the whole goddess were there in front of them, all curves and waves like a Botticelli.

"She plays tennis, I see." Why, Nick thought, am I trying to make jokes? Perhaps because Rita was still as sad as when they'd split up a couple of hours before. And not about anything here, he didn't think.

"It's an apple," she said, looking up at last, and smiling at him now as if she'd been longing to show him around and he'd dropped in right on time. "That's how they know. Paris had to judge three goddesses, to choose the fairest, and each of them offered a bribe. Aphrodite won. He gave her the apple of discord."

"What did she promise him?"

"The most beautiful woman in the world." Something, Rita seemed to say, that neither of them had any use for. Aphrodite wouldn't have had a prayer if it had been up to Nick and Rita.

"Unfortunately for all of them, that turned out to be Helen of Troy."

"Can I pick it up?"

"Sure." And when he did, the look on his face as blank as sleep, she said, "You can see the stem end of the apple—see?—between her finger and thumb."

The hands were heavier than he thought they'd be, as if time were part of the weight, and the surface was slightly rough from the wearing away. The features—fingernail lines and knucklebones and veins—were faint. He hadn't noticed before, but the little finger on the right hand was missing. He flinched when he saw it, he didn't know why. After all, she was missing ninety percent.

"Where did you get it?"

"In there," she said, not looking, not pointing.

"Oh." He sounded as if he hoped they'd be able to get through this without going into all of that. He knew it was *his* room waiting in the dark behind the mirror, but he felt just then no wish to explore it. He didn't need to add another thing to his inventory, and though of course he couldn't speak for Peter, he knew Peter could live without it, too. Rita could *have* it, for all Nick cared. Besides, she had some rights in the matter because, for the present, Frances Dean's room was her room, and didn't that lay a claim to everything in it, ghosts and all? Nick was prepared to abandon all logic. If Rita had come upon an old carved ring of Frances Dean's in a medicine chest, or a tortoise comb that had fallen into a crevice, he and Peter would have insisted she keep it. It didn't matter to him what was in that room. If she'd said it was corpses, that she was a vampire, he'd have scarcely taken it in. That was all on her own time, he would have reasoned. He was mad at himself. I am going to do this, he thought, so that Rita feels no crimes, no grief, no lonely nights, and no impediments to whatever it is she's doing in here. When Nick gave people space, he didn't take no for an answer.

"Can I take a look inside?" he asked her.

"Of course," she said. She understood that she'd been de-

ferred to. "But tell me, why did you bring the parrot? Or did
the parrot bring you?"

"You mean, did he give me the secret word? No. I never
think to look for buried treasure. I'm more in the market to
bury my own. I don't know why the parrot's here, but he
came here by himself. Are there things in there that belonged
to Rusty Varda?"

"In a way," she said evasively. "It's a long story." She was
trying to make him more curious. He talked as if the secret
room was nothing but a box of souvenirs, a jumble of cuff
links and coins and yellowing letters.

"So tell me about it," he said appealingly, and she answered
him with a sigh, "If you insist." By now they were both in a
wonderful mood. She beckoned him along, and she paused at
the mirror's edge to light two candles she took from a shelf.
They entered the inner room. Close on her heels, Nick
watched Rita screw a candle into a holder on a six-branch
standing silver candelabrum. "Medieval," Rita said, and nothing more. "The Bishop's Treasury, Ely Cathedral, 1928," it said
in Varda's diary. But Rita was in a hurry to tell it all, and she
didn't have time to identify things as they made their way. She
scrambled over the crates and boxes like a mountain goat and
slid around the Renaissance stone table and stopped at last in
the sitting-room space at the far end, where she waited for
Nick. He was right behind her most of the way, intent on her,
oblivious to it, like Alice tailing the rabbit. But he was boggled
in spite of himself by the sheer amount of things, and he
paused to gape at the Chinese porcelains ranged, bargain-
basement, on the stone table. By the time he sat down in one
of the great gilt chairs and looked over at Rita sitting at the
cherry desk, the candle throwing light on the Varda diary, he
was suitably out of breath.

Rita began to talk by talking figures. It surprised her how
much she'd filed them away in her head like a story. It was as
if, with all the study and putting together and adding up
columns, she'd been hearing the story piecemeal for weeks
from Varda himself, and now she was spinning it out in the

proper order. About the major acquisitions in the twenties, for instance—the Rembrandt, the Assyrian reliefs, the Shakespeare folios, the lion's share of the china. Tailoring it to her audience, she dovetailed the money disbursed on black market art with the Bel-Air land Varda was selling off in lots for a profit of fifteen hundred, two thousand percent. At the same time, she worked in the highlights of the breakdown and long sedation of Frances Dean. It is like this in here, she seemed to say, because of what it was like out there in the house.

And when the story began to be about the people and not the things, Nick could see Rita sifting the human dilemma out of the catalogue. She caught the thread of the other diary Varda never wrote down. And Nick saw for the first time who they were, the ghosts who haunted Crook House. Sometimes, Rita said, the hopheaded Frances was probably well enough to take a turn with Varda through the house. Now and then, leaning on his arm and gliding in the garden, she must have seemed once more the dreamy girl who'd been in movies. He was forever giving her presents, whenever she was alert enough to hold one in her hands. Here, Frances, have a Degas. Have a Tiffany bracelet. A sky blue dish from China. Anything she'd like, just to keep her here in the outside world. And she must have smiled a mile-wide smile from a silent from time to time, delighted by his attentions. To get through to her, Rusty Varda was glad to buy more and more. A daze was better than nothing. Most of the time, after all, she lay in her room, hospital-quiet, whistling through her lips from the bottom of the ocean.

"It went on like that for twenty years," Rita said admiringly, as if she was impressed by anyone who could stand time on its head like an hourglass, over and over, keeping things the same.

"Why?" Nick asked. He seemed to want to hear a moral purpose, suspecting none at hand.

"Because they loved each other, I guess. Well, *he* loved *her*."

"But it sounds so sad."

"Does it? I thought so too, at first, and now I don't." But she said it quickly, not expecting to be agreed with and anxious to get on. She cares too much, Nick thought. She appeared to believe that what it all came to—the secret room in the hill—was so outrageous it made all the rules. So what, Rita seemed to say, so what if she was drugged up in a stupor and the stuff was all stolen? *Look* at it. But then why was she breaking it up? She got quite grave when she told him the next step, the sending things back to their proper places. In part, perhaps, she was ashamed to be giving away goods that might by law be Nick's and Peter's. As to the contradiction, loving it so much and at the same time taking it apart, it didn't seem odd to her. Varda had reached a romantic pitch as acute as *Anna Karenina*, and now it was time to take down the set. Rita was a great believer in things in their own time.

"Of course," she said, "I don't give a real return address, so I don't know what happens when something arrives. I even go to different post offices." She got up from the desk, as if leaving the figures behind her, and went to the ice-white silk divan to sit down. "The only thing I've heard is a little paragraph in the *Times* this week, about a Toulouse-Lautrec that went back to the Detroit Museum. They had a reward of a thousand dollars, and they didn't know who to send it to. I don't care. I don't want it. Somebody ought to give me a government grant to buy stamps, but that's all."

Then silence. It was Nick's move. "I'm calling the cops," it just might be, or "You're making this up," or "You need help." She'd said too much, she knew it—she'd left him with nothing to add or ask. He's going to try to be nice, she thought with a pang, and all the while he'll be throwing me out of the house. And for the first time she wondered: Would I prefer it if he got mad? She had a sudden picture of him throwing plates at her off the stone table, like a juggling act gone mad. Meanwhile, it was next to impossible to sit there plainly on the sleek divan looking spiritual, like Marie Antoinette awaiting the verdict, because she was up to her hips in silk cushions and felt like a tart. She should have stayed at the desk. In any case, she wouldn't have believed what Nick was thinking.

Whew, he said to himself as he watched Rita's face. Who would have guessed there was so much story blowing about in Crook House? Something as flat as that, as uninvolved and empty of judgment. Not unmoved, though, by Varda's courting of Frances Dean, and properly reeling from the magnitude of the loot. Nick was nevertheless more riveted by Rita than by anything else. She's as lost in this as I am in Sam, he thought, and then he revised his opinion of a minute before that she'd gone too far. Compared with Sam, none of this was a bad thing. No one got hurt, either then or now, and now it was just a public works project, like planting trees by the freeway. Nick wished he had one of his own. No wonder she's not distracted half the time, he thought, like I am—her secret place isn't a fantasy. His sudden picture of her was, by contrast to hers, as calm as a Dutch interior—a row of windows sending in bright light, and Rita there in a white silk dress, holding real things in her hand. Not a single cowboy going up in smoke.

"Well?" she asked, breaking his reverie, as if to say how long was she supposed to wait.

"But why are you so sad?" he asked her back. He was confused. Didn't the treasure make her happy?

"I'm not so sad," she said, more angry than not, now that she thought of it.

"Maybe it's me. You looked a little hangdog when you went off to make the phone calls for the party."

"What do you want me to say, Nick? I was sorry we couldn't spend the day together."

She was crystal clear. It wasn't what she had in mind, but she'd talk about this if she had to. *She* didn't bring it up.

"Oh," he said. "Well, so was I." And he thought: Hold it, I'm two steps behind and making an ass of myself. I'll catch up in a minute.

"Okay, so we're both sad. Poor us. Let's drop it."

"Are you mad?" he asked, still trying to gain time. Of *course* she was mad, but he hadn't a clue why.

"Only because I don't think we'll get anywhere talking about it."

"About what?" he asked, wincing now.

"Us," she said between her teeth, so slowly it ended in a long hiss. "How Rita feels about Nick."

At last he got it. For a moment more he tried to duck it, but it didn't work—there was too much evidence falling all over itself in the wings like a troupe of clowns, waiting to tumble on. The last sixteen days, for instance, went down like a row of dominoes. Rita was his safety zone. While he rode out the hairpin turns of his feelings for Peter and Sam, he came back day after day to Rita, to steady himself. He was about to go sprawling. He'd tripped, he was in the air, and he thought in the long, drowning man's moment before he hit the earth: I've gone crazy. Anyone else would have known by now, but not Nick, because loving had driven him crazy. And he turned on himself the moral rage he took such care to spare others— you're no damn good, he thought, and you've thrown your life away on cheap little sideshows. The human things that were really happening went on and on without him. That, at least, is what the dread in his heart was signaling. But there was something else—though he might have denied it, too, if he hadn't been locked up here—please, he thought, I don't want to give this up yet. As if anything would listen to *him* anymore.

"Just now," he said, swallowing hard, as if his throat were sore from a sudden draft, "I can't think of anything nice you might be feeling."

"Oh, it's not that bad," she said. She wasn't agreeing, she didn't mean him. She meant that she wasn't so far gone, that her heart was more her own than not.

"What are we going to do?"

"How will we go on, you mean." She was following it all far better than he. Let her decide, he thought, because I've fucked it up enough. Whatever she wants. "The same as usual," she said. "I'm not going to corner you in empty rooms and tear off my clothes. Now's my chance, and look how pure of heart I am. I figure, even if we did it, if we ran away to Reno and made it legal, I'd still get over you after a while." She leaned back on the sofa—sank in, really—and put her arms wide along the tops of the cushions. The flare-up was over. "We ought to know when we're both well off," she said with a light laugh. She smiled so winningly that even Nick couldn't say for sure she'd been so sad. If we can just incorporate this, she seemed to say, in our easy way with each other, and laugh and tease and agree and agree, it will all go away. What she said next was born of irony, not heartache, and she did a small lift of her shoulders as if to laugh it off, even as she said it. "I'm a little in love with you is all."

"I didn't know."

"So I've gathered."

"It's because of the last two weeks," he said, beginning to get the thread of an idea. We spent too much time together, I knew it, he thought, and what Rita was feeling was stress. Fixing the blame on the course of situations, he put the whole thing in its place.

"Not really, Nick," she said. "It's been so as long as I've been here. And it's funny, because Peter and I have always been attracted to opposites. I've done a big business in failures myself. Men who've lost their shirts, or men who've settled down to let their lives run out in crummy jobs and four walls in Long Island City. You're really not my type. But I saw you at the pool that day, your back was to me, and I thought: This one's the one. Even though I knew right then you were out of bounds. Does it make me sound like a nut? It's probably never happened to you."

"You're wrong." It happens all the time, he wanted to say, except it sounded so condescending. Sam was only his most fatal case of it. But its happening more than once didn't make him better at it, needless to say. He took no shortcuts through the miseries.

He stood up to go now, cutting it short for her sake. There was no point in making a spectacle of Rita's feelings, now that he'd caught the drift. He had his own thinking to do, to make things right again if he could, and he thought he should leave her here by herself and thus let her know the room was hers and the secret safe with him. She stood up at the same time, to bustle about and prove she was a survivor. She meant to turn over the diary and accounts, for Peter and Nick to study at leisure. From now on, she thought, she was only an interim curator. They both stood up, then, to change the subject. If there had been a Rusty Varda masterpiece at hand—the little Rodin study for Atlas was on the desk, along with a folder of Napoleon's letters, and the porcelain was visible out of the corners of their eyes, just out of reach—they might have fallen into a chat about art like a couple of tourists. But they were suddenly face to face and, like children warned against breaking a thing that is doomed the moment they're warned, they fell into each other's arms.

They had so many motives they practically canceled each other out. He held her first to let her know he didn't run from love. As for Rita, she wanted to put it across that she loved him the other way, too—the painless way. They met in the center of the room like the best of friends, a stone's throw from the outside world. They were guarded by a flame-colored cousin of the hawks that stood sentry over the bones of pharaohs. It was more than they had a right to hope for, so soon after such thin ice. But they had forgotten something. She had been, some two and a half months now, out of the ball game. For sixteen days, Nick had been married to Peter till death do them part. Nick had admitted it early on to Rita, and vice versa: They were neither of them very good at avoiding sex. So the hug that told them they each had a friend went off on its own and floated free, and their motives took a turn for the worse. He embraced her in case she was feeling meaningless in a houseful of men who were stuck on men. She drew him just as close to prove she was a woman, no matter what the odds. They kissed at the same time. Neither did it first.

And they might have stopped cold if the terrible reasons had taken root, because he wasn't really being nice and she wasn't really being tough, and they could both spot a lousy fuck a mile off. On the other hand, they'd been through all the high-minded hugging they needed. So when they pulled apart to come up for air and looked each other over, they might well have decided to quit while they were ahead. They'd done enough acting in bed to last them a lifetime. But by the time they had it in mind to object and go separate ways, their objections no longer applied. In the last two minutes, they had already changed again—their footwork got fancier with the years—and they saw it in each other's eyes. They'd confessed to each other at the beginning that sex was something apart, or sometimes life was and sex wasn't, but they knew what they were talking about. They'd both done it a lot *outside* themselves—that is, it either brought them outside while they did it, as if on wheels, or it drew them outside to do it. So why not put it to the test?

Well, why not, indeed, they decided as they moved to their buttons and zippers. But it was more than that. It dawned on them both at the same time that the easy way they had with one another—casual, guileless, undefined—reminded them of what they felt in bed when love was easy. Easy? Once again, *they* knew what they meant. It was the one-shot lovers—no past, no future—that made them who they were. By means of things of the moment, they saw into the long, long time they lived with themselves alone. What if it's all a delusion? they tended to think in a panic, but by then they were always half in, half out of their clothes, and for the moment their bodies were more insistent than their souls.

Rita let her Irish sweater fall to the floor. Nick undid the front of his flannel shirt and pulled the shirttail out of his pants. If he can't get it up, she thought, I won't even bat an eyelash. I can make love on a Saturday, can't I? he reasoned with himself, and not dredge up the women I used to fail by feeling nothing. Rita and Nick got naked at the same rate of speed, and it had its mysterious side, since they let each other see—in the momentary pauses, the lift of the eye, the faintly smutty cool—exactly what they were like when they went this far. A composure to match the sharpened, concentrated

light of the two candles came upon them with each revelation
—her breasts one minute, his cock the next—and they seemed
as tranquilized as fashion models, as loose inside their bodies,
but selling more than clothes. And with their combined experience, they didn't take each other's measure stupidly.
Though he hardly ever saw anything else in LA above a certain altitude, Nick didn't think skin-and-bones and gold
jewelry was the only way a woman was beautiful. Rita's full
body, the pale of her skin and its swell into roundness, praised
nature for extravagance and luxury. As for Rita, Nick was
almost too chiseled by his years at the gym, his tight skin slick
as a magazine, but she found him touching when he acted like
a cowboy, as if he were dancing and stealing looks at his feet.
They trusted what each other saw. They didn't desire each
other's body, it seemed, half so much as they did the chance to
show who they were.

They stood there utterly at ease, surprised perhaps to be in
it so deep. But if it was the last chance to reconsider that
stretched the moment out, they didn't give it the time of day.
They took their last clear look at each other. Then she came
back into his arms again, and they kissed so slowly that for a
while they were almost motionless. He stroked her hips with
the palms of both hands, then brought them around to the
front of her thighs. She swayed a little. She seemed to hold the
whole of his back in her own open hands, and she felt she
could grip him like the bar of a trapeze, lifting off from the
ground and swinging free. For years each had been the one
who kissed the most, and together they got as serious with
their tongues as players in the finals of a game. I'm still here,
Nick thought, who almost never was after a certain point, and
glad of it for letting him stay with her. Every few moments,
of course, it hit Rita like a brick: I can't take it, I don't *want*
to fuck, I'll hate you, wait and see. Because she wanted him
and not it, she thought. But then it passed, and she laughed far
off in her secret heart for getting overwrought like a girl in a
house on a moor. No big deal, as Nick always said when he

planted his feet on the ground. They were making love in order *not* to be so bloody serious.

By the time they decided to head for the sofa, the critical thing was genitals. They'd kept hands off so far. He wasn't so hard. She could tell by where it fell along her belly what its tension was, but she held off from going first for fear of seeming impatient. His one hand on her breast was lovely, the nipple between two fingers, but the other hand, grazing back and forth so close to her clitoris it felt like a dream just out of her grasp, would not light. The silence was getting thick. So they broke away and turned to the nearest thing they had to a bed, just to keep moving. For a moment he had one arm around her, and her head was on his shoulder.

"*Other* people would say we're nuts," she said, sitting down, lying back. She talked as if they were still all dressed and weighing their options. But she opened her arms and smiled, too, as if she listened to herself with only half an ear.

"People like Peter and Hey?" He sank down on his knees in the cushions, between her legs.

"Oh, no. People in general."

"Would they? They don't fuck at all, do they?" He scratched his chest as he smiled back. They both seemed to recover something by having something to say. They'd be all right because they weren't going to get lost, either of them. In the pauses they learned they had nothing to prove. While he talked, he brushed at the thick hair at his breastbone with the tips of his fingers. She wasn't accustomed to men who touched themselves well, and she gave him another star in her book.

"No," she said, "but—" and couldn't think of a thing people in general had that she didn't. She was all set. As she'd said on the way to the plane in the middle of January, when she waved good-bye to her last Checker cab at Kennedy, she was through falling apart, period. Other people were nice and all, and she was sure the fucking they did was the Garden of Eden to them. She silently sent them all a dozen roses, but otherwise she was glad to be on her own. There were too many doors

long shut between them and her, she decided, for their opinions
to stick. Besides, nobody was nuts who could make it across
the hundred dozen thresholds of Rita's last ten years and still
find a friend inside.

"What about all this treasure, Nick?" she asked, struck by
an obscure thought that they could get it over with in a
second.

"Do what you have to," he said. "I don't want it."

It may have been someone else's cue, but the parrot took it.
He left his perch in the outer closet and flew through the
room. He didn't make a sound, even when he landed, and they
wouldn't have known he was there except for the flash of
color that shot across the dark in his final swoop. They turned
in time to see him disappear behind a Japanese screen in the
corner. He may have come like a curse, of course, to announce
to Nick that it didn't matter if he didn't want the Varda
riches—they had to be dealt with, now that the seals were off,
or they would bury him under the avalanche of their destiny.
Or it may have been a purely sexual flourish, the parrot's
flight, to warn them both of the jungle wet and the choke of
vines they were headed into. Or why not for once a good
omen, ripe with the tropical sleep at the edges of which sex
grew like wildfire, pineapple cider and macaroons instead of
the stinging flies and forest rot? They were both surprisingly
happy to see him. It didn't do on a desert island to get uptight
about the native fauna. It led you to things.

"What's he doing, catching a mouse?"

"No, that's owls you're thinking of," Rita said. "He's looking after the stuff. It's in his blood."

"How do *you* know?"

"Machu Picchu," she said, as if it were an old Peruvian
proverb she'd learned in her cradle. Nick looked bewildered
and would have pursued it, but the echo shook it into place.

"Machu Picchu," squawked the parrot behind the screen of
irises and moss, answering promptly. It was the only time he'd
ever done a trick, as far as they knew, if a trick was what it
was. It sounded like a coincidence.

"See?" she said. "There's nothing new under the sun. It's all very ancient, everything around us."

"You sound like Hey," Nick said, a little as if it might be catching. "He says we all got started in ancient Greece."

"Not me. I just got started a few weeks ago. *We're* not ancient."

"What are we then?"

"We're the middle of the afternoon," Rita said mildly. She reached up both hands and felt at the head of his cock with her fingertips, more than ever as if she were opening a safe. He was so stiff that he took a deep breath when the pressure sent him up. Though the candle was way over on the desk, he could see her clearly, because the white silk reflected its light like the moon. The parrot fluted a night noise behind the screen. If Nick could have spoken just then about why it worked out, he would have said, all jaunty: We did away with the sad part. Maybe, maybe not. They did find a way to spend the day together, which said a lot about their getting what they wanted. And they had to now or never. Today was their last chance.

Chapter 7

"But I *like* clutter," Peter snapped into the phone. "Clutter is what I *do*. If you want a lot of empty spaces, honey, you want someone else."

And he put the receiver back in the cradle neatly, not making a noise, as if he wasn't going to be pushed into a temper. He turned to Rita, who looked up at last from her own worktable. She had just pulled the two oddest colors out of a photograph of a Pakistani rug they'd bought at an auction in La Jolla to put in a house on Mulholland Drive. A purple dark as eggplant and a green like celery. The rug was mostly rust and yellow. You couldn't even see Rita's two colors in the photograph, but Rita had been down on all fours on the rug itself, on the day of the sale, and she knew what knots of color made up the dark medallions in the pattern. Peter, who meant to go right on complaining about the heiress in Manhattan Beach he'd just hung up on, took a deep breath and said, "Holy shit," by way of transition. But when he saw the two squares of fabric in her hand—*chintz*, for God's sake, and purple and green—he flew to her side for a different tantrum.

"What the hell are you doing? Everything has to be beige in Teddy's house, Rita. Colors make him depressed. His parents used to feed him crayons when he was naughty or something. Let me do it."

"Do what, Peter?" she asked sweetly. Then she appealed to reason, her voice like Valium, but all the same she made it do a parody of Peter's rattled state. "So Miss Bank Account thinks you've bought things too big for her little rancho, but is that a good excuse to butt in on my room for Teddy Dray?"

"But you're not listening, Rita. He thinks *brown* is too much color."

"I know. He's putting all that behind him. We reached an understanding."

No question about it, they'd had nothing but trouble in the three days Peter had been back. During all the time he was cooped up in his bedroom, Rita had made a daily report, and together they'd succeeded in putting the lion's share of the current projects into suspended animation. Most of Peter's clients were so cowed by his ruthless search for the truth in their living rooms and so well-trained for delays that they were half grateful to the snake for giving them a respite. Those others who could not live without Peter turned on Rita as if *she* were the snake. They professed to be lost in their own homes like a maze, reduced to tea and toast because they couldn't get around alone. Somehow, though, they gathered the necessary strength to shriek at Rita daily over the phone, demanding things they wouldn't have dreamed of bothering Peter with. And now that Peter was back, he had to have lunch three times a day, from twelve till nearly four, to accommodate the most well-heeled, whose houses were all they had.

Peter complained that they tore him apart, and he always reserved the right to give it all up and go be a shepherd, but Rita knew he really preferred it mad in the shop. He'd dug his own grave this week, after all, by having the party, because he'd made a hundred promises in one night's revels. There were people who wouldn't have known the difference if he'd started back gradually and given himself a couple of weeks to make his rounds. But Sunday night, stoked on the speed of things in Crook House, they had to shout to be heard above the beat from the speakers, and what they wanted was Peter now. Rita got out of the way. It was a relief to pick up the second fiddle again. And yet, as she could see this morning, taking her stand on eggplant and celery, nothing ever went back to being just the same. Inevitably, some of the clients were comfortable with Rita in the house, and they saw no reason to keep pleading for time with Peter and leaving their names and numbers. They decided to forego the master and the chance of media coverage and make do with the winsome shopgirl in the Joan Crawford suits. And Peter was furious.

He didn't say so. He may not even have known it. Rita didn't think he was jealous, didn't see how he could be, since he'd been turning people away at the door for months. It wasn't that he wanted more, or even that he had to have it all, like a king who can't delegate power, driven to drink by details. Mostly, she decided, Peter suffered here from the difference in their attitudes. She kept as madly busy as he—they both required it instead of sleep, which they did only if there was *nothing* left to do, and they dropped—but being busy didn't enervate Rita or test her temper. Peter, who generally couldn't cope if he wasn't knee-deep in refinements, wasn't toughened by things going wrong with people's upholstery. He raged at the loss of quality in first-class life like an old nobleman who'd lived too long at court. Rita considered it a miracle—well, a victory at least, of money over time—when anything worked all the way to the end. So she was very philosophical about the minor squabble and disarray. She was just the person Peter needed.

"Am I a bitch," he asked with some distaste, "or am I a bitch? You're right, you mustn't put up with me. My *mind* is cluttered."

"Oh, but I like clutter," she said, surprised to hear him so much bothered. She hadn't picked up the one other thing from his nagging and hovering that would have raised her protective instinct. The very people who wanted her working for them, who threw out their beiges for her like dowdy old clothes, were Peter's first customers, the people who'd taken their chance on him before he made it. The stars who hired him now, hiring one of their own, took no chance at all.

"I don't deserve you," Peter said, moving to the refrigerator between their two heaped-up tables where they pushed their work around. Hey sent down provisions from Crook House on Mondays and Wednesdays, cheese and fruit and rolls, smoked salmon, a jug of iced coffee. Peter poured out a glass of coffee, creamed and sugared it, and stirred it with a glass rod as he talked on. "Remind me to give you a raise. We also have to hook you up with a retirement plan. You've got to get your *perks*, Rita. You're almost forty, and you don't have any perks. What do you want?"

"Nothing," she said politely, looking off through the shop and out the window at the traffic. It was not precisely true. She wanted a call from West Covina, way off in the middle of nowhere.

"You'll think of something," he said, as if she hadn't answered at all. The stirrer clinked against the glass. "Don't you want a promotion?"

"You mean a title?" she asked, coming back into the room again, leaning back in her Italian chair. "Sure. Vice-president in charge of consumer affairs."

"I mean we could put our names together," he said, "with a slash down the middle. Put up a sign and everything." It sounded almost like a dare. They knew they weren't ready to be partners yet, but it was his way of telling her he'd given up some territory. Neither his nerves nor his ego, he promised between the lines, were going to jeopardize her future. Stars ate up little stars for breakfast, as they both were well aware. But not us, Peter was saying.

"Why don't we see," she said, "when the time comes?" A little too evasive, perhaps, but she turned quite pink at the same time. Peter was satisfied.

"Now I have something to show you," he said, "so close your eyes. It's sort of a present, except you can't keep it."

Everything he did had a set of formalities. She winked at him and swung the chair a hundred and eighty degrees and faced the wall. Faced an Andy Warhol poppy, in fact, framed in yellow chrome. Her mind went like the click of a switch to the big Monet she'd crated up, a field of red flowers done in 1919, when everything but color had gone out the window. He gave it to the doctor who took care of his eyes, whose children sold it to a French racketeer for a song before he was cold. The racketeer sold it to one of Rusty Varda's agents, so it was the first thing Rita had turned up that was legitimate. They could keep it. But she'd right away tracked down the little museum in the Sixteenth in Paris where the mass of the late work went, and she was mailing it to them. As for the poppy, she hardly saw it. She couldn't look at anything much without making connections back to the secret room. It had come to be her memory bank.

"Peek," Peter commanded her. And she let the whole construction of this against that fly out of her head as she spun around again. Propped on her table, wildly out of place, was the Fabergé frame. And the picture inside, snapped out of time by a stray and accidental lens, was as real as a held breath, more so because of the gold and jewels around it. Peter and Rita and Nick were standing in a circle laughing. At first she thought it must be the party Sunday night, because people were milling around, but it took only a moment for her to have the horrors about her clothes. When, she thought in a tailspin, had she looked as bad as that?

"Don't you remember, Rita? It's the party at Jennifer's. The day you arrived."

"Oh, my God," she said, her heart going out to all of them. "What are we laughing at?"

"Everybody else, of course." And for a moment they stared at it in silence, heads to one side, pensive as people must have been when the frame was filled with a Grand Duchess, long ago in the old world. Peter spoke up again. "They certainly look like three of a kind, don't they?"

"Yup. And they don't look like they'd hurt a fly. Someone ought to let them run a small country."

"But they already do," he said.

And they left it at that. It made them feel more emotional things as well, with music they could dance to cheek to cheek, but they steered clear of putting it into words. They always had, about loving each other at least. Peter left the photograph on Rita's table and drifted off into the shop, killing the time before his first lunch. Rita put the chintz and the picture of the rug in an envelope, marked it "Teddy," and dropped it on the nearest pile. It would be lost in the shuffle in a matter of hours. But it was the closest thing to filing Rita could manage, even if it meant a furious search in a few days when she needed it. What next? She attacked a folder of out-of-stock memos from manufacturers, dreading the calls she would have to make to clients, who had to be told they'd have to find something else. But she wasn't getting her paperwork done to be saintly. She was waiting, one eye on the clock and one line open, for the call from the hospital in West Covina. When Peter left, she thought, she'd transfer the photograph over to his table. It wasn't in her way. She wasn't afraid of it. But as with the Varda treasure, she was shut in with something else just now. It was touch and go, in fact—as the hands of the wall clock came together at noon like tweezers, pinching time, she knew that the call she expected and Peter's leaving for lunch were neck and neck.

The phone rang. Lose one turn, she thought. She picked it up and strangled the ring in the middle. When she said hello, she noticed Peter turn his head to listen, looking up from moving a chair closer to a potted plant by fractions of an inch.

"Yes, it is," Rita said quietly. Peter stopped listening as soon as he could hear that it wasn't for him, but he still might finish fidgeting and come within earshot before she was done. "I understand, Mr. Webber," she said. "I know just what to expect." Suddenly Peter was calling her over as if he didn't even remember she was on the phone. He was standing at the chair, peering at it as if there was something spilled on the silk. "Of course," Rita said, "fifteen minutes will be fine." Peter called louder and looked up angrily. When he saw she was still busy, he picked up the chair in one hand and headed in her direction. "Please understand, Mr. Webber, it's my last chance. I'll take what I can get." She spoke as neutrally as a disembodied voice in an airline terminal. "I'll be there at three," she said, and then hung up.

"Rita, why is this chair only four twenty-five? People will think they've wandered into Sears. Change the tag to seven fifty."

"Okay, Pete," she said, reaching for a pen. "I know we have to do our part in the fight against inflation."

"Who was that?"

"On the phone? Nobody."

"Oh. I have to go now. You know what I was just thinking? The first time I was ever really happy was the night we had dinner at '21.'"

"You're kidding," she said as she made out the tag. She remembered it as if it were yesterday, mostly because it was awful. Ten or twelve years ago. She and Peter and a man named Jerry, whom she couldn't recall beyond the smug little smile he wore in fancy places. It was going very badly, anyway, but she figured to set herself up with a *really* swanky dinner before she finished him off. Somehow she'd arranged to have Peter included. She looked up now from tying the tag on the chair's spine, wondering if the past had played another joke. She ticked off the facts. "All I remember is that he wouldn't let us order for ourselves. He sent the wine back. He made a remark about how we didn't have much to compare the place with and he did. And he didn't leave a tip." Then she shrugged as if to say: How do you get happy out of that?

"Really?" Peter said, smiling in disbelief. He either didn't recall what she was saying or didn't use the past in quite the same way. "They could have served us tuna fish, for all I cared. I just kept thinking how I'd *arrived*. I hadn't, of course, not for keeps. I had to go back to eating on earth with everyone else the next day. But I sat there and looked around at all those classy people, and I finally got over my grandfather's curse. He thought everything after Russia was shit. But I finally saw that for some people things were better than ever. That was the night I decided that money could make you happy."

"It sounds like a religious experience," she said. She stood up, and they carried the chair between them back into the shop proper, where everything gleamed and posed, ready at the drop of a hat to double in price. It was very still and very clean, as if the furniture itself found the thought of customers distasteful. They came well-screened, by appointment only. Rita plunked the chair down next to the plant, and Peter eyed it suspiciously, ready to fidget again. But he made no move. Apparently Rita had put it just where it ought to be.

"Well, does it?" she asked him.

"Does what?"

"Money make you happy."

"Oh, who knows," he said, dismissing it now. It was only a road through a boy's small town. Rita walked him to the door and decided to drop it and let him go. Money wasn't really what he meant. She knew it was more the feel of the best. Peter would have been just as glad if going first-class were free, and he didn't care if everyone had a piece. Money to him was not the means of protection and isolation, and thus it never crossed his mind to want a room like Scrooge McDuck's. What made him happy was nice things, and as for money pure and simple, that was all in people's heads.

"Happy I don't trust," Peter said, opening the door and closing it again, because he wasn't finished. It was as if he'd followed her train of thought. "That's what people used to be in my grandfather's day, and it made them dopey and got them pumped by a firing squad. What I want to be is"—and he widened his eyes and held his breath for a philosophical breakthrough, then went on—"okay. That's all."

"Well," she said, "don't worry. You're okay."

"Nick's come back, you know."

"I'm glad."

"I still don't know where he's been. And whoever it was, they must have gone easy on him, because he doesn't seem to hurt."

She felt a little woozy for a second, but held her ground. She didn't hurt, either, she would have said. What was strange was knowing more than Peter, about Sam first, and then about her and Nick on Saturday. Peter didn't know it, but *she'd* come back, too. Not all the way yet, and not from the same place, and not to him, but she was three days full of her own free world and getting better and better.

"Nick's okay, too," she said.

"We all are. I have the pictures to prove it." He winked. He opened the door for real and slipped out, and she watched him bound across the curb to his car like Gene Kelly, wild with anticipation, as if a slew of lunches were a polo match or a fox hunt. But he stopped in his tracks. Something had dawned on him, and he sang out, "Rita!" She stuck her head out. He turned around again, and he looked forlorn and caught short, as if he were going to ask for carfare. His big gray Russian eyes, she thought, are so transparent. "I forgot to ask you," he said, "do you need me to do anything?"

"No. I'm taking the afternoon off."

"Terrific. Let the answering service run the place for a while. They'll get more done if we leave them alone. Go buy yourself something."

"Oh, do I have to," she said. And waving vaguely, she shut the door without even finding out. He thinks I work too hard, she thought as she walked back to her table and her list of things to do. Maybe she did, but she didn't mind. Four or five hours a day, eight or nine in a pinch like Peter's accident—

those were the hours she had to spare, and if she gave over another couple or three to Varda's room, even then she had enough time. She'd be better off in West Covina at three, she knew, because she was going to work till she had to leave, eating Hey's food right out of the tinfoil.

She moved the picture and gave it a last long look before turning away, and it still reminded her more of the party Sunday night than it did the far past when she'd first arrived. Luckily for this brief image, the three of them were laughing like old friends, but as a matter of fact they weren't then, not all three. Sunday night they were. All through the party, they darted back and forth like the Marx Brothers, aloft on a separate level of buzz and jazz from the eighty honored guests. They mugged each other from the middle of different conversations. And when they came together to huddle, they teased one another with the gossip they'd picked up, like kids with trading cards. Peter had it harder than Rita and Nick, because he was the star, so a lot of what went on among them privately was to keep him feeling easy. Hey, ordinary-looking except for a black sliver of eyeliner, glided up to them with a tray of canapés, and said, "If the three of you don't start behaving, you're not going to get invited out anymore." They chorused back, "Who cares?" And Peter said, "It only means more for us."

He gave a party like the Queen of Hearts. The delivery men had been in and out all day, bribed with steelworkers' wages to do it all day Sunday. The living room was reconceived in brilliant reds, with lacquered furniture and screens and lattices and, facing each other across a white sand garden, a pair of opium beds pillowed in peacock silk. What was taken out to make room had been redistributed around the house, adding to the clutter Peter did for a living, and some other things had found their way back to the shop. From where she sat now at her worktable, Rita could pick out chairs and sofa, a chest and a garden seat that had shaken off the air of home and taken on, along with prices that could bring on a nosebleed, the polish of custom goods. Nobody cared if a chair had done time in Crook House. Or no, Rita thought, that's not quite right. They cared like crazy. It was that they didn't consider it secondhand, a thing that had lost its newness and first-bloom flash. Because Peter had actually sat in it, included it once in the floor plan of his life, it got priceless fast, like Cardinal Richelieu's bed, or Carole Lombard's.

She wasn't all the way over Nick. Not the way he'd said he was over Sam, as if it were something not just done in the past and faded but done as well by someone he used to be for a little while who'd passed like a fad. Rita didn't push herself. It worked, thank God, in the secret room, and their making love, such as it was, took away a layer of poses that had run their course and at the same time called a spade a spade. She wasn't going to stop being drawn by certain types—she expected as much, and, if pressed, she took a little to be polite, a lot more if the type was human, too. But she didn't think love had anything to do with it. So all she had to do was get over *wanting* Nick. She could love him as much as she wanted, as long as she didn't mix him up with the class of lover that, take it or leave it, ended up in her bedroom.

And what about Rusty Varda and Frances Dean? Hadn't she cut out a valentine to put around their picture? Somehow it didn't seem like a contradiction to Rita. She still believed in the usual thing, to a point. Two people who were struck by the moon at the same time, maybe in the same dance hall, or like Garbo coming off the train through the steam, when she catches her first glimpse of the count—two people like that still went through love like visionaries on a quest. Rita allowed a little room just in case, with an attitude not unlike Pascal's wager about the slim chance for true love. It was Paradise enough if you could get it. Nevertheless, she declared herself through with being taken in by what her lovers *said*, this after so many years of men who thought they were telling the truth and always being nice. Rita wasn't looking now. Getting the wrong idea about Nick was a warning she didn't ignore. She'd fooled herself and gotten a knock and a couple of bruises and then come out the other side in one piece. She meant to stay that way.

Gee, she thought as she peeled off a couple of slices of red roast beef, I've gotten as hard as nails. She wondered if she even had it in her still to sob at the drop of a hat in a movie. Maybe she'd have to make do with less, with a lump in her throat and an aura of prickly heat behind the eyes. Now that she preferred her feelings in a different key, she was as partial as Hey to the notion of the three of them. And she had to admit, stealing a glimpse, that the picture was right for what they did best, standing in a circle laughing, clustered about with pearls and jewels. All the same, she knew she couldn't stay on much longer at Crook House. She would have found a place of her own already if it hadn't been for the work to do in the treasure room. The three of them, she thought, had a fifty-fifty chance of remaining what they were, but only if the pressure was off from too much forced togetherness. She didn't have the same good cheer about desert islands as she did about country houses looming in English parks—with the latter, at least, you often got a town house thrown in in Belgravia, so that Monday to Friday you lived in the world, and weekends alone in Utopia.

What do you suppose we are? she asked herself idly, arranging raw vegetables on a bed of lettuce as if it were going to be photographed. Not a family. The mere idea made her queasy. Not a ménage à trois, she was pretty sure, though here she wasn't certain how broad the term might be. She thought all three had to fuck with the other two to qualify, and, technically, didn't they mostly do it in the same bed at the same time? If Peter and Rita and Nick were something else again, it got its character from what they broke down to, which was two plus one. Looked at that way, she reasoned, Peter and Nick were the title bout, the star-crossed pair, the group of two that Freud, in the dryest remark of the twentieth century, called a marriage. Rita had nothing to do with it. Part of what they were as a trio, then, was as the bearers of a sort of irrelevance one to another. Or are there three of us, she thought flippantly, because you need at least three to keep one honest? Not that anyone cared if you were honest, and knowing that, you had to either laugh or cry, and you needed three to laugh as well. One to tell the joke and two to hold their sides and whinny. Two because an audience of one was not enough for comedy. One would always laugh to be polite.

But who knows for sure, she wondered at last, staring at the plate with a sudden loss of appetite. She might be all wrong about the three of them, in which case she'd better work it all out tomorrow and make it make sense. Right now she couldn't be bothered. Rita was down to the wire. She still had dozens of major works to get rid of out of the room behind the mirror, but she had a thing to do at three that superseded everything else. It had come out of nowhere and pulled the last three days right out from under her. But she'd known as soon as she made the connection that she couldn't back out of it. It called for hair-trigger timing. She'd pulled apart Aladdin's cave, and now she had to face the genie.

Hey had let it out. When the party was all over and the caterers had left and Nick and Peter had staggered up to bed, she stood in the kitchen and did a double check while Hey counted the silver and tied it up in black felt pouches. When did Frances Dean get bundled out of Crook House for good? she asked him. Forty-three, forty-four, he wasn't certain which. And where did they take her? West Covina. Where was that? Out Route 10, in the middle of nowhere. Why so far? Publicity. They both were talking to pass the time. She wouldn't even have said that Frances Dean was on her mind, though she must have been, what with the party and all. As she and Hey chatted, Rita had begun to think Frances Dean would have fit in nicely in a catered crowd in evening dress, lying back in a vamp's repose on an opium bed—white skin, skimpy dress, no makeup except a smear of red on the lips, the blue-gray circles under the eyes. No one would have guessed it, but a part of Rita identified with the tale of Frances Dean. The helpless girl with the saucer eyes and needle tracks was at the mercy of things, like Rita used to be when she was in love. Listless, given to dreaming, caught without past or future. Frances Dean had engineered her very own silent film to live in. So had Rita, and the only difference was that hers at least had been a serial, an episode at a time, with breathing room in between. Frances's went on and on, the theater darkened day and night.

"When did she die?"

"Hmm," Hey said, as if it was less and less familiar ground. "In the mid-fifties, I think. Yes, that's right." After a certain point, he seemed to say, his memory got sketchy. That didn't register to Rita. She pressed on because she assumed he *had* to know the whole story. Anyone in Hey's position, she knew, would automatically have been splicing together the inches of film that Varda told from time to time about his grandest passion. Besides, she knew Hey didn't miss a trick. Just like her.

"Where's she buried?" Rita asked. It went one of two ways, she was thinking as she sorted two dozen demitasse spoons into slots of felt. They either freighted a movie star back to his old hometown to lie in a grassy yard with a picket fence, or they consigned him to oblivion in a corner of Forest Lawn or Hollywood Memorial, where the big names got the same top billing as ever. Rita was just asking. She wasn't a visitor of graves. She didn't care, which is why she was taken aback by the turn in Hey's mood.

"Why do you want to know so much?" he asked in a sort of quiet fury. "Can't you leave it alone?"

Her mouth dropped open. It was all so safely far in the past, she'd thought, that she couldn't imagine anyone wounded by it still. But a picture popped into her head of Varda and Frances Dean, buried side by side in a corner of LA nobody went to, and only Hey to mourn them and leave an occasional bunch of violets. Under a freeway or something. She looked over at him, and she wondered at last about the secrets he kept. He always seemed to tell everything.

"I'm sorry, Hey," she said, putting out a hand and touching

him lightly on the arm. "I go on and on about Rusty Varda, and I forget that for you it's not just a story."

"It's not that, Rita," he said with a shake of his head. "You don't *want* to know it all. I'd tell you, but you know what would happen? All those pretty movies you have of the two of them would disappear"—and he snapped his fingers an inch from her nose—"like that! It's not a story at all. People change."

Oh, my God, Rita thought, she's still alive. And before she could say a thing, she begged the powers that be not to kill her off before Rita got to her, just for the sake of irony. I'm the one she's been waiting to talk to, Rita thought, the only one since Varda who knows who she is. Hey was saying what they always say when the stakes double: Be satisfied with what you've got. And Rita thought: I will be, once I've seen her.

People change, she warned herself as often as she thought of it after that. She said it again in the shop. She pushed away the lunch she'd only scratched the surface of. She picked up the phone and dialed the man who did their indoor plants. She'd be twenty minutes with him, then ten apiece with the three or four clients who needed daily care. That left her a half hour to stop off at a post office on the way with the Goya etchings on the folly of war. Don't expect a thing in West Covina, she told herself. Just go on with what you're doing. Hey had told her how bad it was, but she went ahead and set it up anyway, trying not to care too much. She was feeling too good after Saturday afternoon and Sunday night not to risk it. From where she sat at the table, she could hear the three of them laughing behind her in the picture. Not *at* her. They were trying to keep her spirits up, because at three she had to go visit a kind of grave. As she said hello to the plant man, she swung her chair around again and saw what it was like when it was easy. It suddenly seemed a million miles away.

The dealer's rep delivered the green MG to Nick's office in Beverly Hills at nine o'clock. He wasn't meeting Sam till twelve, but pretty soon he couldn't stand it, sitting at his desk and staring out the window at it gleaming by the curb. While he cradled the telephone with his shoulder, he lobbed the ring of keys back and forth between his two hands and, without paying any attention, talked out a mortgage problem with a buyer, a seller, and a bank. At ten he chaired his Wednesday meeting with his staff. The four of them exploded into his office, deals coming out of their ears. Compared with them, Nick was calm as a Sufi, and he looked on them all benignly while the properties flew about the room, traded off and pyramided. The agents ran around the Monopoly board with ever greater speed and begged for the chance to set a price on anything with walls. Any of them could have sold the Brooklyn Bridge in a morning's work. Nick gave here and there a word of advice and privately thanked his stars he'd got them all working for him and didn't have to compete. And every few minutes he'd lose himself in the green MG that beckoned him out for a spin.

"Listen, Nick," said Charlie Burns, putting his hands down flat on the desk and leaning too far into Nick's airspace. "I've got a firm one-three on Lookout Grove."

"Not a chance," Nick said, steely-eyed for the moment. Charlie was the agent Nick kept on to remind him real estate was shitwork. He gave off an odor like the rusted underside of rotten cars. Peter refused to be in the same room with him. "One-eight is final."

"You'll never get it."

"Never is a long time, Charlie," he said, still tossing the keys. He kept Charlie Burns around for another reason too, so he could talk tough. The name's Lew Archer, lady—I've been in this town thirty-five years, and I never yet ate an orange off a tree. A million three, a million eight, it was all such hoodlum's language. "That's the top of the world up there," he said expansively. It was the top of Coldwater Canyon, anyway. "We don't dicker for the big ones. They want a grown-up's house, they got to pay a grown-up's price."

When it was over and they'd picked each other's pockets to find out who was winning, they tumbled out again to the four corners of the county, their blood up. Nick was free, and with a whole hour to kill, he headed out early. Free, he thought as he walked to the car, was not the right word. He'd taken off more time in the last month or six weeks because of Sam and then Peter than he had in the whole three years before. He knew he had to stop coasting and go out hunting, and he'd wondered for days if he still had it in him to hustle the same as ever. He had to, didn't he? Money cost more and more, after all. For the first time in his life, he considered taking stock. But not today. He wanted to finish it up right with Sam, and he wasn't going to skimp and try to fit it all in during his lunch hour. A new car had always been for Nick the perfect symbol for starting fresh, and before he gave this one away, he wanted some of the new rubbed off on him. He couldn't go back to a mere MG himself anymore, the LA status system in the four-wheel division being what it was. So he slung himself into the bucket seat to be innocent again, and the smell alone sent him back twelve years to the feel of his first new car. He looked down at the mileage, 3.6, and laughed out loud. Free was the word, all right.

He drove out Sunset to the beach, and though the Jag and the Mercedes could have probably passed him in third, it felt like eighty when he did forty-five. As he took the last long curves through Pacific Palisades, he realized he was on the route he always took for the maiden ride in his own cars. Sunset, with its turns and its country club terrain, was a very showy road, and the show was cars. Nick was twenty-three when he traded a '58 Chevy, two-toned, blue on white like a Chinese jar, for a '63 silver Tempest just off the line. He drove it around for days in a trance of pride, sending out a psychic beam up and down the roads he traveled: Look at me, look at me. Probably nobody did. For one thing, there were always more riveting cars on the road than this year's Tempest. Soon enough he came to see that that included the Jaguar and the Mercedes, too, all the way up the line. In any case, everyone was most possessed by only two cars, the one he had and the one he wanted next. Which, once Nick understood it, sent his innocence up in a cloud of smoke. But he'd say this much for cars: For a moment, at least, for the first long ride out Sunset, they gave it back to you again, which was more than he could say for the kind that disappeared with sex.

He turned north toward Malibu on the Coast Highway. The beach pads hung between the road and the water, elbow to elbow, and Nick could practically watch the prices going up like the rolling dollars on a gas pump. He'd had a place himself for a couple of years before he met Peter, and since it was only a few miles further along, he went faster. He just had time to take a quick look at it before he turned back to meet Sam in Santa Monica. The old house crossed his mind as a pair of numbers: sixty-five, the purchase price, and ninety, what he sold it for. As always, he shook his head and kicked himself, because he knew it went a year ago for two-oh-five. I wonder, he thought, if I've gotten as sleazy as Charlie Burns and don't even know it. Since when, for instance, did he start to see the whole bloody coast as pots of gold, as if he'd forgotten the broken hills and the ocean? Mile after mile, the houses lined up like the numbered lots at an auction. He didn't need a bit of it. He had the windows open, and the wind was in his hair. Buttoning up his lip like Gary Cooper, he thought with only half a smile: The thing about a cowboy is, wherever he rides, he owns it all. No call to act like a worrywart clerk whose head is stuffed with numbers. He convinced himself of everything. So he rose above the rut of money as he zipped along. Forgot, for the sake of the moment's innocence, that numbers turned him on.

It was up ahead. He signaled and made a turn in the driveway. They'd added a deck upstairs, he noted, and faced the wall on the highway with redwood planks, taking the windows away. Nick couldn't see in at all, and he didn't care. He literally only wanted a glimpse. He'd lived in fifteen different places in LA, moving like everyone else whenever the mood struck. If he was in the neighborhood, he touched bases at this one or that one. For him it was just like keeping a diary. In a moment he was heading back south to Santa Monica, all settled in for the flashbacks. He was straight when he bought into Malibu, gay when he sold out. He might have kept it forever, or at least until two-oh-five, except Peter got edgy so close to the ocean. Flipping the pages of an album in his head, Nick hardly recognized himself swinging back and forth—at the beginning, between a steady girl and a hustler once a week, and later on, Monday a man, a girl on Tuesday, and so on. Nobody left a name and number. Nobody was asked to.

And look at me now, he thought with equanimity. Now that I'm with Peter, I've stayed the same for the longest time so far. He used the past exclusively at times like this to congratulate himself. He knew it was bullshit. The lulling smell of newness in the car and the kick of it that took the years away were whistling in the dark. What was really going on all morning was his fear of Sam. He wouldn't own up to it because it was crazy. He'd said good-bye a hundred times before. And he used the car to mush around in the past because he didn't want to think too hard about why he found it suddenly expedient to say good-bye with flashy toys. He wasn't free or innocent at all. He wished he could have said he'd gone too far with Sam and gotten in too deep, but the dread he'd felt about today had nothing to do with second thoughts. It seemed as if it didn't matter what he did. The course of things had a mind of its own now. It wasn't going to stop till it was finished.

He left the highway and climbed the hill straight up to the cliffs that bordered Santa Monica at the ocean. They were meeting in a shelter in the park along the rim, and Nick wanted to leave the MG in plain sight so as to point it out, Exhibit A, at the right time. No hard feelings, Sam, okay? He saw the wooden shelter just ahead, an alley of royal palms going off on either side, no sign of Sam, and at that moment a van pulled out of a parking space, right where he wanted to be. So far, so good. He got out and locked it fast so he wouldn't start to practice what to say. But he took a last look over his shoulder as he walked away, to possess, one more time while it was still his, the past it reminded him of. When he sauntered across the grass to the shelter, an elaborate thing of two-by-fours that held up a shingled roof over a cluster of benches, he noticed the shuffleboard couples padding about, retired and arm in arm. They were all in civilian clothes, and they stared at him openly, probably because he was dressed to the teeth. He wore a pearl gray gabardine suit, Hong Kong shirt, Bond Street tie, and Gucci shoes—deliberately, it almost seemed. He was a long way away from the day he shucked his office clothes in the car to come to Sam on equal terms. Power, not sex, was what he was dressed for now.

He went through the shelter's arch to the ocean side, and there was Sam, leaning forward on his folded arms, on a fence post at the edge. The fence was chicken wire and sagged in places, but the drop-off was so sheer, the distance down so far, that it made its point.

"In the old days," Nick said, and all of a sudden Sam tensed and began to listen, but he didn't turn around, "when they needed to drive a car off a cliff in a movie, this is where they drove it."

"Did you used to come here and watch them when you were a kid?" Sam asked, in some ways the only nice thing he said the whole time, and *then* he turned around. The look on his face was so far off, so uninvolved, he might have been watching the ocean for hours and hours. "You should have been going to baseball games."

"It was before my time," Nick said. "I just heard about it." Varda was who he was thinking of, but Sam might not remember who that was. "How are you?"

"Fine. I'm always fine."

"Good. You want to go for a walk?"

"Why not?" Sam said with a shrug. "We've never done *that* before." Sparring now with everything he said, the look on his face was one thing. He *sounded* as if he wouldn't look at an ocean if you paid him. Nothing there. "So," he went on, "are you getting much?"

"I'm all right," Nick said, sidestepping the reference. "I'm too fucking busy is what it is. Sometimes I think we ought to start over out here and not let the land be owned at all. Squatter's rights. I get so sick of houses I want to live in a tent. In the mountains or something."

"Or on a ranch," Sam said. "With the boys. I bet you're so busy you haven't got *time* to get laid anymore. Isn't that right?"

Oh, please, Nick thought, not yet. Sam was upping the ante in irony, and Nick caught himself wanting time out, to change the tune before they said another thing. He was hit broadside by a wave of the pain he'd bought the MG to neutralize. He called it pain. Guilt was more like it. And irony was fine, he wanted to say, but couldn't they have it subtle and more ambiguous? Like a man being bested in a bargain, Nick had already given up the mood he *thought* they'd be able to do this in. He wouldn't admit it now, but he'd seen the two of them as if from the air, a couple of melancholy men on the cliffs, high above the lordly ocean, worlds apart. Like the clear-eyed lieutenant and the Polynesian girl in *South Pacific*. He scrapped it like a comic routine at a wake. Today is all we've got, he thought hopelessly, so why doesn't he see that what we do now is what we're left with? He'd never, like Rita, read Henry James straight through, but instinctively Nick fell into social forms and complicated manners. He favored ways of saying things that said at the same time: I love you, I hate you, don't leave me, good-bye forever. Who the hell did he think he was? Sam would have demanded if he'd known. He made it clear that the situation at hand wasn't designed to follow Nick's instincts.

"I know I should have called you," he began, but Sam interrupted before he got his excuses going.

"Like I always said, Nick, you don't have to call me at all. Unless you want to fuck. You get off on all these secret agent meetings, but for me it's just a run of red lights between here and West Hollywood."

"I just want to talk, Sam."

"Oh, I *know*. That's what I mean. I don't."

"I can't see you anymore."

"So what else is new?" He turned to Nick, and in the same

motion he cuffed Nick's shoulder with the back of his hand so
that Nick turned to him, too. We can't fight here, Nick
thought sensibly, or if he jumps me, a cop at least will break it
up. And Sam snapped out, "I can't see you either, baby. Get
it?"

"Sam, I don't want it to be this way."

"Oh? Just how *do* you want it to be?"

Fair enough. They stood face to face, and Nick wondered as
he looked into Sam's angry eyes, and then away, if they'd ever
locked eyes since the moment they met. They'd had to then, if
only to telegraph the terms of the contract, that they wanted
to fuck, that one would get paid. Essentially, from that point
on, there was no reason to. Nick didn't know what Sam used
to look at, but for weeks his own eyes, hungry for the whole
of the cowboy's body, had taken a million pictures of Sam in
motion, roused by everything he did. Nick hadn't had the
leisure to get lost in the meantime, fishing the deeps of the
boy's black looks. He was just as able to fall in love without it.

"I still care what happens to you," he said—staring over
Sam's shoulder out at the ocean, as a matter of fact. "I'd do
things for you, or I *would* have, but I knew you'd feel pushed
if I said something."

"Like what?"

"I could have gotten you a job."

"I got a job already," he said fiercely, as if he was being
patronized.

"So you do," Nick said. "But that's what I mean. You don't
want to be intruded on." He thought, I didn't pick it to be like
this, and I won't fight dirty, but I won't lose. It was something
he'd learned from Peter, to be ready on no notice at all to
counterattack. But Peter always smothered it out at the first
spark, before it ate up so much as a handful of grass. Nick
came in late, when the fire was already out of control, explod-
ing the trees like popcorn. He wondered, finally, if Sam knew
how much a man might give away gladly, without a fight.
There must have been those who were left without nothing
when Sam ran off, but since it wasn't money, Sam would have

called it a fair deal every time. Weeks ago, he'd told Nick he wasn't the most expensive. But only to tell him money was cheap. He could *get* a price to choke horses. And his notion of what things were worth placed no value on someone's caring. So you care what happens, Sam must have thought, well that's *your* problem.

"You can't tell me you don't wonder where you'll be in ten years," Nick said. He was surprised Sam let him keep talking. Peter would have locked him out of the bedroom. "You may not *worry* about it at all, but everyone has an idea."

"What'll I be in ten years?" he asked, as if he'd need a hint. "Your age, right? Well, I don't intend for it to matter. Either I'll be dead inside, or I'll be dead, period." And then he grinned, as if he'd had an afterthought. "How do I know? I might be just the same."

"What do you *want?*" Nick asked him bluntly. At least we're talking, he thought, and more than we did when we had no clothes on.

"Didn't I just tell you? I want to be where I am now."

"You'll need money."

"I got what I need," he said, but something changed. He went back to walking and seemed to coax Nick to come along and fall into step. He had the balls to tear up checks in people's faces, probably, but Nick could see that he looked them over first. Make me an offer and I'll laugh till I'm sick. But make me an offer.

"Don't you get tired of the street?" Nick asked. "All that waiting?"

"No," he said quietly, but not trying to cut Nick off. He'd talk about it some, he seemed to say, except he didn't know where to start. "I like it. I *never* wanted to live in a house. Or a tent or anything. The street's where I live, and my room is just a place to keep stuff in. It's like an airport locker."

The Gray Line bus pulled up, and the door hissed open as they went by. The tourists filed out—looking like they all lived in the same town in Iowa, so that you could practically tell who was the grocer, the fire chief, and so on—and they straggled across the grass to the fence, cameras aimed at the Orient. Nick, the tireless LA booster, silently wished them all a happy trip. If he could have stepped out of the three-act play with Sam for a minute, he would have tried to tell them all how it would break their hearts if they saw it at sunset. Which was not to disparage the glorious view trumpeting out even now on every side—a DeMille production of a view, really, because it looked from the top of the cliff like it was twenty or thirty miles across. The ocean, GI green and rough, was probably the biggest thing the Gray Line had. Nick couldn't say himself how far it went, from Long Beach or something at the southern verge, all the way to Zuma on the north. Ahead of Nick and Sam, through the still tall palms, the spring had turned everything very green, and they could see the Santa Monica Mountains and the Malibu Hills both. They'd seen them last from the empty café in Venice, the third time they met. Unlike them, the mountains seemed a good deal closer here, and today they were the deeper blue to which the water aspired. To Nick, when he was feeling the way he wanted to, the coastal ranges were a mystery that ended a long way off. They connected him up with holy places, the Sierras and then the Rockies, and as a result the West took place in his head, all of it. That was when he thought it was heaven on earth.

But why was he thinking it now?

"I guess I knew you'd be all right. You don't need me," Nick said. He was suddenly flying, and it wasn't the Gray Line folk, innocent as they were, radiating niceness, that had picked him up like a helicopter trailing a rope. It was this: He finally knew he was off the hook. He didn't have to keep working at a happy ending. Or not the one he'd envisioned, where they smiled and clapped each other on the shoulder, and Sam drove off grateful, changed, and ready to go to law school. Sam had let him know he didn't care. He hadn't given Nick the time of day since the day at the ranch. And Nick had to admit he was giddy with relief. If he'd thought all along he wanted to *be* someone to Sam, to salvage out of a meaningless ending a moment for them to ache with all their missed chances, he didn't want it anymore. It was a happy ending *because* it was meaningless. What's more, he found he didn't want to be understood. He always had before. I have a lot of commitments, see, and it doesn't mean it wasn't great, but I gotta go. No apologies from now on, Nick vowed. And no more fretting for sympathy.

"I'd just drive you crazy if I tried to hang around," he went on when Sam said nothing. It didn't seem like an ominous nothing, since he took his cue from Sam's own love of distance. "It's better if it's over altogether. We can say good-bye right here. No big deal."

So this is the last time I'll ever see him, he thought, moving off at the slightest angle as he walked, so that they veered again toward the fence. For the sake of decorum, he let the air out of his balloon and came back to earth. It wouldn't do to seem so overjoyed. Like a fancy overcoat, he put on instead the melancholy mood he relished. It's not us, he thought nicely of him and Sam, it's time itself that brought us here. They came up short against the cliff edge, and he looked down at all the little naked people on the beach. If Sam had continued to just shut up, Nick might have given a speech, the parting lover's equivalent, say, of the Gettysburg Address. He didn't seem to know he was hysterical, any more than he did when he drove along in the MG with a sap's lens on his Instamatic. He was a whole lot more narrow-eyed than Iowa. The people who would have done anything for Nick—Peter and Rita at present —would have sworn he never went too far with sentiment. He went farther than Peter, not as far as Rita. They were none of them tacky about it, though, with the possible exception of Nick when he was fixed on cowboys. The question, then, was why today he was getting his feelings off greeting cards. Unless it was that he was as scared as ever. But now he didn't even seem to know it. The fear had made over the world.

"You know," Sam said, "I used to keep count of the times I'd fucked." Nick didn't hear him right away, because he was lost still in his melancholy reverie, where love lasted only long enough to make men fools, and then exiles. "It wasn't hard to keep track, because I did it every day. But I used to try to remember what they looked like, too. Even now I see faces sometimes from back when I started. They float into my head like people I used to know, and it's funny, because I know more about them now."

Nick wasn't sure what to say. Sam didn't seem to be asking if the same thing happened to him. In fact, it didn't. He felt apologetic, as if he'd been found out letting his life run out without a second look. He couldn't recall the face of anyone he'd sold a house to longer than a year ago. Meanwhile, he'd never heard Sam say anything half as complicated. He would have welcomed it a month ago and drawn him out and held on tighter. Now he only thought: What about us? It was almost one o'clock, and if they were going to say good-bye, then someone had to *say* it.

"How do you know them better if you never see them again?"

"I know the type," Sam said. "The reason I stopped counting, I realized after a while how *everyone* was a type. But I still remember the first ones." He laughed, and he put his hands in the back pockets of his jeans and hunched his shoulders as he let out the punch line. "It's the ones I fuck now that I can't remember."

"Sam, there's something I want to give you," Nick said soberly, changing the subject as soon as Sam seemed finished. He didn't want to talk about Sam. He was even a little sick of it. After all, he'd fucked a cast of thousands himself, and he could be just as jaded about it as Sam if he felt like it. He hadn't really been listening. It seemed as if Sam was only bragging.

"The reason I'm telling you—you know what *your* type is?" He turned and met Nick's eyes as he asked the question. They'd get to the settlement in a minute. He had a point to make first. He paused for effect, as if Nick might really hazard a guess what type, and then like a schoolmarm he gave out the answer. "You think I'll turn on you. I'll go tell Peter how you like it, maybe. Or make a scene in your office. You're scared it might cost you an arm and a leg to buy me off." And then another moment's silence. Nick pretended it wasn't worth answering, returning a level gaze as best he could. What did it matter how much Sam knew? It was over with. It didn't have five minutes left. "I bet you got another envelope on you. Should I guess how much is in it?"

"It's not more money," Nick said with a shake of his head. "After all, I'm all paid up, aren't I? The seven hundred was a sort of retainer. And what I'm going to give you now is just because I like you. You've been good for me."

Even to Nick it didn't sound true, but he was damned if he'd admit Sam was right. He *wasn't* right. He'd made it sound like Nick had a horror of blackmail. But it was violence he feared, though he couldn't make it coalesce and make a picture. He wasn't scared for his body. Even at the edge of a cliff, where a lunge and a body block could send him hurtling over like a coupe in a grainy old thriller. He was frightened instead for the life he lived, that Sam would overrun it like an army. But since he couldn't imagine how, it was another reason to shrug it off, pretend it wasn't there.

They both understood it was time to go. They headed back the way they'd come, both suddenly quiet. As if on cue, the Gray Line tourists, signaled by their driver, began to make their way back to the bus, some of them lingering and looking over their shoulders, not ready yet to go back forever to fields of corn with nothing more than a snapshot. This time Nick and Sam had to thread their way through the crowd as they gathered in line. For a moment, the two of them were quite outnumbered, and Nick was struck by the strangest thing. Silence. He'd expected to hear the din of down-home chatter. But as they passed in front of him like a veil, he couldn't tell if they were speechless out of awe or they were talked out and sick of seeing sights. He wanted terribly to know, because he'd begun to get the feeling that everything he'd said about everything all day was dead wrong. If the tourists, after all, didn't act as they were meant to, like the simple folk in a Currier & Ives, then perhaps he was misperceiving more than he knew.

He and Sam were down to the final minutes, and Nick couldn't be sure, even as the countdown ticked away, that they wouldn't go through another reversal. More than ever, today they were holding different scripts.

"Is that woman still staying with you?" Sam asked as they reached the shelter. No reason, it seemed. He was just making conversation.

"Rita," Nick said guardedly. "Yes, she is."

"What does she do for a living?"

"She works in a store. Why?"

"No reason," he said easily. And they passed through the arch to the shady lawn under the palms. The MG was in sight, not a hundred feet away, and now was the right time. No hard feelings, Sam, okay? But Nick held back, stymied by the turn toward Rita. What was the hidden motive in it? No, he told himself firmly, he was only getting paranoid. Sam's world was a hundred percent men, in bed and out. Women didn't even exist. So Nick decided to get on with it, and then Sam spoke again. "Does she want to be rich?"

"Doesn't everyone?" he answered, trying to warn Sam off. "How would I know? She doesn't seem to care that she never had it before, and she isn't killing herself to get it now either. Why? What do you want to know for?"

"I was just thinking," he said, as if it was nothing, "what it must be like to live high up like that. You and Peter are loaded, right? It makes you wonder if Rita wants some of her own."

"Well, that's Rita's business," Nick said, ending it once and for all. He decided Sam was doing it for the hell of it, to make Nick worry that everyone would take him for a ride. It was as if Sam was trying to prove he had more morals than anyone else, and Rita might be a high-price hooker underneath it all. As if she was pawning his cuff links. And if that's what Sam meant, then he was more deluded and out of it than he seemed. He didn't know shit. And Nick said roughly, "Here," pulling the key ring out of his jacket pocket at last. He held it straight out and dropped it. On a reflex, Sam snatched it out of midair, and as he stared at it and put two and two together, Nick decided he needn't have gone to this extreme at all. The remarks about Rita showed Sam's style up for what it was, a punk kid's teasing. If his talk had been a little less foulmouthed, it would have been nothing, like a dirty book with the sex crossed out. Smut was *all* talk. It couldn't hurt a fly.

It was Nick's show now, and he didn't give Sam the chance to get his breath. The moment he raised his eyes to question what it was about, Nick looked away at the car, at the same time pointing. Not with a straight arm quivering, like a sorcerer whipping it up out of the dust. The gesture was as casual, as indifferent even, as one of Sam's. He didn't cheat either and try to watch the shock of it out of the corner of his eye. Let it go. He took no pleasure in a punk kid's toys. He put his mind to higher things, like Peter and Rita and him.

Sam snorted. "Thanks, anyway," he said. "I've got a car, too."

"You got a piece of junk," Nick threw back at him. "Go ahead and take it. You think I'm trying to hold on, but I'm not. It's just a car. Let me say good-bye my way."

"Listen," Sam said, icy cold, and Nick stayed turned away to hear him out. His own cool attitude, aloof and very calm, did not survive the first few words Sam spoke. But he didn't dare look at Sam now because the fear would have shown. All his denials of it died at once. Sam said, "No matter what happens, remember this: I don't want anything of yours. From here on in, I only want what's mine." But what's going to *happen*, Nick thought in a panic—*I* don't have anything of his, do I? And then the keys flew up past his face in an arc, but he made no move, and they fell to the ground. Sam said, "Starting now, you don't know who I am, and I don't know who you are. Good-bye, Nick."

"Wait!" Nick said, but he didn't. He was already striding away across the lawn. It wasn't fair. Nick bent down to get the keys but couldn't see them right away in the deep grass. He had to stoop and run his hands around, and his mind raced: He can't have it all, he's got to go halfway with me, he has to take the car. Then he saw the keys and pounced, but when he stood up, Sam was out of sight. He broke into a run to the MG, but he knew it was no use. There was a ten dollar ticket tucked under the wiper. It was one o'clock on the nose.

The corridors of the Desertside Convalescent Hospital reminded Rita of an air-raid shelter. Cement blocks on either side, painted a shade of beige that must have colored the domes of Limbo, seemed to pressurize the air. She walked behind the day nurse, but because the uniform was closer to a nun's, gray and hooded and bodiless, she could have come from another planet—or, as Hey would have said, another plane. But planet was more to the point, wasn't it, Rita thought, looping back on herself—anything to keep from imagining what would come at the end of the hall—because it was just like an underground passage in a sci-fi movie, too, leading to a rocket ringed with flickering lights. It smelled like—what?—insecticide, she thought, or raw petroleum. It smelled like they were trying to cover up the smell of death. And all the doors were ajar, but not so open that she could see in. They walked and walked to the very end of the west wing. Rita wondered, when they finally stopped at the last door, if Frances Dean had been pushed farther and farther off as the years went by.

"Thank you," she said in a saccharine voice, playing as dumb as she could. "And Dr. Webber. He's been very kind."

"Mr.," the nurse corrected her. She had the wrinkled brow and the bad skin of a believer, but Rita couldn't guess the sect. She seemed too overwrought to read a thermometer and so on. "I know he wanted to interview you first, Miss Varda, but if he can't get back from lunch on time, well, *you* shouldn't be the one to suffer. Please watch the hour. We are very strict about the fifteen-minute limit on coma patients."

"I understand."

"For the family's own good. The patient doesn't care, of course, but we ought to spend our life with the living."

"But she *is* living," Rita said, bristling in spite of herself. "That's the whole point of why it's sad."

"Sad is another word for doubt," the nurse replied. "Where she is now, it's between her and her God."

The last was accompanied by a sanctimonious grip on Rita's arm, and Rita took it with a weak-tea smile, trying to look as if she was undergoing a renewal of her faith. The anger boiled in her guts like an ulcer, but since she was on a special forces assignment, she hid it well and wouldn't indulge it. And then the moment passed. The nurse turned away and walked off in triumph, apparently feeling she'd given Rita the requisite strength with the laying on of a hand. Rita rubbed her arm and chalked up one for her side. She'd assumed all along that they wouldn't let her go in alone, that she'd have to listen to a recitation of medical bullshit at the foot of the bed, and that, to get the moment she needed, she'd be called upon to think quick like a terrorist. And here instead was a free ride. Maybe the standards had dropped all over the place at Desertside. If Mr. Webber wasn't back from lunch at three, for instance, then Mr. Webber must be a drunk.

She pushed the door all the way open and stepped inside, surprised at first by the daylight after the ghost lights that ran along the ceilings in the hall. Corner room, two windows. Otherwise, it was all as Hey had explained, the gunmetal gray steel furniture, the life-support equipment, and—on the low bureau under the window—a dozen roses in a Lalique vase. The roses were part of the contract. Rita wondered, since she was the first to visit in eight years, if they'd kept it up to Varda's specifications: roses, Tuesday; Friday, white carnations. With no witnesses, it was an easy enough corner to cut. And by that time she'd looked at everything else but Frances Dean, so she braced herself and went ahead. She walked over to the bed.

And even then she only glanced at the little body beneath the sheet, letting her eyes run up the tubes to the feeding bottle on one side, the waste bottle on the other. The respirator mask covered so much of the face that Rita couldn't even read it as a face. More sci-fi. The eyes had been closed so long, they looked like the blanks in a skull. And just a few wisps of hair. She looked away at the respirator beside the bed, the tank and dials so foreign to her they could have run anything, from a dentist's drill to a 707. But it was breathing, all right. The sound—it was the *machine's* sound—was like someone very deep asleep, far below the plane of dreams, and with something a little asthmatic about it, too, as if it needed better air to breathe itself. Rita wasn't interested. She cased it only until she saw where the cord came out of one side and snaked along the floor.

She followed it over to the baseboard and yanked out the plug.

She wasn't entirely sure just what would happen. Well, one of two things. Either the lungs would take over, or they wouldn't. But she didn't know about right then, the first few seconds, whether there might be a kind of convulsion as the light went out, or a rattle or a gasp. She stared down at the empty socket for a little, shaken to think she might be a coward after the fact. This was the girl who walked into a store and spotted the very thing she wanted, *zap*, who knew the moment she entered a room what ought to be moved and where. So go on, she told herself, because now is not the time to get like everyone else and play it over and over, because it's *done*. She was aware of the silence as she turned around. But it didn't feel dark like death, since it signified only the stop of the machine. Frances Dean was inert—no more, no less than when Rita walked in. Now she went right up to the bed, once and for all to dry up the fear, to promise she knew just what she was doing, and not for an instant to mourn. Though I suppose I'm here to say good-bye, she thought, so she said it, simple and direct, by way of last rites: Good-bye. She stopped short of adding the name. Frances Dean—any Frances Dean that made sense—was long gone, which was why she'd had to dispose of this impostor. The rightness of the hour caught Rita at last, and she felt as if she'd pushed a boat off the sand where it was beached. Standing ankle-deep in the shallows, she saw it float free, out to the open water. The room was full of relief.

She went to one of the windows. She still had to wait out the next twelve minutes, of course, and once again she could only guess what was happening. As far as *she* was concerned, it was a corpse already. She just knew. But officially, didn't it take the brain six minutes or something to run down all the way? She couldn't remember. What kind of a measure was it, though, for a woman who'd gone under in a stroke twelve or thirteen years ago? Maybe it had to do with the heat of the blood, she thought, its dipping below a certain point. It didn't matter, as long as things were going in that direction. When it came to splitting hairs, it turned into a question for priests and doctors. Every few seconds, she took a look back to see if the sheet had started to rise and fall at the chest, because she might get cheated yet. But the stillness held. If anyone had asked *Rita's* opinion, she would have measured death in just that way, by the keeping still. Clever of her, really, because she could argue then that the woman she'd killed was already dead for years and years. I could plead my own case, she thought, staring out the window at the parking lot, and then I could write a book and make a million bucks. She could, except she'd developed such a fierce protective attitude toward the privacy of Rusty Varda and Frances Dean. She was just like a bodyguard, only it wasn't their lives that had to be protected now, but their deaths.

She'd forced Hey to go over it a dozen times, but she couldn't get a handle on the money. Nick would know, but she would have had to tell him she was coming here today, and she didn't want anyone else involved. The point was—reluctant as she was to admit it—everyone else would have told her not to. They'd say it was because of the risks she would be running, but she had a feeling it was the other thing they'd be thinking, that they thought it was wrong. Not wrong-evil. More like wrong-why-make-trouble. Hey had briefed her for hours between Sunday and now, and he must have guessed from the questions alone, but he didn't want to know in so many words. He didn't know enough about money himself, didn't have the *feel* for it, like a baker who can't get the hang of dough, so he couldn't remember all that he'd heard. Apparently, Rusty Varda set up a trust fund for Frances Dean the year she went into Desertside. Very generous, from twenty-four hour care to hothouse roses. Hey was sure of one thing: It was worded so that the principal went, upon her death, to Desertside itself, since neither of them had heirs. Varda was trying to insure the best for her if she should outlive him, though he didn't expect her to.

Why a separate trust? Rita had asked herself. Now she thought she knew, putting it together with something else. He'd cared enough to keep Frances Dean in West Covina to keep her anonymous. The publicity back in the twenties that tore her apart when she was already down and out on dope was the very thing that led her to Crook House. So he must have had a vivid need to cushion it for her. She was terrified of the media, of the papers and cheap-shot magazines of her own bad press, but she nearly jumped out of her skin as well when she first saw TV, as if she knew how much more helpless people were when the film was turning and the guy with the mike held it only an inch away, no matter how much the victim squirmed. Varda was probably afraid that if he paid her bill out of petty cash and left her the big bucks in his will, the story would get out when he died, and they'd come down on Frances Dean like jackals, no matter how sick she was.

What he couldn't know, Rita thought bitterly now, was how the money would trap the last of Frances Dean. She was worth so goddam much to Desertside that they spared no effort to keep her going. How did they know they weren't being monitored by a posthumous spy for Rusty Varda? So they gladly jailed her in the most expensive system they could find, and to be safe, they probably went ahead with the flowers, too, in case they were ever audited. They'd keep her alive till she was a hundred and ten if they had to. It was worth a couple of million in the end if they did it right. Mr. Webber could lunch from twelve till four. Rita could see as she made her way through the place that Desertside wasn't spending its liquid assets on medical research or geriatric recreation. In spite of the presence of the nonaffiliated sisters, it was clear that money would come to no good here.

Varda may have preferred it that way. He certainly didn't get his kicks from charity. Rita had begun to think that his dying without a will was no accident—he'd already provided for Frances Dean, after all, and otherwise, he may have thought the State of California deserved to have the rest, since he'd made it off California land. Outside of himself and Frances Dean, he wasn't interested in people, so why would he want to bequeath the feeding of orphans and the curing of cancer? And having filled a treasure room in the crook of two hills with a trove the likes of the Valley of the Kings, he probably didn't care about having a library named in his honor, or an indoor pool at a college, or a new wing of anything. Rita didn't really approve of his attitude, and if she'd known him way back when and could have sat him down like she used to do Peter's grandfather, she might have made some headway in bringing him around. It wasn't as if the money ever got to the poor people's pocketbooks intact, or even to the asphalt trucks pouring out a new freeway interchange. Rita would have explained how it all was eaten up by bureaucracy. Twelve million was hardly enough to buy the red tape to tie up a single bill in the Senate.

But Varda *wasn't* around to have his consciousness raised, and Rita had to make do with the Varda and Frances Dean she'd got. It wasn't just the cavalier way with money, anyway. If Rita could have written it as a script, she would have cured Frances Dean, dried her out, and let them marry. Stop it, she said to herself, think nothing. She looked at her watch. Seven minutes. Then she went to the other window, which still looked onto the parking lot, but from here she could see Highway 10 in the distance—LA one way, Palm Springs the other. Well, she thought, no need to go into it here—suffice it to say Rita's script would never have ended at Desertside. It was just that if Frances Dean had gotten sober, they would have lived like kings.

And the images came through, whether Rita liked them or

not, and they had the feel of Harlow in a satin wrapper, eating her chocolates in bed in *Dinner at Eight*. Rita could see the two of them whizzing by this very spot in a Packard, off on a desert lark to a weekend house in Rancho Mirage. They wouldn't stop in West Covina unless they had a flat. And while a man in livery fixed it—the spitting image of Hey—in the parking lot of Desertside, Varda and Frances Dean would have their picnic in the backseat. That is, if they were hungry, because otherwise they'd fuck. West Covina wouldn't even register. Their heads would be too full of grand hotels to make room for it—the Connaught, the Pierre, here and there a Ritz. And what else? Horse races, certainly, and couturiers, topiary gardens and auctions of minor Impressionists. Rita loved to make lists for the two of them to live in. She probably had to today, to counteract the awful room she was waiting in, to her more awful than somebody dead.

She might even have advised Rusty Varda, in the event of a junk-free Frances Dean, to use his secret cave for wine alone. He wouldn't need it for anything else. Rita wondered if it was like telling the Shah not to build the Taj Mahal for a wedding gift, but then right away she saw the difference. The problem lay in the secrecy. It was like mining a mine in reverse, to give it all over to hiding treasure. Like putting the gold back in. Once they'd pulled together and got their health back—Rita had a list of what they ought to eat for breakfast, and a regimen of laps in the pool and sun and steam—then they owed it to themselves to pull all the gold out into the light. Put up a Taj Mahal in LA, or another one, anyway—it was a city where certain neighborhoods had them on every block. Not that one ought to go public for the public's sake, though the wars might all dry up in the fields if the Cézannes and Matisses were hung so everyone could see them. Rather, it was to give them a method for mining the heart that they must dig up and live above ground with their dearest things. If they didn't, then they didn't deserve any of it. Rita's fantasy life had moral laws, all of which tested people in clover as to whether they were worthy. It wasn't all ice cream and cake.

In Frances Dean's prison-gray room, faced with an emptiness that mocked the dreamed-up world in her head, where she figured out the way things should have gone, Rita knew she had to come clean. She wasn't satisfied at all with the Varda and Frances Dean she'd ended up with. She was glad to go this far for them—that is, let out the one of their souls still trapped in Limbo so they could meet, as per Varda's note, in a room where Beauty was held without ransom. But something stuck in Rita's throat whenever she tried to get excited about the reunion of two ghosts. She just didn't buy the idea of afterlife. She was raised a nothing by long-lapsed Catholics, and so she didn't even have a New York Episcopal vision of heaven as an oak-paneled library where the people stare a lot into a crackling fire in a fireplace, while the hansom cabs clop up and down the snow-lit avenue outside. Rita couldn't see it. She'd gone ahead with the killing today so that Varda and Frances Dean would still exist *somewhere* the way they'd always wanted, but the somewhere was—take it or leave it, Varda—only Rita's head. She blew life into them by her rage at what had become of them. In the secret room she didn't want them insubstantial as a dream, but they were.

She looked at her watch. A little less than four minutes left. she wished there was something outside the window she could remember this by, a tree or a couple of little girls with a jump rope, but the parking lot was relentless, the cars in rows, the sun on a hundred windshields. Rita was all that was happening at Desertside, she thought. It didn't have a shred of self to give back in exchange. She turned around again to the little thriller she'd set up. She went behind the respirator, scooped up the plug, and connected it into the wall. Mission accomplished. It wasn't as if the technical part had been all that taxing, but since, like Peter, she was all thumbs except when arranging flowers, she hummed with satisfaction as if she'd just bugged a political caucus or done a brain implant. She gave the room a once-over as she turned to go, but she knew it was clean because she'd brought nothing in and put nothing down. She hovered an instant over the roses, debating one as a souvenir.

They wouldn't miss it. But she held back, since the flowers, at least, were what they ought to be, and she figured they had a right to go on as long as they could.

At the door she paused to pat herself on the back, because in a minute it would be still as death, as if she'd never been here at all. And then she gasped. The machine wasn't going. It hadn't started to breathe again when she plugged it back in, and she hadn't even noticed. She'd fallen in love with the silence. And now she started to shake. She suddenly knew how people could write their names all over a crime and, by force of silence alone, not know it. She darted over to the body of the machine, but it wasn't any use. She couldn't, for Christ's sake, fix the picture on a color TV. And while she'd gotten to think in the fifteen minutes that nobody cared enough to burst in on her and catch her red-handed, as if the act itself wasn't worth a followup chain of events, now she was almost choked with panic. The posse was galloping down the hall even as she turned the dials and, when that did nothing, tried to turn them back to where they'd been. It either had a starter she couldn't pin down, or it held its breath when the patient died. Get out, she told herself, because now they're going to know it's you and not a prettily timed coincidence. As if the roof had suddenly been lifted off, she felt the sear of the desert sun. It wasn't LA at all. They lynched their criminals way out here.

Fixing a rapturous look on her face—my dear Aunt Frances and I, we talked old times and the years fell away—Rita slipped out into the hall and hurried off. Luckily for her, it must have been the dead man's ward, because no door moved and no one made rounds. As far as Rita could gather, it was all done with machines now. The last anachronism was the heart-sleeved visitor, she thought with some small shiver of self-respect, even in the midst of the dread at hand. Striding hard, she might have made it all the way out if she'd kept her eyes straight ahead as she passed through the last swinging door to the lobby. But a man came through the adjoining door from the other side, and she stared full at him and froze as they held ajar their respective doors, in the act of propelling through.

"Oh, you must be Mr. Webber" was suddenly written all over Rita's face. He smelled as if he'd had a bath in Jack Daniels, and he smiled and tipped his head in a manner exaggeratedly courtly. He would have gone right by without making the connection if Rita hadn't stared. She saw it dawn on him. I must be such a hardened criminal, she thought, that I want to be caught and put away, in a room as dreary as Frances Dean's.

"Miss Varda, isn't it? I was just coming to get you."

"What for?"

"So we could talk. I'm Alec Webber." They were both still holding doors on springs, and if Rita had let hers go, they would have had to have their talk in the hall. She pushed on through to the lobby, figuring it would be quicker, and Webber let his door go. "Tell me," he said, "how you found Frances."

For an instant, she thought he meant: How did you track her down to West Covina? But, no. He was asking how she thought Frances Dean was doing. Was she looking well? The question, perfunctory though it was, gave Rita the creeps. The use of the first name got her mad.

"Frankly, Mr. Webber, it makes me want to scream." She knew she'd never pull off the nice-lady act she'd done with the nurse. She was a wreck from the stopped machine, so she had to admit to *something*.

"Don't take it hard," he purred, putting a hand on her arm a moment, on the very spot the nurse had gripped. Things were standardized at Desertside. "It's just another part of life. Who knows if what we're living is more real than the world she's in?"

"*I* know," Rita said. But how long, she wondered, would she hold to her convictions if she had to keep coming? Or if it was her own mother lying there tied to machines like a smothered puppet? She didn't want to know. The scream was pressing against the inside of her skull like a migraine. Rita wanted out. "But I had to see for myself," she continued, stumbling on, casting about for a way to ingratiate so she could end it. "And I know she's getting the best of care, Mr. Webber. That's going to give me a lot of comfort whenever I think of her now."

"So you're his daughter," he said, with an oily shift of gears. "I didn't know he'd ever been married."

"He wasn't," she said, glad for the chance to go into her story, where she felt safe. "I took his name when I grew up. My adoptive parents finally told me."

"And the mother?"

"I don't really know," she said feelingly, "but if you think about it long enough, you start to make an educated guess. You understand?"

"Ah," he said, and looked away. She had him on the run. She'd told him on the phone she'd never made contact with her father, what with one thing and another, and then he died, and now Frances Dean was all that was left of Varda, so since she was visiting here in LA, couldn't she come and see? It's something I'd like to do for my father, she'd said. She backed Mr. Webber right into a corner. But now she'd doubled it into a two-hanky tearjerker, and it became so poignant and intimate that even a nosy, jaded drunk like Alec Webber had to draw back discreetly. "I didn't have any idea," he said.

"If it's true," Rita went on, "then the two of them were even more unlucky than they seemed. They could have used me. I could have taken care of them."

"Were they so unlucky, do you think? At least they were stars for a while," he said, so unctuously she could tell it was one of his pet subjects. For a moment she was crushed, since she would have enjoyed a long talk about her orphaned state and her lonely mum and dad. "You know, we have a lot of movie people in Desertside, and generally they're pretty happy. Everyone lives in the past if they live long enough, and the stars have it all over the others." It sounded as if he still had a tumbler of bonded and branch in his hand.

"You'd think they'd be bitter because it's all gone," Rita said. To her, the image of a corridor of sleepy, broken refugees from silent films was insupportable. Everyone used to be young, too, but with movie stars there was proof of it on film, yellow and jumpy itself with age, but there they were. The silent ones from Varda's time especially were young as kids, their gestures big and amateur—for a few years yet, not surrendered to studios and salaries and the fall of ancient Rome. If they ended up here together, then Hell was a place like this. To get by, Rita thought, you have to pretend at some level that the old have always been old. But Desertside took away that, too.

Webber said, "They love to talk, and people want to hear it. The others go into themselves, because all they have is pictures of their families and the homes they've given up. I'm not saying some are *better* than others," he hastened to add, "I just said happy. You have to have a story people have to know."

"I see your point," she said with a lot of cool, but in her heart relenting, since she saw what he meant. "But Frances Dean's not happy."

"Ah," he said again, and he seemed to relent himself. There was a pause in which Rita measured the distance, ten feet, to the main door. Why was he keeping her? So the day nurse could check on Frances Dean? Then he told her, more or less. "Rusty Varda left you well provided for, did he?"

"I've got more than I know what to do with, Mr. Webber," she said reassuringly, and knew right away she'd made the right move. She thought: He's scared I'll sue to break the trust. He wants me too rich to care.

"Will we be seeing you again?" he asked, steering her solicitously toward the door.

"I don't think so. I spend most of my time in Europe. I'm in art," she said—but airily, so he wouldn't think she was an artist.

"Have you left us an address, Miss Varda?"

"Why?"

"One never knows. I'd like to be the first to tell you—when the time comes."

"Oh," she said, the wind knocked out of her. "I'll send you one as soon as I can. I'm between places right now."

"As you wish," he said ironically. He didn't believe her.

He'd seen her kind before. All fired up for a saintly visit, and then they get punched in the stomach by it, and they never show up again. For her part, when she heard him sound so superior, Rita had an irrational wish to protest how tough she was. You'll see, she thought grimly as she turned to say goodbye. It shocked her. The point of doing what she'd done for Frances Dean was to do it so *no one* would see. If she tried to fight something bigger, the way of things at Desertside or the look on Alec Webber's face, she'd lose. But she had the feeling he wanted to be first with the word of a death because he liked to feed on trouble. Just as he liked to say Desertside was just another part of life, so everyone went away doomed. Oh, Jesus, what if this is all it's going to amount to in the end— that, Rita thought, was what everyone must wonder as they floated across the parking lot on a thin thread of freedom.

Not this time.

You can't hurt me, she thought ferociously, and she pushed the bar on the door. It groaned open, and the frail little breeze off the asphalt was as sweet as a dive in the ocean. She made a solemn promise not to remember any of this. And in that instant she might have done anything, because life was so large outside and Webber was only a speck of darkness. At the end of its arc, the door paused a beat before it swung shut, holding its breath to let her through. She called the last remark over her shoulder as if she were flinging the end of a scarf.

"As far as I'm concerned, Mr. Webber, she's dead and buried already." And the door slammed. "Don't call us," Rita said coyly, "we'll call you."

But with the door between them now, he couldn't have heard that last, even if he could have read lips. Because she said it out to the parking lot, like a proclamation to all things ugly and fruitless. She walked to the car and didn't look back, the fear all gone, knocked out by the saving shot of anger. Anyway, she thought, he was too preoccupied keeping the skeletons safe in the closets to notice what Rita had gotten away with. She clicked herself into the seat belt and started the car.

She locked eyes with the rearview mirror. Now, she said firmly to herself, forget it.

And she did, just like that. She'd done it time and again—with the past when she boarded the plane in New York, with every Varda masterpiece the moment it dropped in the mailbox. She got out of there fast. She'd never be traced because Desertside had too much else to hide. Some things she couldn't forget, of course, because she didn't know them yet. She could kill only what she knew and couldn't be blamed if she didn't see that it wasn't enough. If the past had been in only one place, in fact, she would have been home free. But it wasn't. She sailed up the ramp to Highway 10 and, flushed with a triumph over time, couldn't take in what she was heading back to. Today she'd stopped going cautiously, and the past still had a back door.

Chapter 8

Peter didn't know who let it out about his paintings, but now it was too late to go back, so he supposed it didn't matter. The phone was ringing at ten on Monday when he got to the office. It sounded at first like a hype. For a moment he only waited for it to be over, as if they were selling encyclopedias. Then, when it turned out to be for real, it was like winning a Nobel Prize in the wrong field. They were a gallery in Beverly Hills, and they proposed a show of all his pictures of the ranch for the middle of April. They could do it, they said, any number of ways—but suggested, since he was famous as something else, that they make it a benefit opening night, a percentage to go to a worthy cause of Peter's choice. That way, he'd come off as a model of humility about his work as a painter, and the benefit publicity would drive up star attendance on the first night and insure a clean sweep of the walls as the days passed. If the stars bought, see, then everyone would want a piece. Did he have a better idea? He laughed out loud—genuinely modest, in this at least, but they didn't know the difference—and asked for a little time to think. They didn't like it. Just remember, they said, that we called first.

My God, he thought, and they're not even dry. And then the second call came within the hour. This one bragged about their branches in New York and Amsterdam, and they promised, sight unseen, to take everything he did from here on in. They'd sign him up for life if they could. He said he was already represented. *Who?* they said, because we'll outbid anyone. Peter hung up. Then, while he was talking a client into Roman shades to run twenty-seven feet across a wall of windows, a call came in from a painter's agent. No, Peter said, but where did the guy find out about the pictures? With an audible shrug he answered back, "I don't remember. It's what people were talking about this weekend. What can I tell you?" And by that time Peter could only sit in silence, staring curiously at his trusty heap of fabric samples. Before noon, the *Times* had him on the phone. Because they were his buddies in the "Home" section, they at least took "no comment" for an answer.

"Are you sick or something?" Rita asked when he picked up the phone and said hello to her about a half hour later.

"I haven't been bitten by a snake, if that's what you mean. But I feel a little like Lana Turner on the stool at Schwab's."

"Has someone discovered you?"

"The whole western world has discovered me, Rita. Why aren't you here? It's afternoon already, and I have to hold your hand."

"I'll see you in twenty minutes. I'll wait right here."

"But *you're* supposed to come *here*, remember? It's called a job. Where are you?"

"Right now I'm lying naked on my bed. I'm just about to take a bath."

"Are you sick or something?"

"Nope. Never better. It's just I've been working my ass off to get something ready. Now hurry."

"How did you even know I'd be here?"

"I've been keeping your calendar clean, Pete. You mustn't ever forget how sneaky I am. In fact, if I were you, I'd think about it all the way home. It'll get you all prepared."

"Does it have to do with my paintings?"

"Your what? You mean *Home on the Range?* No, of course not. I thought you'd given that up."

"Me, too. But it seems I might still be needed. I'll tell you about it when I get there."

"No, you won't."

"Why not? We never talk about me," he said petulantly, in case she was trying to imply that he was too full of himself.

"You'll see. There will be only one thing to talk about once you get here. Hurry," she said again, and rang off.

It was true, he had to admit as he climbed into the pickup, that he'd done the course of his career in painting like a shooting star. First he was, and before he knew it, he wasn't. The old revolving door trick. Even by the time he'd strewn the half-done things of the ranch all around the bedroom the night of the party, it was all for the hell of it. Now they were stacked in one of the closets, and he'd raised no cry when Hey took away his easel and paints as well, a couple of days later. But he could tell that Rita didn't understand. She must have come to the conclusion that painting was just a phase he needed to go through, all fanfare and no gumption. In a way, he wanted to believe it himself.

But the fact was, he felt himself go very deep into the paintings only because of his accident. The first of them was crap, the one he abandoned by the fence to go get bitten. So when the second one filled him with power, he figured it was just this: He was better when he painted out of his head. He'd been lousy on location, he reasoned, only because he was cowed by the real thing. But then they got stranger and finer and fuller every day, and something else took over. Even if he was the only one to notice—Rita and Nick scarcely glanced at them, Hey protested they were all the same—Peter knew he was entering a temple. And then on that plateau, where he was expected to coast for a while being great, he realized something. He would only be good after something awful. He whipped up a desert and a sky in his pictures that got across the lightning shock of a rattlesnake's strike. When the trauma passed, the brush was sluggish in his hand, like a stick poked in soft tar.

He didn't grieve when the magic fled his fingers, and he knew he'd be able to do it again at the pitch of the next crisis, like a secret tunnel out of a battle. But in between, he could tell, the surface of the canvas would be flat and indecisive, the work mechanical. He refused to rely on peaks and furies and hurricanes because he had an intimation that a certain kind of painter lived impatiently, waiting for the next fire storm. Through all of this, Peter was not deluded. He wasn't *really* good. He supposed great painters were possessed by their work, and he was jarred to wake up to himself experiencing even a breath of it. But he found, to his considerable disappointment, that he had a metaphysical distaste for being in the grip of forces—the metaphysical version of being squeamish about the splotches of paint on his hands and clothes. He couldn't stand the mess. He was even afraid the fire storm painter produced his own apocalypse every now and then, just to get the juices flowing. Peter saw himself empty and only half alive, waiting for the next snakebite as if for a fix. Or not even waiting but walking naked in the tall dry grass until something terrible took the bait.

Oh, come on, he said to himself, it's not quite so fancy as that. He'd hoped to turn into a laser beam, and he hadn't. He wanted his eye aligned with his brush hand like the hairs on a rifle sight, and he wanted the world broken down into planes and colors alone. It was meant to be done with the mind and not the heart, he thought, and that was that. Peter's two laws in whatever he did were taste and style, which sound as if they amount to the same thing, but for him were like weather and climate, the active and passive faces of the one condition. Certain people criticized his living rooms as too impersonal, and he didn't care because, as far as he was concerned, certain people were too unroomed. He thought of the move from interiors to art as a way of shedding the emotional turmoil of him and his clients, but otherwise there was no difference except in the degree of concentration, like a bowl of vanilla ice cream as against a tablespoon of extract. Serious painters, he knew, would have been horror-struck by his daring to compare the two, and his reliance on taste and style would have called up to them visions of San Marino matrons who bought blue paintings for blue rooms. But again, Peter didn't care because he knew what he wanted. And when he found he couldn't have it—that he was cursed after all with a heart when he painted and hadn't a thought in his head—he had no choice but to give it up.

But he wasn't going over all of this while he drove to Bel-Air in the pickup. His mind went into neutral, as it always did in a car. A blip sounded here and there in his radar and sent up an image from the morning just past, but only because his paintings had so taken over the news of the day. In fact, what was there left to say? He hadn't *suffered* his way out of painting. He'd only thrown up his hands. Rita and Nick had probably *thought* more about why he'd put away his paints than he had—and, too, they'd probably done the thinking in a car. They both had minds that raced when they were on the road, though Nick's was more finely tuned to four speeds from years of practice. Rita was a novice at it, and she didn't so much think as conceive of things whole, which then would hang in her mind in a dazzle, like the setting sun. Peter went blank. He leaned slightly forward over the wheel, and for once he didn't look like Noel Coward. He'd never gotten used to doing it himself, as if the generations of carriage drivers in Russia had refined the skill of traveling roads right out of him.

He made a better passenger. And he didn't mind that other people did most of his thinking for him. He may not even have noticed.

He certainly wasn't going to make the moves on art before he talked to Rita and Nick. Though the thing had already snowballed in such a way as to blur where it all got started, it couldn't have begun anywhere else but at the party. It was clearly the work of his clients, flexing their connections. He thought he'd left the paintings lying about to show that he had a private world they couldn't invade, but the plan apparently backfired. His decorated women wanted him happy, and his two weeks' private convalescence had whipped them up to a frenzy. No matter what he'd been doing to pass the time in his confinement—baking cakes or papier-mâché—they would have been on the phone to people who owed them favors. Peter was the one they'd decided to take care of, as if by common consent. He didn't know if other decorators got the same treatment, since decorators tended for professional reasons to barely be on speaking terms. Perhaps, Peter thought when he couldn't stand it and felt like running away to be a gypsy, it had most to do with the fate of princes. The very rich had always made their money in shady deals—none more shadily, surely, than the princes in Russia—but the money in LA was still too immediate to have shaken off the dirt, or maybe it only seemed that way in the company of princes. In any case, they couldn't bear it if they had to watch Peter measure the drapes, and giving him too much money calmed them down. It may have been, too, that they were trying to buy fate off when they coddled Peter. If the Russians hadn't been able to pay their way out of the slaughter in 1917 with all *their* assets, then nobody was safe. With Peter, at least they were taking care of one of their own. They'd expect the same themselves when they went into exile.

So Peter could do it if he wanted to. The connections would handle the details of doing it right, and even Peter knew they were talking high finance when they started talking galleries in

Beverly Hills and Amsterdam. He and Nick had seen a hundred overnight successes. He'd *been* one. All you had to do was decide to go with the flow and not once wonder if you were any good. And then you spent the next five years trying to get back some say in the matter. Having done it once, he had to think twice—well, Rita and Nick would—about doing it again. He wouldn't say he didn't need the money, in case it might upset the balance of luck, but he'd have to have one good reason besides. And he couldn't imagine anything worth the favors he'd suddenly owe to whichever of the ladies had set him up. Unless the attendant increase in power turned out to be so great it would leave him sailing over everyone's head. In that case, he could close up shop and be a prince full-time. Turn out a painting now and then. The fewer the better.

That's not what you want, Nick and Rita told him when he got that way. Princes, they said, went mad with boredom. He wondered sometimes how they came by their classified information, but he had to believe them. After all, they were the only two people he could be sure of who'd gotten over taking care of him. *They* didn't think so, maybe, but Peter knew it in his bones. They would have referred him to all that thinking they did on his behalf, how it came in time to be second nature. It was the very thing Rita hesitated over before she took the job. And Nick would have added the stores he was assigned because Peter refused, the lies he was always telling over the phone to guard Peter's privacy, the fits of temper he waited out. It was all true. But Peter had done enough thinking to figure *them* out, too, so it wasn't a one-way street anymore. He let them fret and give him advice because they needed to, and in the meantime he was playing his instincts, turning the world to his account. Rita and Nick wouldn't have understood where he was going because thinking had nothing to do with it. It had less to do with putting it into *words* than their lives did. But they must have felt how he'd begun to fight being driven by work, and as soon as they were ready to, they'd see they weren't responsible for Peter any longer.

Though he might still seem to need all the help he could get, it had come to be an act, to put up a wall between him and the people who wanted a piece of him.

He parked the truck close up to the green MG Nick had given Rita. The card said it was from both of them, and that was fine with him. He didn't go out of his way to ask questions either. Meanwhile, it was hard for Peter to get too bothered by the pressure of what went on outside, where the clients and the galleries made the rules, now that he and Nick were in phase again. The days they spent together after the snake were all over, of course, but then they knew it couldn't go on indefinitely. They were back to seeing each other mostly late at night. Time itself had changed. Now it was rife with qualities, the clock replaced by a scale that measured only intensities. It wasn't just making love, though they turned to that again as if they'd been released from a vow of chastity. The body was all the soul they might get. But even more, they realized that it was possible to come back to the full flood of knowing just who they were. That is, they both understood what they'd come to themselves because they could see so exactly how the other arrived. Peter knew, for instance, what Nick ended up with after he'd abandoned his six-weeks' love, just as he also knew it was Nick doing the leaving. Then he watched Nick and Rita glance off one another, probably because they'd never met anyone who looked so much like a mirror image—though only Peter appeared to see the likeness. Afterward, he watched them ricochet away to a safe distance. And all the time he was studying Nick, he saw the clearest picture of himself, as if every move Nick made gave him one of his own. Some things didn't fit, like the green MG, because by his calculations Nick had passed that stage with Rita well over a week ago. But it was still all right with Peter. He didn't have to know everything. Didn't want to.

Crook House made no sound when he let himself in, so whatever Rita's surprise might be, it didn't require a crowd and didn't resemble a party. That in itself was a nice surprise. He took the elevator down and would have walked around to the kitchen to see Hey first, but he noticed something funny in the living room. Don't surprise me in here, he thought. Rita knew it had been the main design of his convalescence, and so she knew it had to be frozen just the way it was for a while. Peter had to brood over it, moving everything an inch or two until he'd got it perfect. When he went up close to the opium beds, he could see it was only a few things dropped on the rug going off into the hall toward Rita's room. As if somebody clumsy had had his hands full. And the thing that had first caught his eye was only an envelope propped in the cushions on one of the beds, addressed to him. He tore it open.

"Follow your heart," Rita had written on a plain white card.

He didn't waste a second on the irony. His eyes darted to the trail of things on the carpet, and then, because they were so strange and dissimilar, he narrowed his look and began at the beginning. First was a pile of coins behind the divan, as if somebody's pocket had sprung a hole. Gold, he could tell right away as he went down on his hands and knees to look, and probably Roman, but he wasn't sure. He didn't touch them, though the note didn't tell him not to, but just in case she wanted things left the way they were. Besides, he'd already decided that when he was done, he'd bring Rita back and go through it again. He stood up and walked two paces, damned if he was going to crawl the whole way. This time it was a piece of jade worked as a belt buckle, carved with a couple of storks. Next, only a couple of feet further on, a pocket watch in a sterling case. Then a powder horn which, if you could believe the inscription, once belonged to Wyatt Earp. And at the turn into the hall, more artful than all the rest, a blue enamel cigarette case with a snake going zigzag across it in diamonds.

The House of Fabergé, Peter guessed right off. He stooped to it and without thinking broke his rule and picked it up. Whatever the crazy thing was that Rita was mixed up in, it had so far produced two pieces of Fabergé. Ever since she gave him the picture frame, he couldn't get it out of his mind that something fishy was going on. He knew how little Fabergé turned up on the open market, and he'd kept the frame to himself, at the back of his desk in the shop, for fear that someone would ask too many questions. The cigarette case in his hand, he knew, had to cost five or six thousand dollars. The other things on the floor weren't cheap, but this was something else. He slipped it into the pocket of his suede jacket. He couldn't just leave it on the floor.

Now what was he supposed to do? He called back into the living room, "Rita?" As if she might be watching him through a chink in one of the Japanese screens. But there was no answer. She was probably still in the bathtub. He turned into the hall to go to her room, and because his eyes weren't yet accustomed to the dark, he didn't see what was there and banged his knee against something that swiveled around and batted him hard on the hip. He jumped, his hand went out and threw up the light switch, and in the instant before he saw the trail continue all the way to Rita's room, he thought, "But this is too much." He meant the joke was over. He knew too well what everything cost, and what's more, it was Rita who had taught him. Here was a telescope that probably belonged to Galileo, it looked so venerable. All the fittings in brass, cherry inlaid with ivory. And Peter knew there wasn't an antique store in LA that could handle it without his having seen it. Things like this didn't get priced. They were already all in museums. For good measure, Rita had draped and tied a string of pearls around the lens like a constellation, and he knew she was gilding the lily willfully, as if to say there was no end to this.

The next thing was big. It fell along the hall seven or eight feet, and it had the shape and heft of a railroad tie. A totem pole, in point of fact. And now Peter guessed Rita was in it so deep, she couldn't even be doing it solo anymore. She could never have lifted this herself. She had to have an accomplice. And what if it was Nick? He stopped. He didn't have time, but he had to look at this totem, it was just too beautiful. He peered closely at the worn, cracked wood where a bear stood on top of an elk, and a wolf on a bear, and then a man. No, he thought as he hurried himself along, it wasn't Nick's style to turn it into a treasure hunt. Nick could never be playful with things that came so close to art. He could make a game of giving away a green MG or anything else you could buy off the floor. But something that carried an air of age and values, one-of-a-kind, always left him stone-cold sober. The accomplice had to be someone as unafraid of the beautiful as Rita, who could pick things up and put them down, who had to have a feel of everything.

Further on, just within reach of Rita's door, was another block of wood, sculpted this time in India. A plump figure in a full lotus, with a look on his face that made him seem like the god of compassion. Exquisite, and any other time Peter would have gazed at it long enough to lay a claim, but a corner of his eye had caught the last thing hanging on the door. A Cézanne watercolor of rocks and a tree, hardly finished, the tree hardly begun, and yet it made Peter want to give up everything and go live there, as if he would never need to move from just that random space of a few feet of forest. Peter's continuous process of picking the best wherever he was took a deep breath. Everything else, all the way back to the coins on the living room floor, was nothing compared with this. The snake-lidded cigarette case was marvelous and frivolous and ritzy, but a real Cézanne showed it up as a curious toy. Peter had two thoughts at once—that value was a very subjective thing, particularly in the presence of what was priceless, and that Rita had gone too far for even him and Nick to get her out of it.

Though he gaped at the watercolor, he must have knocked right away, as if he didn't dare spend too long in a rapture when there was so much to get to the bottom of. But as he was dazed, he didn't remember the knocking. All he knew was that he was an inch from the painting one moment, and the next thing he knew, the door was wide open and Rita was grinning as if he'd come to pay a social call. He was hit just then by a crippling sadness. It all seemed to mean he didn't know her at all, and he couldn't afford to lose either of the members of his team. At the same time, he must have panicked at the thought that if he lost Rita now, what little he had of the past went with her. Take care, he told himself. They stood in silence, staring at each other across the threshold. Rita's grin softened when she saw that he was in turmoil, and as the tenderness welled up in her eyes, Peter felt the color coming back to him, too. In a minute, they looked exactly the same, tuned to each other again and ready to sing a duet. Partly, it was a brave front, but Peter realized it wasn't in him to react to anything Rita did with anything like moral criticism. If she'd had to *kill* to get this stuff, she must have had a good reason. All Peter cared about was that she not get hurt. He'd kill, too, if he had to, to keep her safe.

"You're very clever, I see," she said, pulling him into the room and locking the door behind them. Against whom, he wondered, but let it go. "It would take some men months to follow those clues to the end."

"Would it?" he asked lamely. The sorrow gripped him again like a cramp. He'd like it better if they got right down to it. He didn't think they'd be laughing once they'd started.

"Oh, at least," she said. "Most people wouldn't go any further than the gold coins. A bird in the hand, you know. Then, if they got as far as the telescope, they'd have to diddle around with that." She talked right at him for a bit, but she couldn't seem to stand in one place. She turned to the windows and, starting at one end, went down the row, shutting and locking. "Who ever gets to the good stuff, Pete? And how do they even know when they're there? What percent of the world even knows who Cézanne is?"

"Rita, where did you get all this?"

"You'll see, you'll see," she said, coming back from the end of the windows and holding out her hand. "Come on."

"Wait," he said, his hands stiff at his sides. "None of it's yours, right?"

"I'm trying to *show* you, Pete." She made it sound as if he was getting in the way of a good explanation. But she saw at last how far off the track he was, and she acted quickly to ease his mind. He wasn't having any fun. "Listen," she said, "*we* aren't in any trouble. A lot of this is against the law, but all the criminals have run away. I swear it, Pete, if the cops do anything to us, it'll be to give us medals. Do you trust me?"

"All right." He gave her his hand and let himself be led across the room to the closet. He knew enough now to guess the rest, and it showed what he could do with his mind instead of mere thinking. It had to be Rusty Varda, he suddenly decided, and the stuff must come from a secret cache. Of *course*. It was as if, in some unfocused corner of his mind, he'd always known. There was always something more to Crook House. He understood houses so well that his antennae had at some point picked up the extra space, but he hadn't got around to it consciously yet. Eventually he would have groped his way here, though still it took a Rita to crack the lock. Peter would have had to break through the mirrored door with a hatchet. Now, as Rita ushered him into the closet, he realized that he'd never been satisfied with the Varda story. All that waiting around in Crook House, forty years of it, had to have a purpose beyond forgetting to give away twelve million. Peter used to ask Hey: What did Rusty Varda *do*? Hey didn't know. *Said* he didn't know. Peter abandoned it in the end, but something never ceased to nag at him. Now it came back at full volume when Rita closed the door. Strangely, he felt as if he'd been waiting all his life for this.

"Ready?" she asked, holding a finger up like a magic wand.

"Does Nick know?"

"Yes."

"Who else?"

"Nobody else."

"Go ahead."

She was standing with her back to the door. She brought her finger down to her side and touched it against the button in the doorknob. Click. As the mirror swung open, Peter became aware of a smell that he knew and couldn't name. In a way it was the smell of money, but later he would place it more precisely. A certain kind of Brooklyn Heights apartment, full of the goods of Europe and smuggled haphazardly out of Russia. Louis XVI painted furniture, polished silver, and old masters—the smell of all the princely quarters of Saint Petersburg.

She lit the candles, and they wandered in like Hansel and Gretel at the edge of the Black Forest. For the longest time they said nothing at all. She didn't, of course, have to identify anything to Peter, who supplied a running commentary in his own head, mentally fixing a label and a price on every piece. Rita had by this time sent off twenty or twenty-five packages, but she'd hardly made an appreciable dent. Lots of it was very big. It was one thing to drag a totem pole out to the hallway, quite another to put it through a mail slot. Rita knew she had to expand her operation, which was the main reason she'd decided to let Peter in on it.

But practical matters aside, being there with Peter was like being there the first time again. Rusty Varda couldn't have asked for a better audience. They were kids in a toy shop, kids in an attic, but because they knew the magnitude of the power they stood at the center of, they could hardly get more grown-up either. They were like a king looking out from a mountain at miles and miles of his land. Some of it was sheer possession, of course: All the world they can imagine is theirs, look at the proof, or perhaps there isn't a meaningful line anymore between them and the world. But mostly, in their case as with a kingdom, it had to do with being overwhelmed by a glut of beauty. Nick had told them both that, when he walked up north through a redwood grove, he found himself in the presence of superior beings. For Peter and Rita, it was as if all the artists who did these things were in the room with them, from Rembrandt standing like a tragic philosopher all the way down to the Chinese weaver embroidering, stitch by stitch, the cloth of gold draped on the stone table. It was how Rusty Varda must have seen it, as a meeting ground for artful spirits.

"Where's it all from?" Peter asked quietly, moving off by himself from one thing to another while Rita followed behind, content to go his way and watch it all discovered.

"Everywhere," she said. "Museums, colleges, libraries. A lot of it belonged to the anonymous rich. It's all in a book he kept."

"Where?"

"Keep going. That's my office up there."

She sat him down on the sofa, brought over the book, and put on his head the miner's lamp she'd found in the desk's file drawer. She faced him in the wizard's chair. He was turning to the book, she knew, to take a break, so his mind could adjust to the size of the treasure ground. He wanted to anchor himself in details. And with *his* background, even the diary was gripping, a *Gone with the Wind* reduced to its lists of damages. It could have been an accounting of the Kirkov losses in '17. Rita watched him to be sure she'd been right to tell him. Oh yes, she thought, no problem. Of course, she still had to convince him to agree to keep returning what was returnable. Nothing prevented him from calling a halt to the mail-order business. He could hoard the room from now on as the closest he was ever going to get to the inheritance modern politics stole from him. But Rita didn't think he would. What made the secret room serene was the feeling of being touched by a fabulous story. No matter what else was closing in outside on their actual lives, Rusty Varda's dream sat them down and promised that life wasn't boring at all to those who went after something. Peter was the acid test, since he would appreciate everything here so much, but Rita believed all along that the experience of the place didn't make a person feel possessive. She would let Peter see that they had enough work to do in here to keep them busy for weeks. And the work was enough. It was power over things without the responsibility of owning them.

"There's a Rembrandt?" Peter asked, looking over at her a moment so that the miner's light shone in her eyes.

"You went right by it," she said, as if that in itself was something of an event. "But I put a sheet over it so I could save it for last. You won't believe it."

He took off the helmet and laid it in his lap as he leaned his head back in the pillows. He settled down to being as happy as she was, since it was turning out to be dinner at '21' all over again—actually much much more, because their standards had gotten higher. They'd done enough '21' and the like in the past few years to know the menu inside out. So they prepared to bask in the glow of this place with a vengeance, like a week flat on the beach in Hawaii. And just as Rita had predicted, the afternoon in the real world was canceled. They were going to get light in the head in the next few hours. They wouldn't be any good at other people's houses, not today, even if they could have torn themselves away. They had something amazing they had to work out.

"Do you think they used to come here and have love scenes?"

"Who?" Rita asked abruptly. She hadn't gotten as far as Rusty Varda and Frances Dean.

"Rusty Varda and Frances Dean," he said, reading her mind down to the least inflection. "You don't go as far as *this* just to give yourself a little privacy. You have to have someone to do it for." His head lolled in the goose down, and he spoke up at the rough-beamed ceiling. Rita saw a split she wasn't ready for. It sounded as if they were going to be in passionate accord about the treasure and hardly understand what each other meant by Rusty Varda and Frances Dean. "Like some of my clients," he said. "When they do over their houses, and they feel they're doing it for me, they do a fabulous job."

"I don't know if they were ever actually here inside," Rita said. Which was fussy of her, since she'd fantasized any number of times about Varda showing off the masterworks to his movie star by the light of a single candle. To Peter, she seemed to be trying to say it was only a storeroom in here. But wait, she said to herself, you don't have to protect *them* anymore. The spirits of Varda and Frances Dean were on their own. In fact, Rita remembered just in time, she needed to hear opinions totally different from her own, if only to begin to draw her out of the story. If Peter thought it was folly and she thought it a great romance, it didn't mean either was wrong.

But even if it meant they were *both* right, she had to admit it was a romance made up entirely of yearnings for what might have been. All doom and no all-night kisses. She knew she might have to make do with the notion that, though it was more folly than not, at least it was vast.

"Tell me about them, will you?" Peter said. He must have sensed he was intruding on something of Rita's that was very far advanced, and that she had the prior claim. Just as he didn't have to ask how she'd stumbled on the room or gotten in—it simply had to do with being Rita—he didn't wonder how accurate her information was. If it wasn't the truth, so what. It was better than the actual facts because it came so close to who the people *thought* they were.

"I probably don't know anything you don't know," she said, conveniently letting a little desert murder slip her mind. "But as far as I can guess, she was scared of life, and he was scared of death. So he had to think up something as ingenious as junk was for her. And this is it." She spread her arms helplessly, trying to take in the two thousand years of art as well as the hillside room. But in the gesture there was something of a shrug, too, as if to finish up by saying nothing cheated death, even if it took the fear away.

Then she passed across to him the note that Varda left for Frances Dean's ghost. And then they began to look at the things one by one. And once they were doing that, it was easy for Rita to start detailing the method of her retrieval project. Peter understood everything right away. They went very fast. They would have gone on all day without a break, except that the air usually got tight after an hour or two. So Rita decided they'd work until one-thirty, and then they'd go out into the house for lunch, where she knew they'd be savoring higher matters than food. If they had an image of the whole of Crook House in their minds just then, it must have seemed open and bright and very alive. In the secret room, they were in the heart of something larger, and the peopled house about them was wonderfully calm and humane precisely because it *had* a secret heart. Neither of them could have imagined violence or chaos possible, now that they were in possession of such a completely real inner world. For a little while, they were wholly without the need of dreams.

Which is why some people get bitten by snakes when they least expect it.

Hey knew what was going on in there. He was sitting in the kitchen, his stool up close to the parrot's cage, and when he heard Peter call to Rita in the living room, he knew the two of them would be locked in her room within a few minutes, and then he could have the house to himself again for a while. Rita had told him only to stay in the kitchen till quarter after twelve, so he knew she must have it timed down to the minute. She didn't mind him watching her set up the treasure trail, and she even asked him to help her drag the Eskimo piece out of her room, though of course she didn't ask till it was already out of the closet. She wouldn't have let him see *that*. And Hey smiled mildly, thinking of her precautions. Why hadn't she guessed? He'd been in and out of there a thousand times.

He wondered now and again why he'd never told her, since he'd told her everything else he knew. It was as if, somehow, he had to keep himself out of it entirely to give Rita more space in which to maneuver. The moment he laid eyes on her at the airport, Hey was convinced he'd found the right person to let into Rusty Varda's room. It was destiny, pure and simple. As Holy Brother had promised, he was coming into a time of great release, and Hey could tell on the spot that Rita was part of the ticket. He gave her what clues he could and was delighted to find her skimming along on the same wavelength, pursuing her own investigation before she was in the house a week. Curiously, he refrained from telling Holy Brother what a burden she lifted from his shoulders on the Monday night she figured out the trick to getting inside. But then in one way it made sense, because he'd never gotten around to mentioning Varda's room to Holy Brother in the first place. He said to himself it was all for the dead man's sake. Hey protected Varda's right to a world undelivered by holiness, a world that scorned the universe and made its own nest. But it was also true that he wanted to cover his bets. He held Holy Brother at arm's length in just this one thing, partly to have a secret shelter of his own from *everything*, if it ever came to that, and partly as a test of Holy Brother's power to see through walls. A test Holy Brother had so far bagged.

So Hey was not as duped as the current residents of Crook House seemed to think. The really serious business between Hey and Holy Brother was limited more than anyone knew to Linda. It was the one direction of energy in his life that scared Hey, and nobody else had an explanation that comforted him so much as the notion of visits from *another* life. He had to sit through a lot of smoke and long white robes that faintly offended his sense of theater—he had, after all, studied under Balanchine. The philosophy of Holy Brother was brimful of fateful accidents and wild reversals, and Hey noticed that all the previous lives Brother uncovered in his congregation went on in glamorous ancient times, with Hollywood sets and costumes. No one had ever been just a farmer or a clerk. They were priests of Ra or favorites of the courts of the Louis, or they were extreme and particular people like the disciple Andrew or Marco Polo. But Hey was impressed by the psychological profile Holy Brother drew of two selves dancing in a single soul. He knew now that the presence of Linda had a beginning and an end, and he spent a lot of time just waiting for it to be over and taking it as it came. And when it was over, he planned to drop back to being a Christmas-and-Easter parishioner of Holy Brother. He'd pay his dues, of course, as insurance against another onset out of the past, but otherwise he'd had enough of holy bullshit.

And Nick was wrong when he said once that Hey would rather talk to the parrot than to other people. Wrong because Hey and the parrot didn't talk. Hey wasn't positive what the *parrot* did, but for his part he found it relaxed him just to watch the bird preen and blink and sidle back and forth on his perch. It wasn't that he watched for hours at a time, either, as if it were a fix for a glassy-eyed brand of meditation. He would amble over to the cage while he waited for water to boil, or he'd stop on his way out with the trash. A minute here and there, and it put him in touch with a world as full of form and endless movement as the ballet. The parrot suffered nothing. He wore his beauty in the open and had his million shivers and twitches to execute, and he never tired and never like Hey got so old he couldn't do it without an agony in his joints.

But today Hey sat at the cage a little longer. He was worried and a little wounded about Rita telling Peter. In his mind, he'd turned it all over to her, so he supposed he ought to trust her with all the decisions. He hadn't thought to question, for instance, where Rita was taking the loot, package by package, whenever she left the house. He could tell she knew art, and he was sure it would all get put on the proper pedestal. He would have had to admit that Peter knew art, too, but Peter was spoiled and never serious, and he certainly didn't care a jot for Rusty Varda and the old days. Unlike Nick and Rita, who seemed to feel pangs that something rare had passed for good. Hey would have told Nick months ago, long before Rita, if he could have been sure Nick would keep it to himself. Yet he knew it wouldn't be fair to demand such a vow of silence, since Nick and Peter were the deepest sort of lovers, who passed on to each other everything, no matter how trivial, to get as close as they could to being one. Or that, at least, is how it looked to Hey. And, in fact, Peter's loving Nick so well was in Hey's view what redeemed him, though not enough to make him worth entrusting with the hidden room in the hill. Peter might give it all out to his overdressed, cotton-headed clients. Even Nick might decide to keep it, if only to wrap it up for Peter. It had to go back to the people at large, and Hey was convinced that Rita alone would see it that way.

There was a rustling in the bushes below the kitchen garden, but the parrot got more upset about it than Hey. He stretched out his wings and said "Machu Picchu" very loud. All it was, Hey knew, was a loose dog. One evening at dusk a deer had emerged from down the hill while Hey was cooking, and they had spent a startled moment staring eye to eye before the deer leaped up the hill and away behind the house. People said there were still coyotes in the hills, and a Bel-Air woman, a famous drunk, had once reported to the police a pack of raccoons, a hundred or more, silently crossing her lawn. But that was all at night. At this time of day, it was just a dog. And then the crackling of branches stopped, as if the animal was sniffing out a smell at his feet. Hey forgot about it till he heard the rustle start up again.

One thing didn't seem to make any more sense with Hey than Rita: How could you keep the flame alive for Rusty Varda if you were at the same time taking apart the room where he'd planned to make his last stand, to keep his own fires going beyond the grave? Hey didn't find the two goals incompatible, and Rita would have agreed. They applauded Rusty Varda's extravagant idea, and they both felt their hearts fill to bursting when they lit a candle to go explore it. Rita learned to dream of it in Gothic novels, where brave women came upon ghosts. Hey learned it dancing in the corps de ballet, in a ring around a princess. But they both believed, though they loved the daring of the plan, that it was time to recycle the art and get it back in currency, so as to tempt more visionaries to shoot the moon. Rita and Hey were very democratic. It was like believing that every man can be President. Now let someone try to break Varda's record, Hey would have liked to announce when they gave the public back its paintings and such. He put no more credence than Rita in the notion that Varda and Frances Dean would actually meet when they were dust and ashes. It was a hero's project, the secret room, and it made his life awesome. But now it was over.

This time the noise in the bushes came up like crashing, as if whatever it was couldn't get any purchase on the steep part of the hill below. Hey got up from his stool, very annoyed, and went across the shady kitchen terrace to the dense bushes that fenced it in. Why didn't the dog go find a nice garbage pail at the next house down? If he had to call the Bel-Air Patrol to come and catch it, they'd track dirt all through the house getting it out. "Go home!" Hey shouted. He bent down and picked up a handful of gravel and threw it into the foliage. It made a moment's noise like a hard rain, and the rustling stopped. He scooped up more gravel and did it again. And again. He figured he must have scared the animal silly, and it wouldn't move a muscle till he went away, so he turned around and started toward the kitchen door. It was one of those ordinary moments just before a terrible accident which a man would do anything to retrieve in all its ordinariness. Because suddenly the bushes broke open with a smash like a car going through. He didn't even have time to turn to face it. He saw the parrot go crazy in the cage and bang against the bars, and then the butt of the gun came down, square on the back of his head.

He was out only five minutes, but time did not go easy on him. He felt as if he'd fled into yet another life when he opened his eyes to the scald of the pain. The gradual, gradual calm that had finally come over him during the years since Varda's death seemed to have vanished entirely. And when the first thing he saw through the fog was Sam's face looming grimly over him, he was seized with the certainty that things would never be good again. And that was before he remembered who it was. He tried to talk to plead for time, for anything to stop the throbbing, but he choked on his own horror and gasped and gasped. And when, a moment later, he *really* saw Sam as Sam, he fell through a time warp. He thought it must be the very day Varda died, but with a slight change in the script—now Sam was killing him, too, on the way out. But he wasn't going to be permitted the luxury of amnesia. Sam pulled him to his feet and swung him over so that he sat down heavily on the stool.

"Come on, come on," Sam said impatiently. "You're not dead yet."

Hey could hear the parrot flying against the sides of the cage, making an awful racket. Sam held his arm so tightly it was going numb, but Hey turned around on the stool and forced him to let go as he brought his own hands up to the cage. He held them against the bars, palms open, and felt the wings rush against them and then stop. Hey didn't take his hands away until the parrot made his way back to the perch and settled his wings and shook the disheveled feathers on his head and neck into place again. Then he couldn't put it off any longer. It was here and now and not ten years ago at all, and even worse, it wasn't just a terrible dream. He had to go forward and live through this at a time when he was much better at remembering and imagining. He turned full-face to Sam and looked out coldly, only now opening his eyes wide and not at all flinching when the light sharpened the pain in his head. He determined not to be afraid, no matter what. It all fell to him because it was all his fault.

"Now we're going to play a little game," Sam said, gripping his arm again and pulling him across the kitchen. The dizziness was bad. Hey hung his head loose and let Sam propel him, and he noticed the butt of the gun protruding out of the waistband of Sam's jeans, right above the belt buckle. The barrel of the gun pointed insolently into the crotch, like a symbol that had gone too far. He'd come a long way in ten years, Hey thought bitterly. A simple killing with his bare hands must have begun to seem amateur. So by the time they'd gone through the living room to the opium bed, Hey knew he couldn't save them all by breaking loose and running away on a dancer's legs. His only advantage was that he knew Crook House better than Sam. That was the one way out, and right away he started to wait for it.

"What does it mean?" Sam asked him, nodding at the trail leading out of the room.

"It's just some presents they're giving each other," he said. Clever Rita, he thought, to try to loosen Peter up for the big transition into the secret room, to make it a game so he wouldn't get greedy. Even Sam seemed to know it was child's play. "Take it all and go," Hey said evenly. "Please. Tie me up. None of them will be home to find me till after six."

"Oh, really? You're the only one here today, is that it?" He kicked the pile of coins and they landed silently all over the rug. Hey couldn't seem to stop his getting mad. Sam tripped him and pushed him down roughly on his hands and knees. "Follow it, baby," Sam said. "See where it goes." And Hey just went ahead and did it. The more he held back, the more he'd get hit. He crawled over the buckle and the watch and Wyatt Earp's horn, and he paused only when he got to the hallway, to wait and hope that Sam had had enough.

"Can't you figure it out?" Sam asked. "Let me show you." And he came around behind Hey and kicked the telescope hard. It flew apart, the pieces landing heavily on the floor, the string of pearls sailing ten feet to burst against the far wall. The pearls rained down like hail. "Can't you see where this is all going?" Sam demanded, his voice getting more and more pitiless. He couldn't do a thing to the totem pole, but he picked up the Indian figure and smashed it down and cracked it. Now he was right outside Rita's door. The length of the hallway separated the two of them, and Hey sat back on his haunches and tried to figure how much time he had if he leapt up now and ran. Not enough, of course, and besides, he couldn't leave Peter and Rita now that the nightmare had started to net them in, too.

"What do you want to bet me this is Rita's room?" Sam said, as if it was all too easy. "And you know what I noticed while you were taking your nap out back? This door's locked from the inside."

He paused to let it sink in: There was no hope. Did I want to bring this down on all of us? Hey wondered. But being hurt had made him too hard on himself. Until now, he'd have said he was the only one in danger. The reason he blamed himself was that he knew it was Sam a month ago, when he glanced up from the vacuum cleaner and nearly screamed in fear. He tried to tell himself it wasn't who he thought, and then that night, when Peter was missing, he decided Sam had probably taken him for ransom. Still, he waited to say so till he was sure, trying to wish it away. And then, when it wasn't true and turned out to be only a snakebite, he was twice as relieved as the others. He decided he *must* have made a mistake when he'd recognized Sam, and he'd forced it out of his mind from then on. There was too much else going on, anyway, what with Linda and Rita and waiting hand and foot on the convalescent painter in the upstairs bedroom. Hey knew the nature of fate too well. It didn't pile on the really heartstopping things, like the return of Sam, until one got the feeling one was coasting along on the flats with a view that went all the way to the horizon. Fate had a sense of occasion.

Sam lifted the Cézanne from the picture hook Rita had lightly tapped into the door. He held it in one hand and pounded with his other fist three or four times like a punching bag. Then he stopped and listened, and when there was nothing, he turned to Hey and grinned. He was having a wonderful time. "She doesn't seem to understand how bad it is, does she? Why doesn't she answer the door? Do you think she's mad at us?"

"She took a sleeping pill," Hey said, persisting in lie after lie, because all he needed was for one to take hold. "The doctor says she has to rest."

"Get over here," Sam ordered, and Hey stood up and came to him meekly, waiting for his move. "We'll both knock. I can make enough noise to get through a Seconal." He dropped the Cézanne on the floor, where it landed face up and the glass cracked. Then the two of them banged and hammered the door, four fists, and Sam said, "Louder. Call her." Hey sang out, "Rita! Rita!" in the saddest voice imaginable. If she heard him, she could never have jumped to the conclusion that it was a fire or a landslide. It had to be something to sorrow over. Hey was as furious as Sam. He beat at the door and cried out, and it felt just fine for a while, to bring it all up from his knotted stomach and his shorted nerves like an Indian crouched at a war drum. But then he was seized with exhaustion. He slumped against the door frame, and Sam stopped too, to goad him on. He was breathing deeply. He'd worked himself into a sweat, and he stood over Hey like a player in the middle of a winning game. Hey couldn't breathe at all. He shrank back, terrified Sam would punish him into going on. And then they heard Peter's voice.

"Hey? What's wrong?" He was right on the other side of the door. "Are you still there? Rita, hurry!" Hey knew, as he met Sam's eyes, that Rita was going down the row of windows, undoing the locks. Sam put out one hand against Hey's chest and pinned him there, the pressure so intense Hey couldn't have shouted again, even if it would have helped. Sam's face was wild with triumph, and Hey tried to tell himself it was a good sign. We can't get him mad, he thought. And then, as he heard the lock release on the door, just as they flung it open, he looked away from Sam down at the floor, as if he was ashamed. The heel of Sam's boot was on the watercolor. Hey couldn't see the damages clearly, because everything started to happen, but it registered in his mind that it was ruined.

"*He* said you were asleep," Sam called to Rita over Peter's shoulder as she hurried toward them along the windows. He ignored Peter as if he weren't there. "Maybe you were in bed but wide awake, huh?"

"What do you want?" she asked him roughly, still a little blinded by the light through the windows. "If you're here to see Nick, you wait in *his* room. The rest of us have some rights in this house."

"It's not Nick, Rita," Peter said quietly. "That's all over." He and Rita had never revealed to each other that they'd seen Sam, and they both saw now how loyal they'd been to Nick. Rita still didn't understand how bad it was. She assumed Nick and Sam were still fighting their way out of a sloppy affair, and she thought Sam had gone over to bullying Hey and Peter and her in order to make trouble for Nick. As if any of them would abandon the others for anything now. The angrier she got, Rita figured, the more she was coming to Nick's rescue. But when she looked at Peter and Hey for support, ready to drive him out of the house bodily if she had to, both of them were staring at the ground. She looked down. She nearly let out a wail of pain, seeing the litter of all her beautiful things.

"He's right," Sam said to Rita. "Nick has nothing to do with this." He still held Hey by the front of his shirt, and he still didn't look at Peter. "You have something that belongs to me. Go get it."

"They don't know anything about it," Hey said fiercely. "Lock them up somewhere, and I'll take you in. I'm the only one who can do it."

Instead of answering, Sam pulled him up close, grinned again an inch from his face, and pushed him through the door into Rita's room, scattering the others out of the way. He closed the door and stood there, taking the measure of the room while the three of them grouped at the foot of the bed. Rita couldn't believe it. It must have been Nick who told Sam, but who told Hey? Did Hey know all along? The walls were breaking down everywhere, and Rita's first reaction wasn't fear for the Rembrandt or even for the trusty little band of eccentrics in Crook House. The fears would start attacking in a minute, but just now she couldn't bear it that she'd lost control of the project. She would have let in everyone in the end. But not yet. Now, she thought, she would no doubt begin to stare into mirrors again, instead of walking through them.

"Tell them who I am," Sam said, but looking at no one in particular, as if he was asking the house itself. All three of his present victims would have had a different answer, but Hey was first. His was the worst news, and he spit it out like an accusation.

"This is the punk who killed Varda," he said. And Rita and Peter looked at each other questioningly, wondering what he meant. Sam had only one connection to them, and that was Nick. Hey was rattled, they thought. He was mixing it up with another life.

But Sam seemed to get the idea, and his face stretched tight as he spoke. "How did I do that?" he asked evenly, quite as if he couldn't recall.

"You choked him in his own bed."

"Is that right?" There was no defining the comic quality in his voice, but as things got less and less funny, he seemed to bristle with little laughs. "Now, as I remember it, he was suck-ing me off at the time." And he seemed to plead for reason from Peter and Rita, who flanked Hey like henchmen. "He thinks I don't understand the difference between killing and sex. And I *always* know sex when I see it. I've never yet mistaken it for anything else." He paused as if he might go on talking for hours, but then thought better of it. Still giddy, he took the gun from his pants at last. Then he waved them all across the room and into the closet. He didn't seem to know exactly what he was looking for, but he'd apparently decided it wasn't out here.

Somehow, Rita thought, there wasn't a shred of suspense left in the act of opening up. For a brief moment, the four of them stood in the closet like the crew on a rocket ship in a comic strip, ready to man their stations, all systems go. But Rita closed the door and pressed the button without any flair, like someone ringing for an elevator high up in an office building. And when the door went open, the three of them watched Sam get startled, three against one. It diluted the quickened energy of having someone new to show it to, and, anyway, with Sam they were inwardly vowing to play it down. Peter and Rita and Hey had imagined the secret room so differently one from another that they were bound to be fighting for separate corners of it, covering separate gates to its deepest secrets. In that, too, it was three on one.

Rita lit the candles and handed one to Peter. She'd been such a stickler for authenticity that she'd never used any more light than Varda used himself. She'd started out the first week with what probably were the stubs of the candles Varda had taken in with him on his last inspection. Since then, she'd gone through a dozen more. Sam, she thought, would have to find the miner's lamp on his own, just as she did. She and Peter entered first and stood like acolytes while Hey and then Sam followed them in. Sam made no protest when Hey sat down on a limestone capital from Crete. He took Peter's candle away from him and looked around guardedly, candle in one hand, gun in the other, trying not to show what he felt. He was annoyed at being overwhelmed by the clicking open of the mirror. He had the sense he'd let them see that he was weak.

He was worried for *their* sake, because he wasn't weak at all and didn't want them thinking they could grab the upper hand. They'd get hurt.

The blank look on his face looked awfully shy to Rita, and it gave her a first inkling that he didn't have a clue what the room was about. Already he looked as if he'd been tricked. It wasn't that he'd never seen rare and costly things before and thus felt clumsy, a beggar shuffling his feet in a mansion. He'd had his dose of baronial taste all the while he was growing up, and in fact he was probably the only one of the four who'd had a Cézanne in the library face to face with a gilt and ormolu mantel clock from Fontainebleau. But that in a way was the problem. Because he used to *live* like this—not so splendidly, of course, except it all seemed the same to him—Rusty Varda's secret room looked like the attic of a swank town house. He was silent and tense as he held the candle up and squinted into the warehouse gloom. *This* couldn't be the right place.

"Where is it?" he asked, turning to the light of Rita's candle.

"Where is what?"

"The money," he said sharply. "Stop playing it like a game, Rita. I already won it ten years ago."

Rita frowned. "But there isn't any money here," she said. "I don't understand what Varda told you." She stepped forward, leaving Peter standing next to Hey. She came up close to Sam, so that they stood candle to candle. His calling her Rita helped. He isn't so bad, she thought, as we want him to be. "These are his things," she said, "and some of them are worth a fortune, but not to us. You couldn't *sell* them, because they're hot. And if you took away something to hold for ransom, who would you get it from? *We* don't have that kind of money."

She spoke so gently she might have been about to ask for a donation. She saw what Peter and Hey didn't, that Sam really had imagined a vault knee-deep in silver dollars. Rita had waited forever for a room like this, and so had Sam, and Rita got just the one she wanted, and Sam didn't. It made her feel generous and wise. She felt like a runner safely across the finish line, arms wide to comfort the losers. What else could she do? Somebody had to come in second.

"He used to tell me about it," Sam said, still as if something was funny. "Of all the boys he ever had, I was the only one he told. He *said* so. He used to say he had the pot of gold at the end of the rainbow all locked up in his house."

Rita felt a shiver of something electric passing close to her heart. She suddenly knew she had to get Sam's gangster act behind them. She realized for the first time she had someone here who'd actually heard Varda himself on the subject. Heard it in bed to boot. So Rita worked to alter the tone in the secret room, to have it seem like a normal day so Sam would talk. Because it was the closest Rita would ever come to what it was like when Varda sweet-talked the moon and stars to Frances Dean. She didn't know where to begin, the gun and the break-in having sent them off on the wrong foot. If she could have had it her way, she'd have sent Hey and Peter out to the kitchen to eat the avocados stuffed with steak tartare. Then she would have sat Sam down in her office to cross-examine him. But nicely, and not so he'd feel he was being grilled by a caseworker. It was amazing how much she'd figured out of his story already. She didn't have a clear picture of the relationships with Varda and Nick, and she wasn't much struck by the cold-blooded connection between the two liaisons. Mostly, he'd arrested her with the hint of a ten-year wait. And Rita wrote the book on waiting.

"How did he sound? Happy?" she asked, as blithely as if they were holding cocktails instead of candles, and nobody had a gun.

"No, it wasn't so much that," Sam said, but fishing for it, trying to get it right. "He sounded *safe*. Like he was so high up, no one could reach him." And when he saw her nod as if it fit like a glove, he found he felt safer himself. Sam was more cautious than Rita, from years of no one to trust, and he wasn't ready to let the mood go nice just because *she* wanted it to. He knew the balance of power was with him right now. And he knew she wanted it back. At the same time, though, he could tell she had all the answers to this place. She was the one who could help him redirect his plan, which he had to do in the next few minutes or else. He didn't waste time on having been wrong for the whole ten years. If the getaway car isn't there, then you run. If the clerk wakes up, then you hit him again. Crime didn't pay unless you had an alternate route set up at every dead end.

"Did he say it was a room set aside by itself?"

"I thought it must be a walk-in vault," Sam said, "like a bank." They paused a bit after every exchange, as if to study their positions. He had to admit it would do him good to talk it out about Varda. Though Sam had gotten in at gunpoint, the talking didn't seem odd because Rita didn't. He would have to make a private arrangement with Nick after all, he was thinking, maybe work out some regular payments. He had to exert some control in this house. He'd never really need *money* out of it, any more than Rita did, or, in any case, not to buy things. The Varda treasure was never meant to let him retire from hustling and settle down in a house in the hills with a view of the downtown smog. Security didn't interest him. He only wanted to walk in in the middle of a very big deal, stay long enough to put his mark on it, and split. If it had been silver dollars or stacks of cash, the way it was supposed to be, he might have thrown it all out like confetti from the open door of a helicopter. Or bought up something crazy, a half dozen Cadillacs maybe, and sent them one by one over the bluffs at Santa Monica. He couldn't figure out what was going on in here instead, but he had the suspicion that Rita was feeling around for a deal of her own, a separate peace, or else why didn't she just shut up and let him get nowhere. It might be they could work something out, he thought, something a little more creative than armed robbery. The break-in turned him on, the pushing Hey around and talking surly, but he was just as amenable here as he was in bed to trying something new. Whatever worked.

"Why don't you make me an offer?" he said, breezy and open, and for once the humor didn't seem misplaced. They had to fashion a compromise, and lightly was the safest way.

"This is what you ought to do," Rita said, as ready to deal as she would ever be. "Take something out of here, a little painting or something, and that establishes your credentials. It's like having a share of stock in Varda's company. Then you have to work it out with Nick. Like I say, we don't have the big bucks to pay out for ransom, but there are rewards for a lot of these things. The rest we have to fence somehow, because there isn't any owner to return them to. See what I mean? We're going to have money coming in. What you do is ask for a cut of it."

For a moment, then, they were gliding along like Bonnie and Clyde. Had Rita somehow forgotten the torn and stepped-on watercolor lying out in the hall, its price plummeted to nothing? It was in her, she knew, to get so infatuated with the process of giving a briefing that she neglected her own best interests. But she was gambling here on his innocence, evident to her in the loose, unfocused way he held the gun. His protests aside, games were clearly his strong suit. All his previous crimes, she could see, were a whore's crimes, victimless and brief. He'd stayed a kid by fucking day after day and letting the rest of life go by. That was what it amounted to: He was still a kid, and he needed to hear a kid's story. Nine parts plot to one part character.

"Screw that idea," he said. "You'd have a roadblock up before I got out of Bel-Air."

She talked fast: "Oh, but you're wrong. We can't have the police involved in any of this. We've all been in and out of this room for weeks. I think we're accessories after the fact, but it's very technical, so I don't know. It doesn't matter. There's millions of dollars worth of stuff in here, and to get it they can always think up charges you never heard of." Then what? She took up the tongue of a small-time hood, since no one had ever had to say such things in the drawing rooms of Gothic novels, and thus she had no tradition to tap. "We've got to wipe out the serial numbers, or whatever it is that labels them. Then we get them placed in little old lady antique stores, and then we discover them. It's going to take a long, long time."

"I don't want to do a deal with Nick," Sam said, and she could see his pen was poised above the dotted line. He wasn't fussy about the fine print. He was just protecting his access route to the top man. Which in this case was Rita. "I work for you. I take a cut from you."

"You're absolutely right," she said, nodding so vigorously her candle shook and guttered. "It's the only way to keep things straight." And now that we're in it together, she thought, I wonder what it is. She was making it up as she went along, and now she had to come up with a job that would satisfy him. It was all a play for time, time being the game *she* played well.

"So what do you want me to do?" he asked, just half a step behind her.

"Well," she said, and she looked away as if to mull it over. She and Sam had gotten turned slightly sideways from the others, so as to talk in privacy. Now her breath froze in her throat. She saw the next thing happen an instant before it did, but not in time to stop it. Peter lobbed a Persian bottle across the darker side of the room, and it smashed against the bust of Hadrian close by Rita's office. Sam whirled and fired at nothing, the oldest trick in the book, and Hey came down on top of him before he got the joke. They fell to the floor together, Hey around his neck, and the noise of the gunshot thundered around the room, beating on the walls to find a way out. The candles were snuffed and dead on the floor. They had to make do with the dim, faraway light from the closet. Peter was at Rita's side now, and he tried to draw her off. She wouldn't leave. Sam was face-down in front of her. Hey was perched like a monkey on his back, but he didn't know what to do next. He'd done a dazzling dancer's leap in perfect time to Peter's bottle ploy, but he couldn't seem to get rough. The seconds passed, and Sam heaved his shoulders and squirmed and shook. It was all Hey could do to stay on.

271

"Hit him!" Rita shouted, digging her fingers into Peter's arm. But even as he broke away from her to pick up something heavy, she saw Sam's gun hand struggle free from under him. Before he could use it, he still had to throw Hey off and turn over. She took two steps and stamped her heel hard on his wrist, but because she was barefoot, it didn't do anything but make him madder. He pulled loose, and the arm swung back and forth in an arc. The spurt of rage shuddered through his body. He rolled, and she saw his face. For an awful moment, as Hey lost his balance and fell and Sam was on his side with the gun free, the barrel swept across her body. Her stomach muscles locked. She opened her mouth to beg for something—if they could only start the last part over—and in his eyes she watched the moment pass when it could have been Rita he shot. Then the gun rolled with him all the way over. At last he and Hey were face to face, lying on their sides like a freeze at the end of a dance, and it happened. The fire flashed. The blood fountained out on the front of Hey's jacket. And again the noise. It roared like the blooming flower of a bomb.

Sam leapt to his feet, and Rita dropped into a crouch beside Hey. Sam shrieked, "Don't touch him!" But Rita wasn't any more scared now than she was before the shots. Horrified and maddened and sick, yes, but except for the slow second she was looking down the barrel, not bodily threatened herself. It was just a meaningless accident. Though she would have killed Sam now with no regrets for what he'd done to a man like Hey, she knew it was the game gotten out of hand. And her anger was endless in the face of things that got evil by being stupid, like the final years of Frances Dean. "I told you," Sam barked twice, "I told you." But she wouldn't even look at him. Hey's eyes opened, and he gritted his teeth and took the pain. If they did this right, she thought, he'd make it. The hole was in his shoulder, not his heart, and the blood had slowed to a seep.

"Peter," she said, like a rock inside, "get help. Then bring me some cold towels." When she looked up to get a confirmation, she saw he was holding, cradled like a baby, the Jacobean mace, a wood and silver club that had once belonged to a Scottish lord. Victoria and Albert Museum. It was what he'd picked up too late to bash in Sam's head, but he looked right now like a sad-eyed herald walking in front of a luckless king. He let it down on the floor and turned to go.

"Don't move," Sam said, brandishing the gun to catch his eye. Peter stopped. Rita turned on Sam so sharply that he jumped away, and for a couple of seconds the gun swung back and forth at Rita, then at Peter, like a pendulum.

"When the hell are you going to let it go?" she demanded. "Don't you see? It's *over*."

But he did the very thing she'd done to him. He didn't even look at her, and he went ahead as if she wasn't there. He approached Peter, aiming the gun at his belly with both hands. When they were close together and it was just between the two of them, Sam put a hand to his back pocket and pulled from it a set of handcuffs. He held them out. "Left hand," he said to Peter. "Very slowly." Peter reached over and took the cuffs, but then it took him a minute to open the hinge because his hands were trembling. Rita made as if to stand up, her fury so high she meant to snatch the gun herself, and Sam said, "I'll kill him, Rita. Stay where you are." So she didn't dare move, but she said in return, "No you won't. You go too far, and we have to let you win, so go ahead. Take what you want and get out. But you didn't kill Varda, and you won't kill us."

"Shut up, Rita," Peter said. He snapped the cuff tight around his hand. Then he held it against his stomach as if he was hurt and had to keep it in a sling. He waited for the next order, with nothing to do now but stay alive. He could tell that Rita was as angry with him and Hey for attacking as she was with Sam, though she wouldn't admit it. But Peter had sensed, as soon as they were all locked in together, that Rita was safe and they were in trouble. Sam's eyes glittered with hatred. Peter and Hey both saw it and started to hatch the plot the moment Rita began to deal. They did it with a glance here and there and a couple of pointed fingers, because they could trust the rhythm they already had from running the house together. They both knew the gun would go off. One of them might get in the way. But it seemed to Hey and Peter worth the risk, since Rita was dead wrong about Sam. He didn't kill *her* way, out of what she would have seen as an excess of passion. He'd do it for nothing at all or not at all. And Hey and Peter were as meaningless in the way of victims as any he could wish for.

"What's the most expensive thing you've got?" Sam asked, as if he was an oil tycoon on a shopping spree.

"The Rembrandt," Peter said, and he could feel Rita flinch from where she knelt next to Hey. She would have tried to tell a lie even here. Tried to palm off a cracked Ming jar or a dusty tapestry.

"Get it," Sam said.

Peter moved very deliberately among the crates and boxes. He didn't want to make Sam nervous, and though the painting was so heavy in the frame that he couldn't imagine lifting it, it wouldn't do to begin by protesting. Hey moaned, as if he'd tried to shift positions, and Rita bent over close to him. Sam retrieved a candle from the floor, but he couldn't put the gun down to strike the match. He looked to see if anyone noticed, and when they didn't, he let the candle fall again. By now they were all accustomed anyway to the near-darkness—their eyes had patiently adjusted while they were busy clamoring for power. Slowly, Peter rocked the Rembrandt and balanced it on one corner. Then he dragged it over the concrete until he could seesaw it onto a crate where Sam could take a look at it. He undid the sheet that covered it, which fell aside like a veil, and the clear-eyed Dutchman stared at them all and didn't move a muscle.

"Now get over next to her and cuff yourselves together."

Peter let down the painting beside the crate and propped it sturdily. Walking away, he was strangely shaken by Sam's not looking at it. For Sam, apparently, there was no such person as Rembrandt. Peter had to wonder, when he went down beside Rita and gripped her hand in one of his and somehow got the feeling Hey was dead, whether the painting was worth a thing anymore if Sam should have it.

"It isn't going to be much longer," Peter whispered close to her ear as he shut her up in the other cuff.

"Why doesn't he run?" she whispered back. "He can't get anywhere with a Rembrandt now." But she didn't expect an answer. Peter was right, she thought, to shut her up. It had all gotten out of her range, and if it had gone the same way for Sam, the two of them together might have found the way back to where they were, even in spite of the gunshots. But Sam had cut his losses and gone on, and she was too much overwhelmed at last by the disarray to keep up with him. Hey looked at her when he was conscious with an agony that turned him into a stranger. Anything she could have done to cool him or pillow him, any news she had of an ambulance, would have restored him enough to be recognized. But as she wasn't free to try, she began to be something of a stranger herself. She'd always said she'd been through it all, and yet the suffering she'd done for love was the only kind she knew, and now she knew it had all been in her head. Hey with a blood-soaked shirt was insupportable. She felt like a lone survivor of the kind of disaster that sweeps away men like ants, and nothing is ever going to be the same again.

Peter stared at Hey for half a minute, willing him alive. He could hear Sam pulling at the painting, his energy draining into rage because he couldn't move it any more easily than Peter. Where Rita had fallen so fast from wheeling and dealing and wild defiance to a state where she felt brutalized and worn —as if Peter's "Shut up" had done the reverse of the slap in the face that stops hysteria short and makes a man cool and feisty again—Peter himself grew wilder and more alert as the time passed. He knew what the next step was before Sam even thought of it, and he didn't have much time. Hey would just have to cease looking dead so Peter could go ahead and hold out hope. He didn't know how bad it was, but he refused to believe it was fatal. The snakebite taught him how far he could go on a wound that looked awful.

Hey responded to Peter's stubbornness as if it were treatment. He quivered and came partly awake. He opened his eyes and looked at each of them a moment and then seemed to sigh back into sleep. It was enough for Peter, and he hoped like hell. Unlike Rita, he determined that everything *would* be the same again. Exactly the same. It was what kept Russian princes in exile going.

"I can't do it," Sam said. He sounded at once upset and a trifle conciliatory, as if he might convince someone to jump up and come give a hand. Rita and Peter had the brief satisfaction of sticking to their little group and letting him stew. There was a pause in which Peter felt Sam begin to figure out the risks of going one step further. Then Peter squeezed Rita's shackled hand with his shackled hand, and murmured, "He's going to split us up. Tell Nick not to get mad. I'll leave a sign in the house to let him know you're here."

The whole three sentences came out in a monotone, and Rita heard it as a string of one-liners, like the comic remarks made at wakes, meant to evoke the irony of everything compared to death and not to make anyone laugh. We're caught in a bad cliché, Peter seemed to be telling her, and we're forced into speaking lines out of comic strips. As the crime widened and fed on itself like a mountain fire, they were less and less allowed to talk like themselves, compelled by the tenor of events to be rather formal. It went through Rita's mind in a melancholy way, and the part of her that never stopped grappling with life and what was meant to come of it began to see the scene from very far away. It was an existential event. The great fight to get on with it filled her mind like blood, but it was as if she couldn't speak around the broken teeth. She never dreamed Peter was giving her the orders to get her through the next several hours in Hell. She'd begun to think they were only waiting for Sam to go. It was all she could do not to tick the seconds off, drumming the fingers of her free hand. So when Sam came over and knelt between them and said, fiddling with the key in the lock, "Peter, you're coming with me," Rita drew a blank the size of a movie screen. But wait.

Someone had got to repeat the three things he said, she thought in a panic. Because she didn't know what to do at all.

The steel bit into her flesh, her wrist got yanked, and her watch stopped, all while Sam was struggling to get them apart. She prayed the cuffs were broken. Though she couldn't attach a meaning to Peter's instructions, even as the phrases filtered back, she did still remember "Shut up." So she made no protest when Sam cuffed her other hand. She put on a brave front for taking her last look at Peter. At least he was smarter than Sam, she thought, trying to calm down. She telegraphed to Peter with her eyes that she and Nick would comb the earth to track him down.

Just at that moment, though, he was pretending to Sam to be simple and subdued, so he couldn't very well start winking at Rita. He stood up and, as he went with Sam to the painting, licked and blew at the raw spot on his wrist. The two of them lifted the Rembrandt without any trouble. Rita thought when she watched them carry it out to the closet that they were gone for good. Calm down and count to fifty, she said to herself. And then she'd follow along and get to a phone, peeking around the corners all the way, the receiver clenched between her cuffs. Sam was a dope. If she'd been Sam, she would have cuffed her hands behind her and put in a gag. What was the worst that could happen now? Nobody in his right mind would harm a Rembrandt. If Sam laid a finger on Peter, Nick would kill him. *She* would kill him. Hey appeared to be a grudge from the far past, and Sam was taking Peter along only to further defuse the crackerjack team of Peter and Rita and Hey. In the weird quiet that fell for a bit on Varda's room, she groped to get back her limitless capacity for stories that turned out well in the end. She must have counted to twenty or twenty-five. It'll be okay, she thought. The wrecked Cézanne seemed to fly from her mind a second time, and the hole through the blasted shoulder below her on the floor was a notch less fatal. She was almost high again, ready to fight and win.

But the sounds of things outside the secret room were al-

ways cut off—as if, inside, the hills held their hands over
everyone's ears. So Rita heard nothing, and it was all a trick of
the house. Peter and Sam were in her room the whole time,
working out the best way to get the picture to where Sam's
car was parked. Peter cooperated impeccably, with all his skill
as a mover in space, for the sake of the priceless thing between
them. Even Sam knew right away, when he heard Peter out,
that he was kidnapping his very own museum director to go
with the painting. He understood how great the painting must
be from watching Peter try to protect it. He went back into
the closet to close up the mirror, and he knew he could leave
Peter all alone out in the bedroom. Peter wouldn't run from
the Rembrandt. He wouldn't even risk a scuffle if they were
near it. Sam decided with some relief that Peter was a hostage
with a built-in gun at his head.

Rita thought at first that it must be help arriving. When
Sam slipped through the door again to take a final look, he was
there so suddenly that she didn't think. The light was behind
him, and her heart leaped up. It was Nick! Because nobody
else would have known so soon where to come. And when, the
next moment, she saw her mistake, the breath went out of her
yet again. The back of her neck prickled with the start of a
dead faint. Nothing would have shut her up now, except she
couldn't think what to say, as she sometimes couldn't cry out
in a nightmare. She knew his hand on the mirror's edge meant
he was locking them in, and no one would ever hear her
screaming. The trick to the sound worked both ways.

"Tell him I'm going underground," Sam said across the
room to her. "There's no use trying to find me. I'll call him
tonight."

And then he pulled the mirrored door shut with a click
behind him, and Rita was thrown into total darkness. Her
voice came back like lightning. It may have been that sound-
proof walls were just what she needed. She started to scream,
and she threw herself at the lost light until she was beating the
back of the mirror with her fists. She didn't need to do it long.
In a minute she was listening to her own noise, and the fall into

consciousness brought her up short into silence. Dying away, the echo of the scream sank into the hills like water out in the sun, with only the faintest tremor. It never went so far as to shake things in their frames, but there was a shiver to the room for a moment more before the silence took a grip. Rita didn't even know what the next hysteria was that came after screaming. She sank against the door on one shoulder, and in the pitch dark an image went through her mind of a woman much like herself on the mirror side of the mirror. Pretty and thin and taking time at how she looked. Never the wiser about the treasure there for the taking on the other side.

It would be too much, though, to say she wanted to go back and start over with a suitcase full of the wrong clothes. She only felt how much more she'd chosen over a mirror that stayed in one place, with just one side. She stood in the dark now and saw nothing. If none of it ever happened, she could have stood all she liked instead at the three-way mirror. She had to wonder which way gave her back the most true picture of herself. Maybe neither. But she started to think about it, just as if she was lying by the pool and stirring Campari and soda with a finger. Sealed in the hills with a wounded man, no help in sight till sundown, her oldest friend abducted, she started to imagine what she could have done differently. *That* was the next hysteria. When Hey said her name, she was already so caught up in speculation that she wasn't even shocked to hear him strong enough to speak.

"Rita?"

"What?"

"Are you all right?"

"Sure," she said absently, and then, to be polite, "are you?"

"I think so. Come here. I want to see if I can sit up."

And suddenly she realized. She stood up straight, and her eyes widened. Hands out in front of her, she made her way like a sleepwalker back to her nurse's station. He'd sounded so clear, so matter-of-fact, that it might have been nothing more than a sprained ankle. Just like Peter, she'd refused to entertain the notion Hey would die. And look what happened. He was practically as good as new, up on one elbow already by the time she knelt beside him. She'd do well, she thought, to refuse whatever she could of agony and evil. It might just all go away.

"Get me over to the sofa," Hey said, and he talked through his teeth as he gripped her around, because at first the bones in his shoulder jiggled like sticks. Rita held him up, and they took little steps and said nothing till she eased him down among the pillows.

"It won't be long," she lied.

"Have you got the lamp?" he asked, as if the darkness they were in was after all a cave from *Arabian Nights*. All they needed was a genie. Rita turned to the desk and groped at the drawer pull. She thrust both hands deep inside, much as she'd done day after day for weeks, always certain what she'd find. One hand grasped the lamp, and the other took hold of the diary. It was only a half hour since she'd put them back in place, when she and Peter stopped to eat the lunch they never got to.

"Here," she said. She held it out, but of course he couldn't see it, so she snapped it on. He grinned into the light.

"Now put it on," he said. "You've got work to do."

"How come you're so much better, Hey?" She slipped her head into the lamp the moment he told her to, though she knew it was a waste of time. He didn't seem to understand they couldn't do anything now but wait. They had to save their breath. Not use up all the air. "Are you a Christian Scientist?"

"I'm not a bit better," he said. If he'd left it at that, she would have had the horrors, but he was only being precise. She thought: He's the one realist we've got in this house. He'd monitored his own vital signs since the first shock passed and the pain went into a rhythm. He went on, and he was as tough as the tough guys that turned up to put things right in Rita's stories: "But with *him* here, I thought I better play dead or he'd empty the gun in me. Now, the first thing you have to do is find something good to stand on."

"We shouldn't move around too much," she said, faintly saying no. "It gets very stuffy in here very fast. We have to wait for Nick."

"Nick won't be home till tonight, and you know it." It was as if she didn't understand how tough he was. "We don't have time. We've got to get out of here now."

"Just try to hang on," she said, putting his urgency out of her mind. He couldn't see her eyes for the light, but she saw his. He wanted something. No matter what it is, she thought, I can't. She tried to sound caring and solicitous, and the words tasted awful and cheap. "Let me make you comfortable," she said.

"Oh, I'm comfortable as hell. It's a goddam country club in here." He laughed, short and bitter, and it fell over into a cough that went on and on. Suddenly it sounded like his last breath. He strangled the next words out. "Listen. Please. I'm trying to tell you. There's another way out of here."

Chapter 9

The dirt rained down on Rita's face, but she ducked her head quickly, and it fell on the helmet. The hatch above her head was as heavy as a manhole cover. It hadn't been touched in years, and the ground and the roots of hillside plants had all crept over it. There was a time, Hey said, when Varda would send him up the ladder every couple of months to test the locks and raise the lid—long after it was of any use to Varda himself, who could scarcely climb regular stairs and had no one to make a getaway from anymore. When he built the house, it was meant to give him an alternate route on the day the art cops caught up with him at last. Then he knew he would have to choose just one thing—the Scythian breastplate, solid gold, or maybe the papal crown—and roll away the Roman stone from the entrance to the tunnel behind the screen. And up the iron ladder through the hill, in a space hardly as wide as a well. The going was slow because the tunnel was narrow and timbered like a mine shaft. But it all had a crazy sort of logic for Rita. She thought: if you entered a room like Alice through the looking glass, you might as well leave in the end by a rabbit hole.

And then what? Where did he expect to flee to? Rita wondered as she wedged one foot where two beams crossed. She heaved her shoulders up against the hatch, butting it at the same time with the helmet so that it moved a few more inches. Rusty Varda planned to run away with nothing more than a souvenir of his vast accumulation. That, the clothes on his back, and the money in his pants pockets, like a charlatan run out of town. What was it that turned him on in that? Did he have a second secret room somewhere else? A place to hide in, Rita thought, bare as a monk's cell, quite the opposite of this. When the dirt stopped falling, she pushed again. The dust was deep in her lungs. Her teeth gritted together with a grinding sound, like sandpaper. She decided not. A man wouldn't have more than one secret room. Nevertheless, she knew she was right about how Varda dreaded the day when he'd have to run. Unlike Sam, for instance, he wasn't ever in love with mere running. His own great passion was for putting down roots, even though he knew time came and tore them all up. He wouldn't have been surprised if life turned out to be a passage from a treasure room to a room full of nothing. After all, it was just what happened to Frances Dean. He'd lived long enough to believe it more the more he denied it: You didn't get to keep what you'd got.

"I can't do it," Rita shouted down the tunnel. "I'm going to suffocate!"

"Just *do* it," Hey hollered back. "It's not that hard."

It was hard as hell and he knew it, she grumbled to herself, and heaved and groaned until it gave another three or four inches. This time, when the dirt stopped pouring down, she caught the glint of daylight here and there around the lid. She almost shouted again. She *wanted* to. But she knew how dumb it would sound so soon after all her complaining, and Hey would think it was his insistence alone that got her through. And she hadn't *really* thought she couldn't do it. She'd only called to him so as not to feel alone. She didn't want a shred of help, once she knew the room was built to provide her with·a second chance.

She struggled up another rung on the ladder and suddenly found she could lift the cover free of the hole. She peered out and squinted in the fiery sun, thrilled to find it still the middle of the day. She could feel a tangle of roots that held firm along one side, trying to keep her underground. Any other time, she might have had to climb down and search out a knife to cut her way through. Now she just got mad and pulled the cover loose. She couldn't exactly fling it away, even so. She had to teeter up the last few steps of the ladder, the disk of cast iron above her head. It was the pose of Atlas, and she knew it. She felt like she was holding up the front end of a car, but she could tell in these final moments that it wasn't heavy enough to beat her. She *did* it. By the time she let the cover crash into the bushes that hid the hole, she was waist-high back in the real world, and the lid that sealed the secret room was scrap.

"I'm out!" she cried, though no one was around to hear it, much less applaud it. She had to duck her head back in the hole to shout it down to Hey, but the rest of her was scrambling out before she said half a dozen words. And when she came to her feet and parted the branches, she found she wasn't Rip Van Winkle at all. Everything was the same. She was smack in the center of a patch of desert scrub above the house, away to the right of the cars. With the lavish garden around the pool and the shaded arch running down to the house, it was the part of the hill they never looked at, all overgrown and dusty green. But the view was as lovely as any she could remember. Crook House held its mountain seat. Over the roof, the water in the pool lay still as a pond in the woods. And she could see how the city was strangely intact when she looked away downtown. Bright, with a million shadows. Not a wisp of smog.

She set off down the hill, sliding a foot with every step. She stubbed a toe and didn't stop. To get to the stairs leading down to the house, she grasped two trees, one in either hand, and hoisted herself through. She took the whole flight down in three good leaps and reached the door. Which was locked. But she didn't miss a beat. She moved to the left along the roof, and at the corner she dropped through the bushes above the kitchen garden. The hill was straight down. She went too fast. But there she was—she landed on the terrace floor, and though the parrot rattled the cage as if he was caught in a cockfight, it sounded to Rita as sweet as a speech from *Hamlet*. She could have kissed him for being where he ought to be.

She called the Bel-Air Patrol and not the LA police. The patrol would probably call the police the moment they hung up from her, but that was up to them. She wondered if she was trying still to keep it in the family. She said send up an ambulance, but she didn't say a gunshot wound. She said a robbery, but not a word about who did it. Yet in spite of something that felt like shyness, she didn't think she was out to protect Sam. It was more that she couldn't handle right away the pace and tone of police. They'd be tough and plodding and humorless, and Rita wanted the kid-glove treatment, at least for the rest of the day. She'd had her fill of brute force. Besides, it ought to be Nick's decision. Peter's safety was on the line, and *anybody* might be better than cops. Just now, her own work stopped at getting Hey to a doctor.

When she'd finished the call, she couldn't even remember if she'd given the right address. As she went headlong through the swing door into the dining room, she thought she may have just told them "Crook House" and left it at that. But why would anyone know the name of Varda's house anymore? There probably weren't ten people who knew who *Varda* was. You think too much, she told herself. She shook the worry off, rounding the corner into the living room, because it stood to reason that the luck should swing her way again. And there, as if to illustrate the point, was Nick himself, sitting on the low stone wall that edged the garden of sand. Rita shrieked and flew across the room. Before he could jump to his feet, she threw her arms around his neck. She'd had a running start, and she wasn't taking care, so of course she tipped them over. They pitched back into the sand.

He was shaken and not in the mood. He'd spent the last ten minutes brooding alone, and it made him sadder than he'd been all winter. But he caught her in his arms and let out a hoot and took it all as a joke. For both their sakes, he didn't question if she was playing sexy, consciously or not. Her unconscious was none of his business. Meanwhile, Peter had put in a day and a half drawing the lines in the sand with a pointed stick, but if Rita thought they could roughhouse around, somehow it didn't matter how much they messed it up. Rita was the only one with the necessary radar to get a bead on Peter's designing.

There was a moment when all they could do was scuffle to try to sit up again. They sprayed the sand as if they'd come down from a pole vault. Rita reeled back to get the space to tell him what she could. Nick held on because he didn't understand. He thought he might get a clue if he listened closely. It may have been they were still at the same cross-purposes where they always were, but they could do better than this. And since *she*'d had the shot of power from climbing through the hill, it was all on Rita to fix it. She wanted to bury her head in his neck and let it go. Instead, she sprang away and landed on her feet.

"Everything's ruined," she managed to say by way of generalization. "We have no time. Come on." She backed away in the direction of the hall, beckoning him with both hands as if she was hauling rope. She noticed how all the trail of pretty things had been wiped out. Sam had bothered to pause long enough to get rid of the traces. Rita tried not to think how long it might have taken Nick to guess where they'd gone to. She wasn't even sure she'd ever told him the trick to getting in.

"Not yet," he said playfully, sprawled in the sand. "You wait. Somebody has to tell me first what *this* means." And he held up the unmistakable ring of Peter's keys. He didn't seem to understand she was desperate. It all came across to him as a mock attack of hysteria—so much so that it had the effect of lifting his own bad mood. The keys were the sign that Peter promised Rita to leave behind. Nick had noticed Peter's car cheek by jowl with Rita's when he parked his own, and naturally he figured they were home. But then he'd called their names and poked about, and from the texture of the silence, he could tell he was all alone. He didn't think anything. He supposed they were both plumped up in the back of a client's limo. Or Hey would know, but Nick didn't want to disturb him. He was asleep every day, punctually, from one till three, as if he still lived in an equatorial country.

"Hey's all shot up," she said, and when she saw the light go out of his eyes, she dropped her voice and said as little as she could about the rest. "Peter's gone. I'm sorry."

He stood up and followed her instantly, and something like shame came over them both. They couldn't seem to look at each other as they made their way along the hall to her room. Nick didn't have to ask. It was Sam, of course. When he'd found the key ring fifteen minutes before, on the floor at the bottom of the spiral stairs, it didn't make him scared, but it made him want to cry. He'd sat right down on the garden ledge and thought about Peter without his keys. Nothing was *wrong*—Nick would have known if there was, he thought— but the keys led him to wonder how easy it was to strip a man of his apparatus, leaving him out in the cold. The way to the house, two cars, the shop, and the pickup was narrow as hell and fit in the palm of his hand. And altogether it made him think of Peter alone some day and himself dead—and then, like a flipped coin spinning in the air, it was him alone and Peter dead, but it didn't get any nicer, whichever way he looked. So life was feeling mean and comfortless when Rita blew in and tackled him. It always made him feel guilty to waste his time on death. Besides, it tempted fate. He was ready to hear the ordinary story that went with Peter losing his keys. Ever since getting rid of Sam, he'd needed all he could get of minor matters.

Now he walked through Rita's room in a daze while she went along the windows checking the locks. He stopped in the closet and waited. In the corner where the marble hands had been was the pile of things that Rita had put out that morning to make the trail. Everything was thrown in a jumble, but Nick's eye picked out the cracked lens at the wide end of the telescope and the crumpled Cézanne askew in its frame. So he knew the trove had suffered the same upheaval as all of them, even though Rita had not yet mentioned the Rembrandt by name. She joined him in the closet. As she closed the door, she reached out one hand and touched his shoulder and locked the lock with the other hand. The mirrored door clicked open, but Nick held back. Not Rita. Though she'd lost the miner's cap when they fell in the sand, the dark didn't hold any terror for her anymore. Heedless of gunfire, she rushed in first and called Hey's name.

Nick lit a match and made his way more haltingly. He could hear their voices up ahead in the office, already deep in conversation. He didn't *see* anything different, and then, just as he shook the match out, glimpsed the candles lying on the floor. On the second match, he bent down and retrieved them both, held them together in one hand to light and, as the room brightened, saw a long smear of blood at his feet. From there he could have found Hey merely by following the line of crimson spots as far as the sofa. He came forward with the light, and Rita and Hey looked up at him expectantly—partly, it seemed, to beg him to take control, partly to gauge if he could handle it. He did what he could. The sight of Hey with his front all bloody nearly made him heave, but he sat on the arm of the sofa and joined the group, all for one and one for all. Not that he was squeamish in the least, but he had a sudden horror of what it meant about Peter.

"He says we have to get him out of *here*," Rita explained. "He has to go back in the house."

"Did you call an ambulance?" Nick asked, only now realizing that he'd come into this thing right in the middle. She nodded. As near as he could tell, Rita must have locked Hey in when she went to get help. But why bother? And if it was *Sam* who had locked Hey in, why didn't he put Rita in there with him? Nick tried not to get wrapped up in his own questions. Keep the way clear, he said to himself—at least until they got to Peter. So he turned to Hey, anxious not to leave him out of the talk regarding his best interests. "Don't you think you'd better wait for them?" he said. "We might hurt you if we do it wrong."

"It's not me, Nick," Hey said impatiently. "It's this room." In case Nick thought he was claustrophobic and scared of the dark, he wanted it known that something was more important to him than his health. "I kept it a secret ten years, and I'm not going to let the whole world in until it's time. When this is over, the four of us can talk it out. We can't decide anything now." And when they did decide, he was saying, they'd have to hear *him* out. He had ten years of views to air on the subject. And Rita, who'd seen in Sam a passion as great as her own for what was here, saw yet another. Everything came in threes.

"It's gone beyond what *we* want to do," she said heatedly. "You can't just pretend a painting like that was taken off a wall in this house. It isn't *ours*. It belongs to the Duke of Argyll, for Christ's sake. It's a *Rembrandt*."

Everyone knew it was a Rembrandt. They were having a misunderstanding. Rita was going on the assumption that things would have to be investigated in full. Of all of them, she thought, Hey was the one who should have demanded a swarm of sharpshooters fanning out over LA to get the man who'd laid him low. Yet he seemed curiously loath to call in the help he paid his taxes for, though he had less reason than Rita to try to protect Sam. But where Rita was out to solve a crime, salvaging what she could of the secret world that had come apart, Hey had been brooding all this time over the next round of negotiations. Sam would still have to pay for all his murderous acts. If Hey was lucky, he'd be given a moment at the end to do his own business with Sam, one on one. But right now they were still in the game. It was their move. And Hey was the only one who could plot it, Nick the only one who could make it.

"This is the story," Hey said, and it was apparent he wasn't going to stand for revision. "I was all alone, and I heard a noise. When I came in the living room, I caught a guy stealing a picture." He narrowed his eyes at Rita. "*You* figure out who it was by. But make it sound a little flashy, or they won't believe a thief would give a shit."

"How do we come into it?" Nick asked. "Are we supposed to have walked in and found you?"

"Just Rita," Hey said, putting out his good arm for help. Nick leaned down, and Hey grasped him around his neck and then went on, close to his ear. "You'll be out of here in a few minutes, Nick. You've got to find Sam."

"No, he doesn't," Rita protested, following behind. They went along shoulder to shoulder, like army buddies. "Sam said it specially. Don't try to find him. He'll call us tonight."

Hey retorted irritably, "I know what he said, but it's not what he meant. He only said one thing that matters." And Rita, who could hear the twist the pain gave his words, was sorry she'd spoken up. He didn't say what the one thing was, but it mustn't have been either of the things she'd just repeated. She tried to think: What *was* the third thing Sam had said? But she couldn't retrieve it, and Hey wasn't telling till he'd got where he was going.

They made a slow progression out of the closet. Then on across Rita's room to the hall. She and Nick didn't hesitate to trust Hey's instincts. After all, he'd heard Sam talk through a filter of pain. He'd been the most assaulted of any of them, and he'd spent the longest time alone in the dark. With so much waste and empty space to do his thinking in, no wonder he got the closest to the truth. It couldn't hide long from such a naked eye.

They stopped at the doorway into the living room, and Hey

directed them exactly where to put him down. Then for a moment he was in agony, grunting and panting, his eyes all clouded, but it passed. He got his equilibrium back. And he lay flat on the floor, eying them both and sweating some, and looked as if he were measuring his words down to the quarter-inch. He didn't have the strength for an argument. He'd say what he had to say, and that was that. He was on the very spot where, not an hour before, Sam had forced him to his hands and knees. But if he felt the irony, there wasn't the leisure to indulge it now. The doorbell rang. He nodded to Rita and held up his hand to keep Nick by him.

But I need more time, Rita thought angrily, striding across the room. She had to hear what it was that Sam really said and see if it sounded the same. Maybe Hey was right, and Nick had to go out hunting, but she'd be damned if she'd let him do it alone. The bell rang longer the second time. She wished she could make them wait, whoever they were, and make them nervous. Just now she hated anyone who wanted to separate the people in Crook House, no matter what for. She reached the top of the spiral stairs. But before she opened the door and started the next chain of events, she took a last look down from the rail of the balcony. In the far corner, Nick bent close over Hey, and she had a sense of what she must have looked like a little while ago in the closet, when she was all the doctor they had. But the larger irony wasn't lost on Rita. They were right on the spot, too, where the coins and the jade and the cigarette case had been, right where she'd waltzed around to get things ready for Peter. Consequently, the scene below her had two faces, the before-and-after of an accident. It was just that pointless, and it filled her with rage. So Hey was right after all, she thought grimly. It would kill her to have to wait all day for Sam to call.

She threw open the door, suddenly eager to get this part over with so she and Nick could get on to the chase. Two men in white, wheeling a stretcher, pushed by her. They barely glanced at Rita, since it was clear enough that *she* was in one piece. But if they expected to zip from room to room till they came upon a body, the balcony and the spiral stairs brought them up short. They could see the man they were after, down below, and they turned to Rita for a better route. "Is *this* the only way?" one of them asked in disbelief. Annoyed at Rita, somehow, as if she'd been the architect herself. For her part, Rita stayed cool. She opened the elevator door and acted a bit superior, only too glad to lead them around by the nose. She let them pile in with the stretcher upright. Then, when she squeezed inside and pressed the "down" button, she was closer to them than she wanted to be. They were too clean. She couldn't tell them apart. All the same, she relished the sidelong looks they gave to the *trompe l'oeil* balloon painted around them.

But even in this, her mood went on going up and down. Oh, they were all right, she thought to herself expansively. They just didn't know their way around. And with the tunnel through the hill just added to her own repertoire of passages, Rita was feeling bold enough to find her way anywhere. Let the medics through to do their work. As a secret agent regularly dropped behind enemy lines, Rita appreciated that she couldn't always go it alone. She was part of a team. Taking the optimistic view of the current mission, she was glad to note that everyone was on the team but Sam.

They hit bottom. She opened the door and backed out, holding it wide to give them room. When they went ahead, she decided to run up the stairs and wait to do the same at the front door. Let Nick deal with them for a while. But when she got back up on the balcony and came to the edge to watch, Nick wasn't there. It was just a fallen man, all by himself on the floor. The two carriers made ready and went into position, one at the head, the other at the feet. They must have thought she was crazy to run away upstairs.

"Hey," she called, panicky again, wondering if she ought to race to the cars and head Nick off. She shouted just at the moment they lifted Hey, and a muffled cry of pain was all the answer he gave. He writhed on the stretcher. The two men looked at Rita blackly, figuring the "Hey" was meant for them, ready to backtalk if she tried to tell them how to do their job. She shrank from the railing, frightened by his suffering still. Then they picked up the stretcher, and the cry came unmuffled, but Rita was already bolting. She raced up the outside stairs, even though she knew it would be too late. Nick's car was gone. He must have slipped out by the kitchen garden and climbed around to the front. The very same way Rita slipped in.

Now, going back tensely to the house, she understood for the first time where it all led: She was about to be left alone. She could go to the hospital, of course, and hold Hey's hand in the back of the ambulance, letting her mind go blank to the tune of the sirens wailing. In case Nick didn't get lucky, *somebody* ought to stay home by the phone. What if Sam shot Peter because they ignored the directions Rita thought she heard? She'd wait if she had to. Really, she told herself, all she cared about was getting them back together again and safe. But she wouldn't admit the most curious thing, that she suddenly couldn't bear to be by herself. She, who had gotten so *good* at it. Back in New York, it meant nobody could hurt her too much, because she could always hole up with the scissors and a pile of magazines and plot a course of self-improvement. The talent for being alone had put her on the plane to LA in the first place. And then it insured the single-mindedness of the work she'd done for weeks in Varda's room. The reason she was a great opener and closer of doors was that she'd always been glad to go off by herself, almost from the time she could walk.

She stood on the landing outside the door and listened to them struggle out of the elevator. The feeling of panic persisted. But maybe she ought to call it something else, because it wasn't unfocused, and it told her things. The only way she could describe it was to think of the feeling that grew enormous in a good ghost story. She'd read the canon from cover to cover. There comes a moment of the purest isolation. Somebody realizes that whatever it is is trying to separate the group, to pick them off one by one. Here at Crook House, of course, it was all quite different. Sam was not the agent of anything interplanetary or abstract. He was merely Sam, and he had no power to damage the way they all stuck together. But they'd been through too much today, and if they all got to feeling as lonely as Rita, she thought, they might do the damage themselves. Any one of them might decide that all the chaos started and ended with him alone and so withdraw. One right after another, they'd begin to take the blame. Then, like the brokenhearted simps in soap operas, they'd see where the sins of the past had brought them. Rita knew how quick nice people were to punish themselves. They had to head it off fast before it took hold.

And though at the moment Hey was the worst-off, he was also the one who was just about to be stabilized. He was down as far as he was going to go. He came out of the house feet first, and the two men at the stretcher talked across him in a workers' shorthand. She saw that they'd strapped him on at the knees and hips, presumably so they could stand the stretcher up in the elevator, but Rita shivered as if it were a straitjacket. Then the rest of him passed by her, and she saw his face all colorless and sick. Worse than she thought. She didn't even understand how he could have gone so long and kept so alert, only to fall apart in the last ten minutes. But he managed a slit of a smile when he saw who it was. He reached toward her with his good hand. While she stood there dumbly, the stretcher went on upstairs, and she had to scramble to catch up. She got crushed against the branches because the rescue operation took all the room, but finally they reached the top, and she was able to bend down for a bit and talk in his ear.

"I'll go with you if you want," she said, though she hoped he'd say no and leave her free.

"You stay here," he said gently. "I can't stand the sight of you looking as if I was already dead."

"Tell me where Nick went."

"I don't know."

At that point, somehow, they pushed her aside and lifted

him through the back door of the ambulance. One of the men climbed in after and reached to close the door, while his partner went around the front. Rita regathered her forces and grabbed on tight to the handle. "You wait a minute," she said, as roughly as she could. Then she swung one knee up and pulled herself in. The attendant dropped back to the head of Hey's stretcher, assuming she'd decided to go after all. But she stayed on her knees at the edge, ready to jump back out. The motor started up. "But, Hey," she called, "didn't you *tell* him where to go?"

"No. I only told him what Sam said."

"What was that?" she asked, and the ambulance started to roll, backing out of the drive. The attendant shouted to the driver and then snarled at Rita to make up her mind, so she didn't catch Hey's answer. "Wait," she said again, but the attendant was bearing down on her. She didn't have any more clout. She pushed herself off, but she summoned up a last pleading look and lobbed it at the man in white, just as he reached to pull the door closed.

"Please," she begged, "I didn't hear what he said."

"I'm going underground," the attendant snapped, and the door slammed shut. She had to leap out of the way of the turn. It was a moment before she connected it up: The attendant was quoting Hey, and Hey was quoting Sam. The ambulance lurched off the gravel and onto the road. The siren got louder and louder as it sped away downhill.

Underground where?

She couldn't remember, but she thought he'd said something simpler, like "I'm going into hiding." "Underground" sounded so odd. Not having heard the original, the attendant made it sound like two words when he said it to Rita. Under ground— as if it were a cave. Rita knew she was oversensitive about anything that smacked of a secret place. Sam meant it the other way, of course. For "underground," read "out of sight." It was only to be expected that Sam had all the right connections to the underworld and the cover of darkness. It was only a manner of speaking. And yet, she thought, if that was so, then where was Nick running to? If Sam wasn't being specific, he and Peter could be anywhere, and no one person would ever find them. Nick should have told her. Not so she'd tag along, necessarily, but he ought to have a backup man if something went wrong. As it was, all of them could disappear into thin air, and she'd never be able to trace them. Not a soul would be left but Rita and Hey. That is, if Hey didn't die. And then where would she be? She'd have no claim on Crook House, certainly. Maybe a piece of it would go to Peter's grandfather, but then again it was probably in Nick's name, and a hundred of his cousins would come out of the woodwork and fight for it. She'd be back on a plane to New York before she knew it. Dead-broke and all alone.

She turned from the driveway and headed slowly down the stairs again to the house. Had she always been so close to the brink of irreversible disaster? She'd never given it a thought before. And she wondered now if that wasn't why disaster had struck at last. She'd built up these years and years of false security. On the other hand, was it seemly for her to get superstitious at her age? Nick was the fatalist, much more than she. But that might explain why he was ready to jump when the time came, while she'd ended up left in the lurch. Some people know where the guns are kept. Some others at least know the way to the fire doors and lifeboats. Rita wasn't either sort, she decided. She let herself in and stood once more on the balcony. Now what? Sit by the phone for a call that wasn't going to come? She couldn't even pretend to be standing guard, since the one danger they had to guard against had come and gone.

But whatever else, she thought as the silence swarmed about her, she'd be double damned before she'd do woman's work. She wouldn't keep house or the home fires burning. Fuck that, she thought. But it was only another tune to whistle in the dark. She was talking back to the rapid knocking in her heart. She wanted them all home safe, and she wanted the day wiped out. If only this or that were different, she began to think. And she always spit on that kind of whining and waffling, swore at it and snubbed it. One thing she knew, she couldn't weaken now. She'd better put her mind to it hard, she said to herself as she drifted down the spiral stairs, and come up with the way they'd all gone.

Underground, underground. If they were anywhere else but here, it might be a subway. Or a trapdoor, perhaps, through the floor of a hollow tomb. She walked across the living room and out the French windows to the garden. The angle of vision—through the lush garden shade, down to the toy shop city—was as unreal to her as it had been the day she arrived. She didn't know the half of LA yet. How could she figure out the hiding places? She would have had no trouble at all if they'd been in an English country house. But here she stood by an unruffled pool, the whole world before her, and hadn't the least idea where to start looking. She'd read her way through all manner of underground chambers. In the vast and orderly mansions she used to imagine, the secret room was always just where it ought to be. She shouldn't have been surprised that it wasn't the case out in the world. And though she was probably better at being here than there, just like Rusty Varda, somehow she'd thrown in her lot along the way with her friends in Crook House, and she needed them now more than it.

If she could crack one puzzle, she could crack two. An underground something, off by itself. She could almost see it already, cut right out of the earth. Not a cave. Somebody'd actually dug it with their hands. She stooped and looked at herself in the water. Well, well, she thought, so Crook House wasn't sufficient to be the world. She made a couple of faces, happy and sad like theater masks, and she let go a string of country houses without a backward look. She didn't know why, but she didn't need them. Too much upkeep. Hard to get good servants. Drafty. People who needed the world between their fences ended up driven like Rusty Varda, and just as lonely. Not me, she thought defiantly. All she wanted was Peter and Nick and Hey. Now she could see it was a tunnel, with a room like Varda's at the far end, only not attached to a house. She patted her hair and gave herself a slit-eyed look to see how she looked at a distance. Not bad, not bad. There was really only one kind of place that had the right feel and the right dimensions both. It must be a mine, where the secret room is made by scooping out a treasure. The walls are streaked with veins of gold, and here and there the glimmer of uncut stones comes through, like bits of mosaic.

She could see how it might appeal to Sam. It had a very immediate relation to money, for one thing. Cash on the line. It was tough and ornery, and desperate men tended to throw away their lives to it, digging deeper and deeper. Rita much preferred, if she had to pursue an obsession, a phantom like Rusty Varda's, if only for its craving after the beautiful. And Peter was going to *hate* it down in a mine. No style. No civilized talk. All the more reason to get him out of there fast. She put her hands in the water and threw off the image. Then she cupped up some and splashed her face. She felt better just knowing what it was out there. And she'd needed a time of rest and quiet to sort her thoughts. She was just as glad to be working alone. Let Nick play out his own leads, because she'd get there in her own time. The hard part was over, she thought, swinging on a new mood as if it were a rope over a gorge. All she had to do now was find it.

The afternoon was almost gone by the time Nick turned in at the gate to the ranch. The sun was making a final stand on the westernmost ridge, and the grass was full of a dusty purple. He didn't feel at all as if he owned it. He'd been here only twice, and the course of a whole day had never happened to him on this land. It was purple like the surface of the moon. He hadn't *thought* about it since the day the paintings of the bunkhouse disappeared off the walls of the bedroom and got stacked in Peter's closet. And yet somehow he'd known right off, as soon as Hey laid out the clues, that this was where Sam would take Peter. No other place was bordered so completely by Nick and Sam. In fact, it was already as distant to him as the view in a tourist photograph, or even as Nick and Sam themselves. Nick would have sold it before six months was out, or he would have palmed it off on Charlie Burns and let him sell it. Nick couldn't be bothered driving back and forth to the mountains with clients. Couldn't be bothered being reminded how far he'd gone to strip a cowboy naked.

And when he left Hey's side, promising to bring Sam back alive, and made his circuitous way to the car, he drove breakneck down to Sunset. He had every intention of heading them off before they ever got this far. How much of a start could they have on him? Twenty minutes? But then on the way to the freeway he started thinking. Hey had only had time to give him the headlines of Varda's fatal fling with Sam, but Nick heard enough to lose his faith forever in the niceties of chance. Sam had tracked Nick down to get back in the house. Period. Nick, who was famous for being the guilty party, was suddenly cast in retrospect as the innocent victim. So it didn't just happen that he was stopped at the light that day on Wilshire, when Sam appeared on the crosswalk and caught the wander in his eye. All it was was a plot spinning out. And as it turned out, the most insignificant thing about it was Nick. What with all the years and the people it encompassed, it read like a tale of revenge that passed from father to son, on and on. And for once Nick was the naive one—naive in the shallow, unlikely way of the young man who believes he's loved for himself and not his Lancelot face. Since he'd been so dumb so long, he thought, maybe he'd better not rush right in till he'd figured what it was Sam wanted. When he got to 405, he took it south instead of north. There was only one place where he did his serious thinking, and it didn't seem out of the way.

He took the Venice exit and made for the beach. Headed for the rickety outdoor café where he and Sam had passed a bad hour on the afternoon Rita landed. Had the others known he was going there, they probably would have given up on Nick. What got him into this mess was a lethal dose of out-of-focus sentiment, so it wasn't a very good sign if he had to touch base at the marginal places he'd shared with Sam. But Venice belonged to Nick long before he'd succumbed to the momentary impulse to show it off. He went back to it often, just to remember what he used to want as a kid. None of the others gave the time of day to the wanton children they'd left behind. Peter and Rita and Hey were a good deal offended by the drama and gilded dreams they all grew up on. Very, very tacky. But Nick was unswervingly loyal to the boys he'd been. He didn't sweat the tacky part because he took such care to keep it to himself. Whenever he had a big decision to make, he landed in Venice, all choked up and carrying in his head an armload of 9 × 12's from his past and a lot of beach shop souvenirs.

He drove down an alley beside the café that ended at the sand. It was his habit to spend an hour or two by himself, not finishing sentences, a cup of coffee getting cold in front of him. Or if it was money he had to mull over, he might buy a quart of ice cream instead, and eat it sitting high on a lifeguard's chair. His whole life, he'd looked for reasons to go to the beach. But he didn't actually *think* in Venice. He was like a photographer taking a dozen shots with a fast camera, and one would come out right. Today he was only looking to hold back an hour or so, just so he wouldn't go off half-cocked. Making a stop in Venice was his way of kissing a good luck charm. Like patting the Buddha's stomach. He didn't even need to get out of the car.

If Sam had never cared about Nick from the first, he wondered, what was the use of drawing him close again, unless it was more revenge? And for what? He couldn't very well blame Nick for the fact that Varda's treasure turned out to be nonnegotiable and difficult to fence. Or was it in the nature of Sam's revenge that delivering pain was no fun unless the victim knew his face? Nick could already see he was wrong about being the throwaway character who had no point in all of this. That was just hurt pride. It was maybe true till this afternoon, but not anymore. The money Sam planned to recover in Rusty Varda's treasure house had fattened like a savings account—in his mind, anyway—and the bank went bust without warning and lopped off the future as it fell. So Sam must have thought of getting revenge only now, this afternoon. Against Varda through Hey. And then, for good measure, against Nick for trying to love him.

Nick didn't need five minutes in Venice before he had it figured out. What might come in handy to understand was that neither Peter nor the Rembrandt had anything to do with it. They were no less in danger right now, perhaps, but they'd be out of the line of fire once Nick was face to face with Sam. And Nick didn't think he had to worry about getting shot himself. He had to worry in a much more general way, he decided as he slipped the Mercedes into reverse and went back the way he came. Sam may have already dreamed up a plan that would put the lien on Nick's life for years to come. Blackmail of some kind. It had to be damned good to cheer up Sam on the day his ten years went up in smoke. But if it was only money, Nick was all ready and would count himself lucky. When he got to 405 again, he found he couldn't wait to be going north. Like Hey, he'd come to view it on reflection as a bloodless round of negotiations. In spite of the blood-soaked body he'd left behind in Crook House.

All the way to the ranch, his head was nicely crowded with children playing in the sand, with easy lovers arm in arm and capering dogs and prizefighter types keeping watch in phosphorescent orange trunks. He didn't seem to realize that he hadn't *seen* any of that. Like Rita with her hollow-paneled doors and the winding drive through the deer park, he had such a highly developed sense of place in Venice that he'd lost his grip on the real thing. The beach had assumed the proportions of a benign morality tale, where the seven ages of man sat squinting in the sun and everyone had enough room. It was the perfect setting for the consideration of big investments, certainly, proof of the imminence of milk and honey. In much the same way, Crook House was the right place for Rita's Gothic fantasies. They got her into the secret room, while Nick, whenever he was gentled by Pacific airs, tended to go home and do the thing that would make him rich. But now there was this difference between them. The events of one awful afternoon, because they took place in the room itself, had cured Rita of confusing the books she read with the houses she lived in. Nick was the same as ever. He wanted from Venice a whiff of a rose-colored world, and now he was sure it would be all right at the ranch, just because he understood what Sam was about. He had too much faith as usual in the reasonable flow of events. In that way, the curious detour to Venice was something like a snort of cocaine at the door to a party. Something he didn't do.

He didn't even know where the mine was. He stopped at the crest of the first hill and looked down at the bunkhouse. Nobody there. Sam was being absolutely literal about underground. Nick wasn't altogether sure there *was* a mine. For all he knew, it was part of the realtor's hype that sold him. An actual mine, he'd said, from the 1850s. A band of Spanish priests trying to cash in on the stories that filtered down from the gold rush. Either they were greedy like everybody else, or they wanted ore for the hardware and graven images in their church—the story didn't say which. Cheap Indian labor always available from the mission. Nick had taken it in at all only because of his grandparents' Sunday jaunts in the hills with pick and shovel. They were as dumb as the Spanish fathers, imagining gold so close to the ocean, in such a desert place. And Nick had only mentioned it to Sam because—he couldn't remember why.

He drove downhill past the turn to the bunkhouse. As he came into the floor of the valley, the road filled up with rocks and holes, and even when he only crept along, the car still bucked and quivered like a stagecoach. What little exploring Nick had done was on the uphill slopes, in the opposite direction, partly to take in the view, partly because it was the one good road. He'd turned back from here every time. He figured there couldn't be much to see at the end, since it was obvious nobody'd been this way in years. And the going was so slow, he didn't believe Sam could make it in the MG. The Mercedes, at least, had the soul of a Jeep, but even so, the road was going sandy and losing its grip. At the same time, he'd come in abruptly under the great cold shadow of the west ridge. He couldn't make out the shapes of the stones he hit, and they ripped at his tires and threw him to the side. The dust swirled up around the windshield. He was suddenly scared he wouldn't be able to turn around. So he stopped. And when he got out to get his bearings, he found it was wilderness wherever he looked. The road, except for the hover of dust that smoked in his wake, was hardly distinguishable from all the surrounding waste.

A couple of hundred feet further on, it petered out entirely, and the ridge went steeply up. There was no sign of an entrance to a mine, he could already tell, and if it was off the road and had to be reached by foot, he knew he'd never find it. He wondered if Sam had come to the same dead end. Had he been thoughtless enough not to check it out first? And how mad was he now, with Peter and a Rembrandt crammed in his car and no hideout to go to? Only because he'd come this far, Nick walked on forward to the base of the ridge. It would be dark by the time he got back to Bel-Air. Then he'd get the call. Then go out again. The sense of order and certainty Venice had just given him began to evaporate, and with no warning the anger came. Not so much at Sam as at the layers and layers of complication. Nothing he could do could make it all work. The only virtue he applauded in himself was organization, the keeping of things in their places, and he'd come to a day when it did no good. He couldn't even name the thing he was angry at.

The flat part ended. Just as he thought, there wasn't the trace of an opening. It must have caved in long ago, like a wound closing up, and everything was so far back to normal that no one would ever know. And then if Nick forgot to pass on the bits of the story to the next buyer, the ending would be complete. It would start to be as if it had never happened. And because that was too much like life itself, he threw back his head to defy the indifferent sky before he turned back, to hate it hard, even if it always won. But the cry broke in his throat. Way, way above him, seventy-five or a hundred feet, he made out a light. Not shining like a lantern on a cliff. Glowing, sort of, as if a clump of fireflies were resting in a bush. Or as if the light were coming from a distance, deep inside.

He started scrambling right away. He didn't take the time to look for a donkey path or a set of steps cut in the side of the hill. He'd had enough of roads and plotted courses, anyway. Straight up was the only route he had any use for now. The ground kept sliding away when he stepped, so to keep his speed, he had to grab hold of plants and do it on all fours. He didn't even mind the noise he made. There was such a rustle and scurry of creatures in the bushes around him, trying to get out of his way, that he needed to feel he was clearing the way ahead as he went. He didn't want to face down any wild animals, even if here it was only rats. Or snakes. He flinched in spite of himself, remembering what the ranch had done to Peter. But he figured what the hell, it *couldn't* happen twice, and pushed ahead and didn't listen anymore. After so much wandering, in fact, he liked this part. He dug in with the toes of his Bally shoes and felt the sweat work up on his chest and forehead. His breath came faster. He wouldn't have cared if he'd had to climb all the way up and over. With every foot he gained, he seemed to get closer and closer to what they'd all gone through. His rage and emptiness *went* somewhere. He didn't suffer Rita's swing from mood to mood because his own complaint was typically no mood at all. But now all the blanks were filling up. The business of fate disappeared. When he was alive like this, he scorned it as a game for cowards.

He stood up to see where he'd got to. The light was more to the left than he'd figured, but he was almost level with it already and saw the top of an opening wide as a double door. The dark was falling fast, and the pale yellow light was more distinct. He wondered whether he would have spotted it right away from the top of the hill if he'd come at night. Probably. Why didn't Sam screen it, he wondered, and then he understood. Sam wasn't *hiding* yet. He'd banked on it that they wouldn't send out the police till Nick had talked to him, and he wanted Nick to find his way when he told him on the phone where to come. Nick didn't think he was expected yet. He and Hey had made a lucky guess. "Underground" was a clue, all right, but to Nick on the slope of the empty hill, it didn't seem as if Sam had dropped it consciously after all. And if the MG wasn't there at the end of the road, Sam might be away making the call to Crook House. Which meant, Nick concluded shrewdly, that Peter was all alone in the place where the light was coming from.

There seemed to be a level space in front of the mine entrance, and then it dropped off sheerly ten or twelve feet. Nick was able to move laterally with ease until he was directly below it. The climb up the face of the rock was a little more tricky. How in God's name, he wondered, had they ever expected to get the gold down? A chute of some kind, maybe. His right foot slipped out of a crevice, and he dangled a bit. There was a wrenching in the muscle of one thigh. He kicked off the shoe, and then, regaining the crevice, held out the other shoe and shook it till it fell. How did they get the *miners* up here? He slung one knee over the top and tried to pull himself up until he thought his head would explode. He couldn't do it. He was going to fall. And then it was over, and he was lying on his stomach on the edge of a wide bare ledge.

His face was in the dirt. He coughed and gagged, but in a way he wasn't sorry to begin by kissing the ground. And when he lifted his head and looked across at the opening, he was startled at how far he could see. There was a ghostly corridor, lined at intervals with candles, and it went in a long way and slightly down before it seemed to turn. Even at best, he'd expected little more than a space to huddle in amid a tangle of broken beams. He'd assumed the rest of what there used to be was all caved in. But it was so intact that it looked as if a troop of miners might come marching out, four abreast. The scale of the operation cowed him, and he suddenly felt dwarfed and exposed. He leapt to his feet and rushed to take cover. Flattened himself on the wall to the left of the entrance. Then he had to crouch and massage the soles of his stockinged feet, teeth clamped against the stinging from the rocks he'd run across. He cursed the loss of his shoes. Whatever he did from here on in, he wouldn't be doing fast.

He peered around the corner into the light, and there wasn't a sound or a sign of life except for the candles. He walked in a few paces and looked one over. New. Burnt down to five or six inches and set in a holder cut out of a protruding tooth of rock. But he began to see that everything about this place was finished and sculpted and worked. Between the first and second candle, a niche was carved out, though the saint who'd filled it had vanished. The wall of the corridor was amazingly smooth, almost as if they'd gone to the trouble to sand it down and buff it. It was once painted as well, Nick could tell from the patches and flakes of blue. Even the timbers that braced it were carved in a simple scroll, with here and there a more fully modeled figure, something like a smiling fish. Wouldn't Rita love it here? he thought. But he couldn't pause to imagine how fine it must have been. He had to dart along and get to the end and rescue Peter. Still, he didn't miss much from the corners of his eyes, and a picture grew in his head that it was more like a church than a mine shaft. He might have been walking toward a ruined altar in a country overrun by pagans.

Nick was a real civilian in church, and he hardly ever was in one, so he didn't feel the slightest tingle in the knees. But he had to admit it was superhuman and vaguely threatening. It made him wonder, as he came to the end and glanced back along the empty niches, how many places there were like this. Rita, given her taste in books, in some real way wasn't fazed by there being a secret room in Crook House. The way she saw it, in the sky-high price range, every house of a certain character and size was bound to have one. But Nick expected money to be spent entirely on the surface. If it turned out people were forever digging holes and hollowing out little mission churches and one-man museums, then the very earth under his feet wasn't solid. He couldn't get over how small it made him feel, even as he rushed on through and tried not to notice. And he felt big, for instance, in all the cavernous homes of Beverly Hills. He didn't mean small in the sense of man and God. His soul was a harder nut to crack than that. But where did people come by these lifetime projects? Where did they find the time?

The wall at the end had once been inlaid with mosaic, but most of it had fallen off. Only an arm and an angel's wing were visible still. And at either side of this wall were the openings into tunnels, into what must be the mine proper. The one on the right was impassable, clogged with rubble and dark. The one on the left was candle-lit. Nick ducked to enter it, and immediately had to climb down stairs in the stone. When he got to the passage at the bottom, it was almost as narrow as he was, and the air was hot and smoky. He hated it so much he couldn't move for a bit. But then up ahead he heard music, and he made himself go forward. Not the music of the spheres or the waters in the earth. Disco. AM radio.

The floor of the big chamber, as smooth as if they'd paved it, had gone easy on his feet, but here it was like walking on knifeblades again. He had to brace his hands against the wall, just so he could hobble along. Please, he thought, let Peter be able to leave under his own steam. Because Nick, though he'd brought Hey out from under the hill, couldn't carry a man ten feet like this. The tunnel he was in kept turning so much that he lost the feel of how far he was going or where he was now with relation to where it began. Deeper and deeper was all he was sure of. And he knew they'd have to get all the way out to get away. If they met Sam coming in the other direction, they were both sunk. Just now he wanted more than anything to shout Peter's name, but he waited. He couldn't stand to wait, and yet he was too scared of what it would mean if Peter didn't answer. In all this time he hadn't lost control. Since the moment Rita threw him over into the sand, he hadn't messed it up getting visions of worse coming to worst. But now he was going to see for real. Let him just be all right, he'd said to himself all along, but now he was saying it over and over so fast it slurred, and he felt like screaming. Please, please, please, he begged of no one in particular, as if the way were far too complicated now for anything to be all right.

He nearly tumbled head over heels into the cavern. The last turn was so sharp, the light so raw with smoke, that he found himself hanging again on an edge before he saw a thing. It was his hands gripping the walls that held him up. He was looking down into a deep basin, thirty or forty feet across, the floor ten feet below him. Here the light was from kerosene lamps, and the glow from the walls was steadier and clearer than candles. He could even breathe again, anchoring himself in a wide open space that didn't threaten to swallow him whole. In its way, this room was as lovely and strange as the chapel back at the surface. Rich with gravity and uncut matter, it was serious like the center of the earth. All content and no form.

But Nick wasn't conscious of any of it. Peter was lying below him, untouched and fast asleep, and finally he was free to fall apart. How did he know it was sleep and nothing worse? Simply this: Peter sleeping was his longest-standing definition of nothing wrong. He just *knew*. When at last he called Peter's name, it fell over into a sob. And once he'd begun, he couldn't stop crying.

He never did know how he stumbled down the splintering slope of rock to get to him. "Peter, Peter," he said with delight, as if he'd figured out the missing piece of a wonderful puzzle. But the feeling wasn't mutual. Peter woke in terror when he heard his name echoing over the stone behind the music. Nick was still only halfway down. He felt his way numbly with his feet and couldn't see through the blur of his tears. And Peter waved one hand and hissed, "Wait!" He might as well have answered back and called Nick's name himself, completing the duet. It was certainly too late for waiting. He stood up and held out his arms to this reunion, though to him it seemed the saddest thing in the world that they were together again. Now Nick clung to him and wept on his shoulder. Peter had no choice. He held Nick just as tight and comforted his most unfounded fears, all the while not knowing how to tell him hope was lost. And he stared up at Sam as if to say "You win," but he summoned up enough disdain to cut the resignation. As if to add: "He's mine. No matter what you do, you can't have this. You only thought you had it."

"Hurry," Nick said brokenly, "we have to run." But he said it in a way that was oddly formal. He seemed to know, perhaps from the force of Peter's arms, how still they stood, that they weren't going anywhere yet. And as he became aware of the music again and placed the source of it just above their heads, telling them *Why not dance*, it snapped abruptly off.

"You think that's why I lit all those candles, Nick? So you can run?"

Nick pulled away from Peter, feeling clumsy as a kid. A little ashamed to be watched in the arms of another man. Scared to look at Peter because of Sam, because Sam was all Nick's fault. And then, just as suddenly, old instead of young —because he knew Sam thought of him and Peter as a pair of aging queens. He didn't answer right away. He looked up and saw him first, sitting high on a ledge with a doorway behind. His shirt was off, and he glistened with sweat. The gun was slack in his hand. Even now, Nick saw, the heat of sex was the only thing real about Sam, though they couldn't be farther removed from a bedroom. No wonder desire was the simplest way to think of him. Even now.

"We can run if we want," he said slowly, trying to soften the sting of defiance, "because *you*'ve got to get away. You just lost your place to hide. Cops may be dumb, but how far behind me can they be?"

Sam gave a short laugh and then spoke fast: "You found me because I let you, baby, and you know it." Let's get on with it, he seemed to say. And to back that up, he threw himself off the ledge and skidded down the angle of the wall as if he were a surfer riding on a wave. In a moment he was close enough to touch them. "By my calculations," he said, "you're twenty minutes late. So don't think anything *you* do is any big deal. I know every fucking thing in your head."

Then he started to walk in a circle around them. They couldn't keep his face in focus, and they didn't dare move. So Nick began to take in the litter that lay about in the domed and egg-shaped room. Piles of Sam's clothes. A half-dozen pairs of boots in a line. An unplugged television set. He'd lived with Peter too long in a house devoted to clutter to really believe these things could be all of Sam's wordly goods. But anyone could see that Sam must have been here time and time again. The Rembrandt, propped against a boulder ten feet away, hadn't ended up in neutral territory after all. It wasn't as if they'd met in a field or out on a strip of deserted beach, where they were all on equal footing. They were clearly on Sam's ground.

"You thought I came up here with you to suck your dick," Sam said in a mocking voice. "All I was looking for was a place to take Varda's money. And you know what? You handed it to me as easy as anything else I wanted." He stopped his circling to stare in Nick's eyes a moment, and he seemed in some way unable to place him any longer. Nick looked too much like the dozens of people Sam saw only once. "This mine isn't yours, you know, because you didn't find it. You didn't even believe it was here."

"You want it?" Nick asked dryly. "You can have it."

"Just like this painting isn't yours," Sam went on, dropping back and giving a tap to the gilded frame with the barrel of the gun, "because Varda would have given it to me. I would have had it all."

"But what would you do with it? You got a gallery to hang it all in?" Now he knew Sam had nowhere else to run if all he could talk about was how it might have gone. For Nick, who stood so close to Peter that they touched now and then, there wasn't anything scary here at all except the gun. And what he wanted in exchange for being unafraid was to taunt Sam till he cried uncle. "Maybe you ought to live right here and put it all up around the rocks."

Sam cut him off: "I *do* live here." He turned aside and got busy looking for something in a carton full of junk. "I sleep up there on that ledge. I got a battery tapedeck. And a clock and a flashlight."

"It sounds real plush," Nick said. More and more, he said whatever he wanted. This was the part where he counted on not getting shot. "Maybe they'll let you serve out your term down here. If they give you a little pick, you might tap into a vein the size of Fort Knox and make us all rich."

"Just so you know what I mean," Sam said, preoccupied with his digging as if he hadn't heard. He pulled out a screw-driver and held it up to the painting like a pointer. He might have been about to give a lecture. But he dug it into the paint, ripping it down along Rembrandt's cheek, smiling coldly all the while. The painting crackled, and chips flew off. The right eye was practically gone. Nick heard Peter make a low, low groan, and his own stomach lifted and turned over as if he'd just seen somebody die. It would take a month to fix it right. Even then it wouldn't be perfect again.

"*I* decide about Varda's things," Sam said. He didn't look away, even when he flipped the screwdriver and caught it so he gripped it like a dagger. He jabbed it right through the canvas. And again, and again. Nick and Peter looked away. There wasn't the least trace of reproach on Rembrandt's face. He gazed at the world as patiently out of one eye as he had out of two, searching for something more than an honest man. But they felt they'd failed him all the same.

"Why don't you just say what you want?" Nick said. He still wasn't scared, but he started feeling sad again, the way he had when he'd sat alone with Peter's keys. As if he'd stared down into the pit of all the irrevocable things that could happen, any one of which was enough to kill.

"Money," said Sam flippantly, "the same as everyone else."

"How much?" Nick asked, preparing himself at last to go through the established forms of the negotiation. It didn't matter how much, of course. He'd get whatever it was. But Sam must have followed the train of thought his own way, because he laughed as if Nick had told him a dirty joke. He dropped the screwdriver, and it clattered on the stone. He was bored with being a vandal.

"All the money in the world," he said, "is what I've got coming to me. Varda would have given me everything he had, except we ran out of time."

"Is that so? Then tell me, why did you kill him?" Things he couldn't say before, during all the time he loved him, he found the words for now. He got louder and louder. "Maybe he refused to put it in writing. Is that when the time ran out?" He didn't expect any answer, and he was ready to follow it up with an angry little speech about who owned what. But Sam ran up and raised the gun and whipped him hard across the face. Just once, and then he resumed his pacing. Nick's mouth went sweet with blood from a tooth that cut into his cheek. He held the side of his face and turned to Peter. But if he expected a kiss to make it better, he'd barked up the wrong tree.

Peter said grimly, "Stop acting so goddam smart. He'll tell you if you'll just shut up."

And Nick was so shocked that the pain did stop, or at least he didn't seem to have room for it anymore. He'd been heated up since he first saw Sam, and he hadn't even noticed Peter standing so silent. If he'd thought about it, he probably would have said he was fighting a battle for both their sakes. Now he saw what Peter saw. Somehow, he'd gotten turned around, and he'd started to have a lover's quarrel with Sam. Not to do with love, of course, but how would Peter know? Nick was letting fly with a cheating husband's noises of annoyance: How dare you try to wreck my home, you bitch. Terrible things had been happening all day long in Crook House. Parallel lines had crossed like fences in an earthquake. And what was Nick doing? Getting mad because he couldn't stand it that he'd thrown his love away for weeks on something as vile as this.

He couldn't even speak to say he was sorry. He would have spit blood if he talked right now. He could only flush and look at the ground and hate himself. But Peter wasn't trying to put him through more than it was worth. He reached across the space between them. He tapped Nick lightly on the breastbone as if he were knocking at a door. They smiled a fraction of an inch. Or not even that. They gave one another a certain look. And though Sam didn't watch them as he wandered around, he did seem to wait to let them adjust before he went on. Then he stopped walking and stood behind the painting, leaning on the frame like a podium. He was never quite still, even then. He stretched his naked shoulders and flexed the muscles in his chest, his body in constant motion, however slight. It was like watching a horse shiver and twitch.

"There's no point telling you the truth about me and Varda," he said, as if he'd mulled it all over in a quiet corner and finally thrown up his hands. Almost as if he didn't want to make any friction. "The spic's told you *his* version, right? I know it makes things simpler for all of you to *see* it that way." He shrugged very deeply like a man lifting weights. "It doesn't matter. Not to me, anyway. It's just too bad for you that you'll never know what Varda was really like. He's the only guy I ever met who didn't want to go to heaven."

He seemed to be shaking his finger at both of them, trying to smarten them up. In a way, given the time and place, it was the most perplexing thing of all to Nick and Peter, hearing him show off the range of his wisdom and experience. They had his type pegged from their two different angles, and they would have sworn he'd never known *anyone* "really." Nick thought: That's the fiction we've put behind us in Crook House, isn't it, that we have to go after what people are really like? "People are really like everyone else" is how he might have put it to Sam. But they were much better off not dwelling on it. Nick could have shaken his own finger, after all, and told him off with blood on his teeth, but Peter was right. Shut up. Nick took all the strength he needed from seeing that he and Peter knew better. Otherwise, though the side of his face had started swelling up till it would be by morning fat as an apple, he had left in him still the faint trace of a strange desire. He didn't know why, but now he didn't want to spoil *Sam's* version of the story. It made him feel a little crazy. Maybe the leap of violence, back and forth, had made him remember something delicious that lay between them. He was glad he didn't have to be alone with Sam and follow it out. For once he didn't want to know why.

"I'm going to let Peter tell you where we are now," Sam

said, very businesslike, as if Peter were his apprentice. Nick turned and saw the contempt in Peter's eyes. Apparently, he and Sam had had their own little cold war going before he got here. Peter hadn't started out silent, either.

"What?" Nick asked. He heard it, but he hoped he'd heard it wrong.

"I said: He's planted a case of dynamite." Then Peter went on, but he was stingy with the details, trying to diminish it. "All through the mine, like a string in a cave. He's got the end of the fuse in his sleeping bag."

"Why?"

"That I don't know," Peter said, an edge of boredom in his voice that must have maddened Sam. "He's sending me out and keeping you in. I've told him everything we know about Varda's collection. And then about all our money, yours and mine." He paused and looked at Nick, wondering how he would have done it instead. "It seemed better just to tell the truth."

"But why?" Nick asked again, confused by the fact that there seemed to be a plan. He left the question open so Sam could answer, too.

"All right," Sam said to Peter, "now get out of here."

Nick didn't have a moment to think. Peter hugged him and kissed his hair, and that brought the tears up again. Which locked his voice at the crucial moment. All he could manage was Peter's name. The thing he would have said was too complicated, anyway. In the fullness of the hour, he might have implied that he'd solved at last the dream of the cowboy lover. It wasn't true. It was only that he'd never found himself face to face before with a man he'd broken off with. Five days ago in Santa Monica, he actually felt his temperature drop as he walked away to the car he had no further use for. Before the day was out, Sam was no longer in his system. And that was the way it always was, until now. Before *five* days were out, he was most likely to be found at the baths when not available by phone. So what he'd like to have gotten across to Peter here was something about the timing of desire. How it didn't die fast at all. How it lingered and changed its shape. When he stared it in the face again, everything he'd ever felt about Sam came back at once. It was as if he finally understood what he went through in all his furtive, minor loves. There was more to these things than beginning, middle, and end. And though he couldn't yet put it into words, he knew it meant at the very least that he and Peter were fine. Nothing would ever split them up.

But whatever the certainties Nick might harbor in his head, Peter was certainly going away right now. He crossed the floor and began to inch his way up the slope of the wall. Nick could tell he'd been down here a while, because he knew where the crevices were, and the footholds. When he could reach it, Peter pulled himself up to the door of the tunnel in one great lift, like a swimmer swooping out of a pool. Considering that he didn't go in for exercise, he was remarkably fit and agile in a pinch. It was all those sturdy Russian genes, Nick thought, his mind still wandering wide. Peter brushed himself off and turned around and nodded good-bye, and Nick at least was prompt in nodding back. But Peter's nod was to tell him to watch himself, so it was smart and vivid and heavy with radar. Nick nodded from out of a dream. He was there like a minor relative left on the dock, waving as the ship pulls away to sea.

"Wait," Sam said, and Nick looked over at him hopefully. It was only a test, after all, he thought, to see how strong they could be when they said good-bye. Nothing was final. Sam was just in a mood to play. "Take off your clothes," he said to Peter, and Nick thought: All we have to do is go along, and in a minute he'll stop. He was sure Sam wanted them making protests and fighting back. All the fun would go out of it if they did what they were told.

Peter was perfect. He could have stripped like a hustler and given Sam a surly, slit-eyed look. But he did it as if he were standing alone in his closet at home, quickly and matter-of-factly. With one theatrical touch: He flung each thing out in front of him instead of dropping it in a pile. His shirt spread its wings and lilted to the floor. Jingling with keys and pocket change, his pants dropped like a stone. When he'd cast off his underwear, he stood with his legs apart and his hands on his hips, waiting impassively for the next turn of the screw.

"That should slow you down a little," Sam said in an oddly good-humored voice. "I wouldn't want you just driving off in Nick's car. That's too easy. The cops will still be there, no matter how long it takes."

"Is that where you want me to go?" Peter asked. He looked like a statue in a niche in an ancient temple.

Sam shrugged. "It's where you're going," he said philosophically. "I don't expect to get everything I want. We'll be ready when they come."

"Be careful," Peter said gently, in a voice more appropriate to saying it to Nick than Sam. Nick had a shiver of emptiness, in fact, because he needed to hear it so much himself. And Sam seemed genuinely taken aback. Peter meant to tell him he might be in a tighter place than he wanted or thought. He could do whatever he felt like, but he ought to think it through. It wasn't just a warning. It was as if Peter didn't want him to fail.

"Take your shoes, at least," Sam said. But when he realized they'd have to be picked up off the floor and handed over, he looked at Nick to do it for him. He busied himself behind the painting, not at all ready to pursue any further the tone in Peter's voice. So Nick in his stockinged feet, sore to the bone, retrieved the two shoes where Peter had thrown them and hobbled across the chamber. Peter stooped and held out his hand, and Nick reached up twice.

"How much do I love you?" he whispered, giving over the left shoe.

"More than I know," Peter replied with a sly smile. It was an old song and dance that pattered between them when they lay in each other's arms in the dark. A parody of things they'd said when they started out. "What was the thing you always wanted most?"

"A sidekick," Nick said, quick on the cue. He surrendered

the other loafer. "A guy to knock around with. Maybe get into a little trouble. How about you?"

"Someone to be in exile with, of course." It could have gone on and on, but Peter and Nick weren't the whispering sort. Peter stood up, stepped into the shoes, winked once, and turned and went. He made his way out of sight, walking heavily, like a caveman. Nick let him go without a pang. They'd got off a better good-bye the second time around, and it made it seem as if they were only temporarily caught going in opposite directions. They knew who they were and where they lived in real life.

"Well," Nick asked, stepping up close so the painting stood between them, "now will you tell me why?"

"It'd be different," Sam said, "if it was *your* clothes I'd wanted off." He was getting amused again, the way he had in the secret room before the roof caved in. "I might get ideas if I saw you naked."

"We could use a good idea down here, I think. *Any* idea. What's the dynamite for?"

"To blow things up."

"What things?"

But instead of answering, Sam stood back a bit and spread his arms, like a tumbler just landed on his feet. He meant everything. He doesn't have a plan at all, Nick thought. It was only pretending. And if he was making it up as he went along, Nick counted one for their side. After all, Nick was a salesman. It was his business to get undecided people to do things they thought were their own idea. And Nick had a secret of his own: There was no way Sam could know the part of him that hated him. Sam had seen him only meek and overly accommodating. The last time they'd met, Nick was still giving away sports cars. So he thought he'd be smart and be full of longing still. Keep Sam's guard down.

"The dynamite is here," Sam said, "to give an *edge* to things."

"Listen. I can give you enough money to get out of here.

You know you don't have much time. I've got three hundred on me, and I'll go wherever you want to give you more."

"Wait a minute, Nick."

"It doesn't matter how much. I'll get it. We can meet in San Francisco."

"*Wait*," Sam barked. "If we're going to start bargaining, there's something I need to do first. Don't move."

And he went to the wall and walked right through it. The yellow light around the lanterns played a trick on the surfaces below. The stone seemed to wave and ripple like curtains drawn at an open window. Sam walked into a shadow that grew and shrank, and he reappeared up on his ledge a couple of seconds later. Nick thought, as he strained to make out what Sam was doing in the upper darkness: A couple of seconds was enough to give some men a proper head start. Two clean leaps and a gymnast's body swing would have landed Nick on Peter's ledge, and then he'd be off and running. But Nick had never done much with a couple of seconds. He worked through a state of emergency at his own speed or not at all. Besides, he didn't want to be chased. He could trust the face-to-face to keep him from getting shot, but he might not survive the role of a moving target in a tunnel. Sam, he realized in the meantime, must know every passage in the mine. Like a house where the last survivor lives surrounded by rooms lit only by daylight.

Nick could hear the striking of the match. Then the hiss when the fuse took a bite of the flame.

He shouted "No!" and started to run, and fell. His feet wouldn't hold him. In a flash he was down to nothing, thrown on his hands and knees, all his scenarios gone. He huddled against the floor. His mind went out like the bit of match that lit the fuse. He'd never been alone at all compared with this, and he knew he would die of it. Just at the moment the dynamite blew, his heart would break. But then, turning it into a joke, the music clicked on again and drowned the sputtering out, and he saw that even his death would be taken away.

Why don't we dance, why don't we dance? He put his hands against his ears and screamed.

Sam pulled him to his feet when he ran out of breath. He gripped him by the biceps and laughed in his face. "Are you *that* scared?" he asked delightedly, as if Nick's fear were the thing he'd been waiting for all day long. "Easy, baby, easy. It's *slow*. Like Peter said, I got a fuse that goes everywhere. I just want to shorten it. It won't burn all the way down to the powder for maybe an hour. But isn't it nice to know it's going?"

"Let me out. It's not my fault."

"Stop it," he said, tightening his grip. They could have been just about to dance. "Don't piss me off, Nick. *We're* not the ones who'll die down here. It's for cops. We got another way out."

"But why?" Nick asked, his blood still racing. They'd gotten a reprieve, but it burned and burned. What did Sam know about dynamite?

"You keep asking me that," he said, and he sounded disappointed. Apparently, he'd expected something more from Nick. He pulled away and turned to the painting. Nick slumped down and sat on the television. As he put his head between his knees, it seemed as if Sam were telling it to Rembrandt more than to him. "Today I figured out what's wrong with everything," he said, but you couldn't tell if he was still being funny or not. He spoke entirely in short sentences, and they seemed to Nick entirely unrelated one to another. Nick thought he'd have more to say about Varda's treasure. "There are all these stories that don't end right. Like Ben. And Varda and me. Did you know they worked this mine for eighteen years? It's written on one of the walls like a calendar. Next to it is a map of the whole mine, where they would have dug next and everything. They planned it years ahead. But they stopped. No reason. See what I mean?"

Ben who? Nick thought. He tried to listen, in case there was a clue to where the explosive device was set. He wasn't sure he could chase down the fuse, even if Sam let him loose to do it.

So listen, he ordered himself. At least find out the reasons, see where they go. It didn't matter if they didn't make sense. There wasn't time.

"Everything stops," Sam said, "but there isn't an ending. You know, I wasn't sure what I really wanted when I bought the stuff. I thought I'd maybe blow the place up all by myself. Just sit outside and watch the hill cave in. I mean, once I was done with it. I liked the feel of it, all ready to go—one match, *s-s-s-s-s-s,* 'Bingo!' I think I sleep better with a case of dynamite under my pillow."

"How long have you been here?" Nick slipped in. Turn it back to a conversation, he warned himself. If he didn't, five minutes from now he'd have no say at all. He had to hurry him up.

"Off and on, ten days. With all my stuff, since Wednesday." Five days. Since they'd met in Santa Monica. "I was planning to sit on Varda's money here till the heat was off." He went up close to the painting now. He looked over the damage, putting out a finger to touch the gouges. No emotion. "Now that's changed," he said. "It wasn't the way I thought it would be in Crook House." No recriminations, either. Evidently, no feeling of having been tricked. Not even enraged at losing all that time. "That's when I thought of the mine. Because *something*'s got to have a good ending. It isn't enough if I just light it and run like hell and watch it go. We got to make it a news event."

"But, Sam," he said, as reasonably as he could, "if you kill a cop, they'll get you. You'll be sent up for life. Think, why don't you. If you didn't kill Varda, what you've done up to now is nothing." Forgive me Hey, he thought, I have to. But when Sam turned to listen, Nick caught the glint of defiance in his eye. As if a life term had a certain appeal for a tough guy. As if the minor nature of the crimes so far committed were the crux of the problem. On to bigger things.

"But you're not listening, Nick. We have a chance to play cowboys and Indians for real."

"Grown-ups don't play."

"Is that so?" Sam said, sneering broadly. "What about the guys I work for? What do they do when they're out on the street getting laid?"

He laughed without making a sound. Then he tapped the barrel of the gun against his lips as if he were raising a finger to ask for quiet. They sized each other up again. And Nick caught a sudden picture of himself in a long shot. He wanted the part of the priest who coaxes the tragic young man off the ledge. Give yourself up, it's no go, as the good-hearted clerk tells his punk kid brother. Of course he was playing as much as Sam. He could see he wouldn't get a lot of moral mileage out of acting superior. Sam had already played with everyone from Crook House, one way or another. And if it came to cowboys, Nick didn't have a leg to stand on. As Rita would have said, he wrote the book.

"But why hurt innocent people?" he asked, standing up to face him again, teetering on his swollen feet. The do-unto-others approach.

"Cops aren't people," Sam said idly, bored by the ethics, his mind on something else. Nick, because he hadn't been on Norma Place the day Sam fled Ben's house, hadn't ever seen cops swarm. "You don't understand—this is a victimless crime, like getting laid. If I wanted to *hurt* somebody, I'd go for broke. I'd round up everyone I ever did it with and stand them up against a wall."

"I thought you liked to work the street."

"Oh, I do," he said, and reached over with the hand without the gun. He unzipped Nick's fly and did it up again. Neither looked down. "That's *if* I was out to hurt people. But I wouldn't hurt any of God's creatures. I'm a sucker for living things."

"You hurt us," Nick hastened to remind him. How long now? Six, seven minutes, he guessed. There was a break between two songs just a moment ago, but he couldn't hear it burning anymore.

"*You?*" Sam bellowed. "You're not hurting, Goddamn it. Don't you see I'm taking care of you?" He groped to tell Nick how easy he had it. "All your little pals are safe, aren't they? The worst that can happen to you is you might have to hire new help. A month from now, all it'll be is a caper. You won't even have to have your clothes dry-cleaned. Secretly, you'll be glad it happened. Because it's kicks."

"You think it's so simple. What about how I feel about you?"

"What's that?"

"I mean I care," he said, but casting his eyes down, as if it made him blush. If he hears what a lie it is, Nick thought, he'll shoot for sure.

"Okay," Sam said. "Strip." And Nick was so caught up in appearing sincere, he let it go by. By the time it took and he looked up, Sam had his pants down to his knees. He hopped on one foot while he pulled the other free. He was hard as a rock in a couple of seconds. "I want to do it," he said, "with the fuse lit."

Nick protested, "Sam, I can't." He had no room to maneuver. If he came across repelled by the mere idea, Sam would see how far he'd gone away. The scene had suddenly loosened up and called Nick back. If only he could *think*, he thought, but he faced a naked boy who wouldn't wait. The vanishing fuse had speeded up the time unbearably. Where it hammered Nick's head and scrambled his brain, it seemed to stroke and fondle Sam till it made him at once wild and serene. Though Nick could feel his clothes begin to crawl with a cold sweat, this was his only chance, and he knew it.

"You slay me, baby," Sam replied with unexpected mildness. "You act as if I didn't have the gun. Whatever I want is what we do. I can *make* you fuck, you know." He was moving around again. His cock swung heavily, taut with blood, and he waved the gun as if it were an outer-space device that let him breathe in an airless room. And though he'd shed his shoes along with his pants, he pranced around without the pain that blistered and bruised Nick's feet. "I let your friend Peter go," he said. "You owe me one. So do it."

What the hell? Nick went ahead and did it, mostly to gain

323

the time. His fingers went to his shirt to work at the buttons, and he was startled to find his tie in the way. Overdressed again, he thought ruefully. Meanwhile, Sam seemed to relish being naked in the cavern, fucking or not. As he went from spot to spot, he didn't dance so much as appear about to rise in the air. The music had long since gone into his bones. It was the fuse he took his rhythm from. He was so in tune he could hear it though Nick was deaf to it. He threw his head back and marveled at the dome he lived beneath. In the yellow light, his skin was gold against the tawny stone of the walls. Stacking his clothes on the dead TV, Nick had the oddest sense that Sam had grown so accustomed now to the life underground that he'd gladly give up the skin of the earth. As if he couldn't take the daylight anymore. And Nick had never thought the same of Rita, though he'd witnessed her version of the same intoxication whenever she went into Varda's room.

Nick had never taken off his clothes more chastely than he did right here. He'd never felt before such a horror of being naked. But he didn't want to die with nothing of his own close around him, even though he knew it didn't matter, not if he was going to be blown into little pieces. Once naked, he could feel all over his body the pressure of how it would go, the blowup and then the cave-in, as if he'd be conscious the whole time it was happening. He wasn't giving up. He meant to get out of here alive. But all the miseries of fate still had their hooks in him, even if he didn't any longer count himself a believer. He'd come to the conviction only today that fate was the worst kind of lie, because it was romantic. The whirlwind that had lately descended on Crook House taught him how even everyday things were locked in a drama, a fight to the death, merely by being human. But it wasn't easy to stick to those convictions in an abandoned mine, all of whose ghosts could speak the sacraments in Latin. Destiny seemed to shimmer from the walls like the light that stirred the stones into curtains.

He had an urge to cover his genitals with his hands. He

stood there shyly beside the painting and hoped for the carnal proposal to pass. Sam seemed to have forgotten him, anyway. Caught in his slow, subliminal dance, Sam had gone off with his own thoughts, looking as if he could wander forever in that one space and always find it new. Nick just watched him a moment. Maybe the damned get to like their little cells in Hell, he thought. He could see Sam was just as glad as Rusty Varda not to be going to Heaven. Yet Sam was more of a boy here than he seemed on the street, where he had to act hard and chew on a stalk of grass. Nick had always been aware of him calculating his time, never quite there but only driving through, in transit to a place where no one could follow. And this was it. Sam wouldn't need sex anymore, Nick thought, because he didn't need carfare. Without a dream place of his own to strive for, now that the ranch didn't work, Nick envied Sam his having arrived here. As Nick saw it, he'd gone beyond the daily life of the heart, to a higher plane.

But now Sam turned abruptly back to him—and still erect, as if after all he'd only been biding his time while Nick got ready for bed. Nick cursed himself again for getting lost in other people's heads. He'd wasted another half minute staring at Sam like a movie. Much as he used to when they first met. If it turned out to be half the rest of his life as well, he knew it was his own damned fault.

"I thought you loved me," Sam said tartly, coming close and looking down between Nick's legs.

"Please stop the fuse."

"Is that all it is?" Sam asked, but closer still, so close his cock made contact on Nick's abdomen. Though it might have been a gun, since it made Nick freeze. "No wonder we made a lousy couple. We get turned on by different trips."

"Please, Sam."

"*After* we make it. I'll go put it out as soon as we've both come."

"I can't."

"Relax," he said, and he brought up his arms around Nick's

shoulders and drew him close. "We have all the time in the world. Just think of something else, and your cock will take care of itself. Tell me about your grandparents."

"What about them?" Nick asked brokenly, hardly able to speak for all his confusion. But he wasn't sorry to be in somebody's arms, even Sam's. He was so exhausted that he didn't feel angry and didn't feel scared. He couldn't keep up the high-pitched feelings any longer. Some part of the gun in Sam's right hand touched cold along his shoulder blade, but even that was more curious than horrible. Maybe he'd gotten used to the upside-down of events, the succession of opposites. But he wasn't numb. He felt as if he'd never be able to say exactly what he felt, but he felt it so intensely, it was all he could do to just stand up and hold this boy whom he'd loved and hated too much. Nothing is ever finished, he thought.

"Tell about them digging gold—"

"I can't," he said. He meant he couldn't take in another thing.

"—on Sunday afternoons." And his voice got so plain Nick hardly knew it. "I see them going down these dried-up rivers back in the canyons. They pan the dirt, and they crack open stones, but all the time they're talking. Maybe it's the only time they spend alone together. And they don't expect to strike it rich. All they want to do is stay alive and do the same thing every Sunday."

"How do you know it was like that?" Nick replied, following suit and ridding his voice of inflection. He thought: The only way we know to keep from getting sentimental is not to *sound* that way. He pulled his head away, off Sam's shoulder, but he let their naked bodies stay together. Though he still didn't want to fuck, he had to admit he was calming down. Right now he was conscious of feeling neither love nor hate. It wouldn't last. Now was only a fraction of time, split like a hair. But Sam was right. His grandparents went on their Sunday outings just like he said. Or more precisely, Nick had always imagined it himself in just that way. The sepia photographs handed down to him were stubbornly noncommittal.

Two fat people in denim and homespun, squinting out beneath broad-brimmed hats. You could hardly tell who was a woman. Around them, the dry unpromising hills held nothing secret.

"Now, the priests were a whole other thing," Sam said, looking away from Nick, it seemed, so he could concentrate on the thread of his story. Nick had never heard him talk so much, unless it was fucktalk. And he held Nick now more tightly than he ever had in bed. He's afraid I'll laugh, Nick thought. "They were just like us, Nick. They *had* to hit gold or go out of their minds. They wouldn't take no for an answer." But stranger than anything he said just now was his cock, which began to relax, even as the tension in his grip increased. Nick's shoulders buckled beneath the crush. But it wasn't so bad that he couldn't stand it, so he rode it out. He was altogether a mass of aches and pains that he had to endure because there was no other way. And he was sure that, on the other side of this wonderful connection Sam was trying to share, the whole thing would start its winding down. This was the limit of the danger now. "They had this idea for a church," he said, "bigger than all the temples they found in the Andes. Covered in gold. If they had to, they'd dig till they got to China to find it. Right?"

"Sure," Nick agreed, though he hadn't a clue where it might be going. The priests in Peru were not the same as the ones in the LA mission. He knew that much back in grammar school. So why was Sam mixing them up? Nick didn't have a fantasy for untold wealth. He was much more interested in being rich. He never longed, like Sam and Rita, for the three-sixty view and the total immersion.

"Now let me ask you something. Who got the gold? The Sunday diggers or the priests?"

"Neither one," Nick answered. He wondered why it suddenly seemed twice as sad. Almost no one got the gold, no matter how patient, how pure of heart.

"Can you believe it?" Sam said softly, shaking his head, looking farther and farther off. "That's why I'm so scared."

But now there was no time. It was over, and they didn't

even know it. Nick could see one whole side of the room beyond Sam's naked shoulder. Sam had a view of the other half. And Nick just happened to be glancing up at the way he'd come in because, no matter what else, he had to keep an eye on the way out. He was so thrown by what Sam had just said that he froze like a deer, as if to decide which way to fly. The moment paused on a knife's edge, flush with the moment when Rita's head emerged out of the tunnel. And if Nick hadn't been quite so still to begin with, Sam might never have felt him startle—like a quiver in the region of his heart. But Nick saw Rita, dressed as if for cocktails, and took in who it was, and already Sam was whirling round.

The gun described a perfect half circle, and he shot two shots without taking aim. The bullets hit the face of the rock at either side of Rita's head as if it were all in fun, like a Wild West show. But Sam hadn't meant to miss. His arm was out, straight as an assassin's. Except for the gun, he could have been an athlete stripped for the games. He might have just let fly a javelin in a Roman circus. The noise went on and on like a wind, and none of them heard the disco beat again. Without even trying, he could have picked Rita off with the third shot. She stood as stunned as a bird, looking as if the shots had woken her up. But he froze for a moment of his own when he saw who it was, and by then Nick was ready to strike.

He swung one elbow and thumped Sam hard in the middle of the back. He would have hurt him more with almost any sort of punch, but all he wanted to do was throw him. And it worked like a dose of hypnosis. The shooting arm went rubbery, his head snapped forward, and his torso seemed to lose its muscle. He was thrown for only a couple of seconds, but it gave Nick time to follow up. He hooked his foot around one of Sam's ankles and shoved him forward. Sam went down, *crash*, flat on his face, as if he was too startled to break his own fall. And at last the gun flew from his hand and clattered away out of reach.

Nick wouldn't even have stopped to fetch it if it hadn't landed right in his path as he sprang toward the wall. He bent and scooped it up. Then he caught at the little crevices in the wall as if he'd been up and down it for years. He was sprawled on the ledge before he knew it, looking more or less up Rita's dress. His feet were screaming.

"Run!" he cried out roughly, and she turned and went without saying a word—like someone a sick man sends away when there's nothing to do. He realized he wanted to go out alone. To not be surrounded right now by the best of friends. The flash of adrenaline that got the tables turned and left Nick high on the ledge had dropped. He looked down at Sam, who was doubled up and groaning, his face in his hands. The rocks in the floor had razored him up. He wasn't hurt bad, but he was hurting. He looked a mess. And Nick would have given anything to go back down. He was sorrier now than he thought he could bear.

But it was over. He stumbled into the tunnel and scalded along on the shreds of his feet. The candles were down to the nubs, the air thick as tear gas. He had to go fast or choke. It certainly wasn't the fear that Sam would follow. Nick knew how completely he'd tripped him. Sam would stay curled up like a child until he'd adjusted to his bloodied knees and elbows. Then perhaps he'd cry, this boy without scars. He wouldn't be ready to start out on his own for five or ten minutes, and then he'd escape and go out of their lives, the grin wiped off his face for good. It made Nick mad with grief, who'd done all he could till now to keep Sam young. But in the end, he knew, he had no choice. He came to the final turn in the tunnel without the strength to feel relieved. He crawled up the steps to the chapel, blind with bitter tears, as if determined to refuse the world that could now go on as before. Rita stood mutely at the top of the stairs, and he thought he would tell her the worst, that it broke his heart to have it over with. He'd gone too far to come back whole. Nothing would ever surprise him again.

It was then that the dynamite blew.

The noise was like a muffled cannon roaring in a fog. The walls, before they started falling down, shook off a kind of glitter that filled the air. Nick sailed up the rest of the stairs like Peter Pan. Rita sat down hard on the floor. Time stood still for the last time. Nick forgot about the fuse, just as Sam had said he would, and Sam had misjudged the fuse by nearly half an hour. So in a way they were both right. They'd told each other the truth.

It wasn't just one explosion, in fact, but one right after another, as if the mine and the mountain had only needed a push to pull the world to bits on their own. Nick and Rita, side by side on the floor, were sprayed with pebbles and then with stones. The light was gone. But Nick was as stubborn as ever. He thought of Sam until the roof was coming down in boulders. He wouldn't go back down, but he stared in the direction of the tunnel opening, waiting for Sam to be safe. He *couldn't* be dead, or else what was the point of the pain Nick had given him? Dying wasn't required.

Rita had to take his hand and drag him up and lead him away through the thickening dust and acid smoke. They came out on the ledge at the mouth of the mine, where the dark was light compared with the dark inside. Then the ledge broke off. They slid down with it as if it were an elevator, fifteen or twenty feet. Then even the noise and dust were behind them. The only thing left was the cold night air, and it stung all over, as if he'd landed on a planet where the air could kill. And he knew as he slumped against Rita, blacking out into a third dark deeper than the mine and the night, that everything else would be good as new, but he'd never be warm again.

Chapter 10

Oh, you look all right, Rita said to herself, peering around at all the Ritas in the three-way mirror. She could hardly help but look all right, since if she squinted she could check out in the flesh page 191 of the April *Vogue*. The little nothing of a peach silk dress was two hundred eighty dollars at Magnin's and she hadn't even been able to wear it the night before to Peter's opening, which was far too fancy for afternoon clothes. And anyway, since two-eighty wouldn't have bought the sleeves of the things that turned up at a show on Rodeo Drive, Rita had sensibly given up any thought of trying to compete. She'd thrown on her old faithful, white over green. She steered clear of mirrors and faded neatly into the woodwork. But she didn't really mind. It was Peter's night last night, though he hadn't wanted a bit of it. They'd practically had to tie him into his tux to get him to go. Rita would have begged off herself, but Nick couldn't go because he couldn't stand up for more than half an hour at a time, even now. Rita went so Peter would have a body to leave with. She was glad to do it. She stood apart while they clustered about him. She toted up the "SOLD" stickers every time they were slapped on a frame. In two hours, eight paintings came to forty-four thousand. She took the littlest sips of champagne and thought about today and the peach silk dress. Because today was all hers.

Well, of course it was their day, too, Peter's and Nick's and Hey's. They'd all be right there with her. But somebody had to do the talking, and Rita was whom they chose, four to nothing. She slipped on a pair of pumps and balled up the clothes she'd just taken off. Then she took a look around, to make sure there were no stray slippers or panty hose lying about. But there were only pots and pots of orchids—everywhere. Hanging off the walls and tiered on a couple of stone benches Peter brought up from the shop. She wondered when she'd agreed to orchids in the closet. Lighted by a row of pin spots in the ceiling, they were a perfect fragment of inaccessible forest, dusky and foreign, just as Peter promised. But this morning they also seemed a trifle overdone to Rita. Peter said if you didn't give the art press a little swank at every turn, they'd be bored before you got them where you wanted them. That, and keep their drinks full to the brim. This was the Old Masters division of the art press. They were used to dealing with the sort of rich who made the simply rich crazy with envy.

So her bedroom, because it was the pressroom, was also the bar. She agreed with Peter that it made it more of a drama to bring them in here right away. Brief them first in Frances Dean's room. Shut them in and lock the windows while they sat and wondered what came next. And then the orchids and then the treasure. Before they were done, they wouldn't settle for anything short of headlines. Rita gave it the once-over, counting the ashtrays as she passed on through, shuffling the highball glasses around as if she were racking billiard balls. Peter had done it up like a VIP lounge at the UN. Beige and wool upholstery and Audubon prints. Only the bed was tarted up some—French linen sheets, Star of Bethlehem quilt, as if who would ever want to get up—because Rita would start with the story of Frances Dean, the sleeping beauty, to put them all in the mood. She'd spent the last few nights herself on the opium bed in the living room, to keep out of Peter's way. Now that they were going public, she couldn't any longer cling to a notion as individual as her own room. She was only an overnight guest again. She realized without any rancor, in fact, that after today she'd have to be finding a place to move to. Crook House was finished with her.

She heard a noise like a body falling and ducked her head out into the hall to see. It was Hey. He'd dropped the ice bucket, and now he was on his hands and knees, furiously picking up cubes of ice like a farmer pulling weeds. But with only one hand—the other arm was still in a sling. "They'll never know," he sang out gaily, as if he'd planned it this way all along. "You know they'll never know. It's part of the peck of dirt they have to eat, like anybody else."

"I think this crowd eats dirt like peanuts," Rita said. She stooped to help, glad to have something to do as the morning inched along. She was the only one used to Hey's new mood. Nick and Peter thought he was having hysterics. He broke most things he put his hand to. The socks were all mismatched, and the shirts unironed. The food arrived at the table, Peter said, looking as if it had weathered a 7.0 on the Richter scale between the kitchen and the dining room. And nobody could ever *find* anything, once Hey put it away. But they let it pass. They'd all gone out of their way with one another in the month since the Monday in March. In time, they told each other, Hey would be back on his feet. Time was the key all around.

"Nick wants you."

"Where is he?"

"Upstairs," he said, blowing on his fingers to warm them up. "I swear to God, he's been locked in his closet since right after breakfast. I think he thinks he's back in the mine." He meant to be darkly funny, as if Nick were a combat soldier who still woke up years later in the middle of a bloody battle.

Could they really start to laugh about it now? Rita wondered. What if one of them got offended? "You think it's ghosts?" she asked him lightly. "Maybe something tripped you." And she liked the feel of it. Why not funny? Survivors told the roughest jokes to other survivors, not to the world at large. They talked cripple to cripple sometimes, and the jokes were the sort an outsider couldn't handle. It was better than talking around it. Or acting as if it were over.

"Not anymore. They've all gone back to their graves," he said. They stood up and took the handle of the bucket between them like Jack and Jill. He was so excited about telling her the rest that he almost let it slip again, getting it up on the bar. He was giddy, Rita thought, but not upset. The only one among them overjoyed that Sam was dead. It seemed to set him free. "I didn't tell you," he said, "but Linda went away the minute I was shot. I could *feel* it, Rita. She pulled up her skirts and parted the curtain and let it fall."

"Did the bullet hit her, too?" She realized Hey had been waiting all along for a sign that he could talk. She and Peter had followed Nick's lead in not revealing what they'd felt when Sam laid siege to Crook House. They'd discussed it, of course, all four, and finally decided, three to one, not to report it to anyone. They'd been over the course of the day with Sam a hundred times—that is, the plot of it. They needed to know what it all meant before they could close off the access routes. But no feelings, please.

"Of course not," he said. "But you see, when a lost soul comes back, it gets inside people who don't have anything going. Somebody *boring* is what they like. And a well-kept house, because they're trying to relax." Then he paused abruptly as if to listen, in case the souls in Limbo thought he was misrepresenting the fix they were in. He may have gotten free of the spell he was under, but the superstition had a long way yet to go. "Being shot was just what I needed. But I bet it set Linda back ten years."

"I thought you liked having her around," Rita said. "I thought it was part of your religion."

Hey shrugged. "It was all right for a while, I guess. It was *different*," he said, putting out his free hand to rearrange the highball glasses. Two of them clicked together and cracked, and he picked them up to take away. "I wasn't much good at it, though. And I always thought I would be."

"Good at what?"

"Being a *woman*," he said crossly, as if to say why didn't she pay attention. "I thought it would be like being a ballerina. But it got so I thought about men all the time. Now that must sound *awful*. I don't mean I wanted to get *laid* all the time, or fall in love. That's not something that happens to me." He smiled at his own remark. He seemed to count himself lucky. "But I felt—superior—you know? Men drove me crazy."

"Women aren't so different," she said absently. Best to keep clear, she thought, of Hey's quack theory of gender. It didn't seem any less appalling now than it did when he used too much mascara and walked around as if on tiptoe. Besides, she just caught sight of something in the carpet. She stooped to look closely, but she lost it again.

"The other ghost who's dead and buried now is Varda," he announced portentously. He knew she'd lost all interest, but he plunged on anyway, addressing the back of her neck. "With the kid out of the way, I don't have obligations to the past anymore. The present is all the time I've got. And it's for us. You understand?"

"Us who?"

"Us *four*."

"Oh." Thank God for little favors. She thought he might have taken a sudden fancy to her. She was just about to stand up when she spotted it. She snatched it up fast, intrigued by any treasure that went without a map. It was a little cameo done up as a dangle earring. Pretty—but whose? No woman had slept in here but Rita in all the time Peter and Nick had lived in the house. She rose and held it close to Hey, swinging it just in front of his eyes like a hypnotist. "This isn't yours, is it?" she asked. In return, he shot her his most unamused look, turned on his heel, fled the room, and marched away down the hall. "I didn't *really* think it was," she called apologetically, but he was gone. In fact, she decided, it served him right, trying to fence them in like a gang of thieves and counterfeiters. She understood the mood he was in, all right, but she guessed she'd liked him better when he used to wince and sigh a lot. Before he got to be a hero.

She came out onto the terrace and crossed the garden to the dining room side. She looked at herself in all the French windows as she drifted by. He was a genuine hero, she had to admit, even if he'd only gotten in the way of a loaded gun. It had to do, somehow, with acting the same as ever in the face of great pain. And he meant well, of course, to think the four of them in Crook House were as clean and interlocked as astronauts. She clipped the earring on her left ear because there were no pockets in the peach dress. Her reflection in the living room windows was very faint and very real, and she didn't so much as glance at the view of the city behind her. She would never have admitted it to Hey, but she felt a little betrayed herself sometimes by so much outside world so readily in evidence. It kept calling into question the self-contained oasis they'd inhabited here for the last month. They'd all been recovering nicely, like a solicitous group of people on the down side of a bad cold. Not really bedridden. Cozy in robe and slippers and boiling up pots of herbal tea. Kind of enjoying it.

"Are you practicing what to say?"

She looked up, bewildered, to Nick's and Peter's room, where Nick was standing at the window grinning. She hadn't even noticed, but she'd stopped to stare into the glass doors to the dining room. Stood there maybe half a minute, eyes glued to her own eyes. But she didn't blush to find herself discovered, so long as it was Nick or Peter. They all bumped into each other so regularly now that it came to be something of a need, as if the spells of solitude could be risked, after all, as long as there were others about to set limits. Nick was hanging something up—a blanket, it looked like—to cover the casement. The other window was already dark. Perhaps he was feeling a bit assaulted by the view himself.

"I haven't really thought about it," she said. "I just don't want Varda to sound like a gangster."

Nick shook his head vigorously. " 'Gangster' is all wrong. You want him more of an outlaw. *Western*, like Jesse James. With maybe a hint of the Vanderbilts thrown in, just for class."

"Well," she said, dubious and vague, but committed all the same to clichés of her own, "I want him to come off as a man with a lonely vision. I have to play it by ear. Shall I come up?"

"Not yet. I'm not ready," he said, disappearing behind the blanket as he thumbed in the last tack. "Five minutes," he called.

What are you doing? she almost said, but decided she didn't mind waiting to see. She walked on over to the pool and, in order not to look at the whole of LA, looked at herself again in the water. Nick ought to be at work. He and Peter planned to be home just before the press arrived at one, and they'd had to promise Hey they'd have eaten lunch first. Hey had to get all the servants' work done beforehand, because the apron came off on the stroke of one, when he would be properly introduced as "Mr. Varda's longtime companion." Hey's own phrase. "Let them make of it what they want," he said with endless satisfaction, and Nick and Peter and Rita shrugged and let it go. As for Nick, Rita didn't need Crook House all to herself all morning. What was stranger still, she warned herself, was the notion that she should always know what Nick was about. Why *shouldn't* he spend the morning in his closet?

In the beginning, just after the accident, Nick seemed to

intuit that all he could do for Sam from here on in was to wipe out every trace of him. From his bed at home, his feet up in harnesses, salved every hour, he argued over the phone with Hey, who was still in the hospital. Hey was adamant—now that they were all safe, they had to tell the police. But why? Nick reasoned. The publicity would front-page their lives with the sort of ugly gay innuendo that kept away clients and crowded the driveway with ambulance chasers. And why give it both barrels to Sam's unsuspecting friends and family, wherever they may be? Let them keep hoping he'd turned out all right. Hey had the more serious claim, of course, because he had taken the more serious wound. He thought of it as part of what he owed to Varda, as if the public proof that it was murder ten years ago proved also that somehow Varda might have otherwise lived forever. But he waffled for a couple of days, long enough for Nick to decide it was too late—the authorities would want to know why they'd waited at all. So when Hey came home and they began to have the summit meetings every evening in the secret room, Hey agreed to leave it buried, too. By then he'd come up with his own good reason. "It'll be *our* secret, then," he told them. "We'll give up all of Varda's things, and in return we'll have Sam and the Rembrandt. Just us four."

They could have gone forward, of course, by simply expanding on Rita's cottage industry, the hand-stringed packages without return addresses. They could have cabled the various owners—museums, town fathers, embassies, and idle rich—claiming rewards where available, using Peter's shop as a conduit so that Crook House never got mentioned. But they didn't. They completed the inventory first, down to the smallest diamond stickpin. They separated out those things whose owners were either unknown, long gone, or thieves themselves. Then they considered divvying up that half, but only Peter would have gotten any use out of medieval silver, Burmese ivories, and the like. There was enough to start their own museum, but none of them ever went to half the ones there already were. Besides, keeping it together would cheat them out of the thrill of dispersal. There was too much inertia pent up in Varda's room. All his booty needed to have the dust of museums shaken out of it.

"I'm not ashamed to admit there are things I'd like," Peter had reminded them, twirling a gold-headed cane that Commodore Vanderbilt took out to promenade on Cliff Walk.

"When would you ever use that?" Hey asked.

"I don't always use the things I like."

"I think we have to make a show of it," Nick proposed, "for Varda's sake. If everything gets siphoned off in bits and pieces, no one will ever know. People ought to know."

"I can't allow it," Hey said grandly, not at that point through with his duties to Varda's memory. "He was a great director. We mustn't work it so he's more remembered for being a crook."

And that led to fruitless debate about one kind of fame and another. Nick said the taste in fame had changed since Varda's death, and the smuggling and hoarding of masterpieces would catch the public fancy. There were already crowds of old movie people. If they could still walk, they were out telling stories, and everyone already had the picture.

"I agree with Nick," Rita said finally, speaking from the desk, her hand on the catalogue. She exuded the authority of one who knew the story here, at least, from cover to cover. "Let's throw it open. But not just so people hear about a caper having to do with stolen art. We do it for Varda and *Frances*."

They hadn't had enough of love in life, Rita argued. That was why he'd provisioned so well the journey through to the other side of the veil. And Rita proposed to bring their ghosts together, true to the spirit of Varda's plan, by letting out their story. When Nick and Peter warned her that the press wouldn't tell it in the nicest way, that they'd dredge up the dope story, make it all sound crazy and sad, Rita thought she'd take that chance. "He didn't want to go to Heaven, anyway," she said, staring at Nick. "The best we can do for Varda and Frances is make sure they're linked and let them go."

It may have been sentimental rubbish, but it wasn't too

pretty for Hey. He loved it. Peter thought it was tacky, but he did like the thought of the fuss being made over *his* house, if only so he could pretend it was a nuisance. You can't *buy* it, he always wished he could tell his clients when they coveted something of his that was fine and wanted one of their own. He had a secret wish to surround himself with a whole Russian prince's worth of artifacts and one-of-a-kind, hand-done pieces. Then he could show the San Marino ladies how out of luck they were. And however darkly he tended to paint the press, he liked publicity quite for its own sake. It didn't so much matter what they said, so long as they spelled the name right. Nick's wish was much more basic. He wanted to see the treasure go through the transformation into cash. He wanted to flood the market, send the bidding through the roof, cash in his chips till he broke the bank. An auction of Varda's things would bring out the real high rollers, and Nick liked to keep posted on how they were wearing their money this year.

So they all agreed in the end because they had to. They each had a trove of sentimental rubbish of their own, and they saw there was safety in numbers.

Five minutes up. Rita wondered now, as she turned from the pool, why she wasn't more nervous. Probably, she thought, because Varda and Frances Dean had stayed at a certain remove from her since the day Sam died. Her sentimental projections aside, she was acting—like Hey—more out of duty than as if she were reading *Anna Karenina*. That phase probably ended on the day she pulled the plug at Desertside. She didn't suffer for the star-crossed lovers anymore. Her pals in Crook House took up the slack and the empty spaces. Just like Hey said. Why was she mad at him for saying so?

"You're missing an earring," Peter said.

She turned away from the dining room door a second time. He was coming from the direction of her room, carrying a beat-up wooden box. As to the earring, he didn't miss a trick. "Actually," she said, "somebody else is missing it. I'm just the Lost and Found, as usual. What's that?"

"I don't know. Hey just handed it to me. I think it's the house croquet set."

"What are you supposed to do with it?"

"As near as I can tell," he answered brightly, prepared for all eventualities, "it's a present. 'This ought to go to you,' Hey said, 'because you have the right kind of rhythm.' What kind of rhythm is that, do you think?"

He set down the box between them on the flagstones. The lid had two hooks, and they each undid one and lifted up the top like a captain's chest. It was the juggler's kit. They stooped to it wordlessly and took it apart. A shelf swung out that was constructed something like an egg carton, with hollows for sets of hard rubber balls. Four balls in red, four in green, in blue, in yellow, but ancient and worn-away with use. They looked like the pale, filtered colors of the sky in a Dutch painting. Presumably, if you got good enough to juggle more than four at once, you had to start mixing your colors. Under this shelf was a toy-maker's grab bag of things to throw in the air. Brass rings, steel rings, cones, and batons. A set of frail ceramic birds that whistled when they flew. And then, in a special steel box at the bottom that reeked inside of kerosene, three weighted sticks all charred at one end—for juggling torches. Peter and Rita laid everything out on the ground around them, silent until they were done and the box was empty.

"This is all he brought with him from Hungary," Rita said quietly, though of course she had no way of knowing. But she flashed on an image of a young and dark-eyed juggler standing in line at Ellis Island, a box of tricks in his arms, game to find a circus on the Lower East Side. And if a man like that got old and died, she thought with a sudden flutter of grief and fury, then none of them were safe, even here.

"I'm afraid I'm too old to learn it now," Peter said. He'd have liked billiards better, or bowls or croquet.

"It's a talent, I suppose, like anything else," she said, revolving a yellow ball in her hands. It made her think of the marble apple the goddess held in the secret room. "Like Hey says, you either have it or you don't. Why not give it a try?"

"Because unlike you and Nick, my darling, I don't always have to be acting out the Seven Ages of Man." He stood up and held out his hands to her. "Come on, come on," he said, as if they were on a tight schedule. "Nick must want to show us what Hey gave *him*."

She got up and hurried along, looking over her shoulder once at the props of the clown show strewn on the terrace. Peter was probably right, but what Peter really had against juggling, she thought, had more to do with gypsies and the tawdry decor of circuses. He couldn't see past the tacky part to the magic. And Rita could. The lovely thing it said about Varda was that nothing at all was tied down to stay. Everything at any moment might begin to frolic in the midday air. A juggler was a man who held out hope.

"Why doesn't Hey give *me* something?" Rita asked as they clattered up the stairs in their fancy shoes.

"You don't need it. You find things all by yourself," he said playfully. "Every time you look down, there's a cameo there at your feet." They arrived out of breath at the door, and Peter knocked and opened it. But just before they went in and got lost in the dark, he touched her cheek and added one more thing. "Hey is trying to tell Nick and me that Crook House is finally ours. He's turning over the deeds and the titles. The funny thing is, he's got me feeling grateful."

"Come sit on the bed," Nick said when they came in. He was perched on pillows in his bathrobe, Indian-style, with a movie projector in front of him trained on the opposite wall. The blankets dimmed the light, but not so much so they couldn't see. The air was about as thick as twilight. As they kicked off their shoes and sat on either side of him, he clicked it on, and the film rolled. A man in an Edwardian suit ran up and down in a field, driven to distraction by something they'd missed.

"Wait a minute," Peter said irritably. "Start at the beginning. Explain."

"Most of it's really bad," Nick said apologetically. "You haven't missed a thing. Grainy little one- and two-reelers. I can't even follow the story half the time." Just then, a woman came tearing down the field as if for a touchdown. There was a moment of recognition. Then she and the troubled man danced around for a minute or so, delighted to have met at last. It was about as heavily textured as Mickey Mouse. "I've watched about two hours, and I'm up to 1919, and believe me, he's not a forgotten genius."

But all the same, it was actually Rusty Varda's work, and they couldn't take their eyes off it. He'd saved it all meticulously. Where a hundred other pioneers, too broke to care, had let their reels rot in the attic, Varda transferred every blessed foot to modern film. He'd spliced it up so they ran in the order he shot them. Then he'd listed them all in a log that he tucked in the lid of the wooden box Hey dragged up the stairs to Nick that morning. A box about the size of the juggler's kit. With a sense of method as sharp and passionate as the plan for the secret room.

"How much Frances Dean has there been?" Rita asked tensely, afraid she'd been cheated, about to beg him to please start over. She didn't care about films much, unless they told a story very like a book's. She only wanted to see that face.

"That's why I called you up. She's about to make her debut."

The film in the field ended with a kiss. Then the numbers zeroed down from ten to nothing, and the next film began before they knew it. "Varda Cinegraph Presents *A Test of Faith*." The titles flipped and listed a cast of dozens, and the last line said, "With Frances Dean as The Woman from Paris." She was more real to them suddenly, in just that line. But the film was awful. About a rich old man who'd returned from abroad with a pretty young wife who spoke no English. It all took place at a party he threw to introduce her around his vast Victorian family. A lot of preparation went on in a great big gingerbread house, and the servants whispered darkly about the way things used to be. The sons and their families gathered and went through aimless footage, with sight gags of dumb family pranks and heavy picnicking. When Frances Dean entered at last on the old man's arm, pale and thin and sleepless, confused by all this American cheer and Fourth of July noise, the rhythm went haywire. Nothing seemed to matter except why this beautiful woman was so sad, and there probably wasn't a film in the world that could say.

"This is terrible," Peter said. "She looks like a little girl. No, worse. She looks like a little-girl junkie."

"It's unearthly," Rita said. Beautiful, she seemed to mean, but out of synch, like Garbo and the Keystone Cops.

Nick didn't notice, one way or the other. As he'd done all morning, he was staring stony-eyed at the young male lead, in this case one of the sons, being primed on one side by his brothers to test the young wife, to flirt with her till she was compromised, on the other side smitten in spite of himself. He was all out-of-place in his morning suit, hemmed in as if by armor. But the look was unmistakable. They were different in every movie, but they always looked like Sam. They walked like workmen, and they slouched like whores. Though his heart was in smithereens, Nick had to wonder for one dispassionate moment how so many men could be the same. His eyes weren't playing tricks. Not a single one appeared a second time. He must have seen twenty or thirty, all told. For some reason, Rusty Varda wanted a new one in every film—in his bed as well, presumably. So maybe Sam was right. Varda had asked him back to Crook House again and again, as if in his old age he'd finally found a boy he couldn't leave alone. Finally found the one. What did it mean, Nick wondered, if Sam was right about that?

"It's amazing, isn't it," Peter said, "how people get all their power together? You'd never know how far Varda got from the shit he left behind. A juggler's gear, for Christ's sake, and a crate of second-rate silents—it all seems so puny." He didn't see that both of the others were somewhere else, overwhelmed by the shaking image on the bedroom wall. The fragmentary evidence of Varda's life struck him with how little a man ended up with. Not a typical feeling at all for someone who measured the world by clutter. But somehow it called up his deepest image, of Czarist Russia stripped of estates. It was as if someone had started to play the balalaika. "If we'd never found the room in the hill," he said, floored by the irony, "there would have been nothing to him. Nothing at all."

Rita and Nick nodded agreement. They didn't want to say how jarred they felt, since each believed he was the only one knocked over. They'd worked hard at not seeming extreme for weeks. It was a point of pride that things had gone back to being the same as ever. And acting so had made it so. They're looking right at it, but they don't see it, Nick told himself. And Rita thought, Even Peter doesn't know me well enough to know that's who I always wanted to be, without ever knowing *exactly* who. If she could only have looked like that, Rita thought, she would never have had to waste a minute on herself. She would have been through the wall before she was twenty.

Frances Dean had about her a gaunt sort of flapper look— smoldering, weary, surrendered. And whether it was the dope or just an attitude she was born with, she seemed to maintain complete indifference toward her bruised and sullen beauty. She wouldn't have known what a mirror was for. She might with a tilt of her head have acknowledged a kindred spirit, but women like her didn't talk to women like her. She waited in the garden for the man who looked like Sam. The furtive glances she gave the camera seemed to imply that it caused her pain, just to be watched like that. It was the strangest play for stardom Rita had ever witnessed. As if she'd engaged the camera's power to hurt, and it sent out a beam like a laser that burned her skin. The boy was no match for her. They strolled in a circle, and she did a long speech about the flowers of her country. She touched a rose with one long finger and shook her head because there wasn't any way to say it. Every couple of seconds, every four or five, an idiot title flashed on. He was telling her he'd fallen for her madly. He didn't look it at all.

Peter had had enough. "Hey's right about one thing," he

said. "Rusty Varda is dead and buried." He turned on one of the great terra-cotta lamps next to the bed, got up, and started to leaf through the mail on the bedside table. "She would have made a fabulous fashion model, don't you think, Rita? She's ahead of her time. That look is pure Art Deco."

"You know," she said, "I just realized I don't know the start of the story. Where Varda found her. You don't meet *that* type on a stool at Schwab's." The film on the wall was paler now. The faces were nearly whited out.

"He was probably fucking her, pardon me," Peter said, and he walked to the bathroom door, breaking the light of the film so it rippled across him. "He probably met her on the street."

"No," said Nick and Rita, one on top of the other, but you couldn't say which was the echo. Peter shrugged his shoulders, aware he was being outvoted two to one. He closed the bathroom door behind him, and Rita said to Nick, "Turn off the light, why don't you?"

They watched for a while in silence. It was clearly becoming a situation where nothing was going to happen. Frances kept her distance and told him they had to be true to what they'd got. She groped for the words in her strange new language. No, no, Sam cried, they had to run away. When he reached to take her in his arms, Nick and Rita could almost hear Varda talking through his megaphone, trying to pump in some feeling. Frances skipped away and put a border of rose-bushes between them. She spoke a last passionate speech, flinging her arms about and calling him to honor. In the course of it, Nick and Rita found they'd developed the skill of not reading the titles at all. They might not have agreed at what point it happened, but Frances Dean had started to act up a storm.

It was hard to say what became of the language barrier. It looked as if the film had stopped pretending she couldn't speak English, and the shift could have come out comical, but she *acted* as if she'd found the words because she *had* to. When the brothers and cousins fell out of the bushes, expecting to find her in Sam's arms, she *saw* what they'd tried to do to her. She shot a single strangled look at Sam as she took the old man's arm and went away. Her eyes were full, poised at the peak like the roses. And as she turned to go, they swept across the eye of the camera, hovered there, and seemed to accuse it of the same betrayal. The final shot was Sam wringing his hands, his own life now in ruins, except he looked like he hadn't felt a thing. Frances Dean had pulled off a three-act ballet while the boy was stepping all over his feet.

"Oh, my," Rita said, forgetting for the moment how they'd all agreed it was silly. "Couldn't you tell she loved him, too? For a minute she almost ran."

"That boy is as bad as the kids I went to high school with," he said, dissatisfied and edgy. "I don't understand these movies, Rita. They're all too short to have a story, so they just set up these comic-strip plots, like a Punch and Judy show. But then they try to act them as if they're *Hamlet*. They can't have it both ways."

"Wasn't that a story?" she asked impatiently. "The story was what she was feeling, wasn't it?" Why was she defending Varda's work? She was only going to get melancholy if she started to care in such detail. She'd be holding back tears by the time the press was seated. "It isn't in *words*. It's all states of mind."

"They were never lovers, were they?"

"Who?"

"Varda and Frances Dean."

"No," she said, remembering back when Hey first told her, how instead they were just like brother and sister, as if that were a better arrangement all the way around. The next film had already started, meanwhile. A fancy Park Avenue apartment. Swells in evening clothes. Rita didn't catch the title, and she paid no attention to the setup. She just waited for Frances Dean. And as no Sam had yet appeared, Nick was as free as she was to go on talking. They looked straight ahead at the sepia glow on the wall, each of them primed for a single entrance, and they lounged against the hill of pillows Peter stacked on every bed he put his hand to.

"One thing I don't understand," she said. "Why did you

come home early that afternoon?" Please don't say, "What afternoon?" she thought, though she hadn't mentioned it in weeks, and though anyone might have been excused for thinking they were in the middle of something else just now. But he caught on right away. And he didn't seem to mind.

"It was about the car," he said, and it crossed her mind that back in New York nothing would *ever* be about a car. "I thought you might have had second thoughts, getting a gift that big."

"Should I have? You mean, it makes me something of a kept woman. A man slips me the key to a sports car, and who knows where it might lead?" It struck her funny, and she rocked in the pillows and laughed so lightly that all sorts of things they might have talked out no longer required it. Just then, meanwhile, Frances Dean took her entrance down a staircase, stopping to light a cigarette halfway down, and Rita suddenly felt terrific, as if she and Frances both were traveling first cabin for once, at least for the course of an evening. It was as if they'd have the most wonderful things to tell each other later, when at last they'd get back to the room they shared. I ought to wear silk more often, Rita decided. And incidentally, she hadn't been to a single movie in all this time in LA, not until now, and she thought she ought to go more. "To be honest, Nick, I never gave it a thought. It was just an MG that dropped out of the sky. But I'm awfully glad you started to worry. You were our last chance."

It was a Noel Coward play up on the screen, twenty years before its time, except it was silent, and this one Rusty Varda wrote. To miss the setup, Rita thought, you had to want to miss it. Frances Dean was a famous something—actress, probably—and she expected to be center-stage from the moment she came on. Sam was her opposite number, a famous something else, and they saw each other across the room, did double takes, and got ready for battle. It was a comedy of the old school, where the people fell in love while under fire. And if Frances Dean in *A Test of Faith* had seemed suited only to heavy drama, the maid of sorrows, she cavorted here and told a hundred visual jokes just walking about, with quicksilver timing, one right after the other. Garbo laughs, Rita thought.

"While we're at it," Nick said airily, making his move with his eyes closed, "you can tell me how you found us." In the mine was what he meant. It was a tribute to how well they'd gotten over everything that she hadn't even found it odd that he'd never asked. She hadn't really done much, after all. She'd been the least tested by physical pain, so she wasn't a hero, or by loss, so she wasn't alone. She'd picked up Peter, naked on the ranch road, and driven back down to the mine and gone in and after a while come out with Nick. All she'd done was drive home two naked men.

"Peter showed me," she said, but totally uninterested.

"How did you know to come to the ranch?"

Varda's movie had altogether too much talk, which made it a mess to watch because it had to have too many titles. Sam and Frances were dancing with partners chosen to make each other jealous. They showed off their fancy footwork and then made as if to get carnal, but all the while keeping the beat to a fox-trot. She's a hell of a hoofer, too, Rita thought, vindicated somehow by the fact that the tragedy of Frances Dean was total. It was one thing if she fell apart and was just another pretty face, but it was too terrible to bear if she could have been great. She and Sam found themselves at last on the terrace to have it out, and it was strange to watch them flirting just ten minutes after the scene among the roses. Rita didn't catch it that the man with Sam's face wasn't the same as his counterpart in the other film. She thought the two actors must be a kind of team, like the Lunts. Frances strutted around Sam in a circle and laid out an ultimatum. Then it was his turn, and he poked and poked his finger at her till he backed her up against the wall. He did a better job of being in love, Rita thought, than he'd done in the old man's garden.

"Well," she said a bit sheepishly, turning to Nick, "I sort of went through all your things."

"What things?"

"Your desk, your dresser, your pockets—everything in the

house," she admitted with a shrug, trying to simplify it some. "I'm very good at it, really, because I have this basically sneaky nature. It only took me twenty minutes, and I'd had a look at everything you own. You'd never have guessed. I always put things back the way they were as I go along." She seemed to feel better with it out on the table. She may have come across as less of a hero than she was in fact, but that was all to the good. She was keeping both feet on the ground in this. And then Nick started to laugh. Then they both did. It took care of much of the rest of what was too hard to put into words.

"So what was the clue? You found the deed to the ranch?"

She shook her head. "I came up against a dead end. I could feel it in my fingers, like they were almost going numb. So I sat on the floor of your closet and started to cry. Hard." She could see back to two things at once, down on the floor in two closets—the night she tripped and hit the hollow door and the day she almost lost the trail. It was as if she had to do everything twice before she could see herself plain. "See, I *knew* it was a mine. But nothing seemed to lead me to one, so I gave up. Which sometimes is just what you have to do," she said, so gently she seemed to forgive herself all manner of sins, "because it wasn't till right then that I saw."

"Saw what?"

"Peter's paintings. That's just where they got put away—on the floor against the wall, behind the clothes. I could see maybe three or four at once. All these pictures of the hills around the bunkhouse. So then I knew. All I had to do was call your office and find out where it was." She held up her palms as if to say there was nothing else up her sleeves. It might not be much of a story, but there it was. She wasn't expecting a medal.

"Does Peter know that?" Nick asked. It delighted him, he realized, just to hear the details of how the day turned out for someone else. There must be millions of things he didn't know yet, and now he wanted them all.

"I don't miss much, you can be damned sure of that," Peter

said as he opened the door and came back into the bedroom. "I can't believe you're still doing this grim little retrospective. You know, they'll be here in an hour. What'd I miss?"

"Among other things," Rita said teasingly, "the resolution of *A Test of Faith*. She passes the test, you'll be glad to know. And just now I was telling Nick what a great painter you turned out to be. But you probably know that already, after last night."

"Is that what last night was trying to tell me? I could have sworn it was saying enough is enough."

"We were really talking about the day it all happened," Nick said simply.

"I know. I listened." He looked from one to the other, disarmingly open and full of contrition. "What can I tell you? I have this basically sneaky nature."

When they all began to laugh at once, they each drank in the faces of the others. Though they looked to the naked eye as glad as they did in the picture snapped on their very first evening together, it was better than back to normal now. It's a happy ending, Rita thought, and then she thought, Of course, it's only temporary. But she didn't like it any less for being so. They didn't need more than a moment's rest, at least for now, and besides, there must be more where that one came from. For now they laughed till they'd forgotten why, till they laughed at so much laughing. Peter dropped to his knees at the foot of the bed, weak with it. Nick buried his head in the pillows and shrieked. When Rita's eyes, brimming with tears, alighted by chance on the film, the penthouse and cocktails had vanished, bumped by a western. The good guys chased the bad guys and threw up a lot of dust. So the kiss at the end of the comedy went right by them, but it didn't matter. Rita knew now that Frances Dean was like a mirror, and Rita would have to look into it more, to see how she looked, but not right now. She looked all right.

The laughter died down to fits and starts. They were all three so relaxed from it that they might have just stumbled sleepily out of the steam room. A catnap, in fact, was the

logical next step, and then they'd meet the press refreshed.
The sound of the projector, Rita thought drowsily, was really
very like the sound of the camera. Someone ought to be film-
ing them as they lolled about on this plateau, if only to show it
was possible to be between events. She closed her eyes and so
couldn't see Peter and Nick, but she felt they were islanded
right there with her, just as full of sleep. In a minute she was
going to reach out and touch them both, as if to knock on
wood. In a minute.

When the door flew open, and Nick sat up and tipped the
projector over, she had to come back very fast from far away.
It was only Hey, standing in the doorway, the phone in one
hand, the plug in the other. The film was snuffed out, but it
could be fixed. She knew right away it was only a minor
household crisis. No big deal, as Nick would say. But in the
end, the moment of rest hadn't been long enough, after all.
Nice as she thought she'd be about the way things come and
go, she could see where it all led. The more she got, the more
she had to have.

"Where does this go?" Hey demanded shrilly, shaking the
phone. The cord looped down to his feet like a jump rope.

"Right here," Nick said meekly, waving his hand at the
bedside table.

"And where did I find it?"

"I give up."

"In the garage," Peter volunteered, "where I put it. I hate it.
It's the wrong shade of gray. I've ordered it in white."

"But you don't tell *me*," Hey said angrily. "And I don't
understand why no one's answering, it's driving me crazy. You
expect me to do that *too*, when I got all these reporters
coming."

"I wouldn't dream of it," Peter said. "I am a man without
expectations."

"He's had this phone in here eleven months," Hey said at
last, appealing to reason. "It's never bothered him before." He
crouched behind the table to plug in the jack. He got up,
brought it close, and stood over Peter, who was still half on,

half off the bed. It looked like the start of violence. "The phone is only a thing, Peter. You can't hate the phone. It's for you."

But it took a moment for Peter to make the transition. There was someone waiting on the other end. When he realized it, he sat up and looked at the others helplessly. It might be no one, of course, but it might be a client, and client calls were privileged information, involving as they did the latest-breaking news on various people's reputations. Rita and Nick were on their feet in an instant, bustling to get out of the room. They knew instinctively not to listen in on each other's outside calls. One of the secrets they kept from each other was the hype they used to negotiate the world in general. The rifling of one another's personal effects was pretty fair game. They could eavesdrop if they had to on all the affairs of the heart. But a person's hustle and fast-talk was none of the business of his loved ones. It was the only sure way they had to separate the outer world from the inner.

Nick and Rita shooed Hey out of the room ahead of them, and Peter said hello just as the door clicked shut behind them. Hey kept saying "Wait," until finally they stopped at the head of the stairs, each of them holding one of his arms as if they meant to throw him out a window. Hey said, "You know how much time you have? You don't even have an hour, and you're all just *playing*."

"Don't worry, my dear fellow," Nick said grandly. "We plan to spend the next hour huddled in prayer. In our other life we were Joan of Arc. This time around, they decided to split us up into three, to spread the wealth. Rita got the saintly parts."

"No, *you*," Rita said deferentially, leaning across Hey. "I am only an Onward Christian Soldier."

"You're all *loonies*," Hey remarked, shaking loose the grip on either side. "Thank God you've got me to keep you respectable. Luncheon is by the pool today, so hurry up, before the birds get to it."

"But wait. I thought we were all supposed to grab a burger

on our way home," Nick said. Hey was already halfway down the stairs.

"But you didn't, did you?" And they both shook their heads. "You see?"

Continuing down with his head up, he threw back his one good shoulder and lilted along in triumph. Rita, suddenly startled to be out of the theater, decided in the naked light of day that somebody had to check everything out again—one more time. The ice was probably already melted, and who knew what didn't get done to make way for lunch. Hey had surely produced the lunch to be perverse. She hurried after him, her mind in a spin as if by reflex. She left Nick stranded in the upstairs hall, still in his pajamas and wrapped in a Sulka robe. He was the one in the position to feel the change most sharply —from all of them safe in bed to scattered wide to the four winds. He stepped up to the window at the top of the stairs and saw across the terrace to the table set up by the pool. Set up, as near as he could make out, with the Sèvres and the Baccarat.

It reminded him of something.

He flew down the stairs and out. He had only a few minutes before they'd all be eating lunch, but even so, his speed was something special. Though his feet had healed, he still tended to walk in a gingerly way by habit, every step deliberate. But now he was running barefoot across the cold stones, and he felt a restless tingle in his feet that urged him on. It was as if he'd seen a light and thrown down a pair of crutches. He stripped to the skin at the pool's lip. Before he fell forward in a shallow dive, he glanced at the lavish table and almost shook the memory into place—but not quite. He didn't understand that he was acting out something. Either Sam or Hey could have told him the whole story—about the boys off Hollywood Boulevard that Varda brought up, year after year, for a swim and a naked lunch. But they hadn't said a word. Sam had never had the time to. And Nick hadn't yet sat down with Hey for the long talk they had coming to them, finally to detail the scene between Varda and Sam, when Sam was still a boy without a rotten fate. Well, it must have been a stray remark of Hey's, that very day—after they laid him down in the living room, and Rita went to let in the men with the stretcher. Hey filled Nick in on the sins of the past, but only a couple of sentences' worth. There wasn't room, if he said it at all, for more than the barest phrase about swimming and lunch. But it must have grazed Nick's head as it zinged on by, because now he knew what he had to do to come back to life, though he didn't know why.

He landed with a slap along his body that took his breath away. He did a dead float to the other side, giving himself over to the water's chill. Nick had been up and about for a couple of weeks, so nobody thought of him still as an invalid, but he knew better. Since his hour in the mine, he'd limited himself to minimal gestures, slowed himself down to lull his broken nerves to sleep. It worked, but lately he felt so weak he could hardly climb stairs. It was as if he'd crossed a line that he couldn't go back over. It didn't show on the outside yet. He had gone to the gym three times a week for fifteen years, and he knew he could coast on looking good for months. But to him the muscles were soft as pudding, losing shape, and they didn't connect. Now, as he winged one arm out of the water and started a slow crawl, up and down, he felt it all begin to go the other way.

It was as if he was in a race. He hadn't swum lengths in a pool in years, but he curled and did a flip turn that shot him forward with the spring of a lifeguard. He no longer seemed to be fighting his way out of sleep, so he didn't thrash. His stroke came back intact from his days at the beach in Venice. He was so startled, in fact, to be moving again on his own steam that he agreed as well to the darker side of going forward—to face up to the blindness of all their acts. The flight from that certainty was now his deepest secret. The only way he could hide from it was to act like a man who did nothing at all, because fate appeared to require a moving target. And he wasn't even worthy of the word. What he'd always called fate was a lot of posing and self-deceit, compared

with the thing itself. Sam at the end was a whole Greek tragedy, whirling the world to pieces. Thus Nick's grief required
of him an edge of stillness equal to the force of the chaos. But
the grief was really camouflage, though he swore to love the
boy forever and put the blame on life as murderous and meaningless. It wasn't that at all. Not fate. Not tears. Everything
was a layer of lies ringed around the guilt that seized him as
soon as he knew he'd survived: It was all his fault that Sam was
dead.

Back and forth, back and forth, he churned the water and
clocked the fractions of a mile. He'd thought the guilt at having thrown Sam over would make him even sadder than the
grief, because the guilt turned on him for its nourishment, the
grief on Sam. Yet it hadn't turned out that way. In the end,
the guilt left him all alone, the only man in a fallen world,
where the grief had merely leveled him instead, till he was
brief and frail and doomed like everyone else. He didn't feel
precisely what he thought he ought to, and it threw him. Even
his guilt had to have a rhythm and a plot. If he'd only known,
for instance, that death was where it was leading for Sam, he
would have acted differently. To begin with, he never would
have tripped him up with the final push, which was after all
what killed him, since it left him nursing cuts and bruises
when Nick ran off and the final minute ticked away. Nick
couldn't forgive himself what he saw in the last glimpse from
the ledge, the picture of Sam rolling in pain. Nick's heart sank
on the spot, even as he fled away, to see how easy it was to cut
a man down.

But it wasn't even that, entirely. It was all these contradic-
tory things at once, and yet the guilt that crippled him up on
the bottom line was the guilt at feeling nothing but relief. He
didn't really care, in one way. Sam's death was on his hands,
and all he was able to carry away in the end was the proof that
it was over with at last. All except for the guilt.

If anyone could have thought it through to the end and still
kept swimming, it was Nick. He loved to force the truth
out—the cutting through the masks, the filtering down from

level to level, then the face-off, when the truth suggested something further, toward a meaning he hadn't even dreamed before. He got it all decided now, pulling himself through the pool, faster and faster. Decided it not in so many words. With Nick, the words didn't tend to catch up until later. So what he *saw* when he took to the water was something else. It opened in his mind like a Wild West show.

There was a line of men who were all the spitting image of Sam, walking out of a string of Varda's films like men released from a witch's spell. They were still in costume—cowboy, playboy, prodigal son—but they looked as if they had no memory of the stories they'd been through. They came out clean. They bore no scars—not even a soldier with a splash of red seeping above his heart—and they had no plans. The only thing that connected them one to another was Varda. And now Nick. If they'd stared in each other's faces, they probably wouldn't have recognized the likeness. They couldn't see that far. They were too wrapped up in who they were, and it was in their nature not to go further than looks. They were content to keep the costume while they let the story go.

So maybe Nick was through with Sam, but he could see, as the films had shadowed by him all morning, that he'd only scratched the surface of the type. Maybe he had to play it out like Varda did. He was stuck with the same kind of vision in his head, and he had to track it down. But had he learned nothing? Would he die in the arms of a man like Sam? He certainly wasn't naive enough—and neither was Peter—to think he'd tricked his last trick. He supposed he'd be combing the streets again before long. Maybe the best he could hope for was not to pick up another man who had a prior claim on his house. Perhaps he'd had his brush with the deepest nightmare, and he would be safe from here on in from the violent acts of loving and dying. He could only go forward and see.

He finished what felt like the right amount of distance in the right amount of time. Then he hunched up against the side of the pool and flung himself backward, settling into a float. He rode low in the water, only his nose and mouth in the air, but he could see the dazzle of the sun, even with his eyes closed. One thing he had that Varda didn't—Peter and Rita. They were a hell of a lot more reliable than Frances Dean, and altogether real. He knew, because of them, that the search for Sam was not for someone to love. It was more an urge to affirm a principle—call it beauty, Nick might have said, except he couldn't say it out loud to Peter and Rita, whose taste was more refined, who'd brought it to earth themselves in Varda's secret room. But for their part, the crowd of clear young men in Varda's films had found in the immigrant juggler their ideal lens. He tricked them out of the mirror. They probably didn't feel it consciously when they crossed his path, since they were busy, so long as their beauty lasted, taking everything they set their hearts on. But consciousness was not required. Varda made them into something they didn't understand, and whatever it was they became didn't last much longer than the boys themselves. Now they were doubtless all old men, and the films were as good as lost in a box in an attic. But the principle got proven. Thanks to Varda, it took a grip for a while on the real world. All it needed now was someone to be passed to.

And Nick, who came back to life to pick up where Varda left off, didn't understand that the deal was reciprocal. When the memory of Sam sent him coursing through the pool, it sent up an echo that sounded just out of his reach. And the boy it called back was a harmless gypsy who played a peasant instrument and sang for his supper, who otherwise had no time, no kin, and no inclinations. Nobody but Hey believed that Sam had actually murdered Rusty Varda. Perhaps they went too far for an old man, but it may have been a lucky way to go, the irony more to Varda's credit than Death's. Sam wasn't dangerous until he came up short against the disappearance of the one dream he'd ever gone after. Nick had decided when he broke it off between them that he was the cowboy and not Sam. A month ago, they had nothing left but the distances between them. Sam seemed never to have had any substance beyond Nick's fix for turning out heroes with the golden look of movie stars. But something still stood them face to face, like men in a duel with pistols stepping off paces at the crack of dawn. The cowboy in Nick was a man like Sam.

And though he loved Peter better than himself, though Rita was the only friend to surface in his whole adult life, there was still a quarter of his heart where he turned his body over to anyone who wanted him enough. Then *he* could be the one to remain unmoved while someone loved him. He could watch the thousand twists of the hungering heart, just as Sam had. In the region of dreams that had no end, Nick was Sam and Varda both at once, because he shared the drive that linked them—they never ceased to dig for treasure.

He didn't care now if he never ate lunch, but it was time. A voice from the house calling his name broke through to him. He shook his head free of the water, shook it out of his ears, and suddenly heard in the tone of Peter's shout that more than lunch was yet to be announced. He blinked as he tried to get a good focus on the upstairs window. Nothing stood still, he thought. If he was so ready to go ahead, it seemed he had better go now, because the train was pulling out. He suppressed a last impulse to dive to the bottom and hide forever among the reeds and dim-eyed fishes. He sprang from the pool like a gymnast, landed neatly on his feet, and glittered in the sun. He looked up, ready for anything.

"Are you listening, Nick? I've been promoted. I'm the king of all the Russias." He leaned precariously out of the window, waving his arms as if there were music to back him up. He seemed to want to announce it to the whole of LA, or at least Bel-Air. "Peter Kirkov is now seventh in line to wear the double eagle crown. From the Caucasus to the Sea of Japan," he said, cradling in his arms the desert sprawl from Santa Monica to Long Beach, "the empire is trembling."

"Why? Have the people counterrevolted?" It was a very old joke between them, the matter of Peter's succession. Every time a royal exile died, a chair was removed from the circle, and Peter was a little more alone in the swagged and gilded ballroom. Nick and Peter chose to find it funny. "Did somebody finally prove she's the lost Grand Duchess?"

"Not this time," he said, cocking his head to the side like he did when he painted. "My grandfather's gone."

"Died?"

"'Gone' is how they like to put it. That was the lawyer in Brooklyn calling. There wasn't anything left to leave, of course," he said with a shrug. He was, as he said already, a man without expectations. After all, he'd pawned the icons and caviar spoons himself. "But at the end he directed that all the hereditary titles come to me. I can't tell you what they are, they're all in Russian, but I swear it goes on for a couple of paragraphs."

"Are you okay?"

"I guess so. Are you?"

Of course, Nick thought. Did Peter expect him to go into black for a man he'd never met, just because he was a little oversensitive? He looked up fiercely, to prove he wasn't indiscriminate. But he noticed Peter was gazing over his head, and when he turned, he discovered they were back to being three again. Rita was standing at one of her windows, arms folded on the high sill, looking as if she'd forgotten the way to the room behind the mirror. She'd thrown the casement wide and broken the pattern.

"I don't know," she said carefully. "But I wish it hadn't had to be today." And Nick remembered now that the old man was more to her than Peter. She was his friend. Peter let it go when he left New York, disowning Alexander Kirkov without a second thought. It was something of a tradition in his family. "I was going to write him a letter about you. Tell him how you've done."

"Is that how it's all supposed to end up?" Peter asked in mild surprise. "You let him know I grew up to be King Midas, and he hustles his old bones off to the airport and comes out here to kiss and make up."

She nodded and picked up the thread. "And he moves into Frances Dean's room," she said, "and every day at sunset you walk with him arm in arm around the garden. He talks, like always, about the past. You talk about being the last prince."

"I see," he said. "Very pretty." They talked across the courtyard, Nick thought as he watched them, one and then the other, like courtly characters in a Renaissance play. It was partly the pitch of their voices, raised so they could be heard. "He was lucky to have you as long as he did. You're too good, you know—though I suppose *you'd* say you got back as much as you gave."

"Didn't you ever guess?" she asked. "*I'm* the lost Grand Duchess, masquerading as a shopgirl." The grief was beginning to go, for her as well. Too much life and death had intervened between the time she left New York and now. In some way, everyone there was already gone. Besides, she had no time— something needed doing right away. Like a magician with one more dove in his coat pocket, she had a secret in reserve for this occasion, too.

"It never would have worked," Nick said, not the least put out to follow them into the past. They crossed his borders, and he crossed theirs. "That room is already spoken for. It has an indefinite lease."

"I'll be right out," she said, almost as if she hadn't heard him. "I have to get something in Varda's desk." She pulled the window shut and went along the row, turning locks. When she disappeared, Nick looked up at Peter.

"I bet she went to get the other earring. Though I kind of like the look of one, don't you? On her it's touching."

"She's planning to leave, you know."

"What for?" Nick asked. "To go where?"

"Get her own place."

"Oh. Is that what she should do, do you think?" He bent over and retrieved his robe, but he let the pajamas lie, since he wasn't a bed case anymore. Peter didn't answer right away, and the window was empty when Nick looked back. Was the question so hard that it scared him off? Well, Nick was just as glad to leave it hanging. He put on the robe and sat down at the table, taking the seat that faced the city head-on. Varda's seat, as it happened. He buttered his roll and peeked in all the covered dishes. He wouldn't stand in Rita's way for the world, he thought. She knew she could have a lover in her room, so it wasn't that. She could have a husband and twins if she wanted. Perhaps, he decided, she wanted a separate entrance, all to herself. And she ought to have a little kitchen, to make a cup of coffee in. He reached across for Peter's roll, then Rita's, and kept on buttering, and his mind began to tinker with a model of the house. He didn't for a minute consider the obvious, that she might deliberately prefer a more private place than Crook House. She couldn't. They'd fought for this ground, and they owned it now in a way that none of his clients ever would. He'd sold in his time houses as far as the eye could see, and he discovered that nobody knew how to stake a claim.

"It's probably very hard to live with lovers," Peter said, pulling out the chair that faced west, toward the ocean. "If she really means to make it alone, get by without a man, she thinks she ought to go the whole route and be *all* alone. I'm guessing. Are you planning to eat all three of those?"

"I'm saving time," he said, handing over a roll to Peter, dropping the other at Rita's plate. "I don't think she has a master plan anymore. Which is good. She'll know what she wants soon enough. We won't be here forever, you know, but here we are at last, and we have to see what we can make of it." Did Peter understand he was talking about the house? *Was* he? You can't live long, he'd always thought, in a place you only pay money for. The people who tried to do so tried to buy time. "Does she think *we* want to be left alone?"

"Maybe."

"Serve the soup," Nick said, pushing the ladle in Peter's direction and lifting the cover off the tureen. "We don't, do we?"

"Nobody does. But listen, my darling—we can't tie her down."

"But I promise I won't. I only mean she shouldn't leave for the sake of good manners. We're over that. Should you fly back for the funeral?"

"I can't. It's tomorrow morning," he said, holding out the corkscrew in his left while he ladled with his right. Nick started to work on the bottle. "There's no reason to, really. I wouldn't know anyone, anyway."

"He didn't *want* you to," Rita corrected as she came up between them. She laid a little package next to his plate, about the right size for a watch. A little speech went with it. But again, though she'd had her remarks prepared for months, they came back to her quaintly now, as if lifted from the vanished code of an ancient civilization. New York was nearer by far, it seemed right now, to the glacial palaces of St. Petersburg than Crook House was to New York. "It's like this," she said, looking out for a way to put it casually. "The two of you were deadlocked. He knew that you took a hard line with him, just like he did with you. I think he was secretly glad of it. So he didn't want you to have to walk behind his coffin, in case it would force you to be a hypocrite." And though it was true, she wondered what happened to the graver things she'd put away for this very ceremony—about the treaties that went with love and the tenacity of the past. "He was pretty sure you'd get to like him some day," she said, making up this part, trying to compensate for being matter-of-fact. "But probably not till you're an old man."

"What's in this?"

"I didn't ask," she said, passing around the table to her side, tapping Nick lightly on either shoulder as she went by. "I only promised to deliver the goods when he died. All I know is, it rattles if you shake it. Like marbles, I thought at first. But then they're not exactly round, either. If I had to guess, I'd say it was hard candy."

She drew her chair from under the table and let out a little gasp. On the seat was still another box, twin to both the juggler's gear and the crate of films. But the difference was apparent right away. Whereas Peter's box and Nick's were plain and wooden and practical, meant for the attic, Rita's was richly bound in a faded blue leather, tooled by a Persian who couldn't let go one bare inch. The corners, the lock, and handle were heavy silver. It was clearly the Frances Dean equivalent of the kit a body had to leave behind. And it seemed

363

intended for the family jewels of a robber baron, an ancient
safe-deposit box. Rita put out her hands and felt along the
leather with her palms. It was warm from the heat of the sun,
and it smelled of old books that didn't tell lies.

"Oh, Christ," Peter said, "will you open that after we eat?
There's altogether too much doling out of packages in this
house."

"You're just saying that," Nick put in, "because you don't
know how to juggle. Open it, Rita. See what it is."

She pressed a silver button, and the front opened up like
double doors. When she swung them all the way back, they
could see it was fitted out with dozens of little drawers. The
facing on these was leather as well, but bright Moroccan red,
and the tooling in gold was sharp and flawless, as if it had been
finished only this morning. Each drawer sported a little ivory
knob. Now the smell was deep like brandy. Rita crouched,
then knelt on the terrace floor, so as to be at eye level. She
pulled out a drawer at random and brought it close.

"What is it?"

"Shells," she said, but almost disappointedly. They were
gray and cream and spotted brown, as plain as clams. Not in a
class by themselves. They ought to be shot with orange and
come from a gravelly cliff-locked beach in Cuba. But there
was a trick to get through to the jewels, surely, so Rita pressed
on. She slid the shells back in and pulled the next drawer just
below. When she'd glanced inside, she handed it up to the
table. Nick took it out of her hand.

"Feathers," he said.

Gulls and sparrows, a jay and an owl. And the next was
ordinary stones—too small for weighting paper, too large to
use as counters in a game. Then stamps and penny postcards.
Then a whole drawer full of buffalo nickels, as heavy as an
ingot. They were doing it now in a bucket brigade. Nick took
a look, then held the drawers out in front of Peter, who stirred
the soup and waited for it to be over. As Nick would finish
with one and hand it down to Rita, she gave him a fresh one.
Rose petals, sherry brown and thin as insects' wings. Then

ticket stubs. Price tags. Chestnuts and acorns. By the time they'd gone through eight or ten, the look on all their faces was the same.

"I give up," Nick said, picking over a drawer full of champagne corks.

"If you ask me," Peter said, "she mixed it all together and shot it up. There's probably one drawer full to the brim with syringes."

"But don't you see?" Rita said wistfully—and they could hear the reproach in her voice, though they didn't know it was all directed at herself and not at them. She should have guessed that here at last the jewels were over. "It's not meant to connect," she said. And she put back all the drawers that were out and kept the rest for later. The disappointment hadn't got its hooks into her. The drifter's music had. She found when she cleared her head of the pearls and the dinner rings that she was every bit as tense and eager. More so, since these odds and ends from country walks and old pocketbooks would not distract her with their own worth. "It's only little things she picked up here and there."

"He used to call them her collections," Hey explained as he swept up to the table, a tray perched at his good shoulder. "I see you're getting nowhere fast with lunch."

"Just watch us, Hey," she said. "We're all half-starved." The tone of self-reproach had fled as quickly as it came. She was exuberant now, shutting up the front of the case and lifting it down next to her chair. Then she sat and put a spoon to the soup. "It's really nothing more than a kind of bird's nest. Twigs and hair and bits of string."

"If you cleaned it all out," Peter said, "you could use it as a little secretary. Or a medicine chest or a spice box. But of course you won't."

"Why not?" Nick asked.

"Because she'd rather look through it for Frances Dean. Isn't that right?" he prodded her, but she wasn't about to take the bait. She seemed to have nothing more on her mind than cream of sorrel soup. "I don't honestly think you'd know what to do with her if you found her, but you're the sleuth. A detective always does the legwork for its own sake, doesn't he?—unlike a decorator, for instance."

"Frances Dean is dead," Nick said.

"So is Rusty Varda, but that doesn't seem to prevent us living out his life. And Rita wants to get to a very particular Frances Dean. Fresh out of Indiana. Eating her first avocado and taking a trolley out to the beach. Before she went on the needle. Aren't I right?"

"It's all some kind of an underworld, you know." She wasn't contradicting Peter's rough analysis. It was because she agreed that she had other things to add. "Wherever you look in all of this, it's closets and boxes and caves. Like a world behind a door that no one opens, because it's in a room that looks like all the world there is. I didn't expect," she said, "that I'd end up with something to take away with me."

"Are you going somewhere?" Hey asked suspiciously.

"Be quiet, Hey," said Peter. "Rita's got her own life to live. We don't own her."

"Don't worry," Nick said. "She'll still come and visit us."

She took a sharp breath, intending to go on with it, but her mouth dropped open and then puckered up in a little o. She held the air in as if it were a gasp, because she saw two steps ahead to her own conclusion. Peter and Nick sat straight in their chairs and very still, full spoons frozen in midair. Hey saw his chance. The arm in the sling loomed across the table, and he snatched up all three soups before they knew what hit them. He set down a big bowl of salad in the center. They didn't move a muscle, even when he plucked the spoons one by one out of their hands. By the time he was done, Rita was ready to speak again.

"What I've been afraid of all this month—you see, I thought everything had stopped. Didn't you? All this winding down and settling of accounts," she said, abruptly going into another pause. But they didn't appear to mind the broken train of thought. She picked an artichoke heart from the salad, and in a moment it was as if she'd started a fashion. Nick went in after the mushrooms, and Peter picked off the croutons. Not able to bear it, Hey hurried off. "Ever since that day," she said at last, "I could tell the ground rules wouldn't be in force anymore. No more secrets. From now on, the rooms I was in would have to have windows and hundred-watt bulbs. There are only so many things that are lost. I thought they'd all been found. And then today—," but she let it trail off before the remark was half begun. After all, they'd been through today as much as she had.

"That's what I thought, too," Nick said, nodding slowly, "that it was over."

Peter insisted, "But it is."

"*It* is, if you want," Rita was quick to agree, "but only because the stars of it are gone. The story still belongs to us."

"But you're not Frances Dean," he said fiercely, "no matter how much the idea appeals to you."

"Of course not," she scoffed. He was on the wrong track, but she was happy to risk the rest of what she'd figured out. It had only just dawned on *her* as well, so it didn't count as wisdom won at high cost. Like everything else today, it was free for the taking. "Nobody's anybody, as far as that goes. You think I mean like Hey and Linda. But don't you see, most people spend their whole lives trying to find a story that's all theirs—and they never get it. They go to the movies week after week. They read all the shit in the paperback racks. But nothing takes." Just now, she saw, Peter was the key to it. They needed a resident skeptic terribly, and she didn't want to drive him off by seeming wacky. She'd live alone and like it if she had to, but not here. If they stuck with Crook House, they stuck together.

"Most of the regular stories," she went on, "are simply unavailable. To people like us. *Romeo and Juliet* is not about my first time."

"Or *Sleeping Beauty*, either," Nick suggested. Not by way of insulting Rita, though. He finally understood the degree to which he and Rita had kept the same door unlocked—willing to leave some part of themselves unattached, till the right thing came along to tell them just how their sort ended up. Cowboys were only the barest approximation. So were Rita's Gothic girls in country houses, calling out the family curse. This whole affair, he thought, amounted to a drama he'd made a false start on a hundred times, whenever he fell into bed with a man he'd never met before. Nothing in his life had played itself all the way out before.

"I see what you mean," Peter said, rocking back on the legs of his chair, the little box in the palm of one hand. He tapped it with a finger and got it to make a clicking sound like billiard balls. "We're aliens and spooks, and the stories they tell around the fire don't include us. Or at least not you two. I still have Rasputin and Catherine the Great and all of that in my back pocket. But anyway, I'll give you the fact that now you've got a story of your own. What do you *do* with it? Start buying art on the black market? Maybe you ought to become a junkie, Rita."

"Or a hustler?" Nick added sarcastically, to let him know they could tell their own jokes, thank you.

"I just want to live with it a little while," she said, dropping her napkin across her plate to signal lunch was done. Nick did the same. Then Peter. "At least until the aftershocks are over. It's like Crook House has these scraps of extra footage, all disconnected, all out of order. We're the only ones who can put them together."

"How?" Peter asked, and not quite so suspiciously. A moment ago he would have asked why. Now he could see how richly the other two shared it, and it made him happy. And not jealous, which he'd had a turn at when Nick and Rita went too far for a week. It was the three of them she was talking about. The turmoil that blew up over Varda, Sam, and Frances Dean had paralleled the subtler lines developing between them, one with another, almost like blood ties. They'd finished up distributed into interlocking couples—Peter and Rita, Rita and Nick, Nick and Peter.

"You don't mind if I stay?" she said, glancing over the pool as if to ask it of the city. So Peter's question as to how remained unanswered. Nobody really knew.

"No, no," they protested, both at once.

And in the silence that followed on that, they looked across the table, each of them darting his eyes back and forth between the other two, as if to gauge the relationship each was not a part of. There were no rules from here on in. As best they could, they had to live in a house whose story was over—at least as far as the world was concerned. They began to smile at the same time, but so slowly they hardly detected the change in each other—could hardly feel it, even in their own unclouded faces. Each of them sensed that he somehow completed the other two, though, with nothing to compare it to, how and why would always perhaps escape them. They were just as alone as the three lost dreamers they'd brushed against in dark and smoky passages, all this winter. The difference was, they'd come through to the end together—that is, without being hobbled or put into chains, no walls thrown up by a despot, all their luggage accounted for, and through no special talent of their own.

They heard a whirring above their heads, and the parrot dropped and lighted on the edge of the bowl. They glanced down once, all three, but not for long. They'd passed the point of being startled some time back. Hey was laid up, and the bird slipped out of the cage again and again, whenever they fed him or changed the papers. They cornered him with brooms and threw their sweaters over him. None of them said it was time, but the day came when the gate to the cage was tied wide open for good. They made him take charge of his own life. He beaked at the salad's surface now, skimming off the pumpkin seeds and shreds of mint. Then he popped up and tilted his head and said, "Machu Picchu," though whatever it might have meant to him once, he didn't seem bent on going there now. He homed in on Crook House to eat and sleep, and the visionary gleam he used to affect when he couldn't fly free had vanished.

"Open it, Peter," she told him.

The Gold Diggers

"No, I don't think so," he said, tossing it onto his empty plate, the decision clearly final. For a moment they could hear the stones inside rattle just like dice. "I'm going to wait."

"Not allowed," Nick said. "Everything's got to be out in the open."

"Does it?" Peter asked innocently. "Well, then—I promise to have the two of you by me when the time comes. But it won't be till I'm an old man—which won't be for thousands of years. We'll sit in a row on a park bench somewhere. Then we'll all tear off the wrapping and see if it surprises us."

"But what if it's money?" she pleaded. "What if it's a map?"

"We don't *need* money," he said. "What we're going to need at the end is something for you two to open. When all we've got left is a box apiece of everything we wanted saved."

"It's a deal," Nick said. "And none of us is allowed to die in the meantime."

Rita could see that Peter had raised his last objection. Something very Russian had finally overtaken him. All this talk to do with time, no doubt. He seemed to understand that the lion's share of his melancholy was a long way off. Nick and Rita, who had a daily quota, were a fair bet to put it all behind them in the end. They'd probably turn into pensioners full of eccentric passions. Peter would need them then, she supposed, as much as they needed him now.

"They're *here!*" Hey shrieked from deep inside the house. And they stood up fast, as if on command, ready as they'd ever be. The parrot let out a tight-lipped squawk and took off, skimming low across the water. They watched him float away downhill. When they turned back, there was a bright blue feather on Rita's plate. Without thinking, she picked it up and stooped to the box. She knew right off the drawer where the feathers were kept, and she pulled it open and dropped in the fresh one. When she stood up, she felt the peach dress fall in a perfect line. She put a hand on both their shoulders, and they walked together across the terrace. They all looked thoughtful. Actually, what they were thinking was that they got too serious sometimes. They didn't have to. All they had to do was move along and see what happened.

"I still don't understand what we've decided," Peter said. "What are we going to *do*?"

"Nothing special," Rita said.

"Same as always," Nick concurred.

They were going to live in Crook House. That was all they knew. They were all on record about their chances. It couldn't go on forever—they'd said as much—so how long, then, would be just enough to get the story straight? If it turned out they were staying on only to duck the future, time would find them out. They all knew that. They might be only kids who couldn't bear to go back to school, because the summer sky was haunted with the dreams the real world was never the equal of. But if they were right, and what they'd been through was the story, somehow, of what they were after, then for once they were in a field and not on a road that went only one way. And as long as there were three of them, they'd try to want nothing from one another but the truth. If their living together lasted six months as good as today, they'd be lucky. And they didn't promise it wouldn't be sad later on.

They were at the door leading to Rita's room when Hey burst out. "What are you doing?" he thundered at them, but he couldn't wait to hear. He spoke in a torrent. "Where's your sense of drama? I've just got them *in* there. Give it time. They're pouring drinks. I'll bring them in a tray of food. *Then* I'll call you. You wait here, okay?" They nodded. Then he looked straight at Rita and dropped his voice nearly to a whisper: "Say you're staying."

"For a while," she said.

"Then everything's fine. It's all going to work," he concluded, a bit too rapturously for the three of them. They glanced away here and there and tried to look dispassionate. Hey didn't notice. He beamed at them and spun around and retreated as fast as he had come.

Still in a line, they did a swift and nicely timed about-face.

They must have meant to wander in the garden, leaving well enough alone, to make a show of being on their own. But their eyes all fell on the juggler's kit. The props were scattered around the box, just where Peter and Rita had left them when the movies called them away. They all had the same idea, but Nick got to it first. He scooped up a set of three batons, striped like a barber's pole, and tossed them razzle-dazzle over his shoulder, one at a time. Peter crouched like a shortstop, caught all three, and held them high and took a bow. Rita, meanwhile, running a finger over the shelf of colored balls, decided only the green was right for the dress. They didn't talk. Their smiles went ear to ear by now, but they didn't want to jinx it. They had to get a little bit away.

Rita had two balls going and sent up the third, but they all shrugged off in a tangent and bounced away. While she rushed about retrieving them, Nick twirled a plate on the end of a stick. The trick of it came too easily, though, and he wanted both hands full. Peter had the red balls out of the fitted shelf. Nick took the yellow. They all put up two right away and began to go with the rhythm. They swayed and bobbed like snake charmers. But they had to really let go to do three, and you couldn't call it juggling till they did. They couldn't have done it alone. Having gone so far, though, none of them wanted to be odd man out. One by one, they stepped out into midair, as if off a cliff or an airplane's wing. Nick got it first, and the balls that came under his spell began to loop and go weightless. Rita went into it haltingly, but the motion took, and she danced around behind a veil of moons, an astonished look in her eyes. And finally Peter. He was surely the most reluctant, but he showed a kind of equestrian grace when he entered the inexplicable orbit whirling through his hands. For one long moment, they had all nine in the air.

"Now!" Hey shouted, with a clap of his hands above his head like an itinerant magician. And when they looked over, they felt the colored lights go slipping through their fingers. In an instant, the whole nine fell in a meteor shower. It could have been the worst sort of omen. Where only a moment ago they were out of this world, wrapped in a constellation, they could see about their feet a ruin of bouncing balls, all doomed to lie on the earth. But now was the time to show that, above all things, they were good about time. They came together and threaded their arms round one another's waist. They appeared to take the same simple pleasure in walking away as they did in a float through space. Asked what they'd been up to, they would have told the simple truth as well—they'd just had lunch in the garden. The balls had nearly run down to nothing as the three of them swooped up Hey and paraded into the house. A few balls hopped about like drunken rabbits. But they were still as the terrace, still as the pool—the whole domain of Crook House, high as a cloud above the city—by the time Rita's voice came drifting out the window, telling the story.

Other books of interest from
ALYSON PUBLICATIONS

☐ **EIGHT DAYS A WEEK,** by Larry Duplechan, $7.00. Can John-
nie Ray Rousseau, a 22-year-old black singer, find happiness with
Keith Keller, a six-foot-two blond bisexual jock who works in a
bank? Will Johnnie Ray's manager ever get him on the Merv Grif-
fin show? Who was the lead singer of the Shangri-las? And what
about Snookie? Somewhere among the answers to these and other
silly questions is a love story as funny, and sexy, and memorable, as
any you'll ever read.

☐ **ONE TEENAGER IN TEN: Writings by gay and lesbian youth,**
edited by Ann Heron, $4.00. One teenager in ten is gay; here,
twenty-six young people tell their stories: of coming to terms with
being different, of the decision how — and whether — to tell
friends and parents, and what the consequences were.

☐ **SEX POSITIVE,** by Larry Uhrig, $7.00. Many of today's reli-
gious leaders condemn homosexuality, distorting Biblical passages
to support their claims. But spirituality and sexuality are closely
linked, writes Uhrig, and he explores the positive Biblical founda-
tions for gay relationships.

☐ **BOYS' TOWN,** by Art Bosch, $8.00. Scout DeYoung's four
basic food groups are frozen, bottled, canned, and boxed — but
this warm-hearted story of two roommates who build an extended
gay family is a gourmet's delight.

☐ **CHINA HOUSE,** by Vincent Lardo, $6.00. This gay gothic
romance/mystery has everything: two handsome lovers, a mysterious house on the hill, sounds in the night, and a father-son relationship that's closer than most.

☐ **IN THE LIFE: A Black Gay Anthology**, edited by Joseph Beam, $8.00. When Joseph Beam became frustrated that so little gay male literature spoke to him as a black man, he decided to do something about it. The result is this anthology, in which 29 contributors, through stories, essays, verse and artwork, have made heard the voice of a too-often silent minority.

☐ **TO ALL THE GIRLS I'VE LOVED BEFORE, An AIDS Diary**, by J.W. Money, $7.00. What thoughts run through a person's mind when he is brought face to face with his own mortality? J.W. Money, a person with AIDS, gives us that view of living with this warm, often humorous, collection of essays.

☐ **BETTER ANGEL**, by Richard Meeker, $6.00. For readers fifty years ago, *Better Angel* was one of the few positive images available of gay life. Today, it remains a touching, well-written story of a young man's gay awakening in the years between the World Wars.

☐ **THE MASK OF NARCISSUS**, by Vincent Lardo, $7.00. The murder was one of New York's most sensational. The suspect was a close friend of reporter Mike Manning. Can he establish her innocence without her cooperation? And can he resist the advances of the suspect's son?

☐ **CHROME**, by George Nader, $8.00. It is death to love a robot. But in the desert hideaway where Chrome and the warrior King Vortex meet, a forbidden bond is forming, a bond between man and robot with neither one knowing which is man and which machine . . . a bond that will explode in intergalactic violence and hurtle Earth to the brink of the abyss.

☐ **SAFESTUD: The safesex chronicles of Max Exander**, by Max Exander, $7.00. "Does this mean I'm not going to have fun anymore?" is Max Exander's first reaction to the AIDS epidemic. But then he discovers that safesex is really just a license for new kinds of creativity. Soon he finds himself wondering things like, "What kind of homework gets assigned at a SafeSex SlaveSchool?"

☐ **THE LITTLE DEATH,** by Michael Nava, $7.00. As a public defender, Henry Rios finds himself losing the idealism he had as a young lawyer. Then a man he has befriended — and loved — dies under mysterious circumstances. As he investigates the murder, Rios finds that the solution is as subtle as the law itself can be.

☐ **GOLDENBOY,** by Michael Nava, $15.00 (cloth). Gay lawyer-sleuth Henry Rios returns, in this sequel to Nava's highly-praised *The Little Death.*

Did Jim Pears kill the co-worker who threatened to expose his homosexuality? The evidence says so, but too many people *want* Pears to be guilty. Distracted by grisly murders and the glitz of Hollywood, can Rios prove his client's innocence?

☐ **WORLDS APART,** edited by Camilla Decarnin, Eric Garber and Lyn Paleo, $8.00. Today's generation of science fiction writers has created a wide array of futuristic gay characters. The s-f stories collected here present adventure, romance, and excitement; and maybe some genuine alternatives for our future.

These titles are available at many bookstores, or by mail.

— — — — — — — — — — — — — — — — — —

Enclosed is $_____ for the following books. (Add $1.00 postage when ordering just one book; if you order two or more, we'll pay the postage.)

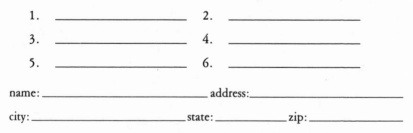

1. _____ 2. _____

3. _____ 4. _____

5. _____ 6. _____

name: _____ address: _____

city: _____ state: _____ zip: _____

ALYSON PUBLICATIONS
Dept. H-44, 40 Plympton St., Boston, Mass. 02118

After Dec. 31, 1990, please write for current catalog.